rilling, noodle-bending adventure that keeps readers guess-
ntil the very end."

—*Kirkus Reviews*

y entertaining. . . . The relentless pacing, richly developed
ters, and brilliant ending make this apocalyptic speculative
an undeniable page-turner."

—*Publishers Weekly*

background in comics shows in this dark, rollicking tale."

—*Booklist*

atile and unpredictable novel will entertain and keep you
until the very end."

—*New York Journal of Books*

le Year has all of the elements of a straight-ahead action
hile exploring faith, politics, and personal responsibility
and a sly, satirical wit straight out of the funny pages."

—*B&N Sci-Fi & Fantasy Blog*

ANYONE

ALSO BY CHARLES SOULE

NOVELS

The Oracle Year

COMIC SERIES

Curse Words
Letter 44

ANYONE

A Novel

CHARLES SOULE

HARPER PERENNIAL

NEW YORK • LONDON • TORONTO • SYDNEY • NEW DELHI • AUCKLAND

HARPER PERENNIAL

ANYONE. Copyright © 2019 by Charles Soule. All rights reserved. Printed in the United States of America. No part of this book may be used or reproduced in any manner whatsoever without written permission except in the case of brief quotations embodied in critical articles and reviews. For information, address HarperCollins Publishers, 195 Broadway, New York, NY 10007.

HarperCollins books may be purchased for educational, business, or sales promotional use. For information, please email the Special Markets Department at SPsales@harpercollins.com.

FIRST EDITION

Designed by Jamie Lynn Kerner

Library of Congress Cataloging-in-Publication Data has been applied for.

ISBN 978-0-06-289063-4

19 20 21 22 23   LSC   10 9 8 7 6 5 4 3 2 1

For my father, who knew I could be anyone.

ANYONE

PART I

CHAPTER 1

A FARM, THIRTY-FOUR MILES SOUTHWEST OF ANN ARBOR, MICHIGAN

NOW

"TODAY, YOU CHANGE THE WORLD," GABRIELLE WHITE SAID, OUT loud, to no one but herself.

She said this, out loud, to herself almost every day.

Someday it would be true. Maybe today. You never knew.

She walked the well-worn path from house to barn, through the side yard and its overgrown grass that was one unmown week, at most, from transitioning to meadow status.

It was evening, almost six, but the sun was still high in the sky—thank Michigan's position on the western edge of the time zone. Enough time for several hours of work before it got dark, and then maybe some rest before the baby woke up.

The bank-style barn loomed ahead, rust-colored and peeling, built into a hillside with an arched gambrel roof above two levels that once, long ago, housed a dairy-farm operation. The thing was ancient, and terrible for the purpose to which she'd put it, but it was on her property. So, rent-free, which outweighed pretty much everything else.

The main entrance, the wagon door, a huge ten-by-ten sliding panel hanging from rollers at its upper edge, was closed and locked. A smaller, human-sized entrance was set into the barn's face, to the left of the big slider, also locked. She paused there for a moment after inserting her key.

"Today, Gabby," she said. "Believe it."

Odors of small animals in small enclosures rose up to greet her as she entered the barn. A flipped switch, and light bloomed overhead from LED bulbs dangling from wires. With it, the sound of mice and rats and rabbits stirring in their cages at the unexpected dawn. Apparatus gleamed: a high-intensity laser, cables running from it to a computer station, and aluminum tables and medical equipment and shelves of research material.

Her lab. Built to her specifications, an instrument designed and fine-tuned and redesigned and retuned for more than a year, using borrowed money on bad terms—but all she could get.

She moved to her primary workstation and powered up the system, the on switch for the laser rig flipping upward with a thick metallic *chnk* she always found satisfying. A little hum, slowly cycling upward. The system would take a bit to be ready to run, which was good.

Gabby needed some time to center herself.

Paul had come home late. That wasn't the arrangement, although he did it all the time. Ten minutes here, fifteen minutes there—it was clear he didn't see it as significant, barely a transgression at all. Then again, he didn't stay home all day with the baby, burning up his energy on caregiving—not that she minded, of course, she loved Kat, her little kitten, she did, but every hour with her brought an almost physical sensation of the dissolution of her focus, her ability to dive deep into the place where inspiration waited. Every single day had to be a masterpiece of mental resource allocation, a careful husbanding of intellectual reserves until the moment she could steal away to the barn to do her work.

So ten minutes here, fifteen minutes there . . . it mattered. It was like telling a marathon runner in sight of the finish line, *Hey, lucky you, we've decided to make it twenty-seven miles this time. No big deal, right?*

But she really believed Paul didn't do it on purpose, and fighting about it would just waste time she'd rather spend in the lab. They'd already had the big fight, the one that mattered, and that was why he was staying out in the guesthouse for a while. Whether that would last, she didn't know, but that's where things were now.

She was just changing Kat when she heard Paul's car drive up, the aging sedan that would have been replaced ages ago but for the financial realities of a family comprised of academics—one employed, one not—and an eleven-month-old baby girl. The car wore its just-over-a-decade of operational life and six-figure mileage decently well, but it made Gabrielle feel a little sad every time she looked at it, a little angry. Unfulfilled expectations in the shape of a 2008 Camry.

They'd exchanged hellos and pleasantries once he came into the kitchen, as between a first-shift factory worker giving way to a late-shift colleague, and then Gabrielle had changed her clothes, putting on her armor, her good-luck outfit: Doc Martens, black jeans with threadbare knees, and a black Bad Brains T-shirt. The shirt always made her laugh—gallows humor, considering what she did for a living. She liked the band, but she loved the gag.

There she was, all black from head to toe, tiny and tough. She laced up her boots and headed to the barn.

Today was a big day. Possibly the last day. Her last chance.

The funding was essentially gone, and while she had made progress in her research, the breakthrough she'd been hoping for had (thus far) failed to materialize. She had changed no games. Nothing she'd achieved would justify another injection of cash from Hendricks Capital. They specialized in high-risk investments all over the state—long-shot research projects and hugely speculative start-ups saturated with the stink of vaporware—but there was high risk and there was just . . . stupid. Irresponsible. Throwing good money after bad. They'd funded her for a year and change, and unless she could demonstrate some strong results, that's all she was likely to get.

Now, the project wasn't a complete waste. Gabby had learned some things, broken some ground. She had enough to publish, assuming Hendricks let her do that, considering they owned the research. Maybe a journal article in *Cortex*, or *Cognition*, or even, dare to dream, *Trends in Cognitive Science*. She could add her discoveries to the great scientific gestalt. Someday, another, better-funded scientist might use her findings as foundational research that let them achieve the true goal. But no more than that.

Gabrielle White: literally a footnote.

Unless . . . today.

Gabby had spent every minute of working time she could scrape up during the past week reviewing, planning, praying, considering ways to reconfigure the gear to maximize the chances of a result that could buy her more funding, more time, from Hendricks. She broke her ideas apart, rebuilt them, tried to find a new approach—a magical, brilliant insight that would synthesize everything she'd learned into a shining whole that would revolutionize the science of the mind.

That was how it was supposed to work. Archimedes in his bathtub, Newton under his apple tree. Every good scientist deserved a eureka moment.

And she <u>was</u> a good scientist. She held a degree in cognitive science from the University of Michigan's Weinberg Institute and a medical degree from the Feinberg School at Northwestern, plus a mostly complete residency in neurology back at U of M's hospital system. All of that obtained after crushing amounts of work, sacrifices by her family and community, grants and scholarships and student loans so enormous she didn't think about them very often, much the way you didn't spend much time considering asteroids on a collision course with the planet.

Gabby tapped a few keys on the workstation's laptop, and her Strong Science playlist kicked off—up-tempo, big drums, big guitars. Not too loud, just enough to get her energy up. She walked along the row of cages resting on a series of lab tables against the wall, looking in at the small, befuddled mammals peering back at her. Some were burrowed in under the wood shavings and paper strips that served as their beds, others were peering up at her, and a few were not doing much of anything at all.

Wilbur, Gabby thought, pulling on a pair of bite-proof Kevlar gloves. She lifted the creature from his cage—a fine example of *Rattus norvegicus*, a classic white lab rat. She could have skipped the gloves. Poor Wilbur was lethargic, barely awake, as far as she could tell. Barely alive, was the sad truth. Beta-amyloid plaque in his brain was rapidly eroding his neurons' ability to function, just as it did in human Alzheimer's patients.

Once, though, Wilbur had been a spectacular specimen, able to navigate mazes in record time and, more important, remember the pathways when reintroduced weeks later to a maze he'd already learned. As rats went, Wilbur was a bit of a genius—until she'd introduced the plaque-causing bacteria to his system. Now, the poor thing was lucky if he remembered to eat.

Gabby walked back across the lab to the laser rig, where a small, dark metal tube rested on an angled table. She slid open the access panel and strapped the gently squirming Wilbur down inside, then sealed it up again. The tube was just a small, dark tunnel, covered in sensors, engineered so that the only light that could enter was the light she allowed.

Gabrielle moved over to the computer console near the apparatus and entered the final sequence she'd designed—the product of all her work over the past year and change, refined into this one, last experiment. She went over it for errors, sent a few trial runs through the simulator to make sure she hadn't missed anything, and checked to make sure the laser was fully charged. It was.

She tapped the space bar on her laptop, paused the music. Time to focus.

A framed picture of the Kitten sat on the workstation's desk. Her beautiful, tiny girl, with a blueberry in her hand and the ghosts of blueberries past smeared over her cheeks, smiling like she'd never felt so happy in her life. That smile echoed through Gabby's heart. She made sure it was always the last thing she saw before she ran an experiment, a final little infusion of optimism.

She looked at it now.

Baby, blueberry, smile, echo, and Gabby activated the system.

The mounting arm for the laser whirred to life, the business end moving forward to neatly insert itself into the tube containing Wilbur the rat. The hum of the apparatus spun up to a higher degree as it prepared to fire a class-four, thousand-megawatt argon laser—chosen for its tight blue-green wavelength that could most easily pass through the eyes and into the brain beyond.

The nervous system's internal communication network was built on electricity and power and energy; one of Gabby's favorite moments in all her many years of education was the point when she realized the brain spoke a language of light.

The entirety of her research program was based around the idea that she might learn to speak that language. Or, if not the language, one specific sentence that could, in theory, cure Alzheimer's disease.

The brain had something like an immune system housed in specialized neurons: microglial cells. Those cells possessed in their tool kit the ability to scrub away the beta-amyloid plaque that destroyed function in an Alzheimer's-riddled brain. The problem was that an Alzheimer's brain lost the ability to trigger those cells to the degree necessary to save itself. It forgot how to speak its own language.

Gabby was trying to find the sentence that would tell a brain, in the language of light, to power up the microglials and put them to work. To paraphrase: "Brain, heal thyself." The laser was her voice. With it, she could initiate resonance patterns within the neurons, gamma waves washing back and forth at specific intervals, an approximation of speaking in light.

Her process was crude: like mashing random letters on a keyboard and hoping to generate something readable. So far, only minor outcomes, shadows of true progress. But every experiment was an opportunity to learn little pieces of how the brain spoke to itself, and slowly, slowly, Gabby had found a few words, developed a little grammar.

It wasn't much. The Kitten had a bigger vocabulary than Gabby's system did. But she'd aggregated all that knowledge into this final test, and she thought she had a good chance of getting a strong result. After all, today could be the day. You never knew.

The laser fired, and Gabrielle leaned forward. Data scrolled across her screen, all systems nominal, nothing unexpected, gamma waves washing through Wilbur's brain in irregular spikes, not the serene curves she'd been hoping for.

She closed her eyes.

So. Today was not the day, and there were no more days.

Hendricks Capital had given her a hell of a lot of money, but her process wasn't cheap. The lab's equipment sucked up enormous amounts of power; each firing of the primary laser consumed four figures' worth of electricity. It added up, cash evaporating over the past year like beads of water thrown on a hot skillet. In fact, this final run had vaporized the very last of her funding, and she'd spent it on . . . well, nothing. Nothing at all.

She was broke, she'd failed, and who was Gabrielle White? No revolutionary. She would have to change her daily mantra. Now, forever, always: *Remember when you thought you could change the world?*

Gabby wanted to scream.

So she did.

She reached out to the power regulators and, without hesitation or regret, pushed them all the way up. To eleven, as it were. The apparatus' hum whipped up into a brutal, stinging whine, then cycled even higher into a shriek. Gabby knew she was running through the rest of her allotted electricity at a ridiculous rate—throwing money on a fire. She didn't care.

Light began to pulse from the end of Wilbur's tunnel, which was wrong. The system was designed to seal, to ensure that only the subject in the tube was affected by the laser and, not for nothing, to protect the eyes of any hapless researcher standing nearby. If she could see light, something was wrong.

Possibly, spiking the power had caused vibrations that had shaken the laser loose from the tube; it didn't really matter. What mattered was this: the experiment, the final test, was a failure on a basic level. The seal wasn't tight, so she had no way to guarantee that her neural stimulation system was the sole reason for any increase in cognitive ability for Wilbur. Honestly, it was unlikely she'd get a positive result in any case, but that wasn't the point. It was bad science. Her last chance, and she'd screwed it up. The cherry atop twelve months of failure sundae.

But . . . something.

The system was still running the sequence she'd entered, flickering through patterns that shifted in millisecond-long intervals. Whatever mishap had created the gap between the nozzle and the subject tube, the opening had to be tiny, maybe just a pinpoint. It was working like a camera obscura, projecting the lights all around the barn, spinning and dancing across the walls, ceiling and floor.

Beautiful.

Gabby tapped a few keys on her control board, and the overheads went out. Her gear was now providing the only illumination in the barn. The lights danced over the arched roof and the support beams like a planetarium laser show, its soundtrack the pulsing whine of the apparatus.

Gabrielle watched, delighted despite everything.

She wished someone else were there, maybe even Paul, because what was the point of seeing something lovely if the only other beings that saw it were Alzheimer's-afflicted rats?

A little glint at the corner of her vision—light reflecting off the framed photo next to her laptop.

The Kitten, Gabby thought. *Oh, Kat would love/*

She was back inside the house, upstairs, holding her baby, looking right into her eyes. She looked into them and saw her own.

The shade they shared was nothing special—dark brown, sometimes deepening to near black, depending on the light—but it wasn't the color. It was the life. The bright desire to see, to know, to wrest understanding from everything there was to understand. She had it, and so did her daughter.

The first time Gabrielle had seen this reflection in and of herself, a rush of emotion had flooded through her—a bucket of joy upended above her head. A recognition that someone else out there saw the world as she did, or at least a hope. She would never have thought it would matter so much, the idea that she wasn't alone in her world and the way she perceived it and what she wanted from it—but it did.

The Kitten was dangling over her crib, held gently in Gabby's hands, a smile lighting up her chubby infant face.

So . . . either she had just lifted the baby up from her crib, or she was placing her gently back down after a feeding or a diaper change or perhaps just a few minutes of holding, of connection.

Gabby had absolutely no idea which it was. She couldn't remember. In fact, she couldn't remember leaving the barn to walk back to the house. She couldn't remember coming upstairs to the baby's room. She couldn't remember anything at all after the barn.

The barn . . . and the lights.

This was wrong. It was completely wrong.

Gabrielle's hands clenched, and the baby's eyes—her big eyes, in the little face—widened in surprise.

Gabby's hands. Were they, in fact, hers? They were thicker, larger than they should be. . . . Whose hands were they, then? That was a question.

She let go of her daughter, and her daughter fell. Not far, a foot or eighteen inches, and she landed on the double padding of her diaper and the crib's bedding, barely an impact at all—but still— Gabrielle had dropped her child.

A moment of stunned surprise as they looked at each other— and even though Kat wasn't hurt, couldn't possibly be hurt, she was definitely shocked, and then, justifiably, outraged.

A lusty, wounded wail poured up from the crib, and Gabby gripped its railing, curling her too-thick, too-big fingers between the slats, specifically designed to prevent even the most curious infants from slipping their vulnerable necks between them.

She turned away from the crib, slowly, hearing her daughter's crying kick into a higher gear. She could feel the thickness, the bigness across her entire body.

On the dresser, her latest knitting project, a thickly woven blue-and-red tassel hat she would put up on her Etsy store once it was done, part of an ongoing effort to bring in extra cash. Next to it, the big navy-blue mug with a bright yellow *M* on it, a University of

Michigan logo item. But she didn't remember bringing it up here, and whatever was in it was still hot. She could see the steam.

Gabrielle completed her rotation and saw her husband looking at her, wide-eyed. He looked stunned, like when she'd told him she was pregnant.

"Paul?" she said, and heard his voice say the word, and saw her husband open his mouth and say the word, but it wasn't coming from him. It was coming from her, but she wasn't herself.

Gabby lifted her hand to her face. Paul, staring at her, did the same thing. She touched her cheek, felt the little scratch of stubble there, completely alien, repulsive, but also not—a sensation familiar from weekends when he wouldn't bother to shave unless they were planning to go out, or it seemed more likely than not that they'd be having sex that night. She watched Paul mirror this movement too.

This made sense, she realized, because she was looking in a mirror, the mirror mounted above the dresser in her daughter's room, decorated with little blue musical notes painted on its frame by the hand she now somehow possessed but had no real right to.

She wasn't looking at Paul. She was looking at herself.

And she was him.

"What the <u>shit</u>?" she said. Her thought, her words, his voice.

A moan escaped Gabrielle's throat, a low note mixing with the higher-pitched cries still coming from the baby, now tinged with desperate, outraged intensity because her mother had not yet picked her up to comfort her.

Her father. Her mother. Her . . .

Gabrielle became aware of a taste—rancid, scummy. Decay, old food, old coffee. She recognized it—the taste of a mouth that hadn't yet brushed its teeth after breakfast, or before bed after a day of ordinary life. Not unfamiliar, she'd even tasted this particular flavor when they kissed, but it wasn't her mouth. It was his. She was tasting the remnants of his day, his decisions.

Her head swam, her gorge rose. Gabrielle's hand instinctively moved up to push back her hair, keep it out of harm's way. She grasped nothing but the short dark hair on Paul's head.

She threw up all over the floor, a good portion of the puke hitting the panda-shaped rug with a wet smack. The taste in her mouth took a significant downturn, stomach acids boiling up into her sinuses.

A glass of water stood on the dresser below the mirror. She hadn't put it there—maybe Paul had, before . . . before all of this.

Gabby took a step toward it, but the effort of lifting her foot was so different, so strange, the thud of its impact landing on the floor so new, the way she was used to walking not the way this odd body walked . . . that she stumbled. She took a second quick step to correct, and her heel slipped in the puddle she had just created.

She fell, hard, unable to figure out how to protect herself in the moment between slip and impact. Her head cracked against the hard boards of the floor, and with the pain came a quick snap into focus.

Gabrielle lay on the floor, feeling the remains of Paul's last meal soaking into Paul's pants.

She didn't understand what was happening to her, but understanding would have to wait. Her daughter was crying, and that had to be addressed.

Levering herself painfully to her feet, she took a cautious step toward the crib. A throbbing pain in her head from the fall warned strongly against moving too quickly before she understood how to walk in this body.

Gabrielle picked up a pacifier from the little table next to the crib. She and Paul had agreed to use the thing in moderation, a conclusion reached after reading mommy blogs and the like warning against stunted emotional development, dental problems, and, of course, all the perils associated with plastics. But this seemed like an occasion that warranted a little pacification. She gave the baby the little nub of silicone, and she immediately calmed, looking at her father with her big, wide eyes, full of life and curiosity, as always.

"It's all right, kiddo," Gabby said, using the term Paul used, not knowing if it would matter or if the baby recognized words at all—one of the biggest mysteries of human development was what infants actually gleaned from the world around them—but not wanting to give her any additional clues that anything was amiss.

"I'll be back in a minute, okay? Just enjoy that pacifier, and I'll be right back."

Gabrielle reached out to touch her baby's head, then realized her hand was covered in sick and pulled it back.

"Everything's okay," she said.

Gabby turned and left the room, getting better at using Paul's body with every step.

It felt like a video game, like a first-person video game, like *Skyrim*. That was her only basis for comparison. She was looking out through Paul's eyes, but she wasn't <u>Paul</u>. She was still Gabrielle. She hoped.

She made her way to the bathroom and stripped off Paul's vomit-soaked shirt. She rinsed out her mouth, avoiding looking at herself/him in the mirror, then brushed her teeth after a moment of indecision about whose toothbrush to use.

She chose his.

Gabby threw on clean clothes, then returned to the baby's room and saw that she was already asleep, contented, the pacifier moving gently in a slow, smooth rhythm. She put her hand on her daughter's cheek, letting it rest there for a moment, feeling the softness against Paul's palm.

Gabrielle flipped on the baby monitor, then went downstairs, out the back door, and across the lawn toward the barn.

If she was in Paul, where was <u>he</u>? And what had happened to her? The real, actual her?

She began to run, still not completely comfortable with the jarring weight of Paul's feet as they hammered the ground.

What had happened to <u>her</u>?

The barn door yawned open ahead, darkness inside, just shadows. Yes. She had turned off the lights so she could watch the plaque-inhibition sequence play out across the inside of the barn. Like a laser show.

The memory of the lights danced through her head again, and Gabrielle's vision momentarily doubled. She slowed to a walk, both to pull herself together and because she wasn't entirely sure she wanted to see what was waiting inside the barn.

But there was nowhere else to go, and she had to know.

Gabby stepped inside and immediately saw herself lying on the plank floor of the barn, exactly where she had been standing when she activated the sequence. A bit of blood was pooling below her head—possibly she had fallen and knocked her head against the lab table when the shift happened.

Her mind seized.

Paul had become Gabrielle, but as far as she could tell, Gabrielle had not become Paul.

As far as she could tell, Gabrielle was dead.

CHAPTER 2

CHINATOWN, NEW YORK

TWENTY-FIVE YEARS FROM NOW

THIS IS THE THING YOU DO NOT DO, ANNAMI THOUGHT.

This is shooting up heroin. This is hooking up with your sister's husband. This is cutting your wrists and swimming with sharks.

She was lying on a flash couch in a darkshare den, about to let a stranger occupy her mind. This would last for two hours. During that time, Annami would be unaware, and her rider could use her body for whatever he or she wanted, anything at all. Drugs, sex, crime . . . anything. Traffic on the darkshare was unregistered, so no one would know Annami was not in her prime while these things occurred. If her rider murdered someone during the share, that landed on her. She would never know who the client was, and the client would never know anything about her.

That was the darkshare.

Annami was young, healthy, strong, beautiful. This was her first run, and her rate was $5,000 per hour. Over time, perhaps that number would go down, depending on what darksharing did to her.

She glanced at Mama Run, the darkshare den's proprietor, standing next to the couch.

"You ready?" Mama said. "Client is good to go."

Annami thought about the life she had created for herself. She had an apartment on Staten Island; she had a good job; she had friends. She had an uncracked pint of lemon gelato in her freezer. Or, hell, it was Saturday night. She could stand up from the flash couch, leave, message Bea or Gilbert or anyone, really, and meet up and let tonight just drift away, a near miss.

But *created* really was the word for what she had. The apartment, the job, the friends—all fiction; a careful, layered composition Annami had constructed over many years. It was both a smokescreen—to hide from Hauser, Bleeder, and anyone else who might be hunting her—and a means to gather intelligence on her enemies. She was a spy, a saboteur, a deep-cover agent alone behind enemy lines.

Her whole life was a story. It was time to write the ending.

But to do that, she needed to make half a million dollars—at least—in a little over a month. The darkshare was the only way.

Mama Run's smile faded just a bit—the woman was getting impatient. She knew it was Annami's first darkshare and was considerate of that fact, to a point, but she was, after all, running a business.

Annami set aside the costume of her life, the happy, smart woman in her twenties who worked hard and fit into the world around her. She let her actual self rise to the surface: one of the few people who knew the truth behind the lie of the world, and the only one who seemed to want to make it right.

She could do anything. Whatever it took. From this moment on, she was steel. She was tough as hell.

"I'm ready," Annami said. "Go ahead."

Mama Run nodded, her smile resurfacing. She lowered the hood over Annami's head.

"Okay," she said. "Client's in the queue. Just be a minute. Remember: three purple peacocks—"

"In a pinnace," Annami said. "I remember."

"Only just in case," Mama's voice said. "You won't need it. Everything will be fine."

Annami stared at the interior of the flash hood, its holo-panels glowing with the dull green of standby mode. The darkshare ran on its own closed-loop networks—necessary to guarantee anonymity on both sides. Not like the lightshare, which registered everything, from flash patterns to transfer duration to names of traveler and vessel. That's why it was safe. Why it made the world go 'round.

She took a breath, held it. When she was little, she'd gone to an amusement park in Ohio called Cedar Point. They had a roller coaster called the Magnum, the tallest in that part of the country. It began with a steep, slow climb, what seemed like a mile in the air, before a fall so intense, so fast . . . she'd held her father's hand the whole time, clutching so hard it hurt her, never mind what it must have done to her poor dad.

She had no one's hand to hold now, so she held her own.

For you, she thought. *I'm doing this for/*

Annami opened her eyes. She saw a wall about eight feet away, mottled and stained, with a spherical light fixture sticking straight out from it, pointing directly at her. It was swaying a bit, just the tiniest bit, like a long-stemmed flower moving in a faint breeze. The light was . . .

No. She was not looking at a wall. A ceiling.

Annami was lying on her back, on something hard. Which, if she was looking at a ceiling, was most likely a floor. She tried to breathe, to move, to begin the physical inventory that would tell her if she was still herself.

But she was afraid, because if things had gone as planned, she wouldn't be lying on a floor. She'd be resting on a returner couch at Mama Run's, with soft, calming music playing in her ears, a mug of steaming tea on the little tray to the left of the couch, and $10,000 waiting to be deposited in a hidden e-count of her choice. Mama Run didn't have to do these things for her runners, but she did, and little touches like that were why Annami had selected Mama's establishment for this idiotic fucking idea in the first place.

You are you, she thought, she reminded.

Lack of oxygen tightened her chest, basic biology competing with Annami's desire to remain suspended in a Schrödinger's cat–style cocoon of unobserved self, and she took a breath. Her body returned to her.

Some pain—a touch at the back of her head, and some in her ankle—perhaps she had fallen badly when her runner left her body. Her legs, present and accounted for. Her feet, also present, at the end of her legs, which seemed like the right place for them. Her arms and hands and fingers, all there . . . but wet.

Annami lifted her hand. It was red, as if she were wearing a slick, crimson glove. Blood.

Scenarios ran through her head, all the warnings she'd heard about the way darksharing could end—bodies harvested for organs, people being used as proxies by masochists who wanted to experience pain but didn't want to use up their own flesh, so many other nightmares large and small.

Annami had blood on her hands, and her continuing personal inventory had informed her that her back was wet from scapula to sacrum, which suggested that she was also lying in a pool of the stuff. So, yes, she had awoken from her very first darkshare in a nightmare. The size remained to be seen.

She thought about the blood. It didn't seem like it was hers, because her head was clear—relatively speaking—and she didn't feel weak. If she had lost as much as the puddle beneath her suggested, she probably wouldn't have woken up at all.

So . . . perhaps this particular nightmare was small. Maybe.

This was the uncertainty of the darkshare; this was the price you paid in order to get paid. Before Annami had pulled the trigger on actually going through with it, she'd made a little list of resulting scenarios in order of horror. The possibilities were endless.

Endless, and waking up in a pool of someone else's blood was definitely on the list. Far from the worst, though. It was, like . . . eleventh, she decided.

She was not: (1) dead; (2) missing any parts of her body (as far as she could tell); (3) in the middle of having sex with someone she hadn't chosen; (4) aware that she had recently had sex with someone she hadn't chosen; (5) chained or otherwise restrained; (6) sick/poisoned (as far as she could tell); (7) falling from a great height; (8) underwater; (9) buried; or (10) lying in a pool of her own blood.

Annami pushed herself up on one elbow and continued to take stock. Still no real pain other than the barely noticeable twinge in her ankle. That was good. The change in perspective also gave her the source of the blood on the floor: a dead man lying about six feet away.

They were in a small, barely furnished apartment, constructed in a style that was still called prewar despite the century that had passed since the end of the Second World War. Crown moldings, hardwood floors with a pronounced warp that wouldn't be helped by the blood soaking into them, a steam radiator for heat she couldn't imagine still worked. The room was neglected, dirty. Little piles of discarded paper, wrappers, and vials washed up in the corners.

Another detail worth noting—a gun on the floor between Annami and the dead man, a little closer to her than him, presumably the source of the hole in the man's head.

Annami got to her feet, wiping her hands on her pants, front and back, trying to scrape off the sheen of blood. She stepped toward the corpse, looking for explanations of what had happened here, how her darkshare runner had used her body, why the dead man was dead.

He was Asian, possibly Chinese, although she wouldn't put money on it, given the warping of his features by the hole in his forehead. Olive pants, dark hoodie, boots with deeply worn, thick rubber soles. On the young side, about twenty-five. Shaved head covered with stubble. Skinny. If he were alive, she'd have said he seemed desperate. He looked like, on balance, the kind of person who made their money by renting themselves out for darkshares, no questions asked and no explanations given.

Don't judge, she thought. *As of today, lady, you're that kind of person too.*

So—no answers from the corpse. Corpses, really. Two people had died here today, at exactly the same moment—the Asian man she was looking at and whoever had been using him as a vessel for his darkshare. That was how it worked.

If one died, both died. The most fundamental rule of flash technology, whether dark or light.

Annami knew she should leave. Right away, right then. But she wanted to <u>know</u>. She'd always wanted to know, anything and everything she could, despite all the things it had cost her.

She squatted next to the corpse and steeled herself to search it for ID or any other clues she knew would almost certainly not be there. Not for someone who died during a darkshare. The whole point was anonymity, on both sides. You didn't know who you were renting, they didn't know who you were—you just paid, did what you wanted or needed while using someone else's flesh, and then it was over.

The apartment door burst open: a crack of splintering wood followed by a hammer blow as the door whipped around and slammed into the wall.

A man half fell into the room, the momentum of the kick that had shattered the door pulling him forward. He had a gun in his hand, a small, dark pistol. He stumbled a little, regaining his balance, then saw Annami, crouched next to the corpse, her bloody hand still outstretched. This new person looked architectural, like he'd been designed to withstand enormous physical forces. A load-bearing man. He snarled something in an angular language.

Annami lunged forward, over the corpse, toward a square archway with more of the apartment visible through it. She didn't know where it led, just that it was <u>away</u>.

A whipcrack noise. Not much of a sound at all. A hole appeared in the wall to the side of the archway as she passed through it. A small puff of vaporized plaster and paint and most likely some trace amounts of lead, given the building's age—all expelled violently as the bullet entered.

Silencer? Annami thought.

That was good, or at least a small victory in the larger calculus of someone trying to shoot her. This new killer wanted to conduct a <u>quiet</u> murder. That probably, hopefully meant that this old apartment was located in some part of New York City with people around, possibly even police.

Not that Annami was looking forward to dealing with police after participating in a darkshare that had resulted in the death of at least one person—two if her hunch was right and the dead Chinese man also had a runner inside him when he died. Still, better the cops than her own bullet in the head.

The next room was just an empty rectangle, with a small,

time-ravaged kitchen visible off to one side through an alcove, outlines against the peeling paint where appliances had once stood. Nothing that would help her. No exit, no back door.

But a window.

She sprinted to it, a filthy, double-hung, ancient thing in a warped metal frame, about three feet wide. A desperate tug on its bottom edge told her that nothing short of the jaws of life would get the thing open. It was too old and covered in too many layers of paint and city soot. It had fossilized.

Annami glanced behind her to see if the killer had followed. Not yet—maybe he'd stopped to check on the status of the Chinese man before coming after her. But then there he was, looming in the archway, filling it, gun raised.

Five more of those whipcracks, as Annami made a sort of flailing sideways lunge. Nothing elegant or planned, just a cringe born of pure survival instinct, like someone jerking their steering wheel after looking up to see the truck that's crossed the dividing lane, far too late.

But somehow, enough. The rounds hit the window and passed through it, creating a spidered pattern in the safety glass. They did not hit Annami.

She and the killer looked at each other, each taking a moment to note the improbability of the fact that Annami was still alive. In another context, they would have smiled, maybe exchanged rueful, amazed headshakes. *Crazy old world. You see that? Holy shit.*

Instead, the killer lifted his weapon and pressed some button or latch on the side that ejected a magazine from its grip so he could reload.

Annami spun back toward the window, lifted her boot, and kicked, hard, the newly holed glass shattering outward under her heel.

She dove through the empty frame, landing on the fire escape outside, feeling curls of rust scrape her palms. The structure vibrated, and for a moment she thought this was it. The whole thing would just crumble into a mist of old steel, and down she would go.

But it held, and Annami got to her feet. She looked below and cursed. Her landing was about four stories off the ground, and the stairs leading down ended in sharp spikes of flaking metal before they reached the third. The lower portion of the stairway had collapsed at some earlier point in the elderly building's history. The fire escape was not an escape, and she maybe would have laughed at that if it didn't mean she was probably about to die.

Annami ran the only direction she could. Up.

The steps shuddered and jangled as she moved. She could see the fire escape pulling free of whatever ancient, dutiful bolts still moored it to the building's facade. She moved faster, taking the stairs two at a time. A shout from below her in a familiar, sharply angled tongue. Through the grating of the steps, Annami could see the killer's head poking through the window, his neck twisted as he looked up at her. He didn't have a clean line of fire, not with the fire escape in the way.

It was only two stories to the roof, and Annami lunged out onto the nasty, tar-paper-and-bird-shit-covered surface, falling onto her hands and knees. She spun, put her hands down to brace herself, and kicked out at the rungs of the ladder she had just climbed.

She connected and kicked again, harder, feeling a sharp spike of pain in her ankle, the one she had possibly injured when her darkshare runner left her back in the apartment. The ladder was loosening, though; she could feel it. Annami kicked again, with everything she had, and the fire escape snapped free from the building, yawning out about four feet.

That final indignity was as much as the old structure could

take. Annami heard a loud screech of metal on stone, and then a tearing noise, followed finally by a snapping, crackling crunch from farther below.

None of those sounds were precisely what she had been hoping to hear: a scream, suddenly cut short. If the killer had followed her out the window, he'd be dead now, entangled and entombed by the collapsed fire escape. The man was, apparently and unfortunately, too smart for that.

Annami forced herself to her feet, drawing in big, gasping breaths, looking around, seeing what she had to work with. The roof was littered with trash, ducts and pumping systems for the building's HVAC system, weathered lawn chairs for desperate, green-starved New Yorkers willing to resort to this distorted, mea- ger version of outdoor space . . . and a small hut-type structure with a door built into it—access from the lower floors for main- tenance.

The HVAC ductwork meant the building had once been reno- vated decades before, probably at some point in the 2010s, when everyone in the world had been convinced that the seas were shortly to rise and engulf coastal regions, and buildings in those parts of New York most likely to be flooded were required by law to put their essential mechanical systems on the roof. That was before a company called NeOnet Global released the tech- nology that allowed the transfer of human consciousness from one body to another. These days, most people called the company Anyone, and the tech it gave the world was the flash.

Among other things, widespread adoption of the flash reduced overall energy consumption on the planet by a third, enough of an edge that alternative power sources and a concerted effort to reduce carbon output had, literally, saved the world.

Annami took a single step toward the maintenance access door, her way out, feeling a twinge in her injured ankle. One step, and then the door was shoved open, exploding outward with that same violence she'd seen in the apartment two floors below. The killer stepped out, looking across the roof, looking for her.

Of course. He was smart.

Smart but unlucky. He'd missed her with his gun down below, and he missed her with his eyes here too, turning his head the wrong direction when he came out the door, scanning the side of the roof she was not on.

This gave her an opportunity, a one-second head start, and Annami used it. Again, she ran.

She was good at running. She had been good at running for a very long time.

Annami pushed past the hurt in her ankle and sprinted toward the roof's edge, keeping the doorway and the HVAC ducts and anything else she could between herself and the killer, hearing those little peppery whipcrack sounds again, seeing holes appear in things she passed. She reassessed this man again.

He was smart, unlucky, and, thank god, a terrible shot.

She reached the edge of the roof and leaped.

CHAPTER 3

A LABORATORY IN A BARN

GABRIELLE SQUATTED DOWN NEXT TO THE BODY—HER OWN FAMILIAR body, which she was not currently occupying, lying on the barn floor, blood seeping from its head. Her own blood. The body looked so tiny. She never felt small when she was inside it, never let herself or let anyone make her feel that way, but now . . . she was just a little thing in a concert tee, all skinny legs and arms and frizz of hair wrestled into an untidy braid, speared in the bright overhead lights like a specimen on a slide.

She felt Paul's knees click in a strange, alarming way as they bent, a weird, crackling release of pressure, and she let that distract her, shift her mind from the horror of staring at her corpse to the experience of being in her husband's body. Were ratchet-wrench knees something to be alarmed about, or just normal functioning? Paul had never mentioned having bad knees—maybe they'd clicked for so long that he no longer noticed. Or maybe it was the other way around, and her knees—smooth-moving, easy, painless—were the exception, and every human being on earth had rickety-rack joints except her.

An itch spiked behind one ear, and she reached up to scratch it in a way she realized she'd seen Paul do a thousand times. She'd thought it was just one of his tics, an odd thing he did, but no. It was a specific response to a physical stimulus wired into his system. Some little wonky nerve ending back there that itched from time to time.

Gabby liked to think of herself as an empathetic person. She tried to look outside herself, consider the worldview and experiences of anyone she was dealing with, walk miles in strange moccasins. Now all of that, every single time she'd ever tried to understand another person's perspective—it seemed clumsy, ludicrous.

This experience, being literally inside another person's body . . . this was understanding.

She was a cognitive scientist. She had spent her entire professional career thinking about the way people's behaviors were steered by their conscious and unconscious minds. But even after only ten minutes inside another physical self, it was obvious to her that a great deal of human experience had nothing to do with the brain. It was the body. Each parcel of flesh and its particular configuration of pluses and minuses created a unique reality.

In other words, it wasn't just the software—it was the hardware too.

The squatting position Gabby had adopted, a posture she could have endured indefinitely in her own body, was beginning to ache. Those crackling knees she was borrowing didn't like the pressure, and the small of Paul's back wasn't too happy either.

She wanted to stand, but she couldn't, not yet. Her own bundle of hardware, the body that, until very recently, was everything Gabrielle White had ever been, needed to tell her something. Until Gabby had that information, she couldn't even begin to process her situation, or consider ways she might fix it.

But she was very afraid, because what she did not know was this: whether her original body was now dead.

"Man the hell up," she said, trying to make herself laugh. It didn't work.

Gabrielle reached out, hesitated, then touched her body's neck. It felt warm—reassuring, but not conclusive. Bodies didn't cool all at once after death. Algor mortis was a slow process—hours—and it had only been what, ten minutes since the shift into Paul's body? No. Not conclusive.

She could feel panic beginning to rise and sought refuge in her scientist brain, asking it to build a wall around the fear, using bricks made of observation and analysis. She had already begun, almost by reflex, to catalog any differences she could note between experiences in her own body and Paul's. There were plenty—just being about eight inches taller brought its own laundry list of new perspectives. Now, she considered the texture of her own skin under her husband's fingertips. If his sensory system detected anything new in the feel of her skin, she couldn't tell. She felt like she felt.

Or perhaps whatever part of her consciousness was her—her essential Gabrielleness—interpreted the sensation at her fingertips as the one she was familiar with, overlaying her template for reality atop what was actually there. The brain was a liar. It lied all the time.

Reality was what the brain decided it would be. It took in sensory input and swirled it all together into a picture of reality, filling in gaps and cutting out inconvenient contradictions. Every human being had a blind spot in their vision where the optic nerve attached to the back of the retina—the brain just plugged that up with what it figured should be there. Or if it decided *sheidl* was actually *shield*, then that's what you read, unless you paid very close attention.

So the reality Gabby was currently experiencing might be hers, or maybe some odd new version of it created by Paul's brain. What would she notice or understand about her current situation that her original body wouldn't, because the mind she was borrowing was a music professor's instead of a cognitive scientist's?

She could feel herself spinning down a thought vortex, trying to find immediate answers to questions she knew she would be considering for the rest of her life.

Gabrielle took in a quick breath, a snap of air.

"It's too big," she said, talking to her body, convincing herself. "You need to science this. Break it down; turn the big questions into small questions. Answer those. Do that long enough, it'll add up, and eventually you'll understand. Science."

In front of her, lying on the floor: the first of those questions. A very small question, which was also the biggest question.

Was she dead?

Gabrielle moved her fingers on the warm, still body, putting pressure on its neck just to one side of the windpipe, feeling, waiting . . . and there. A slow, steady rhythm. A pulse.

The relief was so strong that she fell backward, landing on her ass—her unpleasantly bony, masculine ass—on the wood floor of the barn.

I'm alive, she thought, and felt her mind click over into a new mode. This was no longer a horror movie—it was a problem to be solved, and that, Gabby White knew how to do.

Her first instinct was to call for an ambulance. She even reached into her back pocket for her phone, before realizing that it wasn't there—Paul kept his phone in his front pocket, because that's where men kept them, their clothing being engineered differently than women's, with front pockets large enough to actually hold things. That generated a moment of annoyance, which lasted just long enough for a touch of rationality to sneak in.

The settling of the alive-or-dead question, the escape from that basic panic, had freed Gabby's mind to consider larger things.

What she had here might not be an error. Not a lab accident. Not a tragic mistake.

It might be an invention.

And if it was, <u>if it was</u>, what might that mean for the world?

Her eyes turned to the framed photo on her rig's control station, of the Kitten, blueberry-smeared and happy. What might it mean for her?

A little flare rose in Gabby's soul. Of hope, of ownership . . . of pride.

Maybe she shouldn't call the hospital just yet. Maybe other people didn't need to know what had happened here. Not yet.

Maybe there was time to be a scientist first, to . . . well . . . to see what she was dealing with.

Gabrielle pushed herself into a kneeling position, and Paul's joints dutifully complained, clicking again. She reached out to what had until recently been her head and carefully examined it, looking for the source of the blood. Just a small scalp laceration, not even an inch long, just below her hairline on her forehead. She glanced up and noticed a tiny smudge of red on the edge of the lab table. So—the transition of her consciousness out of her body had been instantaneous, with no time to realize it was happening and take some action to break the fall. Instant bonelessness, and a collapse, and a smack on the edge of the table, and then . . . nothing.

This suggested the movement from Gabrielle's mind to Paul's had not been reciprocated by a corresponding shift from Paul to Gabrielle. She had left her body, but he had not come to hers. Or possibly the transfer was too much for him in some physical or psychological way, and he had just shut down into unconsciousness. Impossible to say yet.

But something in her gut, her analytical instincts, made her think it was a one-way trip. She was in Paul, but he was not in her.

Which begged the question—where in god's name was he? Had she . . . overwritten him? Was he lost forever?

Or, to say it like it really was: had she murdered her husband?

Gabrielle stood and walked to a storage cabinet across the barn, stepping over the thick power and data cables winding their way across the worn boards like blacksnakes. She paused to make sure the volume was up on the baby monitor—it was—then retrieved a medical kit from a storage locker. She slapped it down on an aluminum lab table and pulled out a suture kit.

Moving quickly, she returned to her body. She knelt again, cleaned the wound on her forehead, gave it two quick stitches, and placed a gauze pad over it. She halfway expected her eyes to pop open during the procedure—she purposely hadn't used lidocaine, to see if the pain might wake her (Paul?) up. It did not. She made the stitches as neat and tight as possible. If she could avoid a significant scar, she wanted to try. After all, she'd be looking at it for the rest of her life.

Assuming she ever got back to her own body.

Gabrielle looked at her setup. The laser, the tube with . . . ah.

"Oops," she said, startling herself when she heard Paul's voice. She still wasn't used to that. It sounded different to her than it usually did, in some hard-to-define way, like trying to explain how one wave on a beach was not the same as any other wave but also was.

Gabby stood and opened the end of the tube, to see Wilbur the rat—still strapped down, looking at her with what she read as reproach in his dulled eyes. She freed the rodent and placed him back in his enclosure, where he listlessly ambled across the cage, unsure of what to do with himself.

"You and me both, pal," she said.

She looked up into the dark recesses of the barn ceiling and remembered the patterns generated by the apparatus just before the shift, spinning and whirling across her eyes and her mind.

The lab included an EEG monitoring system, installed on a wheeled cart. Gabby had modified it to take readouts from the many small creatures she used in her experiments, but she still had its original human-sized attachment: a socklike net wired with electrodes, designed to fit over a patient's head.

Gabrielle wheeled the cart across the barn and powered up the system. While it booted, she bent next to her unconscious body and fitted the scanning net over her own head, attaching the electrodes one by one. Unlike when she performed this procedure on her rats, the subject here stayed perfectly still. No surprise there. If her body hadn't awakened while she stitched it up without anesthetic, then getting fitted with a weird sort of hat wouldn't do it.

Electroencephalograms weren't instantaneous—certain tests could take hours—but Gabrielle wasn't looking for a detailed understanding of what was happening in her brain. Not yet. She just wanted to know if something was happening.

The readout came through after about ten minutes, up on the screen of the small laptop integrated into the EEG cart. She scanned it. The system's software automatically weeded out artifacts—little blips generated by electrical sources other than brain activity, like active electronics in the vicinity—which made it a relatively quick process to understand what was happening in her mind.

Long, slow waves in the delta band, no activity in alpha, and essentially nothing in beta, gamma, or mu. Interesting patterns in theta.

Gabrielle had never seen an EEG exactly like this, but if she had to guess, she'd say it felt like a state between a coma and extremely deep sleep, but lacking the REM state that would normally be seen in either. In other words—no dreams. The lights were on, but no one was home. No higher functions at all. No consciousness—no thought. But this wasn't UWS either—unresponsive wakefulness syndrome, once known as a vegetative state before people realized that was a pretty terrible label to assign to a human being.

The main thing, the encouraging thing, was that the EEG

didn't read to her as abnormal or damaged. It was like her brain had gone into a rest state, like a computer in sleep mode. If it was asleep, maybe she could wake it up.

Gabrielle removed the EEG rig from her body's head. She wheeled the cart back to its original spot, using the unnecessary task as an opportunity to work the problem, create a to-do list for swapping herself back into her own body.

First on that list, as on so many lists in her life—money.

Because the lasers that generated the light pulses for her anti-Alzheimer's system pulled down so much electricity from the local grid, Gabby's lab had special high-capacity power conduits installed. But before Consumers Energy agreed to run that line out to a random barn in Brooklyn, Michigan, they required a significant portion of the grant she had received from Hendricks Capital to be placed in an escrow account that would be drawn down every time she turned on the system. It all made sense—if she was going to be racking up five-digit monthly electricity bills, CE wanted to know it would get paid.

That escrow account functioned as sort of an hourglass for the whole project, and Gabby tracked its status more closely than her personal checking account. So she was extremely aware that it was now empty, especially after she'd turned the system up to its highest possible intensity on the experiment that had flipped her into Paul's body.

The conclusion: the last time she had run the equipment was the last time she <u>could</u> run the equipment—and she couldn't solve her current predicament without her system. She knew that much.

Gabrielle reached below her unconscious body on the floor and fished in the pocket of the jeans it was wearing—the back pocket, this time. Another strange moment of intimacy, feeling herself up with someone else's hand. She pulled out a cell phone. Hers, not Paul's.

With it, she logged in to their joint bank account, seeing every penny they possessed, their savings, still shared, a question they hadn't answered yet despite the recent relocation of Paul's sleeping quarters to the guesthouse. Not much, about ten grand—but enough to run the system three times, if she was careful.

Gabrielle transferred the entire amount across to her lab's escrow account with four quick taps on her screen. She set the phone down on the lab table and considered the best way to shift herself back into her own body while somehow bringing Paul back from wherever he currently was.

She knew how stupid it was to even contemplate the idea of doing this alone. She knew it. Further experimentation should be attempted only after exhaustive study, analysis, and understanding of what had actually happened before trying to repeat it—but she also knew that she was teetering on the edge of losing it, the fact of looking out at the world through a body not her own pressing on her mind, not knowing if this would be her existence for the rest of her life and needing to know.

So, screw it. Onward.

Gabrielle ran through a few basic points. One: she had watched the lights swirl around the barn. Two: at that moment, her consciousness had transferred to her husband's body. It seemed, then, that the body-switching process looked for a human mind—a basically analogous brain, thank god. If not, she'd have found herself in Wilbur's body, and considering that made her want to throw up again.

She stood at the edge of the lab table, next to her unconscious body, and took a step toward the door of the barn, then another. She walked back to the house, counting her strides, doing her best to keep a straight line. About thirty paces to the back door of the house, and then another five to get upstairs, where her daughter still lay, asleep in her crib, clutching a little stuffed tiger.

The crib was pushed up against the farthest wall of the house from the barn, and Gabby realized that the theory her pacing had been designed to prove was correct—a conclusion more chilling than the idea that she might have ended up inside a rat. The body switch seemed to be based on distance—the system found the closest human brain to the subject watching the lights and moved the observer's mind into it.

Paul had been closer to the barn than her daughter was when the switch happened. Why? Because in a last flurry of redecorating before the Kitten was born, Gabrielle had decided to put the crib on a wall opposite a window. Only that completely arbitrary decision meant Paul was <u>between</u> the baby and the barn when the switch happened, and thus Gabby had been saved from dropping into the mind of her infant daughter.

Gabrielle was not an expert on developmental cognition—her research was more focused on neurological disorders—but she knew enough to understand that the mind of a baby was not adept at filtering the world around it. Neural pathways designed to interpret existence had not yet formed. An adult mind in an infant's brain might register as an incredibly intense hallucinogenic experience— every sight, sound, and sensory experience dialed up as high as it could possibly go. Insanity. A nightmare.

Not to mention that she still didn't know if this was reversible. Paul might never come back. That would be horrible, awful—she still loved him very much, despite everything—but she could find a way to move on, if she had to. Losing her daughter, though . . . no. No way.

Gabrielle returned to the barn, walking slowly through the rapidly fading light of day.

In the lab, she prepared her body as best she could, considering its comatose, uncooperative state. She taped its eyes open using butterfly bandages from the suture kit, sticking them to the eyelids and across the eyebrows. She felt a sympathetic twinge, thinking about her lenses drying out almost instantly. A few more adjustments, moving the limp form into a position where it would be best situated to observe what she had already half begun to call the flash.

The flash.

Catchy, like the name of something understood, a brand so ubiquitous that it stood in for an entire category of human activity. A noun-turned-verb, like Google, or Skype, or FedEx.

That could be how it was. Gabrielle White, inventor of the flash. She wouldn't be a footnote, any more than you needed to put a footnote after Thomas Edison or Alexander Graham Bell. People would see her name and they'd just know.

Gabrielle White. Inventor of the flash.

If she could make it work. If she could reverse what she had done. If she hadn't just invented a really novel form of mariticide.

Gabrielle moved the projection system forward, setting the nozzle firmly in place against the tube that would ordinarily include a confused rodent but was currently empty. She took a scalpel from the medical kit and sliced the tiniest chunk out of the rubber O-ring around the end of the tube, in an effort to replicate the pinpoint leak that had generated the odd swirls of light around the interior of the barn. Satisfied, she turned the laser on, leaving its power draw at the maximum setting. The familiar hum and whine filled the barn. Gabby set a four-minute firing timer, left the lab, and returned to the house, where she quickly climbed the stairs to her daughter's bedroom and stood next to the crib, as close as she could recall to the exact position Paul had been in when all of this began.

Gabrielle glanced at her watch—Paul's watch—a nice, stainless steel Concord with a minimalist design he'd bought himself for his thirtieth birthday, back before they learned they were pregnant and splurges of any kind became a thing of the past. She tried to calm herself, to put her mind into whatever state it would have been in when the switch happened.

He'd been looking at the baby. Holding the baby.

Gabrielle looked down into the crib at her sleeping daughter and felt all the usual emotions fill her. Protectiveness, worry, and, above all, love, love, love.

She waited. She closed her eyes. If all went well, when she re-opened them she would be back in her own body, looking at the ceiling of the barn twenty feet above her.

After much more than four minutes had passed, Gabrielle opened her eyes. She did not see the barn. She was still looking at her daughter in her crib, now awake, quiet. The baby stared up at what she believed was her father, watching with eyes bright, familiar, and no longer an echo of Gabby's own.

CHAPTER 4

THE AIR BETWEEN TWO ROOFTOPS IN LOWER MANHATTAN, SIX STORIES UP

ANNAMI LANDED HARD.

When she jumped, she had some intention of rolling, tucking into an acrobatic somersault that would bleed away her momentum until she was ready to spring up and sprint away from her gun-wielding pursuer. The sort of thing she'd seen badass young heroines do in vees.

It did not happen that way.

The leap did not snap into graceful slow motion accompanied by swelling music. She was airborne for perhaps a second, barely catching a glimpse of the alley six stories below, and then she landed hard.

The other roof was lower, a five-story building, and that ten feet of drop hit her all at once. Her already-injured ankle twanged as she landed—a sensation so intense she thought she actually heard it—and Annami sprawled flat on the roof, the skin of her palms scraped away. Stinging, brutal, red agony flared up all across her body. Her eyes filled.

She wanted to lie there. She deserved to lie there, after everything she'd endured. Anything else seemed like a clear sign of an unjust universe.

An image appeared in her mind, of herself, prone on her couch at home on Staten Island, digging into that lemon gelato straight out of the container, her thinnie floating above her stomach playing the latest chapter of Anita Jackson's newest epic. The road not taken that night. The road probably barred to her now, forever.

Annami got up. She pushed herself into a crouch, the pain turning into a white sheet folding across her entire self, and she looked.

There. This roof connected to another roof, and another, filling out a long block. She had a path, room to move. She had somewhere to run, and so she did.

She glanced back when she was midway across the third roof and saw the gunman standing at the edge of the original building. He was very still, staring in her direction. One hand was touching his ear—so he had an earpiece or an implant, and he was talking to someone. Probably calling in for help, or reporting in that he had lost his target.

And he <u>had</u> lost his target, hadn't he? She'd gotten away, maybe. The jump across the alley had saved her. The man with the gun didn't want to risk the leap across from his block to hers. It made sense. He was bigger and heavier, and unless he actually had the powers of a superhero in a vee, he couldn't fly. He'd never make it.

Annami made her way to the far end of the block and used a length of rusty rebar to pry open a rooftop-access door. Maybe it was alarmed, maybe it wasn't—she was past caring. She just wanted to get off the damn roof.

No alarm rang, and she slipped inside.

This building seemed newer than the one in which she had awakened from her darkshare. It had an elevator, at least. Annami took it to street level, where she waited in the lobby, just inside the front door. She watched traffic roll by on the street outside, knowing the gunman must have watched her enter this particular building. He was on his way, no doubt about it.

Three yellow cabs rolled by, all unoccupied. They weren't what Annami needed, and she let them go, clenching her fists, ready to sprint for the elevator again at the first glimpse of a giant with a gun. But then, a fourth. She could see its driver through the window, slouching, head lolling against the window, eyes closed as the taxi moved slowly down the street. Perfect.

Annami pushed through the building's door, out onto the sidewalk. She raised a hand. The cab's sensors noticed, and the vehicle slowed and moved to the curb. She yanked open the rear door and slid inside.

"Canal and Mott," she said, surprised that her voice sounded utterly normal. She would have expected a deepening, an edge. She'd been through some shit. She'd seen some things.

The taxi moved back into the flow of traffic, the driver's head lolling back the other way with the movement.

The driver was a criminal.

All licensed cabs were required to have human operators at all times, even the self-driving ones (about half, these days), just in case something went wrong in transit. But nothing ever <u>did</u> go wrong—the software was too good.

The brains inside the taxis were better than most actual cabbies at finding their way through New York City traffic, avoiding accidents, and generally just serving customer needs. But in the early days of the software, people were uncomfortable with the idea of trusting their lives to computerized drivers, and so a law was passed in 2023 requiring a human operator at all times, just in case. It had never been repealed, despite the obvious lack of need for it. So you had yellow robotic cars roaming all over the city with "drivers" in their front seats who just sat there and took in the scenery.

Annami had always thought the law remained in effect more for reasons of supporting the New York City job market than anything else. A gig was a gig, and if some people were willing to sit in a cab doing nothing for eight hours at a time and getting paid for it (and there were always people willing to do that), why not let them? It inched the city closer to full employment, despite how much the cab companies bitched about the requirement.

But then, inevitably, certain enterprising people had realized that with flash tech, one job could be two jobs.

Let your prime sit in a cab all day, while you flashed into someone else and worked a second gig using the body of someone willing to get paid to be a vessel all day. Everyone's happy, everyone's working. The flash economy.

It was illegal, but the sort of illegal that didn't get too much attention. Jaywalking, basically.

And for Annami, the practice presented an opportunity to get a ride while drenched in blood, looking like she'd been mauled by a bear, without the driver asking questions she couldn't answer. Sure, the in-cab video was recording her, but New York, to put it mildly, had too many cameras. It didn't matter how much footage was collected if there weren't enough people to review it. Algorithms looked for obvious criminal activity and sent alarms up through the system, but New York being New York, Annami's appearance was unlikely to raise any flags.

She slouched, trying to find a position that didn't cause some part of her body to flare up into that white-hot pain. No luck. No such position existed.

Annami put her head back and endured, knowing how long it would be until she could clean someone else's blood off her body, swallow as many painblocks as she thought she could handle without inadvertently committing suicide, and sleep, sleep, sleep.

The cab ride passed, Annami attempting to stay completely still, teeth gritted against every little spine-stabbing bump.

Eventually, at last, the taxi pulled to the curb, and a chime announced that they had reached their destination. Annami handled the fare with her payphrase and even added a decent tip for the still-comatose driver. She respected the woman. Working for a living. A lady with goals.

Annami opened the door. She braced herself, gritting her teeth, knowing her battered body would have stiffened during the drive. She levered herself up, groaning, and stepped out of the cab.

Chinatown sidewalk traffic surged into life around her. It was like dropping into a river in the middle of a salmon run, where the salmon were very happy to snap at you in Cantonese or Fukienese or Mandarin if you got in their way. Annami cut across the sidewalk, against the flow, toward a small gap between two street-vendor stalls. One was selling bootleg purses and shoes. The other was hawking vacations to Hainan Island, screens mounted on the booth showing images of idealized, preening vessels available for rental—beautiful physical specimens, male and female, ready to be occupied by Western tourists looking for a few exotic days on the other side of the world. Or a few exotic hours, maybe.

This was another of those illegal operations that didn't get as much attention as it might. If you knew the right things to say to the stall's attendant, the other end of the flash was a Chinese brothel. Still, it was a brothel on the other side of the world, and even these days, the other side of the world was the other side of the world. Live and let live. Or, more particularly, as far as the NYPD's Flash Crime Bureau was concerned, let Chinese brothels be a Chinese problem.

She limped between the stalls into an alley, slick stone underfoot, the odor of cooking oil and spice in her nose, and found a set of steps leading down into a deeper cleft between the buildings. She was well and truly in the labyrinth now, but she knew her way.

Another twenty paces, a left turn, a right, and she was standing before a red door. In its upper-right corner, a tiny, stylized black lightning bolt bordered in white—a copy of the ubiquitous logo of NeOnet Global, but reversed, a negative image of Anyone's. She knocked, and a small window opened in the door at head height. A face peered out, impassive.

"I run for Mama Run," she said. "I just finished a share, but the client's time ended before they could get back here, I think."

"Yeah, I remember you," the face said. "Passphrase?"

"Three purple peacocks in a pinnace," Annami said.

This was the unique identifying sentence Mama Run had given her, in case something went wrong with the darkshare. Common practice in the flash world for verifying who was who; identity rested in memory as opposed to physical appearance.

The window closed, and the door opened.

She walked—no, hobbled, she was really hurting now—into a short, narrow hallway, past the door guard, a compact Thai man named Somchai. The hall wasn't long, perhaps fifteen feet, and it ended in a crimson curtain.

Beyond the curtain . . . a wonderland.

Everything was red—the walls, the floor, the ceiling, the flash couches, the bar, the lights. But somehow, the effect wasn't hellish—it was comforting, cozy, like stepping into a warm home after hours spent out in the cold.

This was Mama Run's place, and here was Mama Run.

"Hey, little girl," the woman said from her customary spot behind the bar. "You look like a dead girl."

Annami made her way across the room. The place was mostly empty, just Mama and a few of her runners waiting for clients. Most were sitting around, looking at thinscreens or their minis, killing time. They looked like what they were—desperate. Not the man sitting at the bar, though.

She'd noticed him both times she'd come here before now: once to scope it out, to meet Mama Run in person and decide whether she would actually hire herself out for something as insane as a darkshare, and then a second time when she did hire herself out for that insane thing. Now she was battered, bruised, and blood-soaked, and she wasn't even that surprised. She knew what she'd signed up for. She was as desperate as anyone in there.

But not the man at the bar, who had introduced himself as Soro on her second visit. He looked . . . easy. Relaxed. Dark skin. Big, dewy eyes set in a face rippled on one side, from his jawline up past his forehead, which she thought was probably an old, healed-over burn scar. A little smirk from this man as he looked her up and down, taking a sip of his drink. Only half his mouth moved—the other side was set, locked in place due to the scar. Maybe the expression was actually a true, genuine smile and Soro was happy to see her. Maybe he was the nicest guy in the world, just killing time in a Chinatown darkshare den where people came to anonymously do the worst things in the world or allow those things to be done to them. Impossible to say.

"You have some trouble on the job?" Mama Run said, as Annami laboriously settled herself onto a barstool. "I told you before you start, these darkshares . . . not so easy."

"Yes," Annami said. "I had some trouble."

"Well, you know I take care of my people. What do you need? Medical suite in back. I can call in my doc."

"Just some painblocks for now, if you have them. And my stuff. I just want to go home. And my money. I want my money."

Mama Run tsked.

"Your money's already in the account you gave me. You know that. I told you that. You got paid the minute you start the run. It's all there."

Annami felt . . . bad, somehow, that she had offended this criminal. But then, she was a criminal too now. Everyone in here was a criminal.

"Hey," Soro said, off to her left.

Annami turned.

"You all right?" he asked. "How bad did it get?"

"The blood isn't mine," Annami said, gesturing to her clothes. "But someone died during the share. I came back to myself and I was in this ancient apartment, and there was a dead guy and a gun. I think my rider killed the other guy, maybe a deal went bad or something. I don't know. Someone else busted in, chased me. They had a gun too. I had to run."

She didn't know why she was telling Soro these things. She knew she shouldn't tell him anything—shouldn't tell anyone anything—but she couldn't stop herself.

The man nodded.

"Yeah. I've had a few of those. But you got away, and believe me when I tell you it could have been worse."

Soro smirked again. Or smiled. Impossible to say.

Annami turned back to Mama Run.

"You're sure there's no way to trace the share back here? Back to me?"

"That's the guarantee, lady," Mama Run said.

She lifted a bottle and poured out a measure of something amber into a short glass. She passed it across to Annami.

"No one knows you, no one knows who use you, no one knows what they do while they use you. That's what this place do. That's the darkshare. That's what I do. If I get any of that wrong, I'm done. So . . . I don't get it wrong."

Annami knew all this. She'd checked out Mama Run's before she came anywhere near the place, verifying that her operation's flash traffic wasn't registered on any node. In the light flash, every transaction, traveler, vessel, intended use, and transfer time was fully logged and available to authorities. But whatever happened at Mama Run's, or happened out in the world while people used the vessels she provided—it was dark, as dark as dark could be.

It was also illegal, much more than cabdrivers working a second job or flash prostitutes. If you got involved with darksharing, as rider or vessel, and you got caught, that was it. Lengthy prison term at best, with your pattern barred from the legitimate flash network for the rest of your life. You'd be a Dull, and in a world shaped, saved, and dominated by the flash, being Dull was being dead.

"Think of it this way," Soro said. "Yes, a murderer rode you, but at least they were good at it, right? Otherwise you wouldn't be here."

The truth of this hit her hard, all at once. Annami realized how close she'd come to not waking up in that apartment at all.

She had ceded complete control of everything she was, everything she hoped to do. She'd risked everything. She'd rolled the dice on all of it, had given herself to a killer who had used her body to do . . . what? She still didn't know, and might never know.

If her rider had been a little slower with his gun, if things had worked out differently, they'd both be dead. That was the system, the way it worked across all flash networks, dark and light alike. If you die while you're in a vessel, then you die, and so does your unconscious body wherever you left it preflash, and so does the vessel.

The first of the Two Rules of the flash: if one dies, both die.

The second: no multiple jumps. If you're in a vessel, you can't move to a second without flashing back to your prime first.

The Two Rules. Hardwired into the flash from the day Anyone released it to the world. To prevent abuses.

Annami reached for the glass Mama Run had poured and took a healthy swallow.

Mama Run nodded.

"Good," she said. "Finish it. Trust your mama."

Annami looked into the glass. She could see her face in the liquid—rippling, golden. She drank the rest and set the glass down on the bar. Mama Run poured her a little more, then looked up to see that someone else had entered the room, a tall, skinny man with a noticeable tremor.

"Hey there, long and tall," Mama Run said, her voice speculative.

"I need . . . need some work," the thin man said, his voice hollow.

Mama Run frowned. She moved out from behind the bar and approached the newcomer, began talking to him in a low voice.

"Can I ask you something?" Soro said. "It's personal."

Annami looked at him, didn't answer.

"Why did you do this?" he said. "I don't expect an answer, really. Not telling people why you're here is the whole point of this place. But I look at you, and I see a woman who isn't, you know"—he gestured at the rippled contours of his burned face—". . . ruined."

Annami watched him take a little sip of his own drink.

"If you want to make money off the flash, there's a thousand better ways," he went on. "Tourist work, maybe. This is New York City. Always tons of tourists coming here. Or maybe even just let people take you for beauty rides. You're young, pretty—lots of people would want that. It doesn't pay like darksharing, but still, it's easy money. Easier than this."

Because I am ruined, she thought. *Because the flash destroyed my life. Because a long time ago, it took my family and left me alone in a world where every goddamn thing I see reminds me that it did and that it's my fault. Because everything is rotting inside, and I'm the only one who can smell it.*

Because there is a secret at the heart of the flash, and the world should know about it.

Because Stephen Hauser is a liar, and the world should know that too.

Because when you spend your whole life thinking about the moment everything went wrong and an opportunity comes to fix things, you take it, no matter what it costs.

Because you're ruined—but maybe everything else doesn't have to be.

"Why do you do it?" Annami asked Soro. "Don't tell me it's because you like the bar. There are a thousand better bars. This is New York City."

"I like how it feels," he answered. "Giving up the control, knowing that anyone riding me in a darkshare probably has a pretty dark reason. Most of the time, I wake up back here, no idea what I was used for. There was another me out there, doing crazy things, I don't know what. It's a rush."

"You aren't worried about the risks? Getting hurt or killed? Catching something?"

"Nope," the man said. "I'm already ruined."

Mama Run returned to the bar, shaking her head. Annami peered through the crimson gloom of the darkshare den and saw that the lanky man she'd been talking to had vanished.

"Poor fellow," Mama Run said. "No work for him here. Not

gonna put a customer in that. We have standards, you know? Dunno why Chai even let him in."

Annami stood and limped to the back corner of the room, where a set of lockers was built into the wall, each with a key-code lock. These were extremely high-tech, tamperproof, with a built-in microwave generator that would destroy the data on anything inside if an attempt was made to break in. All part of the service for Mama Run's runners—you could keep your personal items safe while you were earning and retrieve them when you were done.

She tapped in her access code—all locks were either mechanical or code-based now, biometric security just another thing the flash made obsolete. It even hit money itself—cash and cards still existed, still worked, but mostly you paid for things with your payphrase. Like the passphrase at the door, everything was tied to your pattern, to your memory. To you.

A slim device waited in the open locker, her mini. Annami retrieved it and quickly logged in to her bank account—not her regular account but the anonymous crypto e-count she'd set up to hold her payment for doing the darkshare. Mama Run had been true to her word—the money was there, every penny, less the 20 percent house commission. Some darkhouses charged less—she'd found places in her research that would go as low as 5 percent—but they didn't feel good to her. They felt like black holes. The sort of places the tremor man probably went looking for after Mama Run turned him away. In the black holes, clients were worse, jobs were worse, risks were worse. Darksharing was hellish no matter where you did it—but hell had circles, and some were deeper than others.

Annami slipped the mini into her pocket, wincing as her raw palm scraped against the fabric of her pants, frowning at the weird stiffness from the dead man's blood still soaking them.

Something tiny impacted against her mini as it found its way into her pocket. That wasn't right. Her pockets should be empty. She'd emptied them before starting the darkshare, as per Mama Run's rules. It was a precaution—you didn't want to give your runner access to your personal property. Other than every last millimeter of your body, of course.

Whatever was in her pocket had been put there by her runner, whoever he or she had been.

She pulled her mini back out, then dug around in her pocket and came up with the item. A small, dark rectangle about the size of her thumbnail, with a few electrical contacts on one end. A data. She frowned.

Annami returned to the bar and set the little chip down. Mama Run glanced at it, incurious.

"I had this on me after the share," Annami said. "It's not mine."

"Uh-huh," Mama Run said. "So?"

"So maybe you can get it back to the client?"

"No way to do that," the older woman answered. "Don't know who the client was. No way to contact. That's the idea, remember?"

"I do—but if they come back here to use your darkshare again, maybe you could . . ."

"Little girl, I wouldn't even know if they did. All anonymous. Look, that thing yours now, whatever it is. If client wanted it, client should have put it somewhere he could get it after the share ended."

Soro reached over and picked up the data.

"Don't you want to know what's on it?" he said. "I could help you with that, if you want."

"You can?" Annami said. "I assumed it'd be encrypted."

The man smiled/smirked and pulled out his own mini. He slipped the data into a slot on its side and tapped the screen a few times.

"That's what I mean. I know how to— Huh. Nope. No encryption. It was open. Surprising. Anyway, look."

He held up the screen so Annami could see. A spreadsheet, with rows and rows of data—each row holding seven thirteen-digit numbers, apparently random. But they were not random at all, and Annami immediately recognized what they were.

"Flash patterns," she said.

"Looks like. Probably ripped out of a database somewhere. That's what you were in the middle of—someone was buying stolen patterns, someone was selling them."

Annami considered this. Stealing flash patterns was supposedly impossible—but here they were. Every one of these sequences allowed access to its owner's body via the flash network, without registration or permission required, straight through the I-fi implant almost everyone on earth possessed at the base of their spine, in the S5 nerve bundle, the on-ramp to the neural highway.

Flashing into someone via a stolen pattern was like darksharing but worse, because the vessel didn't have to consent.

Soro removed the data from his mini and placed it back on the bar, lifting his fingers away quickly as if the device was radioactive. The little black thing lay there, evil, the reason at least one person was dead. Annami made no move to pick it up.

"Could be worth a lot of money," Mama Run said, her tone clipped. "If you find someone to buy."

Annami thought about a lot of money and what she was trying to do. She needed a lot of money—that was the whole point, why she had just sold her body. If she had a lot of money she wouldn't have to sell it again.

She reached out and lifted her glass, which still contained the dregs of the second drink Mama Run had poured her. She tipped up the glass, swishing the liquor around in her mouth.

Annami brought the empty glass down hard on the data. The little cube of silicon and plastic and metal crunched and became nothing.

She looked up at Mama Run, who was staring at her, head tilted, some sort of reevaluation or calculation going on behind her eyes.

"Not the kind of money I want to earn. Do you have more jobs for me?" Annami asked. "More clients who might want to use me for a share?"

"Oh, always," Mama answered. "Good strong vessel like you . . . always."

"Good," Annami said. "I'm going home to get cleaned up and sleep a little."

She reached out across the bar, feeling pain in her hands and across her body, and in her soul, like licks from an infected tongue, the filthy rime of whoever had used her hands to kill someone. She flicked the remnants of the smashed data onto the floor.

"And then I'd like you to send me out again."

CHAPTER 5

AGAIN, THE BARN

GABRIELLE INSERTED THE IV INTO HER BODY'S ARM, TAPED THE needle down, and released the clamp on the tubing, allowing fluid to flow.

It had been only a few hours since the switch, and dehydration wasn't a problem yet—but giving her unconscious body some saline wouldn't hurt it, and it let her feel like she was doing something positive.

She placed a hand on her body's chest, feeling the slow heartbeat beneath.

Gabby had performed this test many times, unreasonably certain that her body would simply die when she wasn't paying attention. And then . . . she had no idea. Would she die too? Was her mind linked in some fundamental way to the body now lying on a makeshift hospital bed she had created in the barn from blankets and a lab table?

She didn't know, but she was becoming increasingly certain she would find out, sooner or later.

Gabrielle had tried to switch out of Paul's body into her own twice more since the first attempt, changing the variables a bit each time, burning through the money she had transferred over from their account—their entire savings, painstakingly accumulated over years of self-denial and occasional moments of unexpected good fortune—gone in a single evening, and for nothing. She had failed, failed, and failed again. She was still Paul, and Paul was gone.

The only silver lining she could claw from all of it: if she never figured out how to bring her husband back, she'd never have to confess to him what she'd done.

She laughed, but when the sound came out it was more like a choke, or a sob.

Gabrielle had learned things from the failed attempts—no experiment was ever truly a failure, you always learned something. She knew what she would try next, if she could, but she had no resources left, no <u>money</u>. She was done.

She thought about every frivolous use of her equipment in the year since Hendricks Capital had signed her, every time she had powered up the system to run diagnostics or recheck results or try out a theory she knew probably wouldn't work, burning through funds out of misplaced confidence that she'd <u>definitely</u> find the Alzheimer's treatment before the money was gone. If she'd skipped even one of those, been just a bit more frugal, she'd have another chance right now to use her gear to save her life and her husband's life.

Gabrielle resisted the urge to check her body's pulse again and instead touched the familiar forehead, running her thumb over the stitched-up gash just below the hairline, a bruise now coming up around it. Still so strange to see her own face, especially at peace like this. How many people ever got the chance to see themselves sleep? *Few*, she thought.

But then, she wasn't asleep. She was in a coma, basically. She was . . . dormant.

Gabrielle suddenly realized she might have to catheterize herself, especially now that she was putting fluids into the body. Maybe even a feeding tube.

No, she thought. *If it gets to that point, a hospital. Well before that point, a hospital.*

None of this was her fault. It was an accident. There was no liability. Honestly, she never even had to tell anyone. Thoughts ran through her mind, ideas she hated herself for entertaining but couldn't stop. Hypothetically, if she had to, she could go on living as Paul forever, raising their daughter, visiting her body in an assisted-living facility. She could . . .

Gabby acknowledged a pressure at the base of her spine, a pain, not sharp but constant, and understood why she had been thinking about catheters.

The thought repulsed her. She didn't know why. She'd been as intimate with Paul, with every part of Paul, as any wife could be. But urinating, no, any bodily function at all, even down to eating or drinking—it would be like an admission that all of this was real, actually happening. That Paul's body was hers, now, maybe forever, and she would have to take the necessary steps to maintain it, live in it, grow old in it.

Could she do that? She forced herself to consider it, really think it through. She wasn't sure. As long as the problem remained clinical, immediate, in theory solvable, she could put panic aside. But if it stopped being any of those things, Gabrielle didn't know how long she would stay sane.

It had been hours with no real progress, and she could feel fear creeping in around the edges of her mind. Worse, she had no idea how to make progress. Not as long as she was broke.

Gabby pulled her phone from her right front pocket—Paul's was still in her left. She scrolled through the contacts until she found Jon Corran and tapped the little handset icon.

"Gabrielle?" came the answer, after a few rings. "This is a surprise. What's up?"

"Hi, Jon," she said without thinking, her body tensing as she heard Paul's deep voice coming from her body, a problem she hadn't even considered, focused as she was on the more immediate issue, which was convincing this man to give her quite a bit of money.

A pause from the other end of the line.

"Uh . . . is this . . ."

"It's Paul, Jon. Gabrielle's husband. Just using her phone. She asked me to call you."

"Huh. Hey, Paul. We've met, right? At the—"

"Yeah. The cognition conference, in Memphis. Gabby was giving a presentation."

Gabrielle hoped there hadn't been another time, a more recent time, but she didn't think so. Paul didn't intersect with her professional world all that often.

"That's right, of course," Jon said. "So is she coming to the phone, or . . . ?"

"She's tied up with something. That's why she asked me to call. She wanted me to lay it out for you."

"Lay it out, huh? Okay, I'm listening."

Gabrielle thought, trying to put herself into her husband's head, searching for a way to explain things to Jon Corran in the way a music professor would, someone with no more than a spousal understanding of her work.

"All right. Gabrielle's had a breakthrough. She says it's big. I don't understand the technical side, but she was running a series of experiments that paid off in some significant way. You know, with the rats?"

"I do," Jon said. "Go on."

"She wants to use the equipment again, right away, to follow up, see if she can improve on what she did, but there's some . . . I don't know . . . urgency about it. If she doesn't go now, she'll lose what she's got."

"Okay, so why are you talking to me?"

"Because Gabrielle spent all the money."

"Ah," Jon said. "It's not the money, though. It's my money. Well, my company's money. Hendricks Capital."

"She knows that," Gabby said, trying to inject a sheepish note into Paul's voice—so strange, working with someone else's voice, like knitting with gloves on. "Between you and me, I think that's why she had me call you."

"Yeah?"

"Yeah. She's in there, up to her elbows in this rat's brain—well, not her elbows, the rat's not that big—but you know what I mean. She gets so focused, was just yelling for me to get you on the phone and convince you to transfer over some extra funding."

"Uh-huh," Jon said, unconvinced.

"Look. I know this is ridiculous, the fact that I'm on the phone with you instead of her, but it is what it is. Can we talk about it, at least?"

"Did she give you any details?"

"Hold on," Gabrielle said.

She held the phone to her chest, then called out a question. She didn't know if Jon would be able to hear it, but she had an illusion to maintain.

Her body, lying on the blanket-covered lab table with a needle in its arm, didn't answer. But that was all right. She knew what Jon would want to hear.

"She says ninety percent plaque reduction off sequence four. Does that mean anything to you?"

"Yes. Yes, it does," Jon said, his tone changing from skeptical/amused to . . . business. His tone was business. "How much does she want?"

"A hundred thousand," Gabby answered, without hesitation. With that much, she could run the equipment enough times to test all her theories. She could solve this. She knew it.

"I'll send three thousand," Jon said.

"Three?" Gabrielle said, hearing the hard edge in her voice and knowing it was out of character for her husband in this particular conversation but unable to help it. "She said a hundred. Can you . . . can you help me out here?"

"Paul, you don't know me, not really, but I remember liking you when we met. I also like your wife, very much. But the truth is this—if I sent you a nickel right now, just five cents, I'd have to spend a good few hours in my boss' office tomorrow justifying why I put good money after bad. Sending three thousand, just on your word, not even hers . . . I'll probably get fired.

"But my grandmother died of Alzheimer's, and it was hell on the family. My aunt spent years taking care of her at the end, sort of ruined her life. So maybe you tell Gabby to take her three grand and please, please turn it into something that will help people and, incidentally, let me keep my job. All right, Paul? That sound like something you can do?"

"Yeah," she said. "I can do that. When will you send the money?"

"I'm authorizing the transfer as we speak. She'll have it in ten seconds."

"Thank you," Gabrielle began, but Jon had already ended the call.

She quickly pulled up her bank account again to verify that the funds had landed—they had—and slipped her phone back into her pocket.

Three thousand. Nothing. Not enough.

She could fire the laser exactly once.

So . . . either she figured out how to reverse the switch right here, right now, or the game was up. Keeping all of this secret would be irresponsible. Dangerous. Criminal, maybe.

Gabby made a decision. If this last attempt didn't work, she would call a hospital, and then she would explain to Corran and Hendricks what had happened, and shortly after that she would lose control over this thing she'd found, this thing that could transform the entire world.

This was it. Her one and only shot.

Gabrielle stood very still, breathing in the musk of the barn, the odors of animals kept there long ago and those kept there now. She listened to the small noises, and felt the deepening pain in Paul's bladder, and ignored it. She went deep into her mind, considering all the ways she might fix this impossible, confounding situation.

And she chose.

The laser rig was still in position from the last failed experiment. She just had to power it up.

Gabrielle set the system to run a cycle, typing instructions quickly on the controller keyboard, making adjustments based on everything her failures had taught her. Finished, she tapped the enter key and sent the firing pattern off into the rig. She heard the whine again, building, lapping up on itself, filling the barn with its throbbing buzz-saw pulse.

The lights. The beautiful, flickering lights, filling the barn once again with fractal patterns, dividing and combining, the visuals accompanied by the piercing industrial sounds of the laser firing, a fireworks display scored by a steel mill.

Gabrielle glanced at her body, still so still.

Then she looked up at the walls of the barn, opening her eyes, Paul's eyes, as wide as she could, drinking in the patterns.

They ran across her retinas scattering, recombining a murmuration of starlings in light murmuring into her brain into Paul's brain/

Gabrielle heard a down-cycling whine, like an unplugged buzz saw slowing to a stop. Her arm hurt a little. Her head hurt quite a bit. She opened her eyes, saw the barn ceiling.

She sat up, turned her head, and saw her husband looking at her, his eyes wide, terrified. A darkness on the legs of his pants, spreading slowly.

"Gabrielle?" Paul said.

CHAPTER 6

NeOnet GLOBAL NORTH AMERICAN HUB, MANHATTAN

MAKING PROGRESS, ANNAMI THOUGHT.

She was at her desk, one of about a hundred arranged like spokes on a wheel across the primary flash-network-monitoring floor at Anyone's US headquarters. In her hand, her mini, and on its screen, her e-count balance, healthy and vibrant. A long sequence of darkshares for Mama Run over the past few months had fostered its steady growth. Annami took the minimum possible recovery time between each share, earning as much as she could as quickly as she could. Mama Run clearly had opinions about this behavior, this immolation. Fortunately, Mama kept those opinions to herself—and why wouldn't she, with 20 percent of every dollar Annami earned going to her?

But even 80 percent added up, and Annami had taken to checking the balance regularly, obsessively. A ritual of reassurance, and one of two compulsive behaviors she had developed in the past few months of darksharing.

Annami swiped across her mini's display, closing the account-balance screen.

She resisted indulging her second compulsion, not liking the lack of self-control it implied, already knowing it was a fight she would lose. Annami sighed, then tapped her mini a few times, navigating to another site on the web.

A beautiful man appeared, smiling. His hand stretched out in invitation, in welcome, past the boundaries of the screen, in full, impeccable 3-D, then returned to his side as the man nodded. The loop reset, and the man reached out again. His skin was tinted with the slightest, hard-to-define color—she had heard it described as amber. His eyes were deep, very dark. His hair was silver, yet ageless. It looked like the metal, gleaming. Physically, this man was perfect.

Annami's mouth curled up at one edge, a sneer transforming her face, the exact emotional opposite of the expression held by the man on the screen.

She flicked her thumb across the mini, and a few lines of text replaced the image. Annami scanned down to the most important part—a date and time, unchanged, uncanceled—and felt the slight emotional release that accompanied the completion of the ritual. She also knew that a watch spring inside her would begin to wind again almost immediately, growing tighter and tighter until she found herself once again looking at the beautiful, smiling man. Sometimes it took as long as a few hours, sometimes, in her more anxious moments, just minutes.

It could be worse. A few more jobs with Mama Run, and she'd have enough to pull off the plan and then some. All she had to do was hold out, try not to think about what darksharing was doing to her and making her do. She could stay the course. Just a few more weeks, a few more jobs.

She pushed up the sleeve of her blouse, a nice blue silk piece, the kind of thing she usually wore to work at Anyone—so different from her darksharing uniform of jeans, boots, sweatshirt, no makeup. Annami looked at the scab on her arm, starting just above her wrist and heading up toward her elbow, about four inches long. She had no idea how she'd gotten it.

"Bhangra George. Huh. Are you going to bid?" someone asked from just behind her.

Annami started, caught, pulling down her sleeve. She turned to see the woman at the entrance to her workstation and felt immediate relief. Just Bea, a little smile on her face.

There were, certainly, people who would kill Annami the moment they got even the slightest hint as to what she was planning, but Beatrice Fring was not one of them.

"I dunno," Annami said. "It's kind of silly, I know, but maybe I will. Is that dumb?"

"Nah. Do what you want," Bea said, leaning against the divider wall separating Annami's zone from the rest of the office. "No way you'll win—I'm sure a lot of people want some time inside that lovely, lovely man, and most are probably richer than both of us put together. But if you don't mind losing the bidding fee . . ."

"Nope," Annami said. "It's for charity. I don't mind."

"And you have the reserve?"

Annami nodded. "I've been saving up."

She had pulled together the reserve—the cost of a ticket to bid in the auction—by the end of her third job for Mama Run, and at this point had accumulated almost all of what she thought she would need to win it.

Auctions like this weren't uncommon—a celebrity of one type or another selling a few minutes or hours of time inside their enviable bodies to the highest bidder—and so Annami had been able to run an analysis, look for trends. She used winning bids from comparable auctions, filtered through a number of factors— the current level of fame and desirability of Bhangra George as compared to other actors who had done similar things, the length of time he was allowing inside his flesh (ten minutes), the entry fee, the charity that would benefit (a support group for people whom the flash had zeroed out, along with their families). Putting all of that together gave her a range for what she would likely need to win the auction. Double that, and there—her target amount.

Annami would not lose. She would not lose.

"I know I won't win," Annami said, putting an awkward, embarrassed tone into her voice. "I'm just doing it for fun. Bhangra George is . . . I just . . . I guess I'm a fan."

Bea waved a hand in the air, dismissing her concerns.

"Like who you like, I don't care," she said. "Fun is fun. I like fun. Speaking of which, drinks after work? Gilbert says he found a great place over in Brownsville."

"Nah, too expensive," Annami said. "But thank you. Something else soon?"

"Sure, sounds good—I feel like it's been forever since we last went out, actually. Like . . . months. Have you started dating someone?"

Annami laughed.

"Who the hell would date this mess?" she said, gesturing to herself.

"Gilbert," Bea said, her voice flat and certain. "Also Ruth, and maybe Andy, and that's just the people within fifty feet of us right now. The only reason you're single is because you want to be."

"Is that a problem?"

"Well, no, of course not. I just feel like you don't know what you're worth, Annami. You're gorgeous, the smartest person I know, fun . . ."

I know exactly what I'm worth, Annami thought. *You have no idea how much some people would pay to know where I am.*

A loud, urgent chime sounded from her desk, and Annami spun to look.

"What the hell?" Bea said.

"Node's down," Annami said. "Looks like a big one."

"Ah, shit," Bea said. "Guess I'm not going out for drinks after work either. We'll all be here until midnight."

"Maybe," Annami said, studying the large display that took up most of her workspace, three thinscreens floating side by side, linked to create a single image.

The thinnies projected a three-dimensional representation of the worldwide flash network, varying shades of color depicting traffic in different regions across the planet as billions of people flickered between different bodies for purposes large and small. Surgeons flashing across the globe to perform operations in remote hospitals, trained soldiers flashing into local vessels in war zones for military operations, tourists enjoying vacations in exotic locations via surrogate bodies, the cost of their holiday excesses left to be endured by the vessels long after the happy travelers flashed back home. Dwarfing it all, the endless daily migration of labor from one region to another, people renting out their bodies to people willing to perform the work they themselves did not want to do.

All processed through the trillion-dollar industry that was the flash, the tech that had transformed the world, disrupted everything, from travel to farming to entertainment to law and government. It touched virtually everyone on the planet, the flash patterns of almost every mind on earth stored in Anyone's hypersecure data vaults, shuttled back and forth via either I-fi spinal implants or hardline flash rigs for those unable or unwilling to have the surgery.

The flash network was enormously complex to maintain, even with 90 percent of its traffic managed by decentralized neural nets that handled all but the highest-level processes. The AIs monitored both travelers and vessels for things that could kneecap the system—suicidal impulses, users moving outside preapproved locations and tasks, load balancing, and so on. Payments, rental duration, transfers—almost all of it was automated. But not <u>all</u> of it, which was why Annami and Bea and Gilbert and their colleagues around the world had jobs.

And that was just the light flash, the public, highly monitored side of the tech. No one really knew how many people used the dark flash, the unregistered, unrestricted version that moved through private networks—although Annami's experiences with darksharing over the past few months suggested it was more than anyone realized. She hadn't done the same job twice, as far as she could tell.

"I see what happened here," Annami said, glancing up from her screens at Bea. "Not great."

She pointed at a row of data.

"Lagos got a spike in usage, almost double their usual, and the system tried to offload to the local transfer nodes. They were running high too, the AI couldn't self-correct, and it cascaded. Made it all the way to reserve nodes in Geneva and Kuala Lumpur. The network's always been vulnerable to this. Like twentieth-century power grids."

Annami could see alerts running up the side of the screen; people all over the planet were already getting stuck in bodies past their allotted time, and others were being misrouted—never good. People expecting to flash into a vessel for a scuba vacation in Cairns ending up in a body slated for a day of strawberry picking in Phoenix, things like that. If the problem wasn't fixed, users might start to get zeroed out—their minds sent to destination coordinates 0, 0, 0, aka nowhere, leaving their primes forever unresponsive. Zeroes. It wasn't supposed to happen. Officially, Anyone blamed it on user error at the consumer level—but the system was complex and always handling more traffic than it should. Mistakes happened.

The flash net could have been built with multiple redundancies and traffic managed so it was never anywhere near the breaking point. That's how Annami would have designed it. But Anyone, and more particularly its CEO, Stephen Hauser, wanted everyone on earth to flash. All of their ad campaigns and marketing were built around the idea that everyone could, safe and easy. Whether that was actually true . . . never mind. Flash. Flash. Flash.

Be anyone with Anyone. That was the slogan.

Annami squinted at the problems rolling across her screens. Mounting chaos, but no one seemed to have zeroed out yet. The technicians could probably get it solved, if nothing got worse.

One issue caught her eye—a combat action in Mindanao, in the Philippines. Military flash traffic was highly classified, above Annami's clearance, but easy to spot if you knew what you were looking for.

Highly trained soldiers from some wealthy nation would flash into on-site vessels—usually volunteers from a local army. Then the team would run their mission, using these human beings the same way they might a tank or a Humvee—just another piece of equipment. If a body they were using took a wound in the course of the fight, no big deal, they could just flash back to their primes waiting safe and sound back home. And then their vessels would open their eyes on the battlefield, realizing they'd been shot in the gut or their leg had just been blown off, and . . . oh well. That's war. The cost of doing business.

It was ugly, one of the ugliest things about the flash. It made Annami sick. If she were in charge, it would never have been allowed. But she was not. Stephen Hauser ran Anyone, and he had built the world he wanted.

Annami knew a great deal about the flash. Arguably, more than anyone else alive. Certainly, she knew how to fix the network outage. Instead, she decided to use it.

It was time, finally, to take a step she'd known was coming ever since she'd seen the first advertisement for Bhangra George's auction.

"You should get back to your station," Annami told Bea, reaching her hands to the keyboard. "Sooner we get started fixing all this, sooner it's done."

"Yeah," Bea said without enthusiasm.

She turned to walk away. Annami watched her go, then picked up her mini from her desk. She ran the pad of her index finger down its slim profile, and a datachip emerged smoothly from a slot in its side.

The data was tiny, but the code it contained would be a red flag to the right eyes—no, a burning pile of white phosphorus, hotter than the sun. A blazing arrow pointing directly at Annami's carefully constructed current identity. If her plan didn't work as she hoped, if someone beat her in that goddamn auction, then it would be only a matter of time before they traced the code back to her station, to her system access. Then her anonymity, meticulously maintained for so long, would be trashed. NeOnet Global HR records would serve up her face, and then they'd know. They'd have her.

But, Annami thought, *what are you staying safe for? Isn't that the whole point? That the time for "safe" is over?*

She'd taken a job at Anyone only to learn its systems—the way it operated and maintained the flash network. In many ways, it was a terrible, foolish risk—Bleeder was out there hunting her, and this job basically put her right under his nose. Working at Anyone wasn't a career. It was a means to an end, a way to steal the enemy's secrets.

The idea had always been that a time would come to act—to use all her acquired knowledge in one decisive strike. That opportunity had arrived, in the shape of Bhangra George, and nothing like it was likely to come again.

Annami pressed the data to the edge of her station's thin-screen display and felt the tiny vibration under her fingertip that indicated that the instructional code inside it had been inserted into the flash network's control systems.

Come on, she thought, *find me some Centuries.*

And with that, the clock began to tick. The network was scrubbed constantly in an effort to locate and destroy intrusions of the type Annami had just performed. Yes, the flash was currently compromised by the problem in Lagos, and the techs' attention would be focused on rerouting and rebuilding for a while—but eventually, everything would be back to normal and she'd be found out. Bleeder would come for her, and . . . well. She just had to make it to the auction. She could do that.

Annami slipped the data back into her mini. She looked at her screens again, thinking about the combat action in Mindanao. It was pulling a lot of network resources, and to her practiced eye had strong potential as a failure point. If that node went down, not just the soldiers but also their vessels would go, all at once. If one dies, both die.

She hated that Anyone had let the flash be used for war, but that decision was not the fault of the people fighting and dying on the other side of the world. Annami reached out to the keyboard and typed rapidly, reallocating resources, setting up new pathways and strengthening existing connections to make it more likely that the node would hold until Anyone's techs fixed the network as a whole.

That done, Annami stood. She grabbed her bag and walked across the impressive, domed chamber that was NeOnet's primary North American hub, knowing she was probably looking at it for the last time. A huge mural dominated the ceiling: a stylized human brain, lit up with all synapses firing. The painting was a work by an artist duo known as Threeless One. They built collaborative art pieces by flashing into each other, taking turns seeing what their partner had created while their own mind was dormant, then building and elaborating upon the last round of work.

A three-dimensional holo floated in the air below the mural, displaying node status across the entire network—the same image she had just seen on her workstation's thinnies. She glanced up and saw that another node was down, this one in Cameroon. The problem had stepped up another level—bad for the flash, but good for Annami. The worse it got, the more time it bought her until they found her little bit of code, her Century-hunter.

As Annami walked across the hub floor, she could feel the intensity of the activity around her. Everyone else in the room was focused on solving the problem, bringing the network back online. Everyone but her.

She stopped at the open door to the office of Bertrand Milsen, the hub coordinator, her boss.

"Good luck with the network outages," she called in to him. "I hope it doesn't get any worse."

Bertrand looked up from his own display, a panicked look of confusion on his face.

"W-what?" he said. "What are you talking about? Why aren't you at your station?"

"I'm sorry, Bertrand," she said. "I quit."

"No . . . no, no, no," he said, his face going pale, looking like he was on the verge of full-blown panic. "You're my best, Annami. My best. I need you. Don't you see what's happening?"

He gestured at his display. A quick glance told Annami that another node was teetering.

"Is it money? I can authorize triple overtime—whatever you want. Just tell me. Please."

"I'm sorry," she said again, and she was. Annami felt bad for him. Bertrand was a good boss and seemed like a good man, but she didn't have time for good men anymore. The bad ones deserved all her attention.

Annami turned and walked out of Bertrand's office, hearing his voice calling out behind her. To his credit, he didn't curse her name, or call her a bitch, or anything some people might have done in his position. He just repeated his request that she stay, repeated his offer of money, promotion, anything she wanted. A good man.

She ignored him and kept walking. The money she could make here, even triple overtime, wouldn't get her where she needed to go, not in time. A few more jobs for Mama Run, a bit more immolation, then the auction, and it'd be over.

All of it.

CHAPTER 7

AND AGAIN, THE BARN

"I THINK I'M HAVING A STROKE," PAUL SAID, HIS VOICE UNSTEADY.

Gabby slipped off the lab table and took a step toward her husband. Something pulled at her arm, accompanied by a sharp, slightly internal pain, and she remembered the IV.

A tidal wave of disconnection washed over her—she had a memory of putting the needle in her own arm using someone else's large, strong hands, each of which could span an octave's worth of piano keys. Paul had told her that once, seemed very proud of it.

"Gabrielle?" Paul said.

"I'm coming," she said. "It's all right. Just hold on."

Gabby removed the IV from her arm, slipping the tape off the needle and slapping it on the insertion site as a temporary bandage, then walked quickly across the room to Paul. She put her hands out and cupped his face.

"Look at me," she said, summoning up her medical resident's voice. "Right in the eyes."

He did, and she saw that his pupils were dilated, but that was completely understandable—a stress reaction.

"How do you feel?" she asked.

"Feel?" Paul repeated slowly. "The last thing I remember, I was putting the baby down. And then . . . I blink, and I'm here, and I've . . ."

He gestured down toward his pants. She could smell it, an acrid stink that made her think of rock-club bathrooms in Detroit—Harpos, places like that, where she watched hard-core and thrash and punk.

That was good, though. That was her memory, from before she'd met Paul. He had never been to those places. Her brain was working, and apparently somewhat whole.

"I know," Gabrielle said.

She slipped one hand down to his neck, felt the stubble, had a version of a feeling that was like déjà vu but was not, as she had felt this same stubble with his hands not so long ago. His pulse was strong, fast—again, stress.

Paul reached up to hold her wrists, gently.

"Why were you lying on that table, with an IV in your arm?" he said. "What happened to your forehead? What the hell's going on, Gabby?"

"I'll explain," she said. "As much as I can—but will you please let me examine you? Ask you a few questions?"

"Am I all right?" Paul said. "Where's the Kitten?"

"Asleep, in the house."

She pointed at the baby monitor on one of the nearby workstations, its soft green power light on and glowing.

"She's okay, Paul. We'll hear if she wakes up. Come on. Let me check you out."

Paul nodded and allowed himself to be led to that same workstation, where Gabrielle kept a few basic medical instruments. She ran a quick workup on him—blood pressure, temperature, reflex test. All within normal ranges she'd expect to see.

His eyes never left her.

"You're all right," she said. "But let me ask you—do you feel like . . . yourself?"

He frowned.

"Myself?"

"Yes. I don't have another way to ask. Does anything seem off? Different?"

"Other than the fact that I teleported to the barn?"

"Other than that."

She put her hand on his chest—not the movement of a medical professional but of his wife, someone who cared for him.

He seemed almost startled, which she understood. It had been a while since she last touched him like that. Or at all.

"My knee hurts," he ventured in a tone of someone doing a self-diagnostic test, running his systems. "Throat hurts too. And I'm soaked in pee. Can't forget that. But otherwise, yeah, I feel like myself."

Paul reached up and caught her hand in his, holding it lightly.

"Gabby, whatever it is, whatever happened to me, I need to know."

She stood there, letting him hold her hand, and thought about how she could possibly explain something she did not understand herself—not even a little bit.

Basic, she thought. *Keep it basic.*

"I asked if you were feeling like yourself," she said, "because for a few hours, you weren't. You were me."

Paul tilted his head. He opened his mouth to ask a question, but Gabrielle pushed on before he could ask it.

"I was in the lab running an experiment while you were in the house with Kat. It was going to be my last run—the funds from Hendricks were pretty much gone. I figured I'd just . . . go for it. Go out with a bang. I turned the system up as high as it would go and ran a series on Wilbur. The strength of the laser exceeded the tolerances of the shielding, and it made a sort of projection in the barn. Lights swirling, flashing . . . all over. I looked at them, watched them, and the next thing I knew I was in your body."

"In my body . . . ," Paul said, testing out the words.

"Your mind. My consciousness was controlling your body. Until I figured out how to reverse it."

To his credit, Paul didn't call bullshit on her. He didn't say anything.

"Do you believe me?" she said.

"No," he answered. "You're speaking nonsense. But I can't think of any reason you'd be making it up, either."

He pointed at her arm, where the piece of tape still rested on her skin, a round bubble of blood pushing up beneath it.

"The IV?"

Gabrielle let go of Paul's hand. She grabbed the tape and pulled it free of her arm, a little hiss of pain escaping her mouth. She reached into her medical kit and pulled out an alcohol swab and a proper bandage, applied both to the needle mark.

"My body was dormant while my mind was in yours," she said. "Almost like a coma. I didn't know how long the switch would last, so I set up an IV to keep myself . . . it, I guess . . . hydrated."

She was rapidly realizing that existing pronouns were not up to the task of a situation where one person was temporarily more than one person.

"Your body was dormant . . . but it was still here. Your mind was in my body. Okay . . . so where was my mind? Where was I?" Paul asked. "Actually, no. Before that—are you all right? You're asking about me, but are you okay?"

His eyes flicked up to the bandage on her forehead.

"I fell, I think," Gabrielle said. "When the switch happened.

I'm okay. You did a good job sewing me up, even with those huge paws of yours."

Paul held up one of his hands, looked at it, wiggled his fingers like he was playing an imaginary piano.

"Happy to help," he said, and then he smiled, and Gabby knew he was definitely himself.

"I don't know where you—your consciousness—went," she said. "I don't understand how it happened at all. I have so much work to do. I didn't do any of the things I should have. I should have been taking notes the whole time, but I was just . . . I just wanted it to be over."

"Was it that bad?"

"Not bad, just . . . weird. Really weird. And I needed to know if I could reverse it. If I couldn't do it, I'd still be you, and you'd be . . . wherever you were. Do you have any memories? Did you dream?"

"Nothing," Paul said.

"Tell me if anything comes to mind."

"I will."

A faint cry from the baby monitor, and they both tweaked their heads toward it, like rabbits freezing at the sound of a cracking twig in the distance.

"Kitty Kat's up," Gabby said.

"Good timing. I need a shower."

They walked back to the house, Paul limping a bit, neither saying anything, and Gabrielle went to attend to the baby while her husband disappeared into the bathroom.

Kat wasn't truly up—she had just skipped toward wakefulness for a moment and was quickly soothed back to sleep.

While Paul was in the shower, Gabby took his khakis and boxers and rinsed them in the sink, then draped them over a clothes rack in their room to dry a bit before she put them in the laundry hamper. That took around a minute, and for the remaining twenty-nine of Paul's time in the shower, Gabrielle just sat. Thinking. Smiling from time to time, a smile of disbelief, of amazement.

Now Paul was sitting on their bed, wrapped in a damp towel. His expression was thoughtful.

He pushed one end of the towel aside, uncovering his knee, where a bruise was blossoming. He stared at it for a while, then looked up at her.

"I fell," Gabrielle said. "When I was, uh, in you."

Paul shook his head.

"I believe you," he said. "About all of it. Do you think you can do it again?"

He scratched his ear, the little tic she'd seen him perform a thousand times before but only now really understood.

"Why? Do you want to be in me?" Gabby said.

Paul tilted his head again, the same movement he'd used before, the *Did I just hear that right?* tilt.

She got up, walked the three steps to the bed, and sat down next to him. She put her hand on his chest.

"Gabby . . . ," he said, and she kissed him.

"Shut up," she said. "Don't talk yourself out of a good thing."

Gabrielle wasn't sure why she was doing this—it had been a long time, certainly, but there had been a point not so long ago when she wasn't sure she would ever want to sleep with Paul again.

Now she did, as much as she ever had.

She understood him now, in a way she never had.

They were together, and it was very good—strong, passionate. Paul desperate to have her again after so long, Gabrielle being with him while remembering what it was like to be him.

They lay in their bed, holding hands, recovering.

"I spent all our money," Gabrielle said.

Paul's hand clenched. Just a little, but she felt it.

"What?" he asked.

"I told you. I spent the last of the Hendricks money on the run-through that switched us. I needed money to swap us back. I used our savings."

A long pause.

"Well," Paul said. "At least it worked."

Gabrielle got up on one elbow and looked at him.

"It didn't," she said. "I had to call Jon Corran and beg him for more. He wired me an extra three grand. Enough to run the system one last time. That's the one that worked."

"You called Corran?" Paul said. "How? Weren't you . . . what did you say . . . dormant?"

"Yeah," Gabrielle said.

Paul thought about that.

"Huh," he said.

He put his hands behind his head on the pillow, looked at her.

"This is so fucked up."

"It is," she said. "And we can't tell anyone about it."

"Why not?"

"Because if I can reproduce this . . . if this is a technology, not just some weird fluke, then it will change everything. Everything."

"I know. I've been thinking about it. My brain just starts spinning off, one thing after another this could do. People getting into other people's bodies . . . it's wild."

"Right. So we need to keep it under control, for now. We need to think about this."

Paul's eyes flicked to the ceiling.

"It could be worth a ton of money," he said. "Billions."

"Probably," Gabrielle said. "But the money's not really the main thing I'm thinking about here."

Ideas ran through her mind, and for every wonderful, world-transforming application she thought up for the technology, an equally horrible abuse came to mind.

She had reversed the swap with Paul and returned to her own body.

Nothing had forced her to do that. She had chosen to.

Given the option, some people, people in different circumstances, would not make the same choice.

"We have to keep this between us," she said.

"Forever?" Paul said.

"I don't know."

Gabby got out of bed.

"I just need some time," she said. "Time to understand. Time to think."

She found her bra, slipped it over her shoulders, reached back to clasp it.

The doorbell rang, and she froze. She looked at Paul, saw his eyes, wide and startled, like a kid caught looking for Christmas presents.

"Probably just FedEx or something," she said.

But it was late, past the time when anyone would be delivering anything other than pizza or Chinese, and they hadn't ordered.

"Let me," Paul said, rolling out of bed. He threw on clothes and went downstairs.

Gabrielle finished getting dressed, choosing new clothes. The Bad Brains T-shirt didn't seem so funny to her anymore. She could hear Paul talking, light, jovial. Whoever was at the door, it was someone he knew.

She relaxed a little. Evidently one of Paul's friends, or one of hers.

"Hey, Gabby," came Paul's voice, calling from downstairs. "Can you come down?"

"One sec," she called back, fastening her pants, then glancing in a mirror as she left the room. She was a mess, but she couldn't imagine it would matter.

Gabby walked down the stairs and headed for the front door.

She saw who was waiting, Paul standing next to him, a smile on her husband's face she knew was false.

"Hi, Gabrielle," Jon Corran said, a smile on his face too, one she knew was probably just as false but was much harder to see through. "I hope you don't mind me swinging by. After Paul's call, though . . ."

He stepped toward her and extended his hand.

"I just couldn't wait to see this breakthrough of yours."

CHAPTER 8

THE DARKSHARE DEN OF MAMA RUN

ANNAMI TOUCHED ONE OF THE BANDAGES ON HER FACE, TESTING.

Just a twinge of pain, dull, distant.

The bandages were made of a narrow-gauge elastic mesh, infused with a painblock and antihistamine, designed to reduce inflammation and speed healing, to get to the point where they weren't needed within just hours.

She lifted her drink and took a long sip. She had no idea whether alcohol would mix well with the pharmaceuticals the bandages were pumping into her face, but right then, she felt fantastic.

Mama Run was telling a story about a man who had come into her establishment with a dog, insisting that she configure the equipment to let him swap into the poor thing.

"I tell him no, no, no, can't do it," she said, grinning, her arms folded. "He insists, tells me he'll pay any amount."

"But people have done it, right?" Soro said, his face twisting into the version of a smile his scarred cheek would allow. "It is technically possible."

Annami knew by now that it was in fact a smile, not a smirk.

She'd seen a lot of Soro over the last few months, even more since she quit her job at Anyone. Most of her free time was spent at Mama Run's, waiting for jobs to come in. Waiting, and drinking, and learning more about the darkshare and the people who used it. The place just felt comfortable—a world outside judgment. It was hard for her to look normal people in the face anymore after the things she suspected she'd been doing during her darkshare runs. She'd take inventory of herself as she lay on one of the returner couches after a job, finding strange bruises, strange hangovers, a flu she'd been convinced was the onset of one of the hemorrhagic fevers blazing through India until it abruptly vanished on the morning of the third day.

Annami was burning herself up, physically and mentally. Interacting with people who couldn't see the flames felt just . . . absurd. The differential between what they saw and what she felt was too much.

That's why she liked Mama Run's. Everyone here was on fire.

"It's possible," Annami said. "You can do an animal switch. You just have to configure the gear properly—widen the parameters—but it's idiotic. The brain structures are too different. Chimps and higher primates can work—they have a prefrontal cortex that's at least close to ours. Cetaceans are possible too, but the extra lobe in their brain means information processing creates a completely different physical experience."

She knew she should probably stop talking. Both Soro and Mama Run were giving her appraising looks, learning things from this conversation beyond just some basic information about flashing into animals, things about her, but she was feeling loose and good. Maybe the booze and the bandages were hitting her harder than she thought, but hell, at this point, what was the harm? She had just finished what was probably her last darkshare. She'd even told Mama Run as much, which had gotten a frown from the woman, but that didn't matter. The money in her hidden account should be enough to win Bhangra George's auction, no matter who else was bidding. In a week or so, none of this would matter at all.

Storm's coming, she thought. *Stephen Hauser, Centuries, all you pricks. Storm is* <u>*coming*</u>.

"It doesn't matter how hard animal transfers are, though," she went on. "Some people just want to be dolphins. But if they pull it off, they figure out pretty damn quick it's not what they thought. People tend to panic, no matter how much training they have, and if they stay in long enough, their minds crack, and boom, one drowned dolphin-man washing up on the beach.

"Land mammals are a little easier—at least we breathe the same way—but if that guy who came in here had actually swapped into his dog, he'd have found himself with the reasoning capability of a toddler, with sensory input jacked through the roof.

"Idiots who want to try flashing into an animal think they'll be connected to something more primal, more powerful—they want to go hunting, things like that."

"This guy just wanted to fuck some dogs," Mama Run said. "I could see it in his eyes."

"Sure," Annami said, "that too. But most of the time they just curl up in a ball, shaking, their paws over their ears, shitting and pissing themselves until the share's over."

"Sounds majestic," Soro said.

"Elegant," Annami said.

"Pure."

"The fullest expression of the unadulterated beauty of nature."

They clinked glasses.

"Hey, June, I know we don't really do this here . . . but can I ask you a question?" Soro said, his half smile returning.

"Mm," Annami answered, noncommittal. Over months spent

bullshitting in the bar, it had gotten weird not to give Soro a name of her own. She'd picked June. As good as any other.

"I'll take that as a yes," Soro said. "You don't gotta answer if you don't want to."

He waved a languid hand toward her bandaged head.

"Did you stick your face in a fan? Come in here, your face all mummied up, think we aren't going to ask?"

Annami's hand went to her cheek, feeling the bandages.

"No," she said. "It wasn't a fan."

She remembered.

The artist had a policy when she got requests like Annami's, she'd said.

She always asked three times.

"Are you sure?" the heavyset woman had said.

Annami had glanced down at the sketch on the counter, rough and poor, but apparently enough to give the studio's proprietor pause.

"Yes," she said. "Why?"

"Because life is long," the artist answered.

"I know," Annami said. "I know that."

"Okay, you know that. Good. So, in my opinion, you want to stay away from decisions you can't walk back. Because who you are now isn't who you'll always be."

"I know that too," Annami said.

The artist winked at her.

"Especially in this world, right?"

Annami smiled at the woman.

"Uh-huh. But are you actually trying to tell me you think people shouldn't make permanent decisions? You went into the wrong line of work."

"I didn't say that," the artist answered, folding her arms. "I think they should be sure. The bigger the decision, the surer they should be."

She tapped the sketch on the counter.

"I'd say this requires a significant amount of certainty. So, let me ask again—are you sure?"

"I am," Annami said.

"Okay, last attempt to make <u>sure</u> you're sure before we get this going."

The artist lifted one of the thinnies chained to the counter, each displaying her shop's logo. She swiped it on, then started flipping through the designs on the screen—tribal swirls and hula girls and bar codes and hearts and flowers and words of many alphabets.

"You get a tattoo like one of these, someone sees it, you probably don't even have to explain. Even if it's one of the fancy ones, with a glow or bioactive or something like that.

"But if you do <u>this</u>"—now she lifted Annami's sketch, frowning at it—"you'll be explaining it for the rest of your life. If people even ask. More likely, they'll just make assumptions. It'll mean you can't work any square jobs—and I know maybe you don't want that now, but like I said, life is long."

The artist looked up.

"And . . . don't take this like I'm hitting on you, but you're beautiful, too. Doing this would . . . well, it would change that. Is this a crim thing? Trying to avoid facial recognition, something like that?"

"No," Annami said. "Ask me again."

"Mm?" the artist said, her face puzzled.

"You said you'd ask me three times. Ask me."

The woman gave Annami a long, considering look, then spoke. "Are you sure?"

"Yes," Annami answered.

The tattoo artist sighed, then looked at the sketch, studying it. Her gaze sharpened, no longer that of a friendly businesswoman but a craftsperson about to practice her craft. She looked at Annami again, her eyes flickering over her face.

"I'm thinking fifteen hundred for this. It'll take me a few hours, assuming you can handle doing it all in one session. You ever get a tattoo before?"

"Yes," Annami said. "A long time ago."

She remembered a laughing, drunken night, how the needle hadn't even hurt, how she'd felt so sexy while she was getting the tattoo, so stupid the next day, and then, secretly, sexy again once it healed up. Another life.

"Where?"

"Small of my back."

"Mind if I take a look? Always like to check out another artist's work."

"It got removed," Annami said. "I don't want to talk about it."

"Sure. I see that a lot," the artist said. "Anyway, this will be worse. Small of the back's easy. This, though . . . this will hurt. A lot. Bones are right up near the skin—nerves too."

"That's all right. Do it all. One session."

She paid the fee with her passphrase and followed the woman to a reclining chair in the back of the shop, walking past more framed designs, ways people could make themselves feel savage, whimsical, beautiful, anything they wanted. She was the only person in the shop, and she had the impression its owner had been almost surprised when she walked in. People weren't changing their bodies as much now that they could actually change their bodies. Why get a sexy tattoo when you could pay to be someone sexy for a while?

Annami lay down and closed her eyes.

The pain wasn't bad, but as the artist had warned, every time the needle touched her forehead, her cheeks, her jawline—anywhere the skin was thin over the bone—her entire skull became an angry hornet's nest. A buzzing whine drilled deep into the center of her brain.

She thought about other things, remembering a man who had liked to run his fingertips across barely perceptible lines of ink on her back. Both long gone now, man and tattoo alike.

And then it was over. The artist swaddled her head in bandages, told her not to remove them until the pain was gone, and if she did, not to freak out, because the way the tattoos looked immediately after the ink was applied was not the way they would look after the swelling had gone down.

A walk down to Mama Run's, enjoying the startled glances from people she passed, and then a seat at the bar, where no one was startled—further confirmation of the place's appeal. There, everyone was no one. Not even any questions about what had happened to her—until Soro had asked.

Annami pressed against the bandage on her cheek again—less pain than before. Barely any, in fact.

"I'll show you," she said.

She reached to the edge of one of the bandages and peeled it away, seeing a few drops of blood on its interior, but old, dark. Slowly, she removed the others, wincing a bit at the pull against her skin.

Annami lifted her mini from the bar, twigged it on, and set the display to mirror mode. She held it up and looked.

Her breath caught.

Whorls covered her face from forehead to chin, following the contours of her bone structure, swirling across her skin, with little accents here and there, dots and slashes. Like the patterns of light that were the foundation of flash technology, but stylized, idealized.

She looked fierce. Her face looked nothing like her face.

She could not recognize herself. She looked like a warrior, painted for a final battle against the forces of darkness.

You are you, she thought.

"Perfect," she said.

The sound of argument from the direction of the exit, barely time for Mama Run to frown and Annami to begin to turn— Soro did not take his amazed gaze from her face, she noted in passing—and then a much louder noise, a sharp bang.

Mama Run cursed. Her hands dove beneath the bar and came up with a shotgun.

She called out. Somchai had gone to deal with whoever was at the door, but another man remained in the den's main space. This was Lek, Chai's brother, Annami remembered. Lek moved smoothly toward the curtains leading to the entry hall, weapons appearing in his hands.

Annami had stopped thinking about Lek and Chai very much after her first few visits to Mama Run's. They spent their time on cards and vapor—stim, from the scents Annami caught wafting her way. Just part of the scenery.

It was now clear that the brothers were not just charming doormen but the darkshare den's security, ready to fight and kill. Mama Run's transformed in Annami's mind, whip-quick, from a welcoming place where she drank and bullshitted with Soro back to what it actually was—the home of a hugely illegal and dangerous operation.

"No one is hurt; no one needs to be hurt," a voice, very slightly accented, called from beyond the crimson curtain separating Mama Run's from the rest of the world. "The guard wouldn't let us in, so we had to force our way. He's fine, though, and you will be too. This is nothing. We just have a question."

"Fuck your question!" Mama Run called out. "This place is owned by the Three-Fold Blades. You cause trouble here, it all come back to you three times as bad, whoever you fuckers are!"

"We know that," the voice said, "and we have immense respect for this operation and the valuable purpose it serves. We use it ourselves. That's why we're here. We just want to follow up on a business transaction that went wrong. We know it involved one of your runners, but we don't know which one. We're looking for some lost property, that's all.

"We're all businesspeople here," the voice continued. "We'll happily pay for any information. Twenty thousand just for talking to us, and a hundred grand if you have what we need."

This offer gave Mama Run pause.

She glanced at Soro and Annami.

"That's good money. But if this goes bad, there's another way out, through the back. You follow me while my people keep these fuckers busy, okay?"

"You don't want to, uh, show us the way out right now?" Soro said, but Mama Run had already shifted her attention back toward the curtain and her still-unseen visitors.

"Send one guy," she said. "Hands up, no weapons. I see anything I don't like, bang bang, okay?"

"Absolutely," the voice called back. "But I'd like to come in there with a colleague. He was involved with the transaction, and, honestly, I'd feel more comfortable if he came along. No weapons, I promise."

Mama Run considered this.

"Hands up," she repeated.

"Hands up," the voice said.

"Fine, okay. Come in. Money first."

"Done."

Slow footsteps from the hallway, and then two shadows appeared on the red wall, people with hands extended above their heads. One thin, the other broad, blocky.

Two men entered the room, and Annami understood immediately what was happening. She could also imagine several versions of what was <u>about</u> to happen, cataclysms one and all.

The first man was slim and tall, white-haired, his features precise. The sort of man who regularly considered and adjusted the state of his eyebrows. One hand held a small, thin object.

"I have a credit chip here for the twenty thousand," he said. "Just tell me where you want it."

The second man was large, powerful. With his hands held up above his head, he looked like a bridge stanchion. He was . . . architectural.

His eyes roamed the room, dismissing Lek, who still had his pistols out and leveled. They flicked across Annami's face, then moved to Soro, and Annami released a deeply held breath.

The tattoos, she thought. *Maybe he won't recognize—*

The big man's eyes came back to her face and widened slightly.

He barked a few words, and the first man's eyes snapped to Annami. He smiled.

"Huh," he said. "What are the odds?"

"What?" said Mama Run. "What you say?"

The thin man inclined his head toward Annami.

"My friend Gerber says the woman there was the runner involved in the transaction we're talking about. It seems pretty likely she has what we're looking for. You mind if we ask her?"

Annami looked at Mama Run, who was staring back at her thoughtfully.

"Sure," she said, "but it'll cost the full hundred."

"Done," the man said.

The bottom dropped out of Annami's gut. Mama Run was her friend. The older woman had patched her up after some of the uglier darkshare runs she'd done, given her medical care and kindness. They'd spent hours drinking and talking together. The woman was . . .

No. The woman was nothing to her, and never had been. That was now abundantly clear.

The thin man slowly reached into his coat and produced a second credit chip. He slid both across the floor to Lek, who picked them up and ran them through a slot on his mini, doing it one-handed so he could keep a gun on the invaders. Lek nodded at Mama Run, who relaxed a bit. She gestured at Annami with her shotgun.

"Ask what you want," she said.

The thin man approached.

"Hello," he said, "my name is Olsen."

Annami didn't answer.

"You were doing a darkshare for Mama Run not long ago. It went bad. Someone died, the run ended, and my colleague here"—he pointed over his shoulder with his thumb at the giant, who was looking steadily at Annami, the guards, Soro, Mama Run, everything at once—"showed up. You ran, which I get—he's an intimidating guy. But an item was being bought and sold in that apartment, and it wasn't there when we went back and looked. The only explanation is that you have it."

"I—" Annami began.

"A data. Flash patterns. She had it, then she smash it," Mama Run said.

Annami whipped her head around, anger creasing her face, pulling a twinge of pain from her new tattoos.

"Calm down," Mama Run said. "Better to just get this over with, whatever it is. Dumb to lie. Just business. Trust me."

"Trust . . . you . . . ?" Annami said. "I don't think so."

"She's right, though," Olsen said. "The faster we understand where we stand, the more quickly we can come to a resolution."

Annami looked at Soro, who had his hands on the bar. He was watching her, his face unreadable.

"That chip was valuable," Olsen said.

"I didn't know," Annami said. "I didn't want any trouble. I don't want any."

"Who does?" Olsen answered. "But we need to be made whole. I have people to answer to. If you don't have the chip, we'll find another way."

"She has money," Mama Run said.

"Oh?" said Olsen. "How much?"

"A lot. From her runs for me. She keep it all. I know."

"No," Annami said. "That's not . . . that's not going to happen. I need it."

"Yeah?" Olsen said, a note of sympathy in his tone.

Annami felt like she was sliding down a greased chute, unable to stop or even slow herself.

"Listen to me," Soro said, his voice low and insistent. "It's only money. You can make more. There's always work."

He looked at Mama Run, who was leaning against the back of the bar, much more relaxed. She seemed to know how all of this would play out.

"Right?"

"Lots of work," she said, and Annami understood that for Mama Run, this was rapidly turning into a happy accident that would prevent one of her best employees from leaving the business. "Maybe a different kind of work, with that stuff on her face . . . but there always work."

"We can put you to work too, if that's preferable to paying us," Olsen said. "Maybe a different kind of work."

She looked at Soro. He nodded.

"It's the only choice," he said.

Minutes later, Olsen was gone, and Annami sat in silence, tears burning the still-raw skin on her face.

Cataclysm.

She had nothing. Her account was empty, and she barely had a week left until the auction. It had taken everything she had to gather enough money to be sure she would win. She had burned herself down to <u>nothing</u>, let her body be . . . be <u>used</u> . . . and now she only had days. Not enough time. Nowhere near.

She had failed, and Hauser and Bleeder and all the rest had no idea she'd even tried to come at them.

Everything was lost.

She was nothing.

CHAPTER 9

THE FARMHOUSE

"Ninety percent plaque reduction off sequence four. That's what Paul told me," Jon Corran said, smiling. "Incredible, Gabby. Triples your best prior result, doesn't it?"

Gabrielle cursed herself for giving Jon specifics when she'd called him to beg for money. Then again, if she'd been vague, he might not have given her any money at all, and she'd still be in Paul's body.

They were standing in the living room: playpen and ratty couch and scatters of toys and childproofed power outlets. Gabby's craft table, where she wove pretty multicolored baskets and created knitwear to sell on Etsy and eBay for extra income, covered with scraps of wicker and yarn. And tension, of course, so much that the idea of three people fitting inside the room at once seemed utterly bizarre.

Gabrielle was embarrassed at the state of her home, even though she knew there was so much more she should be worried about. Jon was a nice man, kind, but that didn't mean he wasn't judging her because a few Cheerios were visible on the rug, courtesy of the Kitten's poor motor control during snack time.

Just get past this, she thought. *Get past it and you'll have everything you ever wanted. You can hire a thousand maids.*

"Why don't you sit down, Jon?" she said, gesturing to the couch. Gabrielle turned to Paul.

"Can you make some coffee?"

"Oh, I'm all right," Jon said. "I'd take a pop, though, if you have a Coke or something."

"It's for me," Gabrielle said, looking back at Paul and smiling. "I'm wrung out. It's been a pretty crazy day."

"On it," Paul said.

He put his hand on her shoulder, then turned left and headed into the kitchen.

"Okay," Gabrielle said, sitting down in the armchair near the couch and mustering up a humble expression. "This is embarrassing."

Jon raised an eyebrow.

"Oh man," he said. "I knew it was too good to be true. What happened?"

"This is why I sent Paul into the kitchen. I feel like an idiot."

"You're the furthest thing from an idiot, Gabrielle. That's why we work with you. I'm sure it's not as bad as you think. Just tell me what's going on. You okay, by the way? Your head, I mean."

Gabrielle reached up to her forehead. She'd forgotten all about the bandage—her brain had done its job and shoved the pain to the back of her mind while more pressing matters intruded. And now it was just one more weird thing to explain to Jon Corran.

She liked him, actually. He was a good guy, as far as money guys went. Smart, thoughtful, patient. He was a little younger than she was—late twenties. She didn't know his specific title, maybe a director of something or other, but she had the impression he was like an FBI field agent, sent out from Hendricks Capital's main office in Detroit to check in on the fund's various investments. Limited ability to make decisions, but still an important part of the power structure.

And right now the man who could ruin everything, no matter how likable he was.

"I'm fine. Just tripped. As far as the experiment . . . I mixed up a couple of rats. Wilbur and Stan. I did a run on Stan, but I thought it was Wilbur. So when I got the results and checked them against the benchmarks, I got excited. Stan's plaque advancement is much less pronounced than Wilbur's. I thought I'd achieved more than I actually had.

"Like I said . . . I'm an idiot."

"Huh," Jon said, his forehead wrinkling as he considered this. "Same color or something?"

Gabrielle blinked.

"What?"

"Stan and Wilbur."

"Oh, yeah. Easy to mix them up. Well, it's not <u>easy</u>, I'm not that dumb—I have the cages labeled—but the baby's been keeping me up. I think I was just a little tired."

Gabrielle said this and realized she <u>was</u> tired, exhausted, and that the cages <u>were</u> labeled, and Stan and Wilbur were in fact not the same color at all. Wilbur was white, Stan was black. She was making things worse.

"So that extra money Paul called me for . . ."

"I wanted to repeat the experiment right away, see if I'd really cracked it. That's when I realized my mistake. I was going to call you tomorrow, but I was . . . just . . . I feel stupid, Jon."

"Nah," Jon said. "I'm the stupid one. I drove all the way out from Detroit."

Paul returned from the kitchen with two steaming mugs and a can of pop under his arm. He handed one mug to her, then passed the can to Jon.

"You want a glass?" he asked.

"I'm good, thanks," Jon answered.

Gabrielle tasted her coffee. It was exactly the way she liked it, just the right amount of everything, from milk to heat. She looked at

Paul, now leaning against the doorframe. He smiled and lifted his own mug.

"So it was really nothing?" Jon said, cracking open his pop.

"I was so excited there for a minute. Paul can tell you."

"I thought she was going to burst into flames right there in the barn," Paul said smoothly. "It had me excited too, and I don't even understand what the hell she does out there."

Jon raised a hand, like a kid in school.

"Okay, but let me ask one question. When Paul called me, begging for money . . ."

"Was I begging?" Paul said. "I don't know if I was <u>begging</u>."

"He asked for a hundred grand and said it was urgent. Like you needed it right then. Right that second."

He lowered his hand and gave Gabby a puzzled little smile.

"If you already had the good result, and it was documented, then what was the rush? Your system out there in the barn records everything you do. You send us the reports, every month."

"Oh, you know," Gabrielle said, remembering with a huge mental forehead slap the auto-archiving data system. The entire secret, or enough to put together the idea that there <u>was</u> a secret, right there, spooled to a hard drive for safekeeping out in the barn. "I was excited. Didn't want to wait to keep experimenting.

"The good result with Stan—what I thought was a good result—used up the last of the money you'd given me, and I wanted to make sure I could duplicate it. The idea of waiting for approvals, going through the paperwork for another tranche of funding . . . I just wanted to, you know, cut out the middleman."

Jon glanced around the living room. It felt involuntary, just a flicker, but Gabrielle thought it felt like he was buying himself a moment, thinking about how to respond. He didn't believe her, and in a minute he was going to ask to see the archive, and that'd be that. Game over.

"Man," he said. "I was excited there too. The whole drive over here, I was thinking maybe this was finally it."

Jon leaned back on the couch.

"My grandma died of Alzheimer's. I mentioned it to Paul on the phone, but I don't know if I ever told you. My aunt ended up taking care of her for the last four or five years of her life. Kind of ate them both up, I think. My aunt used to laugh, drink a lot. Probably drank too much, but she had fun. She was beautiful too. Now . . . she's just tired."

"I think a lot of people have stories like that," Gabrielle said.

"Mm. But that story is mine. And so when your prospectus came across my desk, I pushed it through. Convinced Mr. Hendricks to fund you. He was going to pass, but I made it happen."

"Thank you," Gabrielle said. She wasn't sure what Jon wanted her to say.

"You're welcome," he answered. "I just wish it had worked out."

He stood up.

"Okay. I'll get back on the road. I'm sorry to have disturbed your evening—next time I'll just call."

Gabrielle felt the beginnings of relief. Somehow, improbably, she'd pulled this off.

Jon stretched a bit with his hands on the small of his back, grimacing a little.

"Man. Long drives just kill me," he said, then looked over at Gabrielle. "Before I go, can I get your backup of this last run of experiments? I wouldn't mind taking a look, just to see how far we actually got."

Quick, burning panic.

"The raw results?" Gabby asked. "Don't you just want the normal digest at the end of the week? I was going to do a full summary for you guys, process everything so it's easier to understand."

"Oh, absolutely," Jon answered, "and believe me, we appreciate it, but I've been going over these reports for long enough now that I can usually get the gist. Hendricks is going to ask me why I wired you guys that three grand, and I want to have my story straight when he does. You don't mind, do you?"

Gabrielle's mind went white. Game over.

The baby, from upstairs—the thin, keening cry that meant she was awake and had some desperate, immediate need. There were times Gabby hated it, usually when her mind had finally drifted into that state where she could actually get some deep thinking done— but right now it was a lifeline, like her daughter had read her mind and given her exactly what she needed.

"Kitty Kat's up. Can you grab her?" Gabrielle said, looking at Paul. "Bring her down?"

"Yup," he said, and headed for the stairs, not hesitating, even though getting the baby out of her crib after putting her down wasn't the usual program, barring a diaper emergency. Bringing her down into a well-lit room full of fascinating grown-up voices risked her not seeing the need to go back to sleep at all.

But Paul had agreed without a word. Maybe he could read her mind too.

"Sorry," Gabrielle said, turning back to Jon. "You know, I can't believe I don't know this, but do you have any kids? I don't even know if you're married. I apologize. We've been working together for too long for me not to know that."

"Totally fine," he said. "And no. My partner, Aaron, and I have talked about adopting down the road, but we're not really there yet. I don't think he's ready to give up vacations and big nights out and all that. I'm not sure I am either, if I'm being totally honest. Maybe in a few years."

Paul came downstairs, holding the baby. Gabrielle got up and walked over.

"Diaper?" she asked, looking at her daughter's smile at seeing her mom.

"Nope," Paul answered. "Bottle, I think."

Gabrielle flicked her eyes up to meet Paul's gaze, one very intense look that she hoped he could read. She knew Jon was watching them both.

"You want me to make it?" she said.

"I can do it," he answered, and then looked over to Jon. "But I don't want to delay our guest. Would you mind holding the kiddo here for a minute while I warm up a bottle? That way Gabby can get out to the barn and run off that backup for you, so you can get back on the road."

"Uh . . . ," Jon said. "I guess, sure?"

Gabrielle lifted the baby, flashing Paul a tiny smile, and presented her to Jon.

"Thanks. She'll be no trouble. If she gets fussy, just play peek-a-boo with her."

Jon took the Kitten and sat back down on the couch, holding her awkwardly on his lap. Man and infant stared at each other, neither particularly convinced that this was a good situation.

"Back in a few," Gabrielle said.

She left the house and walked toward the barn, moving quickly, but not so fast that Jon would get suspicious if he glanced out the window—not that he wasn't already, that much was clear.

Gabrielle flicked on the lights in the barn, seeing evidence everywhere that the story she had told Jon was an obvious, idiotic lie—from blood on the floor to discarded IV materials to two obviously different-colored rats named Stan and Wilbur—but she didn't have time to clean any of it up. She pulled her laptop open and started to type as quickly as she could, making errors, slowing down, focusing, forcing herself into a Zen state.

She had two tasks here. First, a data dump to a USB stick. That was easy, but it was slow, with gigs of information to transfer. Everything, from the earliest days of development of her Alzheimer's treatment protocol—she had no idea what would be useful down the road, and this might be her last chance to access any of it.

The progress bar crawled, a tidal creep.

Gabrielle closed her eyes, shifting her mind away from the agonizing wait, from the fact that if Jon walked into the barn before it was done then the future she could see so clearly would also be gone. She hadn't had time to consciously start analyzing what the flash could mean, but her subconscious had been working hard. Applications, new technologies, complete paradigm shift, all flickering through her mind in a tide, ideas leaping from one to the next so fast she couldn't keep up, and above it all, one idea.

It doesn't have to be like this, she thought. *The world doesn't have to be like this. I can give my daughter something else. I can make it all so much easier for her, so much better.*

The laptop chimed and Gabrielle gasped, coming out of her fugue. She yanked out the memory stick and slipped it into her pocket, then began her second task. More typing, precise, no mistakes this time, deleting, moving, adjusting, creating a new picture of the day's data.

She could hear Jon and Paul talking outside, getting louder— walking toward the barn.

Gabby put all thoughts of discovery out of her mind. She focused on her task, became a robot programmed with one overpowering directive: to complete the data transfer before Jon Corran entered her lab. She could do it. She would do it. For the Kitten, and for herself, and for everyone.

A few more keystrokes and she was done. Gabby slipped a new drive into the laptop's USB slot and activated the download. Much faster this time, as she was only transferring a few days' worth of data as opposed to years. Fifteen seconds and it was done.

Jon entered the barn, Paul at his heels holding Kat, flashing her an apologetic glance from behind Corran's back.

"Hey," Jon said. "All set?"

"All set," Gabby said.

She gave Jon the doctored drive, even gave him a quick hug, thanked him for everything he'd done for her, all the support, and promised to get him the full digest of the final phase of the protocol within a week. She remembered to act remorseful, to ask him if maybe he could see if the door might be open for Hendricks to put any more money into the project, and smiled ruefully at Jon's chagrined head-tilt response.

Just as if she still cared about Hendricks Capital or its money, as if the other data set, the real one, wasn't burning in her pocket like a live coal.

She waved at Jon as he drove away, headed back to Detroit, and then she walked into the house, where Paul waited. The baby was upstairs again, asleep after her bottle.

"I don't know what you were trying to do out there, but I guess I hope it worked," he said.

Gabrielle reached into her pocket and pulled out the thumb drive.

"I do too," she said.

"What is that?" Paul asked, looking at the drive.

"This," Gabrielle said, the little hunk of inert plastic and silicon still feeling hot against her hand, "is the future."

She grinned, a cheek-stretching smile that was just a tiny echo of the bright, white-hot joy that surged through every part of her.

"Today, baby," she said, sitting on the couch next to her husband. Utter happiness.

"I changed the world."

END OF PART I

SIX YEARS FROM NOW

DIGITALTRENDS.COM—Reader, I've been a tech-sector journalist for more than two decades. I was in the room in San Francisco when Jobs unveiled the iPhone. I was second-row center when Elon launched SpaceX. I have been on the front line of the next big thing for my entire professional career. I've seen it all.

Yesterday, I was introduced to the most substantial technological innovation I have ever seen. I am stunned, reeling, barely able to type. I hope you will forgive me for using the first person here, but I think you'll understand once you get a sense of what we're talking about. In many ways, this is all about *I*.

I was invited to a junket for a company I'd never heard of before—NeOnet Global. Sounded like telecom (it's not). You get a lot of these in my business. A cell phone start-up, a software developer convinced they have the next killer app . . . whatever. It's never anything too impressive, even though they all use the same adjectives—*revolutionary* comes up a bunch. Hyperbole up the wazoo, pardon my French. Usually, these are an instant no. I'm twenty years in. I like my own desk, my own bed. Let the kids do the junkets if they feel like it. But this one wasn't too far from home, just up in Boston, good old Route 128, and there was something about the copy on the invite. Usually, you can smell desperation— "Please, please cover this. . . . We worked really hard on it and spent too much money."

Here, though, just confidence. "We have decided it is time to reveal how NeOnet Global will reinvent the world." And then, four words: *Be anyone with Anyone.* Great logo too—this lightning-bolt thing.

I was intrigued. Plus, they paid for me to take the Acela up from New York. Can I be bought? No, absolutely not. But am I more inclined to attend your junket if you make it easy, fast, and comfortable? Guilty.

Up I went on the appointed day and met a number of my colleagues in the invention-journalism biz milling around before the presentation. No one knew anything about what this company was doing, but we all agreed that it felt different, worth the afternoon, at least.

The setup wasn't that different from how it usually goes. Stage, some seats, minimalist design, subdued electronica piped in. The presentation began, and we met Stephen Hauser, who introduced himself as the CEO of NeOnet Global—"But we just call it Anyone," he said. "You'll see why in a minute."

Hauser is charming, self-effacing, handsome, utterly relatable, and has that manic gleam behind his eyes all these guys seem to have. That's not a criticism, by the way. You need to be at least 40 percent maniac to run a company in the tech world.

He told us why they call the company Anyone. Friends, this is where I might lose you. He said they had a process that could transfer a person's consciousness into another person's body. "Like borrowing someone's car," he said. "You're in control of their body. While it happens, their mind is dormant, and your own body is essentially asleep." So it's a one-way exchange—but not a one-way trip. It's completely reversible, and according to Hauser, completely safe. He said they call it the flash. The person who sends their consciousness out is a traveler; the person they inhabit is the vessel. He threw around a few more buzzwords, but that's the basic setup.

You could have cut the skepticism with a knife. Advances like this don't come out of nowhere, and it just sounded like . . . like it was impossible. Like it could not be. Almost like it should not be—and I'm agnostic when it comes to that stuff. Tech goes where it goes.

Anyway, Hauser clearly knew we all thought he was nuts, so he started with a demonstration. A curtain went up, revealing an apparatus—like a chaise lounge with a server rack next to it and a sort of hood attachment. Reminded me of a hair dryer in a 1950s beauty shop. Big, thick cords running off the stage. Behind it, one of those huge video screens that tend to be the backdrop for these presentations, like the whole wall was just a massive monitor.

He told us he was going to flash into someone in Salem, eighteen miles away. That, of course, rang a bell—an Alexander Graham Bell. The first long-distance telephone call, in 1877, went from Salem to Boston. Clever, Mr. Hauser—positioning this flash tech alongside one of the most influential inventions in human history.

The flash is bigger.

The trick here, of course, was, how would you know if the transfer actually worked? There was no way to verify—until Hauser gave us one. We could whisper a few words to him, tell him a secret, he'd flash up to Salem, and the vessel on that end would reveal the info, to the delight and astonishment of all.

A bunch of us did it—and it worked every time.

Hauser looked like he went to sleep on that chaise, or maybe into a coma, and upon the screen behind the stage, the vessel (a charming, attractive man who lacked only the mania to be a CEO himself) revealed what we'd said. I tried to beat the system—instead of telling him the secret, I wrote it down and showed him the paper, just a number with some significance to me—108. My thinking: if he was bugged, that'd beat it. I showed Hauser, he flashed, and the vessel promptly announced 108.

Okay, fine, but Penn & Teller and David Copperfield (dating myself a little there) pull off more impressive tricks six nights a week in Vegas. But let me tell you something. The person on that screen, up in Salem—before Hauser flashed into him, his eyes . . . like a normal person. But after . . . there he was. Hauser. Same mannerisms, same glint behind the eyes. Yeah, you could game that too— just acting. But then you ask yourself, why? What would be the point of such an elaborate fake-out?

Three or four of us did the secret-whisper trick. If that was the end of it, I think we'd have gone home, written something up, wondered what we'd actually seen, laughed it off. But that wasn't the end.

Hauser got up off that chaise, and he looked at us, the dozen or so journalists who had shown up that day. And he gestured to his weird beauty-salon server-rack thing, and he said, "Would any of you like to try it?"

I did. I did try it. I can try to explain what it's like to be in a new body, to live as someone else even briefly, but words fail. And, I suspect, all of us will know soon enough.

The flash is real. It is *real*.

My friends, it's a whole new world.

PART II

CHAPTER 10

THE DARKSHARE DEN

SORO—WHOSE NAME WAS NOT SORO BUT DEREK—WATCHED June, whose name he was pretty sure wasn't June, cry.

It wasn't some big drama, not like how people in his family or girls in the neighborhood would do it. June wasn't putting on a display, angling for sympathy, showing everyone how bad she'd been hurt.

No, this was about June. No one else. The woman sat on her stool at the other end of Mama Run's bar, fists clenched, her whole body clenched, eyes screwed closed, with tears running down those new tattoos whirled across her face. Tears dripped onto the bar. Soro was a few feet away, but he could hear the sounds they made.

A tear hitting a bar. Hard to think of a smaller, bigger sound.

Soro knew he should look away, but most people who dark-shared were past tears. They were numb in all the ways you needed to be to walk through Mama Run's door in the first place.

Not June, though. Whatever she was feeling, it was deep, and he'd never seen anything like it. He couldn't stop staring.

Mama Run was watching too, leaning her wide ass against

the shelf behind the bar, her arms folded. She was frowning, dis-approving, as if she wasn't the cause of the tears, as if she hadn't just given every dollar June made from her dark runs to the first shitheads who'd come in and asked for them. *Just business*, Mama had said. But she'd also let June smash the data with the flash patterns in the first place.

Mama could have said something back then. Told June to hold on to the data, in case someone came looking for it. The woman was clearly new to the world of very bad things, and it would have been kind of Mama Run to ease her in, help her avoid a few of those virginal mistakes—but that would have kept June out of trouble, and trouble was why people worked the darkshare.

Mama Run pushed herself off the shelf, all quick and an-noyed. She took a glass, then reached up behind her for a dark green bottle. She poured out a measure of liquid that glowed tawny and rich in the low red light, then thunked the glass down on the bar.

June's head jerked up; her eyes flipped open. She seemed shocked, like she'd been slapped. She looked at the drink, then at Mama Run. Her face twisted into a snarl, radiating heat. Like staring into a fire, the new tattoos rippling across her skin. June's hand moved, a sharp backhand, and the drink shot back over to Mama Run's side of the bar, exploding into Scotch and glass.

Mama's mouth opened, but she didn't say anything. June stared, her face hot, her eyes cold. Mama Run shook her head, then bent to scrape the larger pieces together so she could throw them away.

"Hey," Soro said.

June turned, the full force of her hitting him hard. He swallowed.

"You want to go somewhere else?" he continued.

"With you?" she said, frowning.

"Yeah. But not like that," he said, holding up a placating hand. "Just another place. Another drink, maybe."

"Fine," June said. "Good."

She stood up, turned, and walked out of the darkshare, past the flash couches, past Lek and Chai, who had gone back to playing chao dai di now that the excitement of Olsen's visit was over, past all of it, without even a look. No more tears. The lady was sharp now, a knife.

Soro got up from his stool to follow.

"See you soon," Mama Run said, her tone flat.

"Yeah," Soro said. "Probably."

Outside, June was waiting, the tears gone, scrubbed away. All of that was over, looked like.

"You know a place, or . . . ," he ventured.

"I do," June said. "Come on."

She walked to the corner and turned, heading east. They cut along Canal for a while, June not speaking, her hands stuffed into her pockets, then a left turn to go north on Chrystie and a right a few blocks later to enter the Lower East Side ramble.

Soro looked around as they walked, up at the twenty-story condo buildings looming in aluminum and glass, each one different, with fancy boutiques and cafés burrowed into their ground floors. Money, money, everywhere, far as the eye could see.

"You know a bar around here? You sure we'll be, uh, comfortable?"

What he was actually saying: *I don't know if I want to spend my cash drinking with the sort of people who drink around here, and I absolutely don't want to pay what those drinks will cost, mostly out of principle, and even more than that I have a huge fucking scar on my face and people already stare at me everywhere I go, which is bound to be a hell of a lot worse in some shitty, fancy cocktail bar down here . . .* But it didn't really seem like the time, and he was doing this to help out a woman who had just lost something she went through hell to earn—more dark runs in less time than anyone he'd ever seen. If she wanted to drink pricey booze in the company of pricey assholes, he could roll with it. At least for a round or two.

But then June turned down a side street off Allen and stopped in front of the type of establishment Soro would have sworn had gone extinct across all of Manhattan twenty years back, and from the Lower East Side ten years before that.

A real-deal, honest-to-god dive bar.

Ugly, weathered wood facade, neon in the windows advertising beers he wasn't sure they still made, letters above the banged-up steel door reading CONRAD's. All set at the base of a six-floor brick building, a rotten tooth in the gleaming grill that was the rest of the block.

"Is this like a theme park or something?" Soro asked. "Fake nostalgia?"

June glanced at him, smiled a little, which still looked weird on her face superimposed against the tattoos, but she probably didn't know that, and hey, a smile was a smile. She opened the door and gestured for Soro to go in ahead of her.

"You tell me."

Soro stepped into Conrad's dim, brown light. On his first breath, he knew there was nothing fake about this bar. A pungent, mushroomy odor of ancient beer, and under that just the faintest aroma of puke and urine. People had been drinking in this space for a very long time.

June followed him in, surveying the interior with the first hint of anything like pleasure he'd seen from her since they'd left Mama Run's. A few tables, a timeworn bar with a timeworn man behind it, a popcorn machine with some little plastic bowls stacked next to it.

Music was coming from a banged-up old digital jukebox, some ancient R & B dance track Soro recognized but couldn't place. June liked it, though—her head immediately swaying with the beat, fingers tapping her leather jacket.

"Guy who owns the building hates change," she said. "He's like a hundred and three, and he's turned down every offer everyone's ever made for this lot. Last I heard was two hundred and fifty million."

"Just for the lot?"

"Just for the lot," June confirmed. "I came here on my first trip to New York City, a long time ago. Same back then as it is now. Heard this song too, I think. Beyoncé."

"You're not from here?" Soro said.

"Nope," June said, but that was apparently as far as she was willing to go.

They each paid for their own beer and found a table. Not that it was hard—the place was almost empty. June sat, staring into her glass, brooding. Soro watched her, thinking he'd just wait until she felt like talking. If she ever did.

The beer was fine.

Soro looked around the bar again, now a little bored. He scratched his neck—the spot where the burn scar on his face met the untouched skin near his collarbone always tended to itch. Something toward the back of the room caught his attention.

"Hey, you want to play darts?" he asked June. "Something to do, you know? We don't have to talk or anything."

June glanced up from her beer at him, then over to the dartboard mounted on the wall at the back of the bar, a little chalkboard next to it for keeping score.

"Huh," she said. "Sure. Sharp objects sound good right about now."

Soro nodded. He got up and went to the bar, retrieving a set of darts from the bartender, the stiff foil fletching printed with the Union Jack.

June was waiting for him at the dartboard and had moved their drinks over to the closest table. She'd also chalked up the scoreboard with the numbers fifteen to twenty and the word *bull*, right down the center in a vertical line, with an *S* up at the top on the right and an *A* on the left.

Soro-who-was-actually-Derek noted that *A* almost certainly didn't stand for *June* but decided not to bring it up.

"Cricket," Soro said.

"Yeah," June answered. "That okay?"

"It's the only darts game I know, so yeah."

They started to play, and it went the way a round of darts went, more luck than skill. Each slowly knocking down numbers, trying for triples and doubles, closing things out, keeping score, working through their beers, not talking, just taking turns.

Soro won, but it was pretty close. June didn't seem too bothered about it. She was back to staring into her now-empty beer mug.

"I'm going to get a refill," he said. "You want another beer, it's on me. No rush. Just let me know."

She looked up at him.

"Why?"

"Uh . . . figured I'd buy you one, since, you know, you just lost all your money."

"Yeah. I sure did," June answered, and went back to staring at her glass.

"You want to talk about that, maybe?"

She gave him a look.

"Okay, fine," Soro said, holding up his hands. "I don't know you well, not the details, but we have spent a lot of time hanging out together at Mama Run's."

"Mama fucking Run," June muttered.

"Yeah," Soro said. "She's a piece of shit. Your mistake was thinking she wasn't, because she treated you nice. Everyone in there is trash, even me. Especially me. But it's pretty clear you're not, and you were doing all those dark runs because you needed something you couldn't get any other way. I think you just lost whatever that was, and that has to be hard as hell, and I'm saying, if you want to talk about it, even just, like . . . emotionally . . . you can. I think maybe you'll feel better."

"Why do you care if I feel better?"

"Oh, I dunno. I'm a human being?"

"Mm."

June sat back. Her eyes flicked over to the dartboard.

"Tell you what," she said. "Whoever gets three bullseyes first can ask the other one whatever. Any question, and you have to answer."

Soro shrugged. "Okay, whatever. Just let me get another beer."

He got up and returned with a new glass, and June offered him the darts.

"You go first," she said.

Soro threw, missing with all three. One got close, the second socked firmly into the triple-ten bar, and the third hit the wall to the side of the dartboard and skittered off onto the floor.

He walked up to the board, pulled the two darts out, and picked up the third from the floor, then handed them to June.

"Your turn," he said.

"Uh-huh," she answered.

June didn't stand up. From her chair—which was well behind the throwing line, so she was technically still within the rules—she flicked the darts up, one after the other. The movement was casual, her hand on the darts light, just her fingertips touching them. Each flew in a slight upward curve, then tilted down and thunked perfectly into the bullseye, creating what looked like a little flower sticking out of the center of the dart-board.

Soro stared at that flower for a little while, then turned to look at June, who was watching him, a little smile on her face.

"Were you . . . what the hell? That first game we played, when I beat you . . . did you throw it?"

"No," she said, standing up. She walked to the dartboard and retrieved the three darts. "I just wasn't playing the same game you were."

She walked back to the throwing line.

"Ten," she said, and threw. The dart hit the ten—not its slice on the board but the actual number, right through the oval of wire that made up the zero.

"Seventeen."

Thunk—nestled right up in the seven's point.

"Triple fifteen."

Triple fifteen.

She looked at Soro.

"I don't usually tell other people what I'm aiming at."

She walked forward, got the darts again, and handed them to Soro.

"I had fun, you had fun—you got to win—what's the differ-ence?"

June sat back down. "Anyway, you owe me an answer."

Soro shook his head and sat, placing his beer and the darts down on the table.

"Questionable," he said. "You hustled me. But I didn't see it coming, so that's on me. Go ahead and ask."

"Why are you ruined?" she asked. "Why do you darkshare? You told me it was for the rush of it, back at Mama Run's, but I think that's bullshit."

"That's two questions," Soro said.

"Yup," June replied, "but I think it's only one answer."

Soro snorted. He thought for a minute, swigged his beer to buy some time. He didn't talk about himself, but he also knew that was mainly because he never let himself get into a position where anyone would care enough to ask.

He moved his hand to his face, running his index finger down the familiar ripples of his scar.

"This happened when I was little. It was an accident, but it was the sort of thing that wouldn't have happened if I was . . . I don't know . . . somebody. The kind of kid people care about what happens to them."

June didn't say anything. She just watched, those big, dark eyes staring out of the strange lattice that had become her face.

"I didn't get much education, nothing to really make me somebody, if you get my meaning. Never had the opportunity. But I know I'm not nobody. I know it.

"So, you know . . . I do the dark runs. It's like a logic thing for me."

June tilted her head a little, not seeing the logic.

"Anyone who uses a place like Mama Run's, who hires runners like us . . . ," Soro went on, "they do it because they really, really want to. Or, like, they need to. With how much it costs, and how dangerous it is—no one does that shit casually.

"So when I let those people use my prime for their runs, it means I'm part of something that's really important to someone. I'm . . . what's the word . . ."

"Crucial," June said.

"Yeah. Crucial," Soro said. "But it's also good because it lets other people do all the work. Like, I could try to go to school, learn something, get a skill set. But this way, I don't have to do anything but let it happen. I just lay back, be crucial, and get paid."

"So you're lazy," June said, laughing a little.

Soro liked that laugh. He hadn't heard it in a while.

"Laziest man in New York."

He lifted his beer.

"Also," he said, not really knowing why he was revealing this detail, considering she had told him nothing about herself and didn't seem likely to, "I'm a Dull. I have a heart defect. I get too excited, I could drop dead. No warning. Boom."

Soro drank, finishing his beer, his eyes on June and her suddenly wide eyes, feeling pleased with himself that he'd finally managed to shock her.

"But . . . ," she said. "Does Mama Run know?"

"Nope. Didn't volunteer that piece of information. If I had, you think she'd let me run for her?"

June slowly shook her head, processing. Soro understood that. People didn't generally volunteer that they were Dulls. It was like telling someone you had cancer. Or you were a sex offender. Or both.

"But whoever uses you," June said, "if your heart gives out while they're in you, or while you're in someone else . . . either way, you're taking someone with you. They die too. That's like . . . I don't know."

Soro shrugged.

"One iffy little valve in my heart means I can't use the light flash. Ever. I don't even have an I-fi.

"But you know as well as I do that in this world, if you can't flash, it's like you're crippled. Like you don't matter."

He touched the burn scar on his face.

"I already got enough of that as it is. Dark runs might be all I'll ever get, but at least they get me out of my skin. They let me matter."

"But how do you rationalize the risk to people who run you as a vessel?" June asked, still clearly a little stunned.

"Eh," he said, waving his hand a little, "anyone who darkshares knows it's risky. That's why it's criminal, lady. Maybe I'm just a little riskier than most."

He smiled, that weird contortion he knew looked bizarre but was all he had, so he did it anyway, like his personal signature.

June stared at him, an expression on her face he couldn't quite figure out, something like disgust and awe mixed together, which, all things considered, was better than just plain disgust.

She stood and walked away, and he thought he'd probably never see her again. But she went to the bar, not the door, and came back with two full glasses.

"On me," she said.

They sat and drank for a little while in silence.

Fuck it, he thought.

"Hey," he said. "You needed all that money from Mama Run's for something specific, right? It wasn't just about getting rich?"

June hesitated, then answered, surprising him.

"Right. And I don't have time to get more. The thing I needed it for will happen in, like, a week."

Soro considered that. He looked at June, this odd woman who hit what she aimed at.

There was another reason he did the dark runs, one he was less likely to admit to than any of the others—he liked helping people who had nowhere else to go. He . . . dumb, scarred, ignorant Derek Lincoln . . . made dreams come true.

"That gang that took your money. Olsen and those fucks. I recognized them. A friend of mine used to roll with them. They operate out of a place in Red Hook."

June's eyes narrowed.

"And?" she said.

Soro smiled at her.

"And maybe we should go pay them a visit."

CHAPTER 11

THE DETROIT RIVER

JON CORRAN DIPPED HIS PADDLE INTO THE RIVER: A FLAT SHEET OF darkness that swallowed the thing utterly, like a dimensional portal in a sci-fi movie. He tried to bring it back out as smoothly as it had gone in, soundless and sharp, even as he rotated the handle in the arc that would bring the other blade down to the water, on his left.

His goal, the art of it, was to make no impact on the river. Just move along it like he didn't exist.

It was impossible. Everything touched everything else, and in keeping with that principle, a few drops of water spattered the surface as he maneuvered the paddle back into the water. Still, there was something noble in the effort, a serenity, like raking a Zen garden.

Corran had driven home to Detroit from Gabrielle White's farm out past Ann Arbor, arriving home in Creekside about three in the morning. Too late to try for sleep. Better to go to work early, power through, and leave early—although he knew he wouldn't leave early. He never did.

But first, the particular peace of a night paddle. He got the kayak out of its rack in the garage, ran it down to the slip out back of the house, threw in what he needed—a thermos of coffee, a Ziploc bag with a few energy bars, his little tool kit. He mounted the battery-powered, bright white light on the stern (visible for at least a mile as per US Coast Guard regulations), and out he went.

Usually, the water roughened once you left the canals and entered the main channel of the Detroit River. Not tonight. It was still, a held breath, a meditation, requiring barely any effort to glide along its surface—and Jon couldn't enjoy it. Was barely even aware of it. He was thinking about Gabrielle White and everything she'd said and done while he'd been at her house.

The thumb drive she'd given him was in his bag at home, waiting for him to take it to the office and begin trying to understand what it had to say. He thought he could, too. It was a matter of pride for him to be able to follow the basic tenets of the research accounts he oversaw for Hendricks Capital. In his experience, scientists didn't have much patience for explanation. Their minds moved fast and deep. Like the river, in fact. He didn't think it was fair to force them to slow down just to make sure he understood everything they were thinking and doing, any more than he could expect the river to take his wants and needs into account.

Gabrielle's project was no exception. He'd put in the time, reading everything he could about Alzheimer's, the state of the art on the cruel inexorability of the disease and possible avenues of treatment. He now knew more about beta-amyloid clumps and tau tangles than anyone this side of the Mayo Clinic's neurology division and had a detailed understanding of the toll the disease took, not just on the afflicted but also on their caretakers, usually family members.

About six months back, after doing all that reading and understanding what the disease really did to people, he'd taken his aunt to Paris for a long weekend, to thank her for everything she'd endured in his grandmother's final years. If he could have, he'd have done more.

The upshot—he thought he'd be able to read Gabrielle's data, but he didn't think it would tell him a particularly interesting story. He thought it would match Gabby's explanation, nothing unexpected or strange at all. But that didn't square with the vibe he'd felt back in that farmhouse. Paul had been kind, clueless, distracted, like the few other times Jon had met him. Gabrielle, however, read tense. Like she was caught, and she knew it, and was trying to find a way out.

But caught doing <u>what</u>?

He couldn't figure it out, and it was bothering him. It had bugged him the whole drive back from the Whites' farm and was the main reason he'd decided to come out on the river, to find a little calm, to let drifting along the surface help him drift through his mind.

Jon glanced east, toward Windsor. The sky was getting light. He considered moving out onto Lake St. Clair, maybe briefly becoming an illegal immigrant to Canada via a landing on Peche Island for sunrise coffee and one of those energy bars, but . . . no. He wanted to get to the office, look at that thumb drive.

He spun the kayak around and headed for home, hugging the shoreline for a mile or so until he made it to the entrance to Fox Creek and turned in. A short trip along the shallow, fragrant canal, beaten-up homes leaning toward the water as if they were trying to look at their own reflections, the water thick with sediment and decades upon decades of people putting literally anything they wanted into it. Trash Venice, Aaron called it.

But even Trash Venice was a Venice, Jon considered, as he pulled up to the little dock extending out from the deck behind his home. The house was rickety, it was old, but it was on the water, and where else would he and Aaron be able to afford something on the water?

People didn't think of Detroit as particularly coastal, or nautical, but it was and always had been. The river, Belle Isle, the lakefront, the weird pseudo canal district of Creekside, where he lived—all a massive part of the city's past and current life, even more than struggling auto manufacturers or urban blight. Developers and hipsters and gentrifiers were bound to find the neighborhood eventually. When that happened, he'd probably be priced out. But for now . . . he had a house on the water.

Music inside, and the smell of coffee. Aaron was up, singing along to one of the pop songs he liked, something Jon recognized but couldn't identify. A radio song. Aaron was hitting the melody perfectly, arguably doing a better job than the original singer—although Jon acknowledged his bias in that department.

Jon stopped a few steps inside the back door to listen, as the song moved into its belter outro chorus. Aaron was right there with it, and then he stopped, poking his head out of the kitchen.

"Thought I heard you," he said. "You went out this morning?"

"Yup," Jon answered. "Got back late from Ann Arbor, figured I'd feel worse after an hour of sleep than none at all."

"We'll see what you say this afternoon. Coffee?"

"Yes please," Jon said, and walked into the kitchen, waiting as Aaron poured him a cup.

"What is it?" Aaron asked, handing him the mug. "You're brooding."

Jon took a sip—near scalding but delicious—then answered.

"I went to see Gabrielle White last night. To check on her research. She said she'd made a breakthrough, but when I got out there, she claimed it was all a mistake."

"Okay . . . so?"

"It all just feels weird. That woman doesn't make mistakes. She's brilliant."

"Why would she lie?"

"Exactly. And if she is lying . . . I don't want to think what I'd have to do next. I really like Gabby. I like her husband too. Even their kid. I just hope it's a misunderstanding."

Jon set his empty cup down on the counter.

"Anyway. What's your day like?"

"I'm recording in the morning, working on some new ideas," Aaron answered. "Then I have an engineering session this afternoon. Might keep me late. One of those bands who think inspiration can't strike unless they've been hanging out in the studio all night gorging themselves on shitty Thai and shitty beer."

"Heh," Jon said, moving past him, giving him a quick peck on the cheek as he went. "As long as they pay you for all that time."

"Oh, I always get mine," Aaron said. "Shower. You smell like canal."

Forty minutes later, Jon was on Jefferson Avenue on the outskirts of downtown, the curved slab of steel and blue-tinted glass that was his boss' headquarters looming up from the skyline. The truth was, though, he'd already been in Hendricks territory for four or five blocks. Gray Hendricks had been buying up Detroit real estate at fire-sale prices for more than a decade. Some of it he rehabbed, creating things like the Hendricks Capital headquarters building currently dominating Jon's view. Other properties he was holding, waiting for the city to catch up with his ambitions, at which point he'd either build something else he needed or sell off lots at 1,000 percent profit.

Jon parked in his designated space in the lot beneath the Hendricks building and rode up to his office. He had Gabrielle White's drive in the USB slot on his laptop before he'd even fully sat down.

Datalogs appeared on the screen, time-stamped entries of Gabby's final round of experiments and the results. Incremental increases and decreases, all well within the margin of progress she'd been seeing since the protocols began—which was to say essentially no progress at all.

Exactly what he was expecting to see. Exactly what she'd told him he'd see.

He sat back, his arms folded, trying to push through the numbers on the screen to see the story behind them.

Jon clicked the window closed, considering.

He decided to look at the only other data he had access to, just to see if it might jar something loose. He pulled up a browser and logged in to the bank account into which he'd been depositing funds over the year and change Hendricks Capital had been underwriting Gabby's research. He saw the $3,000 he'd sent the previous day, almost immediately debited by the power company as Gabby ran her gear that one last time. As expected.

And then, something unexpected.

Another $10,000, wired into the account from an external source. A different account—owned by Gabrielle and Paul White. About an hour before the three grand he'd sent.

He thought about the pop they'd offered him. Generic grocery-store-brand cola. He thought about their couch, torn and patched and stained. He remembered the spools of yarn and half-finished pieces of knitting on their table, and recalled that Gabby had once told him she sold homemade hats and scarves and socks on eBay to make extra cash. He thought about their baby, and all the ways an infant had to hoover up money day after day.

And yet here was $10,000, wired into the operating account and gone in an hour, after what had to be a feverish run of experiments using Gabby's laser rig, none of which were reflected in the datalog she'd given him.

Jon stared at his screen, considering everything this new information had to mean.

He had a decision to make, and he made it, without even hesitating very much. He liked Gabby and her family, but he liked his job too—and if he was being honest with himself, he was pissed.

She'd lied to his face.

Jon stood and walked down the hall to another office, in the corner, door closed. He knocked once.

"Come," Hendricks said.

Gray Hendricks was an imposing slab of a man. Dark skin, almost reflective, shirt and tie that seemed too tight but couldn't really be, because he could afford to have his shirts tailored and then throw them away after one wearing. Sleek, hairless scalp, and slate-hard eyes.

If you asked the man, he'd tell you he was single-handedly bringing Detroit back to life. Jon wasn't sure he was wrong, either. He'd poured millions upon millions into the city through his real estate ventures, and that was just the start.

Among other endeavors, Hendricks Capital provided seed money to hundreds of research and small-business operations all around the city and state. Gabrielle White and the other clients in Jon's little corner of the operation were just a fraction of the total think tank Hendricks funded. His garden, he called it.

Most of the seeds Hendricks planted failed and died, of course, but every so often they blossomed—and then the harvest. Very little for the gardeners who created the ideas and saw them through, and very much for the man who owned the garden.

Gray Hendricks saw no issue with this policy, moral or otherwise. He was always up front about his terms with anyone who took his shilling, and he often invested in ideas that were the longest of long shots. For example, for about eight months, Jon had been assigned to oversee a man in Royal Oak who claimed to be building a time machine. That one . . . had not panned out. But it had kept a lunatic and his small staff employed for a little while, and hey, you never knew. If the man had succeeded, Hendricks would now own a time machine. Worth a roll of the dice.

It was odd to work for him, sometimes. Jon Corran considered himself to be an upright, honest person, moral and good and fair. Gray Hendricks, by reputation . . . was not. The story was that Hendricks had made his first real money loan-sharking in some of the city's worst neighborhoods back in the eighties. He supposedly did it in the true, brutal way, not just a loan shark but a great white, breaking legs and cracking skulls as required. It was all rumors, never confirmed.

But whatever path brought Hendricks that initial stake, he grew it by opening a chain of payday-loan operations, then getting lucky with a majority investment in a software start-up run by some genius kid from Southfield who had lightning in a bottle and was willing to trade it to Hendricks for an amount that probably seemed like a fortune. He wondered what that kid thought when Hendricks sold the company three years later for more than a hundred times what he'd paid.

That first deal was the spark that eventually flared into the Hendricks Capital incubator portfolio. Hendricks was still a loan shark, except now he was lending time and taking his interest in inspiration. If there was such a thing as a slumlord in the world of intellectual property, it was Gray Hendricks.

But he slept like a baby, every single night. Jon knew he did. Hendricks was saving Detroit, after all. Just ask him.

And Jon . . . well, just because he worked for Hendricks didn't mean he had to be Hendricks.

"Corran," Hendricks said, looking up from whatever he was reviewing on his desk. "What?"

No pleasantries, no small talk. Hendricks saw no point in it, which was one of the few things Jon could say he unreservedly liked about the man.

"Gabrielle White discovered something big, and she's trying to hide it from us."

Hendricks blinked, once, long and slow.

"White. She's working on the Alzheimer's thing. I thought the woman was smart. Our contracts have her so sewn up we probably own every crap she takes. Hell, we probably own her kid. She's got a kid, right?"

"Yeah, she has a kid," Jon said. "And she definitely knows what the contracts say. She's an extremely together person. Probably could have drafted them herself. But still, she's doing it."

"You're certain? How do you know?"

"She uses our capital to run her gear for her experiments. It's a hugely power-hungry rig, so we funded an account that gets drawn down every time she turns it on."

Hendricks waved a hand in a *get-on-with-it* gesture.

"She used up everything we gave her yesterday," Jon said. "Then she called for a bridge loan. Wanted a hundred grand. I gave her three thousand. She used that too."

Hendricks waved his hand again, more insistently.

"But before that—after she used up the first tranche and before the bridge—she deposited ten thousand of her <u>own money</u>. Used all that up too."

Hendricks' eyes narrowed.

"You see it?" Jon asked.

"Of course I see it," Hendricks said, frowning. "She got close to something big right when she ran out of cash, wanted to try to verify the results before she had to bring it to us. She deposited that ten K, didn't get what she wanted, then she called you for more money. Obvious. But what I don't get is why she thought she could get away with it."

"I don't think she knows we can see the activity in that account. She thinks of it like it's hers, since we just wire funds into it and she decides how to use the money. But our guys set it up, back when the deal started, so of course we have the passwords and so on. That feels right to me. Gabby White is a genius, but geniuses tend to have blind spots."

Hendricks shifted in his chair, his eyes looking past Jon, out at some target far in the distance.

"Whatever she figured out, it has to be big," he said. "To take a risk like this."

"Has to be," Jon said.

"Huge."

"Yeah."

Hendricks considered.

"Whatever it is . . . ," he said, his eyes sharpening, shifting back to Jon, "it's mine."

CHAPTER 12

AN ALLEY IN MURRAY HILL

"What's this place?" Soro asked.

Annami thought he didn't sound nervous, just curious. Like he was requesting more information to be able to adequately assess the situation. She had the sense that illegally entering other people's property at well past midnight wasn't something he found particularly unusual. Maybe nothing he did regularly, but familiar enough that he had the basic rhythms down. Like skiing. You really only needed to learn how to do it once. The only variable was the height of the hill. The incline.

This was in fact a very steep, very tall hill—but Soro didn't need to know that yet. She needed his help and didn't want to take a chance on his backing out.

"This place is a loading dock," Annami said.

"I know, June. I can see that. Whose?"

"Later," Annami said.

She heard a little rustle next to her, a sound she took to mean that Soro was not content with that answer.

"You told me that Olsen's gang has its operation down in Red Hook," she said. "Fine. But we can't just go in there and ask for my money back. We'll have to be . . . persuasive, and in order to do that we need some particular gear, and I only know one place to get it.

"It'll be okay," she said. "Follow me."

She pulled a baseball cap from her coat and snugged it down over her head. She and Soro slipped up a short set of steps that led to the dock proper, a concrete pier at the end of a long, angled pit where truck drivers once used extraordinary skill and precision to back their rigs up to the big metal sliding door for loading and unloading. These days, the maneuvering was mostly handled by AIs in the trucks' processing units.

"You can relax," Annami said. "At least for now. No camera up here."

"How do you know that?" Soro said, his voice low.

Annami pointed down. Cigarette butts littered the ground.

"People smoke out here. They like to keep it secret so the company doesn't cut their insurance. They tilted the cam a little to give themselves some privacy."

Soro frowned.

"Security never fixed it?"

"Security guys are out here smoking with the rest of them. They adjusted the drone coverage pattern too. Their little secret."

"And yours?" Soro said, raising an eyebrow.

"Yeah," Annami answered. "One of many. For example . . ."

She stepped to the human-sized entrance set next to the larger loading door. A keypad was mounted just above its handle. Annami tapped in a nine-digit code. A soft chime, and the door clicked open.

She walked through, holding it open behind her for Soro.

He seemed consumed half with admiration, half with alarm.

"How did you know that code?" he said.

"I used to work here," Annami answered. "They're supposed to change it all the time, but like I said, the smokers use this spot, and they figured they could all trust each other, I guess. Honor among addicts."

She moved into the darkness of the freight area: high-ceilinged, concrete-pillared, their footsteps echoing back at them.

"Come on. I don't want to be here long."

"Where is <u>here</u>, June?"

"Does it matter?" Annami said. "You've already committed the crime."

"A little. If this is a bank, I'm more likely to get shot than if it's, like, a library."

"It's not a library," she answered.

"Excellent," Soro said, shaking his head.

Annami led him to a door that opened into an employee break room, with a coffee machine, lockers, a little sink, cheap table and chairs. Along one wall was a rack of navy-blue jumpsuits on hangers. She walked to this, flipped quickly through them, and chose two.

"You're a large, right?" she said, and tossed one of the jump-suits to Soro.

He caught it easily. "Yeah."

Soro looked at the insignia sewn to the chest on the jumpsuit, a stylized yellow lightning bolt with the letters N and E and the number 1 incised above it in red. He sucked in a quick breath, really more of a gasp, then flicked his eyes up to Annami.

"Wait," he said. "We're at <u>Anyone</u>?"

"Yeah," Annami answered, pulling her own jumpsuit on over her clothes. "NeOnet Global North American hub number one. Get dressed. If someone does see us, it'll be better if we just look like two late-night maintenance people."

"If someone sees us, we're dead," Soro said. "I can't believe you brought me here. Why didn't you tell me?"

"Because you wouldn't have come," Annami said, "and I need your help."

Soro glanced at the door, frowning.

"Well, fuck," he said, and began pulling on the jumpsuit.

Annami zipped up her own. It was a little tight, but she wouldn't be wearing it long, hopefully.

"There's a storage room on this level that has everything I need," she said. "We'll load up the bags, and then it's back out the way we came in. It'll take us, like, ten minutes. Can't be longer, really—security makes a sweep every fifteen or so."

"So, what if I'd left just now?"

"Then the job would have taken me twenty minutes, and I'd be screwed, so thanks very much," Annami answered.

She walked to the locker room's exit, the door leading deeper into Anyone, and pulled it open, Soro following. They walked along a brightly lit hallway, moving naturally, not too fast, not looking around, acting as if they belonged. Annami had the benefit of having walked this exact path many times before, but Soro was just as smooth as she was.

He was a natural.

Annami liked him. She knew better than to like anyone. But she liked him.

The storage room she needed wasn't far. Locked, but again, Annami had the code. She was almost surprised that it still worked, but then realized it didn't make sense to change every code in the building every time they let one employee go.

She moved quickly through the room, slipping through aisles delineated by tall metal shelves loaded with boxes of various sizes, each with its own bar code and serial number. Every few seconds she would indicate a box, and Soro would take it, placing it in one of the dark nylon duffel bags they'd brought with them. When the first was full, he handed it to Annami and she slung it over her shoulder, continuing to point out items she needed.

"So this was just a . . . shopping trip?" Soro said quietly. "What is all this shit?"

"The stuff that will persuade Olsen to give me my money back."

"That is not an answer," he said.

"I'll tell you once we're out of here," she said. "I promise. I know it's a big deal that you're helping me. I mean it. Thank you."

"Uh-huh," Soro said. "You about done?"

"Completely done," Annami answered, selecting one final box, a small white cube about two inches on a side. She tossed it to Soro, who caught it and slipped it into his duffel, then zipped the bag closed. "Let's go."

They moved to the storage room's exit, the duffel heavy on Annami's shoulder, the irregularly sized gear crammed inside it shifting clumsily as she moved. She pulled open the door and stepped out.

Bertrand Milsen was standing about five feet away, in the middle of the hallway, holding a steaming cup of what might have been coffee but she knew was tea because that's what her former boss drank, his eyes wide, mouth a little open.

"Who—" he said, and then a little flash of recognition and puzzlement across his face. "Annami?"

Soro was right behind her, and of course he'd heard Bertrand use her name, not June, the one she'd given him. That was a piece of information she wished he hadn't received, but it was too late. It didn't matter, really. She had a lot of names.

"What the hell are you doing here?" Bertrand said, his focus coming back, his hand moving toward his pocket, probably reaching for his mini to call security. "What did you do to your face? And who's he?"

She looked at Soro, who had unzipped his jumpsuit and placed his hand inside it, around waist level. His eyes were very tightly focused on Bertrand. She realized that Soro trusted her to a point, but he trusted himself more, and had taken certain precautions to ensure that he wouldn't get into a situation he couldn't free himself from.

What that meant: Soro had a gun, and it was maybe already in his hand, under that jumpsuit. Tension grinding tighter, the two men's eyes locked on each other.

"No," she said, lifting her hands, holding one out to each of them, palm out. "I can fix this."

"Annami," Soro said, his voice calm, quiet, placing emphasis on that name, making it clear that he'd heard it, marked it down in his mind, "I hope so."

"I'm not stealing anything," she said, addressing Bertrand. "I just need a few pieces of flash gear. Just for, like, a day. I'll bring it all back."

Bertrand made a little involuntary noise, a snort-laugh.

"No," he said. "I don't think so. I don't even know what you took, or why you need it, but there's a reason this stuff is kept under lock and key. You know that as well as anyone."

He took a little step backward, tensed his arm a little, the one holding the steaming paper cup.

"Don't," Annami said. "Don't throw it. My friend has a gun, and I don't think getting splashed with tea will keep him from using it. We need to talk this out. I want you to let us go without calling security, and you want to get out of this without getting hurt. I'm telling you there's a way that can happen."

Bertrand's arm relaxed a little, and she sensed Soro pulling back a tick too. He wasn't calm, he wasn't <u>comfortable with the situation</u>, but she didn't think his finger was actually on the trigger anymore.

"You're still having that problem with the network, right?" she said, her eyes focused on Bertrand, her voice calm, like they were talking over a glitch in his office. "I don't have access to the same monitoring tools I did when I worked here, but the feeds are talking about it, and the system just seems to be running slow overall. I can feel it. That's why you're still here at three in the morning."

Bertrand nodded.

"Yeah. All over the world. It got worse after you left, too. It's spreading. We've had a few folks get zeroed out."

He shook his head.

"I probably shouldn't tell you that. But people will figure it out on their own soon enough. If we can't contain the cascade, we'll have to pull the whole network offline and reboot. I can't imagine what the fallout from that would be."

"Or," Annami said, "you can give me your mini and half an hour."

Bertrand's eyes narrowed.

"No way. Half an hour? Not possible. You can't fix this in half an hour."

"You know I can, Bertrand. Remember what you said?"

She smiled.

"I'm your best."

Bertrand thought for what seemed like a very long time. He took a sip of his tea, thought some more, and, at last, nodded.

They retreated into the storage room and pulled some of the larger boxes off the shelves to serve as makeshift stools. Annami took Bertrand's mini and set to work.

The device was already logged in to the network, and before anything else, Annami checked to see whether the bit of code she'd inserted into the system on her last day at Anyone was still present and still doing its work. It was, growing fat with data like

a tick. She considered sending it to herself then and there but resisted the impulse. The code was set to fire its payload off to her
mini automatically a day before the Bhangra George auction, and
she wanted to give it as much time as she could. The Centuries
were elusive targets, and the longer she waited, the better the
odds her code could find proof they existed.

Annami began tying off the network's infected veins and ar-
teries, rerouting healthy traffic through clean backup and maintenance pathways, emergency pipes and utility pipes and legacy
pipes from the earliest versions of the flash. It didn't even take
thirty minutes. More like twenty, and then she handed an amazed
Bertrand back his mini, hope dawning on his face.

"There," she said. "Network's back up to about eighty-five percent effective, and I've isolated the issue so it won't spread. That
should take some of the heat off while your techs work to purge
the infected zones."

"Holy shit," Bertrand said. "Annami . . ."

"My pleasure," she said, standing and hoisting the duffel bag
over her shoulder. "And you'll have all this gear back soon, I promise. I'll messenger it to the lobby. You'll stick to the deal?"

"Yeah," Bertrand said, still looking at his mini as if it were
some sort of holy relic. Evidence of the existence of God. "I will."

"Okay, good," Annami said. "Because if anyone comes after
me, the first two words out of my mouth are *Bertrand* and *Milsen*."

Her former boss looked up, nodded, annoyed.

"Jesus, yes, Annami. I'll stick to the deal. You don't have to
threaten me. I'm a man of my word."

"I know you are, Bertrand. See you around."

She and Soro left with the bags, slipping back out through
the loading dock and the alley and out into the streets of Murray
Hill and then down into the subway, where they hopped on the
Second Avenue subway heading north.

They found seats in a car at the far end of the train and sat next to each other, the two duffels on the ground between their feet.

Neither speaking, Annami running through the next steps of her plan in her mind, everything she would need to do in the little time she had left.

"Holy shit," Soro said, after a while. "Who <u>are</u> you?"

She looked at him, raised an eyebrow.

"Didn't you hear? I'm Annami."

Soro shook his head, processing that. Processing everything.

"What now?" he said.

Annami pulled out her mini. It was a quarter after four in the morning. She frowned.

"I guess I have to kill about five hours," she said. "Maybe I'll get this stuff home, try to sleep a little."

"Yeah?" Soro said. "Then what?"

Annami leaned back in her seat, putting her head against the window and closing her eyes, feeling the rattle of the train as it moved beneath the city.

"The pet store," she said.

CHAPTER 13

EARL V. MOORE BUILDING, THE UNIVERSITY OF MICHIGAN, ANN ARBOR

THE PIECE WAS A BACH CANTATA, SO WELL CONSTRUCTED THAT IT essentially played itself. Paul had chosen it for the midterm figured-bass examination for exactly that reason. The music had an internal consistency so strong that it virtually forced a performer to play it correctly. It was completely tonal, every passing note and chord moving to the next so naturally that it was almost more math than music.

That was why he loved Bach. The logic in the compositions was all but visible in the air as they were being played. You could see the music rippling together in great inexorable sheets, no note able to be anything other than what it was within the overall composition. The <u>logic</u> of it.

But not just logic. Also, somehow, it was beautiful.

There: the mystery of Bach. The music was perfect, like something designed by an artificial intelligence, machinelike and precise—but also heart-stirringly beautiful. Human in the deepest possible way.

The mathematical elements made the piece good for a figured-bass exam, which involved quick calculations of the chord inversions to be played beneath a melody, but the beauty made it easy to listen to twenty times in a row as his students plowed their way through.

That had been Paul's theory when he'd selected the cantata for the exam—no matter how badly a student messed up the piece, it would never be unlistenable, never torturous to sit through. Bryan Wentz was gamely disproving this notion as—again—he hit an A-flat. The cantata was in G major. A-flat wasn't the ugliest possible note Bryan could have chosen, but it was up there. He listened to the poor freshman fumbling along for another few bars, then decided to put the kid out of his misery.

"Okay," he said. "Enough."

Bryan pulled his hands from the keys and let them rest in his lap.

"You don't know how to do this, do you?" Paul asked.

"I'm sorry, Professor," Bryan said, wincing a little. "Honestly, I just can't motivate myself to get it under my fingers. It's not, um . . . figured bass just doesn't seem useful. I don't think of the notes this way. I'm a—"

"Guitarist," Paul said. "I'm aware. Go take a seat."

Bryan returned to his desk. Paul watched him go, looking out at the other students. More than half were also guitarists, and they all seemed to find the idea of learning extremely technical Baroque classical composition methods beneath them. His theory classes were always packed with guitar players these days, convinced they didn't actually need to learn anything. They could just "figure it out by ear."

He'd heard a story once about Eddie Van Halen getting a D on a composition he'd turned in for his own music theory class decades back, when he was just a kid, before he became the biggest guitar hero of the eighties. The professor had decided the tune was too poppy, too modern. Eddie had walked up to the piano, played the piece, then turned around and asked the class if they liked it. Applause, and Eddie walked out, headed for sold-out arenas and twenty-minute solos, never to return.

Paul was pretty certain these kids had heard that story too.

"I get it," he said, addressing his students. "Figured bass is extremely difficult. It was originally a shorthand for people like Bach to use when they were writing a composition so they could get it finished quickly. All they really had to do was jot down the melody and a few numbers here and there to explain what the harmony was supposed to be, and people who knew how to read it could play the piece just from that. Bach and his fellow composers of that era had to generate tons of music really quickly, and this was a way they could do it."

He looked out at his class, saw the jaws clenching, the eyes narrowing as his students, most of whom weren't yet twenty, found more evidence for their already entrenched opinion that he was old, old, old.

"So," he went on, ignoring the rapidly closing faces across his classroom, "you're wondering why the hell I'm making you learn how to do it. It's not something people use today, and you won't be composing choral pieces for Catholic masses unless your careers take extremely strange turns. But there is a reason."

Paul stepped up to the piano and tossed off a run with his right hand, adding in a few seventh chords and a major ninth with his left. Jazzy, nice. Never hurt to remind them that he wasn't just the guy who yelled at them about Haydn and Handel. He could play too.

Nine instruments, he thought. *Including guitar.*

"You can't think of this thing as just a piano," he said, continuing to play. "It's a keyboard. Literally. Just like a computer. No better machine has ever been invented to translate your musical ideas into something other people can understand. Nothing is more efficient. Not violin, not winds, not guitar."

He tossed a quick glance over at Bryan Wentz, gave him a quick grin. He shifted from whole chords in his left hand to an ostinato, just some minor groove. A little ominous, with a touch of syncopation to make it dance.

"When I ask you to learn figured bass, I'm not asking you to learn how to play the piano. I'm trying to teach you how to type."

He hit a big, ten-fingered E major chord and let it fill up the room. He lifted his hands from the keys and turned to look at the class again.

"Look, I'll be honest. About half of you failed this midterm."

Groans from the room.

"But I'm your teacher. If you failed, I failed. So, here's what I want to do. Take the weekend, work on this. It's honestly not that hard—you just have to put in the hours. We'll do it again on Tuesday—but that time, it'll count."

He lifted his hand to forestall the questions from several students who knew they'd passed—Cassie and Jim and Wendy, who had not only nailed every chord inversion perfectly but had also all managed to instill the piece with some life, some emotion. They'd produced actual music.

"If you passed on the first try, you can skip the composition exercise that I'd have assigned for Tuesday. Everyone wins."

His three prize students let themselves relax back into their seats, comforted that their excellence had been properly and duly recognized.

"Now get out. Go rehearse with your bands or do whatever it is you actually want to be doing."

The students filed out of the classroom, leaving Paul alone—but not quite alone. He looked at the top of the grand piano, where the Kitten sat in her car seat, blissfully asleep.

Paul stretched out his hands and began to play again, more

Bach, settling his mind with the beautiful progressions of the pre-
lude to *The Well-Tempered Clavier*.

He used his freed brain space to think about Gabrielle. She
was in the university's engineering labs at that very moment, using
equipment they'd both called in fairly big favors to access. Gabby
was known to the people there—she'd worked at the University of
Michigan for years before leaving once the baby came—but she
didn't work there <u>now</u>, and there was a not insignificant chance that
if the wrong person saw her down there, maybe someone who held
some sort of grudge from the old days, or maybe just someone who
thought rules were important and should be followed, that he'd lose
his job.

Not that Gabby had taken that into account or was likely to care
if she did. His wife had vanished deep into the Mariana Trench of
her own mind. He'd seen it happen over and over again during their
years together, when she became utterly focused on some new idea
or project. She was drowning in her own thoughts, flailing for survival in a sea of ideas and connections and inspiration. When she
got like that, the basic human niceties became not just inconvenient
but nonexistent.

He lifted his phone and checked the time. Gabby had asked
for three hours, but he knew that three could and would become
five or six.

The Kitten stirred, and Paul took his hands from the keys. He
lifted his daughter from her seat and held her close against his chest,
smelling the sweetness of the top of her head. A few little coos and
she settled deep into baby sleep, down away from the world, dream-
ing infant dreams.

Paul hadn't dreamed when Gabrielle had swapped into his
body. He couldn't remember anything at all about the experience. It
was like his mind was a light bulb. On, then off, then on again. His

throat still felt raw—Gabby had told him she'd thrown up during the switch—and he was very aware of the bruises and soreness on his legs from the tumbles and falls she'd taken while . . .

While using me, he thought.

It was hard to think of the hurts across his body as his injuries, his pain. They felt unfair, like things she'd done to him. Not on purpose, certainly, but nonetheless, things she'd inflicted upon him. Paul knew that was ridiculous on a logical level, but that was how his irrational self, his emotional self, felt about what she had done. It was . . . a taking.

Being married to Gabrielle was a constant series of swings between joy and despair. She applied diamond-like focus to anything she cared about, working to perfect it like a sculptor working marble, but she also felt things deeply. She had a strong sense of injustice on levels social and personal, and because so much of her time was spent alone, in her head, she spent hours chewing over arguments, letting them grow and evolve in her mind until she was ready to unleash them. Usually on or at Paul. It didn't matter if he was the target or not.

It was exhausting.

But also beautiful.

Gabrielle White <u>loved</u>. She burned bright. Sometimes a hearth fire, sometimes a cutting torch.

They both knew their arrangement was far from ideal. Gabby had left her residency at the university hospital to become the primary caregiver. That was their agreement, and it made sense. Paul was on tenure track, was making more money, and Gabrielle could continue her work through private funding—which had happened, via Hendricks Capital. It all made sense, but it still rankled the ever-loving shit out of his wife.

Paul was a music professor and historian, a composer who felt fortunate to get a quartet performed in public a few times a year.

The only chance he had at changing the world was by having some influence in the musical life of a student who went on to do great things. And that was fine with him.

But Gabrielle White . . . now, she'd planned to make an impact from the very start. Not just planned, but _expected_. If it wasn't through the Alzheimer's cure, it'd be something else. He knew what she said to herself before she started work each day—he'd heard her say it a few times. That little motto of hers.

His wife had a great deal to prove to the world, which he understood, considering where she'd started and everything she'd overcome. And of course just the nature of herself, in a world that had to be convinced and reconvinced that women like her deserved any real opportunities at all.

Shut a door in Gabby White's face and she'd kick it down. And then maybe she'd set the building on fire.

But Paul was on that tenure track, and so when the Kitty Kat showed up he stayed at the university and she left and it was fine at first, she'd gotten the funding from that gangster Hendricks, but then when the results she was hoping for didn't materialize and the funding was running out and she knew she was right, that there was an answer if only she could _see_ it, desperation and frustration taking root behind her eyes and then the arguments, arguments they'd never had before, fierce, much more cutting torch than hearth fire, and eventually Paul sleeping out in the guesthouse, that ramshackle shack that was barely better than being outside, and who the hell knew what would happen when the season turned and it started to get cold—she wouldn't make him keep sleeping outside, would she? And then this _new_ thing, the body switching, and god only knew what that might mean, and the sex out of nowhere, and everything else had been set aside, and she'd made him lie to Jon Corran and sneak her into the labs, and he'd done it because he loved her so much and wanted her to have absolutely everything her brilliance deserved . . . but here he was holding his daughter and smelling her sweetness and he was standing on a frozen pond and Gabby had a hammer and was just hitting the ice, big cracks forking out with every impact, and she wouldn't stop.

He knew her. She would not stop.

That was why and what she was.

Paul cleared his throat, feeling the rawness there from the time his wife had placed her soul into his body.

"Come on, kiddo," he said, carefully putting Kat back into her car seat and placing it into the stroller frame next to the piano. "Let's go see your mama."

The engineering labs were across campus from the music school. The day was gorgeous, very warm for October. Fall hadn't really hit yet, plenty of green still on the trees, with gold and red and orange dappled across them like Jackson Pollock slashes.

Paul swiped himself into the Lurie Biomed building, the security guard leaning over her desk to lavish well-earned and completely appropriate praise on his sleeping daughter.

Gabrielle was up on the third floor. Paul found her by following the music—a song by one of the early-aughts hard-core bands she liked was drifting out from under the door of a lab. Lawrence Arms or Alkaline Trio or something, one of her aggressive-guitar, big-poppy-chorus bands. Paul didn't enjoy all that the way Gabby did—he was a musicianship guy—but he got the energy. For her, music seemed to be a way to build a buffer between the world and her mind, the thicker the better. For him, it <u>was</u> the world. But that was okay—music could be anything, everything, for everyone.

Paul pushed open the door to the lab and stopped. He'd never seen this room before, and it was odd. Small, for one thing, and the walls were strange, covered by something like aluminum foil with a copper mesh over it, like a tightly woven chain-link fence. The ceiling as well, and the floor, beneath plexiglass plates laid down to protect the stuff. As he closed the door, he saw that a curtain made of the same material could be pulled across the exit, ensuring that every surface in the room could be shrouded in the copper mesh.

"Oh . . . hey," Gabby said, looking up at him, shouting over the music. She seemed surprised to see him. She tapped the space bar on her laptop, and the snarl of guitar and sneer singing evaporated. "What are you doing here?"

Paul pushed the stroller over to his wife's worktable, trying to understand the object resting on it amid scattered bits of wire, tools, tape, and electronics. It looked like a welding mask, with a foot-long metal cylinder protruding like a unicorn's horn from an assembly mounted over the visor. Wires ran from the end of the cylinder— the tip of the horn—and into a laptop not far away on the table. Paul recognized the information on the screen from his casual familiarity with his wife's work: a pattern template for the flashes of light that would, ideally, reduce the amount of plaque on the neurons in the brain of someone suffering from Alzheimer's disease.

"It's been three hours," Paul answered. "I texted you I was coming over."

"Uh, right," Gabby said. "I didn't get that. Look around. Signals can't get through this. That's the whole point."

She gestured vaguely and dismissively into the air around her, which Paul interpreted as a reference to the foil covering every surface.

This was the Gabby he—well, he didn't hate her. Even after everything, he couldn't imagine a world in which he hated this woman, but this was the Gabby he preferred to spend as little time with as possible. The one who cared only about running down the idea in front of her, not caring who she trampled along the way.

"Any progress?" he said, keeping his tone light.

"I think so," she said, attaching another wire to the end of the horn. "I need to run some tests, but . . . I think so."

"What is that thing?"

She lifted the mask, inspecting it.

"It's hopefully a way to test the body-swap effect without using the argon laser."

She tapped the horn.

"This is a high-intensity LED, with a bunch of different settings. Quick flashes, slow flashes, steady, dim, bright, whatever. It's got eighteen diodes that can be triggered in a number of different ways to create those effects. It's off the shelf—you can get these at hardware stores—but I rewired it so it's programmable, and then hooked it into my system for the Alzheimer's plaque-reduction patterns."

She gestured at the laptop, which had a little thumb drive sticking out of it. Paul shifted his glance over to the welding mask–like assembly.

"And this?" Paul asked, tapping it.

"Welding mask. Completely sealed up. Wanted to make sure the light went where it should, nowhere else. You don't want to trigger the switch by accident."

"No," he answered, his tone very dry. "Wouldn't want that."

Paul sat down on the stool next to her, knowing that she was barely aware of his doing it, her attention focused completely on the device she was tinkering with.

"Hey," he said. "Can I ask you something?"

"Sure," Gabby answered, not taking her eyes off the wire she was adjusting.

Paul put his hand on her arm, and she looked at him, her eyes narrowed.

"It's important," he said, keeping his voice soft.

She nodded and set the mask down on the table. She turned to face him and waited, all forced patience.

"Did you not want to tell Jon Corran about the . . . what did you call it? The flash. Did you not tell him because it would mean the technology would be recorded as existing now, and if we get divorced, it would mean you'd have to share any profits with me? But if you waited, then you could keep it all for yourself?"

Gabrielle's face softened into genuine surprise. No, more than that—almost hurt, shock.

She took his hand.

"Paul . . . no. First of all, I'm not sure divorce law works like that, and second, I'm not thinking that way. Not at all. You and me . . . we're a problem for another time."

"A problem . . . ," Paul echoed.

"No. Not a problem," Gabrielle said, forceful. She squeezed his fingers. "I didn't mean that. We have some things to work on, but we love each other, and we need each other, and if that's been a little eclipsed recently, believe me, it's in the forefront of my mind right now. I love you."

Paul nodded, not quite ready to say it back.

"So why . . . ," he began, gesturing toward the half-finished mask.

"Because Jon Corran and Gray Hendricks don't deserve the flash."

"But they paid for it."

"No. They paid for a cure for Alzheimer's. This isn't that."

"I might not be great with divorce law, Gabby, but I am certain they have rights to anything you invented with their money. If they find out, they'll come after this tech. And you. And us."

Gabrielle's jaw set, another sign he knew well—it meant a mental digging in, a fortification, a complete unwillingness to consider any point of view other than her own.

"They don't <u>deserve</u> what I made, Paul."

She lifted the mask.

"If my process is repeatable, reliable, it will be the most important technological advancement since the invention of the transistor. It could revolutionize transportation, governments, medical technology . . . I come up with new applications every time I blink."

"But it is not <u>yours</u>, Gabby. Gray Hendricks has a reputation."

"I know his reputation," his wife answered, annoyed. "You've told me before. You told me when I made the deal with him in the first place."

"Then I didn't do a good enough job," Paul said. You didn't grow up in Detroit. You don't really know. Hendricks was the king back then, no one you'd even think about fucking with, and I can't see how coming up in the world like he has would have changed that. He just has other people do the really evil stuff for him now. And you signed his paper. You have a <u>contract</u> with the man."

Gabby leaned forward, her eyes very focused.

"Fuck the contract. I am not giving the flash away, and there is no way Hendricks Capital will come for it unless they know I have it. And they <u>won't</u> know. I falsified the test results I gave to Corran, redacted everything about the switch."

"Is this about the money? I can see how there'd be a lot of—" Paul began.

"Trillions," Gabby said, utterly certain. "But the money isn't the point. It's about who steers this tech once it's deployed. Who decides how it's used. Because I'm telling you, the potential for abuse is horrible. If Hendricks is as bad as you say, there's no way he should have it. I should be the one. Because of who I am."

"I'm not following you," Paul said, feeling himself coming up against what, in his head, he called the Wall—the spot where Gabby's mind raced ahead of his, leaving him conceptually the tortoise to her hare.

"Look. It's this," she said.

ANYONE

153

She took his hand and pressed it against her cheek, his coffee-with-cream skin making a sharp distinction against her much darker shade.

"You know I'm a black woman, right?"

"Might have noticed, once or twice," Paul said.

"Everything I say or do in this world takes that into account. I am a mother first, then a scientist, a wife, and a black woman."

Paul took note of the order, but decided he was just happy to be included.

"People in my field, people in the grocery store, people in general—they see that list backward. Maybe they don't see anything at all past the first thing—a black woman. It's all they need to see."

"But with this"—she gestured with her free hand at the mask she'd made—"maybe that changes a little. I'm not saying racism goes away. That's idiotic. But if you can't tell who's inside the skin of the person you're talking to, maybe you can't judge them so quickly based on the color of that skin. You have to judge them based on who they are. How they act."

She moved his hand to her mouth and kissed it.

"Black, brown, white, gay, straight, boy, girl, trans, young, old, disabilities . . . none of that would work how it does now, with the world putting you in a box from day one just because of your face, your hair, whatever. I mean, my god, Paul"—Gabby pointed at the Kitten, still asleep in her stroller—"imagine the world this could give her."

Somewhere, beneath his mounting disquiet at what his wife was proposing, Paul felt hugely satisfied that she was telling him these things. She didn't just love him—she trusted him. Gabby obviously cared about the flash with everything she had, and she was giving him enough to ruin the whole thing, if he wanted.

He touched the mask.

"This works?"

"I hope so," Gabby said. "I have to test it. It's important. I need to do it now."

"Why?" he asked. "Why now?"

"Because . . ." She hesitated. "The first flash was an accident. I didn't mean to do it. It just happened. But if this mask works, it means I understood what I did, refined it, and repeated it. I can legitimately say that I am the inventor of the flash.

"Hendricks and his lawyers are going to say that I'm not, and they'll think it's easy to take from me, because of this."

She touched her cheek again.

"Because I'm just a black woman."

Gabby bent, fiddled with a wire.

"But this mask thing, if it works," she said, "means I deserve to keep it. It'll be worth however hard I have to fight to keep it."

"I get it, babe," Paul said. "I'm with you. How would you test it?"

She gave him an apologetic look.

"Ah," Paul said.

"That's why I'm working in here," she said. "This room is a Faraday cage. Electromagnetic signals can't get through the wire netting on the walls."

"I thought the flash worked with lights," he said. "Is light, uh, electromagnetic?"

"No, it's not, but it's more than just light," Gabby said. "Some other kind of signal is clearly moving. The visual pattern sets a consciousness loose from its native mind, and then it goes out looking for the nearest similar host mind. I think."

"So if you used the flash outside this room, you could end up in some random person's mind."

"Exactly," Gabby said. "I want to try this here. With you. Like we did before."

"We can't do it the other way? Me going into you? I don't like the idea of going dark again."

She shook her head.

"If only one of us can stay awake through the process, it should be me. So if something goes wrong, I can try to fix it. Think of it this way—we'll be like the Curies, or the Salks. There's a long tradition of families experimenting on themselves for the sake of scientific progress."

"Hooray," Paul said.

He thought. He looked at his daughter. He looked at his wife.

He picked up the mask and handed it to her.

Shortly after, with the baby safely deposited with a colleague a few floors up, Paul lay down on a table in the lab and closed his eyes. When he opened them, he was in darkness, with the mask over his head. He pulled it off to see that he was now sitting on a stool across the room, with no sense of how much time had passed or how he had gotten there.

"Okay," Paul said, looking at his wife getting up from where she'd been lying on the floor. "It works."

Gabby didn't say anything, just looked at him, as excited as a kid on her birthday.

"Guess we better figure out how the hell we're going to keep it," he said.

His wife reached up and took his hand.

CHAPTER 14

THE BACK ROOM OF MR. O QUICKSHARE, RED HOOK, BROOKLYN

THE BACKS OF ERIK OLSEN'S HANDS HAD SPOTS ALL OVER THEM. Small, pale brown dots, none so prominent on its own, but if you noticed one, you began to see others, and your entire perception of the hand changed. What was an ordinary human appendage became a sickly thing, a signpost of age and decay. It got worse the longer you looked. The crepe paper texture of the skin, which took full seconds to smooth back into shape after being pinched. The thick, thickening tendons beneath that skin. The slight yellowing of the nail beds.

Olsen's hands were those of an old man, which was frustrating to him, because he did not feel old, and he did not act old. He maintained constant vigilance against time's efforts to erode his appearance, manipulating every changeable element to make sure the exterior reflected the interior. It worked, largely. There were still plastic surgeons, despite the flash generally making it easier for the people who could afford such alterations to simply slip into fresher bodies when it was necessary to appear in public.

Certain celebrities had vessels on constant call for the purpose, who often became well-known themselves.

If you were rich enough, you could spend most of your time in a younger self. Sometimes vessels signed long-term contracts— renting out their bodies on an exclusive, nonstop basis for a year or more—deciding that sacrificing some period of their life was worth financial security once they returned to their primes.

The fees for such a thing were astronomical, and despite a lifetime diligently devoted to criminal pursuits of various flavors, Olsen was not quite wealthy enough to afford a full-time vessel. He used short-term services, of course, almost everyone did. Vacations from the self, spending time in whatever flesh appealed— but he did not greatly enjoy it. The moment to return to his own body always came, and the disjunction between soul and body never felt more prominent than when he slipped back into his own aging prime.

Or, for that matter, whenever he looked at his hands. Not much to be done with the hands, he'd been told by the doctors who'd worked on his face and body. The spots could be lightened via lasers or microdermabrasion, but the rest . . . not much.

But as he looked at those hands now, silhouetted against the glowing thinscreen floating a few inches above his desk, Olsen smiled. Displayed on the screen was a man's head, rotating, with an image of his body beside it, also spinning slowly. The man looked to be about twenty. He was wearing a T-shirt and jeans. Nothing special. Olsen flicked a finger in front of the thinnie, and the clothes vanished, leaving the man naked, arms slightly spread to either side.

Pinching and spreading gestures zoomed in and out of the various body parts on display. Olsen applied a critical eye. The man was uncircumcised, which was fine, easy to adjust later if he wanted to.

"Nice, eh?" said a voice from the thinnie. A man, with just a slight accent. Greek, Olsen thought. Maybe a Turk.

"Yes, nice," he agreed. "What do you have that's younger?"

"How much younger?" the screen asked. "You know we get too young, it moves into what we call a gray area. The law says anyone below eighteen cannot consent to long-term shares."

Olsen knew this should be interpreted as an opening to negotiations, not as an expression of any true moral qualms. Assuming a price could be agreed upon, the Greek, or Turk—the Mediterranean, he decided—would happily provide a clean, young vessel of essentially any age, within which Olsen would spend the rest of his life and provide excellent, twenty-four-hour medical care to his prime until it died.

When that day came, Olsen would die, as would his youthful vessel, whoever that unfortunate man might be. That was the way it worked. The first of the Two Rules. If one dies, both die.

No vessel for a share like this ever actually gave their consent, over eighteen or not. It was a death sentence. It was also hugely, incredibly illegal. Olsen knew it, and the salesman knew it, and the vessels certainly knew it. They were usually people who had been kidnapped from their economically depressed hometowns, or possibly who went to work with a legitimate-seeming flash-based company in hopes of saving money and achieving whatever dreams they had. Instead, this. Sold forever to wealthy men and women who wanted to escape their aging bodies.

Or wealthy men and women with inconvenient illnesses, or who had simply aged out of being able to use the flash at all. Anyone set a hard limit of seventy years old for participation in the flash, after which special waivers were required to use the system. These could be obtained only in emergency situations or for individuals who were either particularly healthy or particularly skilled. Eventually, though, even those were no longer available. Very few people over seventy-five flashed—at least in the light-share. Eventually, everyone turned Dull.

The upshot—all this nonsense about consent was simply a pretext for the salesman to jack up the price, higher with each year of reduction in age of the vessel Olsen chose.

That didn't matter, though. Olsen had the money, thanks to a visit to Mama Run's darkshare den that had proved to be infinitely more profitable than what he would have earned selling the stolen flash patterns he had gone there to retrieve. He had no idea what the woman he'd taken the funds from had been planning to do with the money, and he did not care.

Yes, he would have to make some sort of obeisance to the Three-Fold Blades for daring to invade one of their places of business, but that was in itself business, and it was worth the cost and hassle.

Especially since if all went well, he wouldn't be the person enduring that cost and those hassles.

Olsen's eyes flicked to another thinscreen floating up on the wall to the left of his desk. It was a security feed, showing the front room of the legitimate front for his business, Mr. O Quick-Share, a low-rent set of flash booths designed primarily for day laborers from foreign countries who flashed into vessels in New York to perform menial jobs before returning to their own bodies for the evening. The laborers did the work and split the proceeds with the vessels, or simply paid a rental fee. It was one of the lowest tiers of the flash economy, used only by people too poor to afford the I-fi implant, and Olsen always felt a mild distaste that he was associated with it. Still, it was a mostly cash- and crypto-based business, due to the varying nationalities of the people involved, which made it excellent for laundering the proceeds from the other businesses he ran, primarily extortion rackets and thievery.

Olsen's son, Lars, was sitting at the front desk, his feet up, chatting with Gerber, the reassuringly enormous man who served as the primary enforcer for Olsen's little syndicate. Other members of the group (Olsen refused to call it a gang, at least in his head—he thought the word just sounded uncivilized) were clustered around, hanging on Lars' every word.

The security feed had sound—Olsen could listen in, if he chose, but he knew what he'd hear: an idiot boasting about a woman screwed or a brawl won or a scam pulled. Nothing he hadn't heard before, and nothing he felt particularly inclined to listen to again. He hoped Lars would rise to the challenge of running the organization once his father was gone (well, not gone, but changed, and living a new life somewhere else for whatever amount of time he had left). If not, though . . . not his problem. He'd raised the boy. Now either Lars would grow up and take responsibility for himself, or he wouldn't. Either way, his choice.

Olsen turned his attention back to the business at hand: the thinnie above his desk still showing the naked, young—but not young enough—man.

He moved his index finger half an inch, returning the prospective new vessel back to a clothed state.

"Younger," he said, finally answering the salesman's question. "Sixteen, if you can do it. I miss my teens."

A grunt from the screen, which Olsen took to mean *all things are possible.*

"Not cheap, and it'll take a little time," the salesman responded. "Hard to find a sixteen-year-old kid up to the physical standards of my organization who will want to make this deal. We'll need a deposit. Twenty percent."

Olsen understood from this statement that the Mediterranean was almost certainly going to send his teams out to kidnap a sixteen-year-old boy and bring him to New York City so his body could be sold into a sort of endless, unconscious slavery. He wanted a deposit to make sure Olsen was serious enough about moving forward to justify the expense and risk of acquiring a good subject.

"That's fine," he said. "Send me the account information, and I'll transfer it over."

A flicker of movement from the second thinscreen, the security feed. Olsen glanced at it, then frowned. Small, dark shapes were moving into the main room, scurrying across the floor. Lars was still in the middle of his story, so his audience hadn't noticed yet, but as Olsen watched, one of his men—a tough, hardened criminal—almost fell over himself in terror as he realized a swarm of what certainly looked like rats was heading toward him and the others.

His reaction triggered a domino effect, and the rest of the gang began to scramble backward. All but Gerber, who stood and watched, impassive—he was rarely passionate about anything, in fact, which was a factor in his overall excellence.

Two figures appeared at the far end of the room, a man and a woman, both wearing dark goggles and odd metallic mesh hoods. The woman held something in each hand.

Three-Fold Blades, Olsen thought.

He was reaching for the intercom to shout out a warning when the woman tossed out the items. They looked, in the half second Olsen saw them, like balls made of tiny light bulbs—and then a splash, a <u>surge</u> of illumination, a coruscating flicker that reminded him of the sound of popcorn popping, if such a thing had a visual equivalent. It filled the outer room, whiting out the thinnie's screen, but not before it shone out into Olsen's office and bored deep into his eyes and into his mind and/

And/

On the floor. Crawling, but running, too—hands are feet. Can see something past his eyes, is something stuck to his face? Sticking out of it, like a mask.

Hot. Running hot. Heart pounding. Can feel it. RUNNING. Hands are feet. So fast.

Rats, there are rats all around, but giant, as big as he is, and people, mostly slumped to the ground, even bigger. If the rats are giant, these people are too big. Enormous.

Too hot. What he sees is split, the colors strange, like a photo negative, and blurring into nothingness not far out. Vision to either side, he can see so far to either side, almost behind him, and there, behind him, a gigantic worm, a snake, pale and horrible, twitching, twitching, and INSIDE HIM. He can feel it moving as he sees it move, and he doesn't even have to look behind him to see it move.

A feeling, over and over again, from the sides of his head, intense, like touching his tongue to a battery. Things are sticking from his face—attached to him, he knows that now—twitching, horrible, twitching like the pink worm.

He thinks he is female. He smells the males and wants them, wants to be with them in the darkness, tails coiling together. He wants to find the food he can smell everywhere, wants to take it down into the darkness, to get out of the light, to get away from these LIGHTS and find the dark, to eat and mate and eat and mate. He sees a rat, a rat like him, and he knows it's the one he will be with, down in the dark.

And he sees one of the giant people, monumental, unconscious, being pulled out from among the others, and he knows it. He recognizes it. The puller, another giant, dark, bending down, pulling something shiny from its belt and reaching to the unconscious giant's hand and making a quick movement—he can see movement easily, yes—and then the smell of blood, the richness, and he wants it, but he also knows, somehow he still knows whose blood it is, and he leaps forward, teeth bared, the pink worm (his TAIL, he knows what it is now) giving him balance, ready to tear into this horrible giant monster (PERSON, it's the WOMAN who did this to him) who dared to hurt the body he knows is also his.

A pressure closing around him, enclosing the middle of his body, and he bites, finding his sharp teeth barred by the material of whatever is holding him. He gnaws away at it, knowing that he'll get through in time, and then he'll have all the blood he wants and a flash of light, coiling, bubbling light that he's never seen before but understands and/

And/

Olsen screamed, the sound ripping out of his throat, so deep and elemental a signal of his horror that it seemed likely to almost rip <u>out</u> his throat. He was just acknowledging a searing pain in his left hand and the fact that he was handcuffed to one of the flash couches out in the front room of the quickshare when he was slapped, hard, by something that felt much harder than a hand should be.

"Shut up," a woman's voice said, and Olsen did.

He looked up at her and realized that what was happening to him had nothing to do with the Three-Fold Blades. The woman had tattoos all over her face, and he knew who she was. The one he'd stolen from, after she'd stolen from him. Just business. The way things worked.

She did not seem to see it that way.

The woman was wearing what looked like chain-link gloves. That's why the slap had been so hard, and that's why . . . he froze that thought, unwilling to let *That's why I couldn't bite through them when I was a rat* make it into his conscious mind.

"You're going to give me back my money," the woman said.

"Fuck you," Olsen spat. "You took from me; I took from you. We were square. There was no need for . . . for . . ."

He looked around, seeing his men, his gang, even Gerber, stolid, reliable Gerber, all unconscious on the ground, while the rats housing their souls and minds huddled in corners, squeaking miserably as the second attacker, the man, rounded them up one by one and placed them in a large wire cage.

"That one's his son," the man said, gesturing toward Lars' insensate body with the black rat he was holding in his own pair of chain-link gloves, before placing the animal—person—in the cage with the others.

"Okay," the woman said. She moved to the cage, reached in and picked up a rat. This one was spotted, brown and white.

Like the back of my hands, Olsen thought, almost laughing.

"We don't know which rat got your son," the woman said. She glanced at the cage as if she was counting. "Ten percent chance it's this one, give or take."

She held up her free hand, which held a stun gun, electric prongs crackling. She shoved it into the rat, which convulsed.

"NO!" Olsen shouted, eyes wide, casting his eyes to his son.

One of the other bodies slumped in a sort of relaxation Olsen had seen before—the last gasp, literally, of an empty prime when its vessel died. One dies, both die—even if one is a rat.

It wasn't Lars, though, thank god. The dead man was fairly new to the organization, one of Lars' cronies, someone Olsen barely recognized.

The woman tossed the dead rat at Olsen. It landed between his legs with a meaty slap, a smell of charred fur wafting up to his nose.

"My money, please," the woman repeated. "Next rat I fry, it's one in nine it's your son. Then it's one in eight. Then—"

"All right," Olsen said. "Bring me the thinnie from my office, and I'll put the credits on a data."

"Yes, you will," the woman said. She nodded at her partner, who walked to the back of the room and disappeared into Olsen's office.

"How did you do this?" Olsen asked, desperate to know. "You can't flash into animals. This isn't possible. None of this is possible."

The woman just stared at him from behind her dark goggles, silent.

The man returned from the back room holding the thinscreen from Olsen's desk.

"Uncuff me and I'll make the transfer," he said.

"You wish," the man said. "Give me your access codes, and I'll make it happen."

Olsen frowned, his one slim hope of using the thinnie to call for help, to fix this, to do anything at all . . . dashed.

He read off his codes, and despite Olsen's expectations, the man pulled only the funds Olsen had taken from Mama Run's. Not a penny more. He slipped the data holding the cash out of the thinnie and held it up toward the woman, grinning.

"Got it," he said.

"Good," the woman answered. "Just one more thing."

She walked over to Lars' body and reached under its arms. Grunting, she dragged it over to the rat cage.

"What are you doing?" Olsen demanded. "Please . . . I did what you wanted."

The woman ignored him, and Olsen knew at that moment how much he loved the foolish, braying idiot he'd raised. He realized that he was almost certainly about to watch Lars die in front of his eyes.

"I can give you more money," Olsen said. "Whatever you want. Just don't hurt my son!"

"He needs to be quiet," the woman said to her partner, and the man shoved a piece of cloth into Olsen's mouth. It tasted like chemicals, like cleaning products.

So now Olsen could only watch, through eyes gone watery from the astringents saturating the rag in his mouth, as the woman held Olsen's unconscious son up close to the cage holding the rats. The creatures inside were attentive. Still, wary. They weren't acting like rats—which made sense, because they were not rats.

"This prime is one of yours," the woman said. "I need to know which one. If you don't tell me, then I'll leave you in with the rats. If I find out what I want to know, then I'll switch you back. I promise."

With a slight grunt of effort, she lifted Lars and pressed his face up against the bars.

"If this isn't you, go to the back of the cage."

None of the rats moved, and the woman turned to frown at her partner, standing guard over Olsen.

"Dammit," she said. "They're too far gone. Rats don't have language centers in their brains. I'm not even sure they can understand what I'm saying."

"Look again," the man answered, a wondering tone in his voice.

The woman looked back at the cage, as did Olsen. The rats had moved to the back of the cage, as ordered. All but one, a dark-furred animal that was staring at Lars' face—its own face—as if hypnotized.

"There we go. That wasn't so hard, was it?" the woman said.

She pulled a bag from inside her coat, made from what looked like the same material as her gloves. She reached into the cage, extracted the rat that was Lars, and placed it into the bag.

"Wait," Olsen said. "You can't take him. You said you'd switch him back."

"No," the woman said, gesturing at the cage, where the remaining rats sat, very still, "I said I'd switch <u>them</u> back."

She cinched the metal bag closed, then handed it to her partner, its occupant squirming and squeaking. They passed out of Olsen's field of vision, and he thought that was the end, that it was over, that they were leaving. His gang of rats apparently thought the same—a chorus of terrified noises from the cage.

But the woman returned, now holding a pair of the same dark goggles and metal mesh hood she was wearing. She placed both on Olsen's head—goggles first, then hood. He could still see, but the world had gone very dark, like the light in the room had been reduced to a single candle. He watched as the woman placed another hood over Lars' unconscious head and then removed another of the odd light-bulb grenades from inside her coat. She twisted a dial on its side and placed it on the table with the cage.

"This will go off in sixty seconds," she said, turning to Olsen and pointing at it. "It'll put the rest of your people back into human bodies."

"The right ones?" he asked.

"Maybe a few," she answered. "They've all got a one-in-eight chance."

"And my son?" Olsen said, pleading.

"His prime will stay here, with you. I'll keep the rat. He's security, so you don't do anything stupid. Like a hostage. I'll switch him back in about a week. Don't worry, Olsen, I'll take good care of Lars here. Just put his body on an IV, maybe get a doctor to check on it. He'll be fine."

The woman walked toward the door.

"I understand the importance of family," she said.

CHAPTER 15

A LAW OFFICE, DETROIT

"THIS IS ALL CONFIDENTIAL, RIGHT?" GABRIELLE WHITE ASKED.

In the experience of Sara Kring—which was substantial but not endless, being as she was an eighth-year associate at the Detroit firm of Barton, Oestreich & Yoo, LLP—a lawyer being asked about confidentiality preceded a story that, while invariably fascinating, landed the listener squarely in the center of the endless web of ethical rules and regulations to which attorneys were subject.

In short, it was a brightly waving red flag for a huge pain in her ass shortly to ensue . . . but it could also signify new business, and that was the thing. New business. You'd endure quite a bit to bring in some billables under your own name, especially as an eighth-year.

"Well, let me ask you this," Sara answered. "Are you here looking for a lawyer, and if things go the way you want, you'll hire me?"

Gabby nodded once, tight, not a millimeter of movement more than was required to convey her intent. That little gesture, the precision of it—that was the woman she remembered from college. It was the nod of a woman with goals, and no time to waste getting to them.

Her husband, Paul, sat in the other chair, the one she'd brought in from another office because her own was too small to comfortably fit two. She didn't know Paul well. Hot but bookish, artsy. Not her type, but she understood why Gabby had picked him. He balanced her out—a one-man aromatherapy session.

Paul seemed nervous.

"Then yes. Attorney-client privilege applies," Sara said. "Speak in confidence, with confidence."

Sara smiled, sliding into the reassuring affect she'd seen more senior attorneys at the firm use for years.

Gabby nodded again, the same tight motion, then started talking.

"You remember the contract you helped me with, little over a year ago, with Gray Hendricks?"

"Of course. The IP deal. You were part of his incubator portfolio," Sara responded.

It was a pretty standard VC agreement, with zero room to negotiate. Her role as Gabrielle's attorney was mostly just to explain what the various provisions meant, to make sure her client knew what she was getting into. Hendricks wouldn't change even a single word. The lawyer on the other side had said as much, telling Sara he'd be happy to clarify "any provisions she didn't understand" (the prick), but specifying that the agreement's language had been thoroughly vetted in prior deals and required no revision.

In other words: take it or leave it, lady. Gabby had taken it.

"Did Hendricks not hold up his end of the deal?" Sara asked. "Did he not pay what he was supposed to?"

That could be interesting, she mused. The contract, as she remembered it, was ironclad on both sides—Hendricks Capital was bound just as firmly as Gabrielle White. If Hendricks hadn't paid out the specified amounts, it was grounds for a suit, or at least some threatening demand letters that might end in a settlement. Nothing that would end up on the front page of the *Detroit Legal News*, but something.

Sara was eight years in to practicing law, the point in the firm's traditional career path when decisions were made on upper floors about whether she would become a partner, be gently but firmly urged to move on to a new position somewhere else, or worse— assigned to the limbo of an of-counsel position. Of-counsel was code for "skilled attorneys who couldn't generate business and so were expected to grind out the rest of their careers doing partner-level legal work while the actual partners took three-hour lunches and made three times the income—in a bad year."

It did not look good. Sara didn't have the connections she needed to really bring in the bacon for the firm. She wasn't best friends with any rich kids due to inherit their parents' businesses, she wasn't dating a hedge fund manager willing to send some legal work her way, and her own family had zero connections to the upper-tier Detroit Athletic Club set. Her parents were still sort of stunned she'd made it as far as she had.

None of this was how it was supposed to be. Sara Kring was a graduate of the University of Michigan's law school, nationally ranked as a top-ten institution year after year. Back when she'd started, her future was assured. This wasn't how it was supposed to be.

But it was how it was.

Sara Kring had one client of her own: Gabrielle White. And as much as she liked the woman, respected her drive and intelligence and ambition, and enjoyed the fact that they had shared memories and tragedies and triumphs from undergrad, Gabby's matters would never generate much in the way of billable hours.

Take the Hendricks Capital deal—the whole thing had been, like, a six-hour job. In the end, Sara had knocked it down to three when she saw the expression on Gabby's face, pregnant with her daughter, out of work, as she realized what six hours of attorney time would cost her.

Despite the jokes about her profession, despite the clichés, Sara wasn't a monster. She was just a lawyer, trying to make her way.

"Hendricks paid," Gabby answered. "Everything he said he would. Even gave me a little extra, at the end."

"Okay, so what's the problem?"

Sara reached for a pencil and flipped to a clean page on her yellow legal pad, quickly writing Gabby's name and the date on the first line.

She looked up to see that Paul had reached out a hand toward her and had an odd half smile on his face.

"Uh, no notes, okay? How about we just talk, for now."

Sara raised a mental eyebrow, all the way to the sky. Interesting.

"Sure, Paul," she said. "No notes. For now."

She looked back at Gabby and raised an actual eyebrow.

"Okay, so . . . ," she said.

"I just want to know if there's any wiggle room in the Hendricks deal. Hypothetically."

"That's a big question. Those papers were as locked down as any legal documents I've ever seen. They gave you money, and you were supposed to use it to try to invent something. If you pulled it off, they owned whatever you made, and you got a little piece of any profits going forward. So . . . wiggle room for what, exactly? Who's supposed to be wiggling here, you or Hendricks Capital? And where is the destination of said wiggling?"

Sara paused, then said one more word, with the same particular emphasis Gabby had used.

"Hypothetically."

Gabby considered those questions, her eyes narrowed. "Is there a way for Hendricks not to own whatever I invented?" she asked. "For me to keep it?"

"No," Sara said. That much she knew, even without reviewing

the contracts. "You get your little percentage, you stay involved, but they own it and control it."

"What if I want to keep it anyway?" Gabby said, which earned her a sidelong glance from Paul.

"What the hell's going on?" Sara said. "Enough with the dancing around. I can't help you if I don't know—" She stopped herself.

"Actually, no. It sounds like you're planning to perpetrate a fraud. Privilege doesn't extend to helping you commit a crime. If it's something you'd already done, sure, but I'm not allowed to sit here and help you plan how to break your deal with Gray Hendricks."

Paul nodded, as if this was something he was expecting.

"All right. Thank you, Sara. We appreciate it."

He made a subtle sort of move, like he was about to stand up but hadn't quite pulled the trigger on it yet, when Gabby put a hand on his arm.

"No, hold on," she said.

Gabby leaned over, partially disappearing from view behind the edge of the desk. Sara heard the sound of a zipper, and watched Paul's face collapse into an expression of utter dismay.

"Hon, this is not a good idea," he said.

Gabby reappeared, holding on her lap the small gym bag she'd brought into the office, now unzipped. Her hands were inside it, and her jaw was set—another Gabrielle White facial expression Sara Kring recalled very clearly from their college days. Paul could say whatever he wanted, but Gabby had decided that her idea was in fact a good idea, and that was that.

"It's all confidential, Paul," Gabby said. "Sara said so."

Sara knew that she should clarify things for her client. At this point in the conversation, she had made her objections clear, explained that she couldn't help Gabby commit a crime. Technically, she should reiterate the idea that her client was moving down a road where Sara could not follow, and that she could in fact be compelled to offer testimony against her at some point.

But she really, really wanted to know what was inside that bag.

Sara shrugged.

"Sure," she said.

Gabby pulled out an odd contraption from the bag. As far as Sara could figure, it was a mask with a flashlight attached to it, with the light-up end pointed in toward the area where the mask's eyes would be, if they weren't covered. Wires ran from it to a laptop, which Gabby also removed from the gym bag. She moved the name-plate pen set Sara's dad had bought her when she graduated from law school and set the computer in the newly vacated space.

"Put this on," Gabby said, offering the mask.

"What is that?" Sara said.

"It's easier just to show you."

A heavy sigh from Paul. Sara glanced at him, confused. He didn't seem worried anymore. More like . . . resigned, aware that there was no way to fight his wife once she got moving in a direction.

"Is it like a VR thing?" Sara asked, taking the mask and inspecting the homemade, taped-together hodgepodge.

"Yes," Gabby said, flipping open her laptop and typing quickly. "Paul, you're good for this, right?"

"Always," Paul said, unconvincing in the extreme.

Sara shrugged and placed the mask over her head. Complete darkness. It smelled stuffy, like old sweat, and the flashlight threw off her balance, pulling her head forward.

She heard another burst of typing from Gabrielle, then she said two words.

"Thirty seconds."

"Okay," she heard Paul respond.

Another few keystrokes, and then it sounded like Gabby got up and left the room, closing the door behind her.

"Uh, Paul? Are you there? What's going to happen?"

"Just don't freak out," he answered. "Don't, you know, scream or anything."

Paul could not have selected a more alarming set of words, particularly while she was wearing a getup almost certainly designed for sexual deviancy. Sara reached up to yank off the mask, but then the thirty seconds were up, and bright lights flashed before her/

She was sitting on the other side of her desk, watching her body slump in its chair, her head in that ridiculous mask falling forward, the end of the flashlight thunking into the legal pad and propping her up like the stem on a wineglass.

Just as Sara became aware of the massive difference in her own physical being and prepared herself to scream until her throat tore free, a hand slipped around from behind her and clamped firmly over her mouth.

"It's all right," Gabby whispered in her ear. "I promise you. Everything will be just fine, but you have to stay still. Relax. Look at this."

Gabby's free hand moved in front of Sara's (?) eyes, holding a little compact mirror. Sara looked, wanting to understand, and saw Paul's face in the mirror, with Gabby's hand covering its mouth. Behind this alarming, incomprehensible image was Gabby herself, hovering over Paul's (?) shoulder.

She flicked her eyes up to meet Gabby's and saw her nod.

"Stay relaxed. I'll put you back, right now. Okay?"

Sara made a noise of assent, and Gabby let her go.

"What . . . what . . . ?" she said, stopping when she heard herself speaking with Paul's voice.

Gabby reached over to Sara's body on the other side of the desk, carefully removing the mask and gently placing her head down on the legal pad. She could have been sleeping. Sara hoped she was.

The mask went over her head again, and Sara realized that the smell this time was a little different. She couldn't put her finger on it, but apparently the way Paul processed the odor was not the way Sara did. Despite herself, she found that fascinating.

"Thirty seconds," Gabby said, and thirty seconds later it was done. Sara felt the press of her desk against her cheek and pushed back inadvertently, the casters on her desk chair rolling her backward until she hit the rear wall of her office.

She snapped her head up, to see Paul, his expression apologetic, almost ashamed, setting the mask down on her desk. She was just realizing she had <u>been</u> him when Gabby stepped back into the office, closing the door behind her.

"I know I just burned our friendship to the ground," Gabrielle White said, "some of it, anyway—"

"All of it," Sara said. "You didn't even <u>ask</u> me."

"—but the stakes are too high," Gabby went on, as if she hadn't heard. "I needed you to understand that this is not hypothetical. I actually did this. The tech exists. Ten days ago, in my lab, I made it."

She sat back in her chair.

"I want to know how I can keep it."

Sara Kring considered. She used her heels to laboriously pull her chair back to her desk, in that awkward crabwalk you had to use for the purpose. The bright sunshine yellow of the legal pad shone up at her, empty but for the name of the woman who had . . . well.

What had Gabrielle White done?

Above the sunny, lined pages: the name and logo of her firm, printed on every legal pad in the place. Barton, Oestreich & Yoo. Commonly shortened to just BOY, as in Boys' Club, as in the place to which she had tied her future and also the place where she had no future.

Until now, perhaps.

She looked up, back at her client.

"I need to review the agreement again, to see if there's anything we can do. As I recall, you were working on a treatment for Alzheimer's. This obviously isn't that. Perhaps there's some wiggle room there.

"Honestly, though, I doubt it. My suggestion is to just wait. Don't go public. Down the road, like a long time down the road, at least a decade, you file for a patent. Your job during that decade, Gabby, is to figure out how to refine the tech, alter it, hide its origins to make sure it's impossible to connect it to the experiments funded by Hendricks Capital."

Silence from the other side of the desk, until at last, Paul spoke.

"And . . . that will work?" he said.

"Fifty-fifty," Sara answered. "At best. Gray Hendricks is not stupid."

"Yeah, well," Gabby said, snapping her head down and back in that tight, controlled nod, her jaw set, eyes narrowed, "neither am I."

CHAPTER 16

NUMBER 20 UNION SQUARE EAST, MANHATTAN

GOOD LIGHT IN HERE, BLEEDER THOUGHT FOR THE HUNDREDTH time. He and the Eaters had been using this building as their headquarters for more than a decade, and he never got sick of the light, which poured down through skylights sixty feet above, illuminating what had once been the Union Square Savings Bank building, then other banks, then a theater space, well into the twenty-first century, and now . . . the home base for his team, who were tasked with . . . well, call them outside security consultants for NeOnet Global and leave it at that.

Number 20 had been designed by the same guy who created the Lincoln Memorial. Bleeder had looked it up once. You could actually sort of see it in the construction. The building's interior was a huge open space, all marble and columns. His team had subdivided it a bit, adding a medical clinic and a few other zones to the back, but mostly it was just all big, echoey openness. The place was inspiring and intimidating in equal measure, and Bleeder loved it.

He was sitting at his desk, running a whetstone over one of the other things he loved—a thirteen-and-a-quarter-inch Italian switchblade picklock stiletto, with a sinuous kris blade that looked like a snake waving its way up out of the abalone handle. The thing was almost a hundred years old, and the steel in the blade was particularly hard, which meant sharpening it took a lot of effort and time. Bleeder didn't mind. Good tools were worth the effort to maintain them, and sharpening his knife was the perfect sort of mechanical, low-maintenance task that freed his mind for deeper thoughts.

For instance, his Eaters, and which one would take over when his time as Bleeder was done. He wasn't old yet, but he was older than he'd once been, and this job could get physical. It was a young man's game, and he didn't ever want to be the relic sitting back at headquarters issuing orders while the rest of the team went out and did the fun stuff. No—Bleeder fought with his squad. Bled with his squad. That was the job.

There were twelve men on the team—always twelve, plus Bleeder. They all lived in Number 20, sleeping in the bedrooms built into the back of the building when they weren't on shift, like a team of firemen. A decent comparison, even if Eaters were more likely to set fires than put them out, as a rule.

He could see five of the twelve from where he was sitting. Zahn, Escobar, Perez, Edgar, and Chan, all busy with the tasks of the day. Maybe one would get the download when his time was up, maybe it would be one of the others. Interesting to think about.

Bleeder's mini chimed—a text from Alice, asking about dinner later. Dr. Hong was the team's doctor, and she lived in Number 20 as well, in an apartment that Bleeder had spent quite a few nights in recently. She was one of the reasons he wasn't looking to hang up his stiletto just yet. Just too nice to have her right nearby.

"Huh," Zahn said from his own desk, where three thinnies floated side by side.

"What?" Bleeder called over to him.

"Come take a look," Zahn said. "This is interesting."

Bleeder closed the blade and slipped it into his pocket as he stood, then made his way over to Zahn's desk. The man—in his early thirties, like most of the Eaters, slim built and a bit of a slob—was staring at some sort of report that had come up on his central thinscreen.

As Bleeder approached, Zahn pointed at the report.

"We got a ping from FCB. They're working a case, and we got copied on it."

The Eaters had a special relationship with New York's police department, particularly its Flash Crime Bureau. When cases were opened that had certain tags assigned—anything suggesting nonstandard usage of the flash or unusual expertise with the technology—a copy of the report was automatically sent down to Number 20. Zahn was tasked with reviewing them as they came in, to see if they might point the team toward the target that was arguably their primary reason to exist—a certain young woman who had vanished seven years back and now could be literally anyone. Especially these days.

The Eaters did a lot of things—whatever Stephen Hauser needed or wanted, really—but finding that woman was the task set above all others. The CEO of Anyone made sure they had every resource they could ever need to accomplish it, including the special arrangement with the NYPD. There were many quid pro quos on both sides of the deal—the Eaters getting these reports was just one.

"What'd they find?" Bleeder asked.

Zahn looked at him.

"A bunch of people showed up at a hospital in Brooklyn with about the worst cases of dislocate sickness the doctors had ever seen. They're getting treatment—antipsychotics, the whole deal.

So far, not too crazy—but it's the story they told the doctors that got the FCB involved. They claimed someone had swapped them into rats and then turned them back. They didn't all end up back in their primes, and it messed them up."

Bleeder considered this.

"Sex thing?"

Zahn shook his head.

"No—according to FCB, a gang thing. These guys were mostly muscle for a low-level operation based in Red Hook. Extortion, stolen goods, generally small-time. Apparently, they pissed off someone who's really good at flash tech."

Bleeder was not an engineer, not a technician. His expertise lay in other areas. He had only a layman's understanding of the way the flash worked. That said, he knew that human-to-animal consciousness transfers required a large amount of equipment and computing power. Nonhuman flashing was reserved for people like Hauser and his friends—the few people rich enough to afford it and deranged enough to want to try it. A bunch of dumb goons from Brooklyn would never get near that sort of gear under ordinary circumstances.

But if someone had figured out how to do animal swaps in a less exclusive setting, or had actually weaponized it . . . that could be a game changer.

"Do they know how it was done?"

"They said she used this," Zahn replied, and gestured at one of his other thinnies, pulling up an image of a small round object that looked to be made entirely of miniature LEDs, wires, and maybe a small processing unit inside at its core.

"She . . . ," Bleeder said, flicking the image to enlarge it and examining it more closely.

"She," Zahn confirmed.

Well, that was interesting. They hadn't had a real lead in years—their target had dropped off the map after she escaped from the Shermans, may those doddering old idiots most certainly not rest in peace. This could be an actual clue, or it could be nothing, just the latest in a long line of false leads.

But worth a look.

"That's Anyone tech, isn't it?" Bleeder said, pointing at the device.

"Yes," Zahn said. "Even the wires. All specialized stuff used for the internal networks. Not commercially available."

"Huh," Bleeder said. "How about that?"

He turned away from Zahn.

"I'm going to head down to One Police Plaza. Seems like the boss should get his property back, don't you think?"

"Sure. You want company?"

"Nah," Bleeder said. "This'll be a friendly visit. No need to bring the troops. You guys can be pretty intimidating, you know."

"Damn right," Zahn said, turning back to his thinnies.

Bleeder took the subway downtown. He'd first visited New York more than thirty-five years before, back in the early aughts, and from then to now there was still no better way to get around the city. If the subway had a stop within five blocks of where you needed to go, you took the subway. That was Bleeder's philosophy. One of them. He had a few.

The NYPD's Flash Crime Bureau took up most of the fourth floor of One Police Plaza, the headquarters for the whole department. It had a broad remit, getting first crack at every crime committed within the five boroughs that had any connection to the flash. That included everything from darksharing to fraud, slavery to identity theft, which had a very different definition now than it had back when Bleeder had first known the term.

Sometimes people just skipped—tried to disappear in a body not their own. Removed their I-fi and began to live as their vessel, or as some new identity somewhere else.

The FCB was massive, a department within the department, with its own subdivisions for crimes financial, technological, physical, and so on. Crime had to be completely rethought in a flash world, and expertise rebuilt from the ground up. Detectives were taught to question suspects in a fashion designed not just to discover facts but also to discover and verify true identity, as well. Fingerprints, DNA, eyewitness testimony, camera and drone footage, biometrics . . . none of it functioned the same way in the justice system as it had prior to the flash, and new strategies had to be devised.

One of the primary tools the FCB used in its fight was fairly free access to NeOnet Global and its records and technology— Anyone and the cops worked hand in glove, most of the time. But that level of cooperation came at a price, and Bleeder was there to call in a marker.

The officer assigned to the Red Hook case was a detective named Gerry Pak. Bleeder was taken to the man's desk immediately upon entering his Anyone ID passphrases into the FCB verification system. Pak was bearded, a little worn. FCB could be a tough, frustrating assignment, Bleeder had heard.

An officer deposited Bleeder at Pak's desk, one of many on the floor. The detective looked up from his screens, his expression open and curious—probably a good quality for an investigator to have.

"Hello, Detective," Bleeder said, offering his hand.

Pak reached up, shook it, and gestured to the open seat on the other side of the desk.

"Hey. Your name is . . . Bleeder? Is that first or last?"

"Both," Bleeder said, sitting down. "I was first, and I'll be last, too."

That got a frown from Detective Pak. Police officers, as a rule, did not like to be fucked with.

Oh, well. Sorry, Gerry.

"What can I do for you?" Pak asked. "Anything for Anyone."

"Exactly. That's a good philosophy," Bleeder said. "I'm here to talk about that case you picked up in Red Hook. The rats."

Pak leaned back, raising an eyebrow.

"How do you know about that?"

"I run a special security detachment for NeOnet Global. We get access to FCB files that deal with unusual uses of flash tech. The thing in Brooklyn came up on our system. I wanted to talk to you about it."

The detective frowned, clearly not liking the idea that his precious cases were sent out to someone he probably considered little better than a rent-a-cop.

Oh, well. Sorry about that too, Gerry.

"Okay . . . fine. What can I tell you?"

"It's more about what you can show me. I need to look at the device."

Pak hesitated, then shrugged. He opened a drawer in his desk and removed a plastic evidence bag, within which was the device from Zahn's screen back at Number 20. Pak offered it to Bleeder.

"Go ahead," Pak said. "Our techs haven't gotten a chance to check it out in detail yet, but I showed it to a friend down in the lab. He said he'd never seen anything like it. It'll be a while before we have any information on how it works. We're pretty slammed right now. Those network outages you guys were having in the light flash sent people over to darkshares, private networks . . . makes my job a lot harder, to be honest."

"Sorry about that," Bleeder said, examining the little globe-shaped thing through the plastic. He'd never seen anything like it either—but he was no expert.

He stood, which got an alarmed look from Pak.

"What are you doing?" the detective said.

Bleeder held up the bag.

"I'm taking this," he said. "I'll get it back to you soon, but I want my people to look at it first."

"Absolutely not," Pak said, also standing now, holding out his hand. "That's evidence in an ongoing investigation. I don't care who you are. Hell, I don't <u>know</u> who you are. Give me that bag right now, or I'll have you tossed in a cell."

Bleeder gave him an amused smile, an *Aren't you adorable* look that was received rather poorly by Mr. Gerry Pak.

"Detective, come on. You know the way this works. Cops have been working closely with NeOnet Global since before the FCB was even established—hell, we've been working with you guys since before there was an Anyone at all, way back in the Hendricks Capital days."

Bleeder slipped the evidence bag into his pocket, which elicited an outraged sort of squawk from the other man.

"Anyone gives FCB total cooperation on your cases," Bleeder said. "High-level access to anything you need, without subpoenas or administrative stuff gumming up your investigations. You submit a request about who was using the flash on the three hundred block of East Eighteenth Street on August third at 2:58 P.M. . . . boom, you got it.

"That's not all, either. How about those nice discounts on flash usage for FCB personnel? You ever take vacations on Anyone's nickel, Detective? Flash into some of that primo skin in Hua Hin or Aspen or Dubai? It's all logged and stored. Easy to look up. Could have that in about thirty seconds. One call on my mini."

Pak's lips tightened.

"This is bullshit," he said.

"No," Bleeder corrected, lifting his index finger. "It's friend-ship. We're all on the same team. You need things; we provide them. And when we need things, you provide them right back."

He patted his pocket.

"I need something else, too. A conference room, just for a few minutes, so I can make a call. Secure—no mics, no cameras. Can we do that, Detective?"

Pak nodded, his mouth still tight—but he knew he'd lost. No point in prolonging things. The detective's clear goal now was just to get Bleeder out of the FCB as quickly as possible, and the way to do that was to give him what he wanted.

The requested room was made available. It was really more of an interrogation cell than a place for meetings, with green walls the color of pond algae and a battered table with steel rings bolted into it for securing suspects during questioning. It didn't matter. No cameras, no mics—that was the point.

Bleeder sat in one of the chairs and unrolled a thinscreen he pulled out from inside his coat. He set it to float above the scuffed surface of the table and called in to Anyone headquarters over on Twenty-Third. While he waited for the connection, he pulled his stiletto and sharpening stone from his inside coat pocket.

"Bertrand Milsen," he told the switchboard menu, popping the blade and rasping the stone along it. The hub coordinator was a good place to start. The guy was a solid engineer and might be able to tell him what the device was for, or where its components had come from.

Bertrand's round face swam up on the screen—annoyed at first at an interruption in his schedule, and then his eyes noticed the switchblade, and annoyance was replaced with a mixture of awe and fear.

"Uh . . . hello, sir," he said. "How can I help you?"

"Relax, Mr. Milsen. I'm just trying to figure something out here—the FCB is investigating a crime that might have involved some of Anyone's flash tech. I was hoping you could help."

Bleeder put down his knife and sharpening stone, then pulled out the evidence bag from inside his coat. He held up the little light-bulb sphere to the thinscreen, letting Milsen get a good look.

"The FCB recovered this from the scene. It was built using your gear. Do you recognize these components? Any idea how they might have gotten out of storage, or what this thing was built to do?"

Milsen's face went pale, the hi-res screen on the thinnie capturing his reaction perfectly. This man was guilty. Guilty of what, was yet to be determined—but guilty.

"I didn't . . . sir, I mean . . . the network was on the verge of collapsing."

This had all become very interesting. Bleeder set the evidence bag down on the table—Bertrand's eyes were locked to it, following it all the way down—and picked up his stiletto.

"Mr. Milsen," he said. "Tell me a story."

CHAPTER 17

AD ASTRA COFFEE, CORKTOWN, DETROIT

SARA KRING STARED OUT ACROSS THE COFFEE SHOP, GENTLY FEELING her bicep. She didn't see her rapidly cooling skim latte, she didn't see the scruffy creatives at the other tables—outfitted in flannel and noise-canceling headphones, busily coding and designing and writing on various streamlined pieces of electronic gear—and she didn't see the space-themed decor or the truly gorgeous chalk mural against the shop's back wall, erased and redrawn monthly by a new artist no matter how beautiful it might be. She didn't see any of it because she was thinking about how weak her arm felt to her just then and remembering when it had been strong.

She hadn't been in Paul White's body for very long—maybe a minute—but she couldn't stop thinking about what it had been like, and everything she wished she'd had time to do. If Gabby had let her, she thought she'd probably have stayed in Paul for much longer. Hours. Days. Weeks, months, years.

If Gabrielle White could figure out how to properly bring her technology to market, everything would just . . . flip over. Society's written and unwritten rules about gender, sex, equality, and so much more would evaporate in a moment, replaced by . . . well, she didn't know yet. She was a lawyer, a profession not known for its vision. If Gabby could—

But there was the problem. Her friend was brilliant, but in a specific, savant-like way. She'd never struck Sara as being particularly business-minded. Even if Gabby could hold on to her . . . what had she called it? The flash. Good name. Even if she could keep the flash secret for a decade, develop the tech, and keep it from the terrifying and all-powerful (as far as Detroit was concerned) Gray Hendricks, odds were that someone else would come along and take it from her. A bigger, meaner fish.

And, of course, since Sara had tied her wagon to Gabby, once someone came and took the flash, it meant neither would reap any of its benefits, financial, physical, or other.

Sara had been thinking about ways she might convince Gabby to let her flash again—into Paul, or anyone, really. Maybe she could offer herself up as a test subject. Gabby would need one. Not many people knew about the flash, and the more she told, the better the odds of the secret getting out.

And it would get out, Sara knew. It was inevitable. Then what? Maybe Gabby would end up explaining why she'd tried to keep the flash from Gray Hendricks, and who had given her advice on how she might do that—her loyal attorney, Sara Kring.

Career over. Disbarment. Maybe even jail time.

Maybe it wasn't too late, Sara thought. *Maybe she could tell Gabby to . . . no. No one could tell Gabrielle White anything.*

Sara touched her arm again, flexing a little, remembering. She'd never had a thing for Paul White. He was always just . . . fine, there, a human being. Gabby's husband. Intellectual and sensitive and not her type at all—but she was getting turned on thinking about him. No, not about him. About being him. She'd taken a moment to feel herself up during the switch, while Gabby's back was turned, back in her office, and it was . . . nope. Shift away from that.

She looked around at the coffee shop again, forcing herself to see it. None of it seemed real, and that sensation wasn't just confined to Ad Astra Coffee. The world as a whole felt flimsy, fragile, a stage set. Sara had knowledge about this technology that would change everything, a society-reinventing tsunami . . . and yet no one around her did. All these idiots at this coffee shop, drinking their lattes and chatting and being completely unaware that many of the old rules about what was possible, what existence as a human being <u>was</u> . . . were about to vanish. Ancient history.

Sara wanted to ride that tsunami. She wanted the new rules, when you could be whatever you wanted to be, and no one could tell you no because of your face, your body, anything. Because you were a woman. She wanted that, to be a huge, important part of it. The idea of waiting a decade, at best, for that new world to arrive . . . agonizing.

There had to be a way to move things forward on an accelerated timeline, or maybe figure out a way to get some ownership out of Gabby. Take a little equity stake in the flash in lieu of fees. Even 1 percent would make her rich beyond her wildest dreams. Even a tenth of a percent. She'd have to think about it.

Assuming, of course, Gabby didn't blow it all somehow, which she would. Gabrielle had been the treasurer in their sorority for a semester, and bills had gone unpaid, dues uncollected . . . just a mess, from a business perspective. The woman's mind just wasn't wired for it.

Sara picked up her coffee cup—now cold, barely a sip gone. She stared at it.

She extended her arm out to the right, to its full length, and slowly upended the cup, letting the coffee and foamed milk pour down to the floor in a long beige cascade.

There was a sense of people reacting around her—or trying to. No one knew how. This was beyond the pale. Such things were just not done. The social contract, the <u>rules</u> . . . my <u>goodness</u>.

But Sara Kring was operating under the new rules, and as far as she was concerned, the new rules were no rules.

She stood, slung her purse over her shoulder, stepped delicately around the spreading pool of coffee, ignoring the outraged barista saying . . . something . . . to her, who cared . . .

. . . and left.

CHAPTER 18

SEAVIEW ONE, LOW-EARTH ORBIT

STEPHEN HAUSER LOOKED DOWN UPON THE WORLD HE HAD BUILT and saw that it was good.

Far below, a few hundred miles or so—Stephen could never remember the exact distance—a tiny white dot of light moved across the dark side of the planet, approaching the terminus where night became day. A plane flying east across the Pacific Ocean, into the dawn, on its way to Tokyo or Beijing or Bangkok.

He couldn't see any other aircraft, which wasn't surprising. Partly because it was extremely difficult to see something as small as a plane from this high up, but also because people didn't fly like they used to. Why strap yourself into a tube and lose all that time and suffer all that inconvenience when you could just flash yourself into a new body at your destination?

People still flew. Hell, people still took rockets up into space from time to time. That's how he was up here at all. It wasn't like it used to be, though. Nothing was. Sometimes that surprised him, just how easily the idea of putting your mind into someone else's body had become normalized. It reminded him of the way smartphones had become absolutely ubiquitous in the 2010s, the way you would walk into a coffee shop or down the sidewalk and see everyone staring into their own little personal entertainment and distraction devices. Everyone on earth seemed to have surrendered their awareness and attention to the things overnight.

The flash was the same. Good for business.

Be anyone with Anyone.

He'd come up with that tagline, back in the early days of the company. And had it worked? My god, had it ever.

Stephen closed his eyes and stretched, letting himself roll gently onto his back. He liked zero g, and this body was particularly good, well acclimated to low-earth orbit. Probably somewhere in the middle of its rotation. Vessels generally stayed up here for about six months before they got sent back down to Earth and a new set came up to replace them. Best way to avoid debilitating bone loss, lingering radiation effects, that sort of thing.

It was a good system—healthy, strong young people sent up here to act as vessels for anyone physically unable or unwilling to handle the stresses of launch and reentry. It worked well for researchers unable to endure astronaut training, or artists, workmen, anyone who couldn't or wouldn't handle a ride into orbit.

Stephen had developed orbital flash into a new line of business for NeOnet Global, too—space tourism, realized at last. The tagline, again one of his: *See the world with Anyone.* Maybe a little overclever, but it worked well with the accompanying visual, just a killer shot of Earth as seen from orbit.

He'd given the world to the world. Those who could afford it.

Enough could, though, that Stephen had built himself a home up here, a place he called *Seaview One*. The megarich on Earth aspired to acquiring private islands for themselves. Stephen Hauser, owner and CEO of Anyone, had a space station. The ultimate house on the water.

"See anything interesting?" a voice said behind him, and Stephen opened his eyes.

"Trying," he answered.

The man floating near the entrance to the observation dome was young, strong, and handsome. No one he knew, at least on the outside. Just a vessel. The inside, though, he knew very well. Most of the world below knew him, too. This was Bhangra George.

It had to be George, because no one else was up here other than *Seaview* staff, and none of them would ever be so familiar with him.

This was the little calculus of the flash, another thing that had become a constant part of modern life. Running an analysis on everyone you met to determine who they might be behind their eyes, where they fit into the social ecosystem. Were they who they appeared to be, or someone else? Even he had to do it, and he'd brought the technology to the world.

"Anyone else arrive yet?" Stephen asked.

"No, but soon," George answered. "Are you ready?"

It was a rhetorical question. There was nothing to do, really. Stephen was throwing a dinner party. The sum total of his effort had been to decide on the guest list. Everyone he'd asked had agreed immediately. No one ever declined an invitation to *Seaview One*.

"Can I ask you something?" Stephen said. Another rhetorical question.

George made a languid gesture, immediately recognizable as his. Body language was an important part of the calculus. The body might change, but the way you moved in it generally didn't, barring a massive difference in the vessel's body type. Even facial expressions seemed to carry over, the personality of the person you knew swimming up from beneath the unfamiliar features.

"Why are you doing this stupid auction thing?" Stephen asked. "It makes no sense to me."

"Didn't you hear? For charity," George answered. If there was such a thing as a rhetorical answer, that was it.

"Uh-huh," Stephen said. "So pick up your mini and make a donation. Why do this? It's risky, letting a stranger ride you. It's beneath you."

"What's beneath me hasn't been your business for years, my dear. And on top of me, and inside me, and all over me. Anyway, the press coverage has been beyond all expectations."

"Because no one actually thought the great <u>Bhangra George</u> would pull a stunt like this."

"My concern, Stephen, was that no one was thinking about the great Bhangra George much at all anymore."

"What are you talking about? You're one of the most famous people in the world."

"For things I did ages ago."

"No, that's not right. Your last movie . . . what was it . . . the historical thing about the impeachment trial. That was massive."

"That was four years ago. I've starred in three films since then. Can you name one?"

Stephen considered. He could not.

"Exactly," George continued. "I'm an elder statesman, in entertainment terms. Everyone loves me; no one wants me. Not the way they did."

"And you think selling ten minutes in your body to a stranger will fix that?"

"No. It probably won't. But it feels good to have them talking about me again. It's vanity, which I am decidedly not above. And what's the harm, really?"

There was potential harm in it, Stephen knew. He and George and a handful of others were not like everyone else who used the flash. The odds of that fact coming to light were vanishingly low, but nevertheless. Harm could be done. On the other hand, he understood the essential fragility of the immensely famous, talented, and wealthy man floating on the other side of the observation dome, the earthlight shining up on him through the open canopy below, and he saw no real reason to fracture it.

"You can always start over, you know," Stephen said. "If your star's fading, just become a new star."

"Not yet," George answered, an edge to his tone. "Not again. I've never gotten this far before, and forgive me if I don't want to just slough off the version of myself that actually made it. Life shouldn't be too easy. You understand, don't you?"

No, Stephen wanted to respond. With the resources at George's command, he could probably become equally famous in a new, young body without much effort. That was the whole point—reinvention, resurrection, choosing your fate, not trusting it to small quirks of luck or birth. George was one of the very first Centuries. He had transcended destiny, and it made Stephen sad that the other man couldn't see it.

Life shouldn't be easy. But there was no reason whatsoever to make it hard.

"Sure," Stephen said. "I understand completely. I'm sorry for pushing it. Just wanted to ask. It's soon, right? The auction?"

"Yup," George said, a little smile appearing on his face, a smile Stephen knew very well, a ghost of amusement past. "It'll go out live, across the world. You wouldn't believe the deals my people made for me. I'm getting offers for new roles, too—some very interesting stuff. I'm not ready to abandon old Bhangra George just yet, Stephen, and neither is—"

A chime sounded, from an artfully designed speaker overhead—or what passed for overhead on *Seaview One*. The floor was the ceiling was the floor was the wall, in most of its spaces.

"Sir, I'm sorry to disturb you, but your guests are arriving," said the voice of the station's chief steward. "They're gathering in the lounge."

"Good," Stephen said. "We'll be right there."

He reached for a handhold on a nearby wall and used it to turn himself so he was facing the observation window again, the large, curved dome made from some clear, ideally indestructible polymer. He knew that the station's staff actually went out there to clean from time to time. The most expensive window washers in history.

"That world down there . . . it's yours, you know," George said, drifting up next to him. "You built it."

Stephen watched the glimmering planet turn so far below. He looked for another plane skimming through the sky, and saw nothing. More than 82 percent of the human population had used the flash at one point or another, with most of the 18 percent of nonusers represented by people under ten years of age, deemed too young to safely flash. Stephen had lobbyists working to bring that age down to eight and get other restrictions relaxed, like the limits on pregnant women using the tech. He thought in time that 18 percent could be cut in half. Parents were getting their babies the I-fi implant as soon as six months after birth; early attachment to the spinal nerves decreased risk of mis-transit, dislocate syndrome, and zeroing. The risks were already almost nonexistent, but why take a chance? Get those kids ready to flash as soon as possible.

"It is my world, isn't it?" Stephen said. "Not so bad, is it?"

"No. Not so bad," George agreed. "Come on, conqueror. Time to party."

They pulled themselves through the hatch leading out of the observation dome and through a few passageways, all sleek design—*Star Trek*, not *Apollo 13*. They flew to the slowly rotating circular entrance to *Seaview One*'s central module, the drum-shaped area that provided spin gravity, enough for a floor and ceiling to present themselves, and drinks to stay in glasses and food on plates. Important, when hosting.

Several men and women awaited them inside the chamber, each with a drink in hand, provided by quietly circulating station staff. Music trickled into the room, jazz, a Lee Morgan album Stephen particularly liked.

The atmosphere was utterly saturated with the calculus of the flash, and Stephen enjoyed it very much. Every guest knew that the other people in the room must be important and powerful, or they wouldn't be there at all. But *Seaview* had a rule—a very simple one—no introductions, not until dinner was served, in the dining room one chamber, where place cards waited at every seat.

So these people, each occupying attractive, strong, fit, utterly anonymous vessels, had no idea at all who they were talking to. It could be a business partner, it could be a bitter enemy, even a spouse.

Stephen knew every one of them, of course. The rail-thin, dark-skinned woman was pharma magnate Baron Gates. The crew-cut blonde was Anita Jackson, creator of a popular type of flash-based entertainment where audience members from all over the world competed for a chance to flash into the popular roles for an episode or longer, until they were voted out and someone new got a chance to take on the character. The stocky redhead was Abd al-Hakim, aka the Solar Sheik, controller of a vast power-generating empire across the Middle East. A particularly beautiful man of Mediterranean extraction was former US senator Freddy Mingus. And several more.

Every guest a Century. His sentries, helping him guard the world from chaos. His people, every one, his property, despite all their power.

From the hatchway Stephen watched these titans dancing around each other, trying to put names to bodies, trying not to give offense but also striving mightily, with every word, to give everyone else a sense of their massive achievements, power, and influence. It was a game, and Stephen Hauser was the only one who enjoyed it. He knew his guests always hated this part of an evening with him—but they came anyway. No one ever refused an invitation to *Seaview One*.

Abd al-Hakim looked up as Stephen and George entered the room, his eyes narrowing for the briefest moment. Perhaps that was just a reaction to the arrival of two more people whose identities he'd have to divine . . . but then again, perhaps not. In a way, this entire evening was about the sheik. Stephen had wanted to spend time with him in person, in a setting that could be plausibly denied as anything but a social occasion. Anyone had informants in every major corporation and government in the world—call them agents, call them spies; it was simple enough when you controlled the flash. One of his agents inside Mr. al-Hakim's empire had recently presented Stephen with a very interesting theory about some recent actions the man had taken.

Tonight seemed like a good way to get them confirmed. The Solar Sheik was good at controlling his emotions—anyone who ascended to a position of global power had to be—but when you were in an unfamiliar vessel, those reflexes were somewhat muted. Reactions, emotions slipped out. Stephen wanted to look the man in the eye, see what might be learned.

Baron Gates wandered over, the low gravity causing his cock-tail to ooze slowly up against the sides of the glass. The woman's eyes flicked between him and George, settling on Stephen. She extended a hand.

"Hey there, Mr. Hauser," she said. "Thank you for having me. Always a treat to come up here."

Gates was no fool, of course, and Stephen supposed he had his own tells, his own secret self that came to the surface no matter which body he was wearing. Everyone did.

"Glad you could make it, Baron," he said, shaking the extended hand.

"You fixed all that instability in the flash network, right?" Gates said. "Wouldn't want it to go down while we're up here."

Stephen frowned in mock—but not entirely mock—outrage.

"You think I'd have invited you people if there was even the slightest chance of an outage?"

Gates lifted a long-fingered, mollifying hand. "No, of course. You're right. Just wanted to ask. We're pretty far from home, you know."

"We're on a closed circuit," Stephen said. "Flash traffic to and from *Seaview One* doesn't run on the main network. There was never any danger."

"Should have known," Gates said. "Anyway, I'm looking forward to dinner. I could be wrong, but I'm pretty sure you've got Candy Patel over there—no mistaking that accent."

She inclined her head toward a slim, male Korean vessel chatting with Anita Jackson. Gates—again—no fool, was correct. It was indeed Candy Patel.

A small vibration against the inside of Stephen's wrist, a very particular code—three short buzzes and a long one.

He lifted his arm and glanced at the mini strapped there to confirm what he already knew. Only one person had that code, and would only use it in a very particular circumstance, especially considering that Stephen was up on the station.

Abd al-Hakim would have to wait.

"If you'll excuse me," he said. "I need to go. Enjoy the dinner."

Gates blinked once, a look of surprise coming across his face.

"What?" he said. "You aren't eating with us?"

"No. Something's come up."

"You realize that's just . . . rude as hell, right? Even for you."

"Yup," Stephen said. He walked away from Gates. As he passed Bhangra George, he tapped him on the shoulder.

"Take care of them. Make sure they have a good time," he said.

"Will you be back?"

"I don't know. Probably not."

He held up his arm, showing George the mini on his wrist. George nodded. "Ah," he said. "Good luck."

Stephen left the chamber, slipping over to a flash bay a few modules over. Two minutes later and he was opening his eyes back on Earth, the eyes he'd been using as Stephen Hauser for some years now.

He sat up from the couch where his prime had lain awaiting his return from low-earth orbit, and saw Bleeder there, a respectful few paces away.

He had changed his body since the last time Stephen saw him, but it was of the type Bleeder generally seemed to prefer. Compact, powerfully built, but not obtrusively muscular. Like a coiled steel spring.

Bleeder shifted through vessels more than anyone Stephen knew—a privilege of the position he held within the organization as one of the very first Centuries—but they were always obviously him. Bleeder was just . . . violence, and readiness, and competent disdain.

"I found her," Bleeder said, without preamble. "She was actually working at Anyone, at the main node station in New York.

Right under our noses. She stole a bunch of gear. Her supervisor caught her in the act, but she made a deal with him to fix that outage from last week, and he covered it up. I looked at the personnel files, and it has to be her. I'm putting together the retrieval team now."

"Huh," Stephen said, utterly stunned.

After all this time, he thought. *I can't believe it.*

"Who is she?"

"Annami," Bleeder said. "She calls herself Annami."

CHAPTER 19

THE OFFICES OF HENDRICKS CAPITAL, DOWNTOWN DETROIT

"I'M HERE TO MAKE A DEAL," THE LAWYER SAID.

Gray Hendricks considered the woman sitting on the other side of his broad, cluttered desk. Ill at ease but not unconfident, in a nice navy suit with a few well-chosen accessories. A brooch on the lapel, some delicate flowery thing. An attorney in uniform.

He knew who she was—Sara Kring—and he knew who she represented. Gabrielle White, a woman who had been much on his mind of late. So it wasn't surprising that Kring would pay him a visit, nor that a deal was on offer. Gabby White had something, and Hendricks assumed she had asked Kring to figure out a way to change the terms of her contract with Hendricks Capital so she could make more money off that something—which had been invented using Gray Hendricks' money.

Fat fucking chance, lady, he thought. *A deal is a deal is a deal.*

Still, he was interested in what Kring might have to say, what logical or emotional structures she might build in an effort to convince him Gabby White was entitled to more than her fair share. She didn't have a prayer, but it would be fascinating to watch her try. That's why he'd taken the meeting. He loved this sort of thing. A nice break in the day.

Hendricks looked up at Jon Corran standing not far away, arms folded, frowning. The man knew that this White deal going sideways was on him. Gabby was one of Corran's projects to manage, and so the buck stopped there, right at his desk. It had been weeks since Jon brought him the news that the woman was trying to steal from him, and yet they still didn't know what she had. Corran said he was working on it, going through her lab records more closely and watching to see if White filed any patent applications, but apparently the woman was keeping her head down. So, what did they actually have? Nothing. Vague suspicions and some weird bank transactions.

Until they knew something concrete, they couldn't bring legal action, and Hendricks wasn't quite ready to handle this the way he would have back in the old days. Maybe down the road, once they'd exhausted all other options.

In any case, Gabrielle White going off the reservation wasn't technically Corran's fault, but that didn't mean he wouldn't get the blame. That was the way things worked at Hendricks Capital. The way they should work everywhere, actually. If he had a motto, and his company had a motto, it was one word: *responsibility.*

For your actions, for the city you live in, for the people around you, for the things you agree to do, for the choices you make, for whatever portion of the world you can get your arms around. Responsibility.

"What do you think, Jon?" Hendricks said. "Lady wants to make a deal."

"I think the lady already has a deal," Corran answered. "Or her client does, anyway. All nice and neat, on a piece of paper with Gabrielle White's perfectly legible signature on it."

Kring opened her mouth to speak, but Gray held up a hand.

"I want to show you something," he said. "Then we can talk."

He pushed himself up out of his chair, feeling his weight settle into him.

This body, he thought. He was so much more aware of it than he used to be. It announced itself to him all the time, in a thousand different ways. Acid reflux all afternoon after a perfectly innocent lunch, a meatball sub, something he could have eaten ten years earlier with zero consequences. Waking in the middle of the night with an aching back. A weird twinge in his wrist, like a bee had taken up residence in there. Just an overall heaviness, a slowness, an entropy, an inertia.

Inertia. He knew about inertia. Detroit was all about inertia.

Gray moved around his desk, passing a puzzled Sara Kring.

His office was all windows, tall, providing views of the city beyond, with its little core of prosperity near his headquarters building, a modern, six-sided confection locals called the Drixagon. Ford Field to the north and Belle Isle to the east, right in the middle of the Detroit River. Lake St. Clair barely visible beyond that, with a bit of Windsor at the edge of vision. But outside that core, the core he had single-handedly built, the rot began. The blight.

Neighborhoods that still had not recovered from decades of neglect and corruption and auto-company erosion and white flight and Devil's Night fires and all the rest of it, the confluence of despair and bad luck and changing times that had turned Detroit from jewel to apocalypse. Whole streets that looked like war zones, burned out and boarded up. Vacant lots returning to wildness, abandoned, rusting pieces of what had once been homes poking up above wildflowers and grass two feet tall. Hendricks liked to drive those streets in his Escalade, taking the pulse of things, and he'd once seen a hand-painted board on a telephone pole advertising various meats for sale: raccoon, squirrel, possum, anything that could be snared in the new forest arising out of the old city.

Gray Hendricks was fully aware that his standards of edibility did not have to be shared by every resident of the city. He knew plenty of people liked raccoon just fine. Put it on their tables at the holidays, in fact, especially folks who had come to Detroit from the South. Something of a delicacy.

Nevertheless.

Detroit began its slide in the late sixties with the riots, and then, inertia. Once something's moving in a direction, it wants to keep moving in that direction. The bigger the thing, the more inertia, and Detroit was very, very big. Forty square miles.

Hendricks' father had been a salesman who drove all around the city and its outlying areas, from the Polish outpost of Hamtramck to Indian Village, where all the cops lived, to Corktown with the Irish and Mexicantown with the Mexicans. He saw it at its best, and loved it, and instilled that love in his son. They'd drive around on weekends, and even though most of what Lou Hendricks saw in his head was already long gone or in decline, he would describe it, all that had been lost, and then Gray could see it too.

That was why his office was all windows. He could still see it— that old, lost, shimmering Detroit—and he wanted everyone else to see it too.

"Where are we going?" Sara Kring asked as they moved down the hallway outside his office, Jon Corran following a few paces behind.

"You've heard about how I keep an eye on downtown, right?"

"Ah . . . yes," Sara answered, a bit hesitant.

Hendricks understood that. His reputation in Detroit was mixed. Some people complained, said he was overstepping, even as they brought their families to newly opened restaurants and shops in the city center, and went ice-skating on the rink he'd paid for, and didn't think too much about how ten years before, or five, they'd never have even considered going downtown, for fear of a mugging or worse.

Did they think that just . . . happened? Did they think the crime went away on its own?

"I'd like you to see my security operation," Hendricks said. "How it works."

The attorney raised an eyebrow.

"I'll take a look at whatever you'd like me to see, Mr. Hendricks, but I'm not sure how your security setup is relevant to the reason I came to see you."

"You will," he said.

An elevator ride to the basement, and they entered a control room, with full-color video screens covering three of four walls. One large monitor in the center, surrounded by smaller displays on every side, all showing the streets of downtown from various angles, including a number of shots from high overhead, almost like satellite views.

Two technicians sat in chairs before the monitors, each with a large keyboard surrounded by a constellation of joysticks and trackballs. They turned to look as Hendricks, Corran, and Kring entered, their eyes widening.

"Mr. Hendricks," one said, a woman named Ellie whom Gray liked quite a bit, in that employer/employee sort of way. She was good, sharp, efficient. "You didn't let us know you were coming."

"Should I have?" he asked her. "You doing something down here I shouldn't see?"

"No, sir, of course not," Ellie answered. "What can we do for you?"

Hendricks turned to gesture at the lawyer.

"This is Sara Kring. K-R-I-N-G. An attorney with Barton, Oestreich, and Yoo."

Ellie nodded. He knew she had no idea what to do with that information, but she assumed he had a reason, and so she just accepted it. Good, sharp, efficient.

"Can you tell Ms. Kring how the system works?" Gray said.

"Of course," Ellie responded. She gestured at the largest screen, displaying a zoomed-out overhead view of the city, centered on downtown but spreading out for miles in either direction.

"This is a real-time image of Detroit. We keep a plane overhead, flying circles over the city with downward-facing optics, twenty-four hours per day. It records everything that happens on the streets—high-res visual spectrum during daylight hours, and state-of-the-art night vision once the sun goes down."

"Wait . . . twenty-four hours a day? How much does that cost?"

"By your standards, a lot," Hendricks said. "Go on, Ellie."

Ellie gestured at the other screens, the smaller ones arrayed around the central image.

"We have about ten thousand additional cameras in place throughout the city. Every intersection, sidewalk, alley, you name it.

"All the data from those feeds, including the overheads, comes in here, to a server in the basement, in real time. We've got facial recognition, automated ID and tracking, you name it. All the bells and whistles."

"Are you wondering if this is legal?" Hendricks asked Kring, who was looking at the monitors, her eyes flicking from one screen to the next. "It is. It's all public. No different than filming something on the street with your iPhone."

"I know it's legal to gather the footage," Kring answered. "How do you use it, though?"

"Show her the one from last week," Hendricks said.

Ellie nodded, turning to her keyboard and typing rapidly. A new image appeared on the main screen, another overhead shot of a downtown street with cars moving along it.

"Nothing, right?" Ellie said. "Just a street. But let me zoom in."

She rolled her fingers across the trackball built into her control panel, and the image fell downward, a vertigo-inducing plunge from thousands of feet up. Down, down, with no loss of detail, ending six inches above the sidewalk.

Now the screen showed a scattering of glittering crystals with a blue-green tint at their edges, familiar to any resident of Detroit—or any city, really. Automotive glass, from a window that had been shattered prior to a car being burglarized or stolen.

"We got a call from the Detroit PD about a car being stolen on the twenty-two-hundred block of Woodward, right here," Ellie said. "They got there when the owner reported it, but obviously the car was long gone, and the thief too.

"But here's what the system lets us do."

She moved deftly, zooming out again with the trackball to provide a view from perhaps fifty feet above street level, and canted one of the joysticks to the left, and time began to flow in reverse. Cars and pedestrians moved backward, the angle changing slightly as time passed, with a wobbling motion reminiscent of a ship at sea, the image flipping back and forth between full color and a grayscale but still detailed view from the night-vision cameras.

Eventually, the image slowed and a dark SUV backed smoothly into an empty spot on the side of the street. A man wearing a dark hooded sweatshirt got out, moving quickly, agitated. Ellie zoomed back in on him. The man appeared to pull a sort of tool out of the open front window of the car, a short metal rod, and there was a spray of silvery glass from the sidewalk, leaping up to reassemble itself into the SUV's driver-side window.

"Nothing too amazing yet, right?" Ellie said. "If you've got a camera in the right place, you can rewind the footage, no big deal. But watch this."

She moved her hands back to the control system, touching another joystick, and the image began to proceed in real time again, forward. The man in the hoodie slipped into the SUV, and it pulled out of its parking space and drove away. This time, though, the image moved with it, following it up the street.

"Since we have full-time coverage of everything, we can pan the image to follow anyone we want, anything, switching from camera feed to camera feed. So with this scumbag . . . ," she said, smiling as she moved the joystick, the image tracking the SUV as it turned a corner, "we can start at the moment he stole the car and then just watch him, see where he goes."

The SUV rolled through downtown, into a more industrial section of the city, where it pulled into a warehouse and was lost to the cameras.

"Can't look inside, even if we had infrared," Hendricks broke in. "That is illegal. Even for me."

"It's okay, though," Ellie continued. "The SUV never comes out. That's a chop shop. We sent the cops there, and they were able to recover the vehicle and a number of other stolen cars, too."

"What about the thief?" Sara said.

"Watch," Ellie said, sounding satisfied.

The image fast-forwarded again, and the hoodie-wearing man reappeared, stepping out of the warehouse and onto the sidewalk. He turned right and walked to another car, which he entered and drove away, all of this followed smoothly by the system. The shot followed the car as it drove through the city to a home in Oakwood Heights, one of the few standing amid empty lots and burned-out husks.

"And that's it," Ellie said. "This is all about four hours before the SUV was even reported stolen. We gave the cops the guy's address, and then . . ."

Another fast zoom forward through time, and police cruisers appeared on the street outside the house, officers moving in and bringing out the man who had stolen the car.

"Amazing, huh?" Ellie said. "Because we keep the footage logged and the planes going twenty-four-seven, we can roll to any point in the past, zoom in on anyone, follow them wherever they go. It's like a time machine."

Sara Kring didn't answer, just silently watched the image on the screen, as the police cruisers rolled away from the house, their captive safely locked away. Gray thought she probably understood what he was trying to tell her, and more, why he'd given her name to Ellie so clearly and precisely. The camera system was good for bringing down the crime rate in Detroit, but that wasn't all it could be used for. Why, you could watch anyone, follow them, see everything they did. Anyone at all.

"Let's go back upstairs, Ms. Kring," Hendricks said. "I'd like to hear what you came here to say."

Detroit would never solve its problems by itself. It didn't want to. The long, inertial slide down into oblivion was too far advanced. The city needed someone to take control, someone not bound by the rules of propriety, or a need for reelection, or anything else. The city needed someone to take it by the scruff of its neck and shake it, to force it to turn itself around. Someone to take <u>responsibility</u>. It needed Gray Hendricks.

He knew that he was causing some people pain in service of a better future. Everyone from that car thief to Gabrielle White. He was also aware that the choices he was making were creating an obscene amount of wealth for himself. He saw no disconnect between those goals. Life was a tally board, and if, at the end, you've done more good than bad, even a quarter percent differential, then it was a life well-lived, and you'd have nothing to be ashamed about.

"All right, Ms. Kring," he said once they were seated back in his office, with Corran leaning against the wall, arms folded, listening, a background element. "Let me say one thing before you start. Gabrielle White and Hendricks Capital have a contract, and we expect it to be honored, or we'll make things exceptionally difficult for your client.

"That said, I'm a businessman, and if you think you've got something to offer, let's hear it. What sort of deal does she want to make?"

The young attorney tilted her head. She took a deep breath. It felt to Hendricks like she was gearing herself up for something difficult or risky—which it was. Breaking a deal with Gray Hendricks was always a bad idea.

"The deal's not with Gabby," she said. "It's with me."

Hendricks raised an eyebrow and glanced up at Corran, who seemed equally puzzled.

"I've already got a lawyer," Gray said. "Many lawyers."

"It's not that. I know what Gabrielle White has, and I know what it's worth, and I want to help you get it."

Hendricks considered this.

"You're selling out your client?" he said. "You'll get disbarred. Disgraced."

"Yes," Sara Kring said. "I know. But I've decided it's better than the alternative, for Gabby and for me. Besides, being blunt, if you and I can make a deal, then whether I can practice law won't matter at all.

"Gabby's invented something incredible. It will change the world, and that's not euphemism or hyperbole. This is like the telephone, airplanes, the internet. She wants to keep it for herself. Her mind's set on it. But I think she'd be smarter to work with you. If you're willing to cut a deal with me to make sure I participate in the upside, and Gabby gets her share too, I'll work on her to come to the table with you. She trusts me. I can make it happen."

Kring leaned forward in her chair.

"You might be able to get it on your own, through the courts," she continued, "but if you did you'd lose what you really need—her. She's the genius. Even if you did get a judgment, it'd take years, and you're not getting any younger, right?"

Hendricks' lower back chose that exact moment to send out a little zing of pain. No. He was not getting any younger.

"You seem to be a very practical woman, Ms. Kring," he said.

"I just see things how they are," she said.

"Okay, then," Gray said, smiling at her. "Let's change the world."

CHAPTER 20

THE LAST DIVE BAR IN MANHATTAN

"Will you ever tell me what this is all about?" Soro said.

"What do you mean?" Annami answered, her attention on the screen mounted behind the bar, currently displaying a much-hyped retromatch in which she was actually pretty interested.

"Come on," he said, a little edge of annoyance in his tone. She turned to look at him.

"You can do things with the flash like no one I've ever met. That stuff with the rats at Olsen's place . . ." Soro went on.

A little rustle from the cage on the seat next to Annami, where Lars the man-rat rested, her insurance policy against retaliation from Olsen before the auction. Any other bar in New York would have an issue with that—but not Conrad's Lower East Side Tavern, thank the lord.

"Even just the way you acted down there," Soro continued. "Ruthless, like. And the money . . . you used to work at Anyone, and it sounded like a good gig. Why did you quit that to start darksharing for Mama Run? None of this makes sense, Annami."

He shook his head.

"I don't mind helping you. Promise. It's interesting, and I don't care about the risk or anything like that. I just want to know what I'm doing. I mean . . . what's the point?"

They sat in silence. Annami considered what she owed this man. Probably a lot, by any accounting you chose, but that didn't matter. She wasn't going to blow everything she'd worked for just to make him feel a little better, a bit more included. The stakes were too high, and she was too close.

Soro made a small grunting noise, a sound of frustration. He stood aggressively, grabbed his empty beer mug, and headed for the bar.

Annami looked at the screen again. Pete Sampras was playing Roger Federer on a grass field built to resemble center court at Wimbledon. The two champions were a decade apart in age, which meant they had never played each other in their respective primes thirty and forty years back, but the flash solved that. They each transferred into vessels in their midtwenties, skilled tennis players in their own right, and then they went at it.

Skeptics said the retromatches couldn't replicate what it really would have been like, and Annami herself thought that was probably true. Muscle memory mattered, and at the level of players like Sampras and Federer, the ability wasn't just mental but also keyed to infinitesimal physical refinements built up over thousands of hours of doing nothing but playing championship-level tennis, living in bodies molded and carved and optimized toward winning Opens. Neither Federer nor Sampras had played like this in decades, and what they'd lost in that time wouldn't come back overnight.

But it was still pretty awesome. Everywhere Annami looked, she saw things the flash shouldn't be used for, things she would never have allowed if it were up to her—but retros . . . those, she'd do.

They had become big business, and not just in sports. Musicians too old to play like they used to, singers whose voices were shot . . . the flash gave the world a chance to catch another glimpse of old glories. Ordinary age restrictions on flash usage were lifted, and vessels gladly signed death waivers to allow themselves to be inhabited by elderly geniuses of various stripes. It was worth the risk—vessels for retros were generally handpicked and often saw their own careers spike after the event. If Adele wants to borrow your body's voice for her big comeback concert, odds are you're not so bad yourself.

Sometimes it went wrong, of course. Sometimes the performer's original body died during the retro, and the vessel dropped dead at the same time, in the middle of the guitar solo or dunk contest or victory lap or pommel horse. All part of the fun, the frisson; all part of what made retros so popular. If one died, both died.

Sampras was winning. Already up a set.

Soro returned with a full mug—just one—and sat down. He pulled out his mini and began to fiddle with it.

"I'm not," she said.

He looked up. "What?"

"I'm not going to tell you what this is all about, or why I'm doing what I'm doing. It's my business, and it needs to stay that way for a thousand reasons. But it doesn't mean I don't appreciate everything you've done for me, Soro. If you want money, I'm happy to do that. I have plenty now, after Olsen."

He tilted his head a little, the implication clear—*You have plenty now because I told you where Olsen was*, he was saying. *Because I risked my life breaking into Anyone, and then the crazy shit down in Red Hook. Because I haven't told anyone about what you did.*

Annami thought about this man, whose every choice seemed

geared toward trying to matter in, and to, a world that had de-clared him Dull.

Soro shrugged.

"It's fine," he said. "Don't need money."

That made Annami think about needing things. What did she need? The Bhangra George auction was in two days, and so odds were, in two days she would be dead. She couldn't let herself care very much about that. She was steel. She couldn't let herself care about anything. Not the things her body had been used for while darksharing, not the fake-but-still-pleasant life she'd abandoned, not the fact that she had killed a person back at Olsen's—that rat she'd tased—without thinking, just acting, doing what had to be done.

It was exhausting, being steel—like the first days after a baby's birth, trying desperately to make sure all its needs were ad-dressed, that no mistakes were made. She had no choice, though. The moment she let herself care, her entire soul would lock up and die.

You are you, she thought.

She thought again about what she might need. In this particu-lar context, in these last days, what did a woman of steel require?

She reached over, touched Soro's face, tilting his head up from his mini. His eyes widened, narrowed. He was surprised. So was Annami, actually. They'd never touched before. She couldn't re-member the last time she'd touched anyone.

You think that's a shocker, buckle up, she thought.

Annami kissed Soro.

He tensed. Made a small noise and pulled back a little at the violation of his boundaries. Then he got over it and leaned in, and their tongues were touching, and she felt his hand on her leg. Just staying there, just above her knee—moving upward at a rate so slow it probably couldn't be measured with existing technology.

It's been so long, Annami thought.

It had been. That was also why she had to stop. The dark-shares were one thing—she had no idea what her body was being used for, and she could convince herself that she wasn't responsible for those acts. They weren't her choices. But this . . . this was all her.

She pulled back from Soro, crinkling her face in something between embarrassment, shame, and, above all, guilt, feeling a wall of awkwardness slam down between them.

"I'm sorry," she said. "I'm sorry. It's just been a very long time. I just . . ."

"Ah. All right," Soro said. He took his hand off her leg. "Listen, you've got a lot going on. I know that. It's as obvious as all that ink you put on your face. I like you, but I'm not in a rush. Whatever works. Even if it never does. That's okay too."

Soro smiled at her, that weird screwed-up smile that she'd come to enjoy, that she found herself working to give him a reason to unleash. Then he looked off to the side as if none of it mattered. But of course it did.

And she <u>wanted</u> to.

No rush, he'd said. She'd be dead in two days, most likely. And it had been so <u>long</u>.

"I just . . . can't. Not in this," she said, gesturing to her body.

Let him assume whatever he wanted. Disease, disfigurement, it didn't matter. This world had the flash.

"Can you, though? With your heart, I mean?" she asked.

"Of course," Soro answered. "On this side, I'll be sleeping like a baby. Resting heart rate the whole time. Nothing's going to happen to me. Well. Except for whatever you think up."

They went to one of the stalls in Chinatown, because they

were the closest place either of them knew, and suddenly they were in a hurry. The agent, a kindly middle-aged woman, asked them in barely accented English what they wanted.

"We have it all," she said. She pulled out a thinscreen displaying many people, bodies, nude and clothed, all shapes, colors, and genders. You could have the experience alone or as a couple, whatever you wanted. They had it all. This stall was just the storefront for the operation—a flash setup was somewhere nearby, in an apartment or sealed-up retail shop, and the madam would escort them to it once they had chosen their vessels and paid for their time.

"She didn't even try to hide that this is the front door to a brothel," Annami said in a low, excited voice to Soro as they flicked through their thinnies, searching the decks of flesh for something that caught their eyes. "We could be cops."

"You don't work a gig like this without getting pretty finely tuned instincts," Soro said. "She can tell we're excited for real, I guess. Cops wouldn't be."

Annami realized that she was, in fact, excited. And then the guilt, again.

"Or more likely she's just paid up for the month and knows the cops won't hassle her," Soro added.

The operation wasn't technically illegal from a prostitution standpoint—every vessel on the Chinese side had signed up to use their bodies this way, had a contract, and saw a good cut of the proceeds. The problem wasn't morality—it was international trade. New York had its local workers, in their own registered brothels, and the cops wanted to make sure the sexflash went to them. But those brothels were part of the lightshare, and Dulls couldn't use them—Soro, for instance, with his heart defect.

The Chinatown stalls weren't darkshare dens—everyone involved knew exactly what would happen to them—but they ran on their own network and served a similar need for anonymity and access to the flash that the lightshare didn't or couldn't.

A woman on the screen caught Annami's eye. She stopped scrolling. Most of the available options were Chinese, which made sense considering the brothel's physical location on the other side of the world, but this woman was darker-skinned, with features that made Annami think of someone like Genghis Khan. Tall, too, which she liked. The woman seemed strong. Like she could break you in half. Like steel.

She reached out a finger to select the vessel, then hesitated. She glanced at Soro, tilting the thinscreen toward him so he could see.

After all, shouldn't it be someone he was attracted to? Annami had never gone through this process before. She knew it wasn't uncommon in the flash-altered world, but every other time she'd had sex had been in her own body. She didn't know the etiquette.

"It doesn't matter," Soro said, looking up from his own screen. "For me, this is about you."

He held out his thinnie.

"But if you want to pick my vessel, that's all right," he said.

"Surprise me," Annami said, pushing his screen away with an extended index finger.

He did. She thought he'd be all rough machismo in bed, taking what he wanted without much consideration, but it didn't turn out that way. He gave as much as he took, and what he took was what she offered.

It was good, so much better than she'd expected it to be, despite it having been so long that she was basically a virgin again. It helped, she thought, that her vessel responded instantly to Soro's touch, revving itself up faster than she ever had in her own. Maybe that was some sort of enhancement, chemical or technological, or maybe Annami's own emotional contribution to the situation (so long . . .), but the body was <u>ready</u>.

She needed this. To feel someone connect with her, even if it wasn't really her. It felt like a melding. It felt real, and the insertion of the two vessels, both beautiful, gave it an extra orgiastic something. It made her bold.

Soro was acting bold, too—or maybe that was how he always was.

She did things, things she'd only ever considered hypothetically, in a giggling-over-drinks-with-girlfriends kind of way, the would-you-evers. She let him do those things to her, and her to him, because none of it really mattered, but it felt like it did.

She came, and then, a little while later, so did he.

They were resting, on a big pink bed in a small room somewhere in China, sheets kicked to the floor and the air saturated. She put her hand on his.

"More," she said.

One of the benefits of the flash was that if your vessel wasn't tired, neither were you. You could stay up for three days straight, then flash into a well-rested vessel and feel fresh as a daisy. No fatigue toxins.

Annami and Soro made the most of that particular perk, methodically working their way through much of the brothel's menu, zipping back into their original bodies only long enough to choose new vessels for the next phase of the festivities. They had to—the second rule prevented flashing into a new body from a vessel.

They were men. They were women. They were other options, everything they could be, but always themselves. They burned through hours together, and a truly astonishing amount of Annami's money, but that didn't matter. Annami had a lot of money.

Finally, it was enough.

Annami and Soro rested on a different bed in another small room in China, this time blue. Her vessel was a stocky, swarthy, muscular man, and Soro was in a zaftig blonde with very pale skin.

"Huh," he said. "That was something."

"Yeah," Annami said. "Thank you for that. I needed it."

"You think?" Soro answered, his personality clear even through the voice of his vessel, his words layered with wry amazement.

She looked at him. She felt connected, in a way she couldn't remember feeling for, well . . . so long. She didn't want to be cautious anymore. She wanted to have someone to trust, and that couldn't happen unless you entrusted them with something.

"I'm doing something important," Annami said. "There's sort of a . . . problem with the flash, and I'm trying to fix it."

Soro got up on one elbow, his vessel's expression alert, the postcoital haze gone.

"Wait. Are you actually <u>telling</u> me something right now? I thought you didn't do that. You told me back at Conrad's you never <u>would</u> do that."

"I changed my mind. You changed my mind."

"I'm that good, huh?"

"You're good. But not at sex."

Soro raised an eyebrow.

Annami shook her head.

"Ugh, I'm sorry. This is weird. I'm just . . . I don't talk to people about anything that matters very often."

She took his hand.

"The sex was great. Fantastic. But what I mean is that you're good. You're a good person. You don't even really know me, and you've been there for me every time I needed you. I just think you deserve a little more information."

"Fine by me," Soro said, running a fingertip down her arm. "You make a man curious, Annami. Okay, problem with the flash. You worked at Anyone. Couldn't you just fix it there?"

"No. It's bigger than that. Have you ever heard anyone talking about Centuries?"

Soro's face—the vessel's cute, pale, blue-eyed face—was blank.

"A hundred years, you mean?"

"No—they're people. A certain type of people. Anyone . . . made them, I guess. Or Stephen Hauser did. They're good for him, bad for everyone else. I'm one of the only people who knows they exist, and Hauser wants me dead so I'll never be able to talk about them. He has his people looking for me. There's one in particular, his main hunter, a guy named Bleeder."

"Wait," Soro said. "The CEO of Anyone wants to kill you? Why the fuck did you work there?"

"I needed to learn as much as I could," Annami replied. "They didn't know who I was. I took precautions. Anyway, the Centuries, the way the flash is now, even you being a Dull, it's all tied together. The world shouldn't be like this. I'm going to try to make it better."

"You're gonna fix the whole entire world, and once you do, I get to flash for real?" Soro said, raising an eyebrow.

"I know how it sounds."

"Doesn't matter. Be my guest. Fix the world."

"I'm trying . . . and you're helping. I want you to know how much that means to me. Even the fact that you're listening, not calling me crazy. It matters. I've been alone . . . for a long time."

Soro smiled, not his burn-scar smirk but a real, true smile.

"My pleasure, ma'am," he said, affecting a sort of cowboy drawl for no reason at all. "I ain't goin' nowhere."

Annami kissed him, then sat up, stretching, getting a moment of disorientation as she adjusted to this vessel's eyeline being lower than her usual.

"We should get back," she said.

A thinnie sat on a table next to the bed, displaying a list of options—food, drink, additional partners, stimulants, costuming, lubricants and oils, vinyl and silicone and metal paraphernalia of every description—anything a patron of the establishment might desire during their erotic explorations. Interestingly, though, no condoms, no birth control or prophylactic measures of any kind. Presumably the vessels attended to the unenticing details of preventing pregnancy and disease in their off-duty hours, and of course, there was no risk of any of that for the customers. This was all fantasy, all the time—until your time was up.

At the bottom of the thinnie's screen, a little running countdown, discreet, displaying the minutes or hours (or, based on the number of digits, even days) left until the session timed out and a return to original bodies via the flash rig wired into the walls of the room itself—no need for I-fi. After which the vessels probably took a long, hot shower and had a well-deserved nap.

Next to the timer was a little icon reading END SESSION.

Annami picked up the device. She realized how much time she'd spent with Soro—almost a full day. The auction had drawn appallingly close, and the weight of everything she needed to do before it happened crashed down on her all at once. Among other things, the scheduled data dump from the Century-hunting code she'd left in Anyone's mainframe had probably already been sent to her mini, and it would take her a while to analyze.

"This has been amazing, but I need to get back to the real world," she said. "I hope that's all right."

She turned to Soro and saw that he was already gone. His vessel was lying on the bed, the large blond woman's limbs sprawled and eyes up and staring. Dead. Obviously dead.

Annami blinked/

She was back to herself, in her own body, but not lying comfortably on a flash couch in the New York City end of a transcontinental brothel. She was on her knees, and her hands were behind her, bound at the wrists by something tight cutting into her skin. That little pain was dwarfed by an agony in her head, pulsing with her heartbeat, so strong she nearly blacked out with every throb. It was centered on her cheek, which she could already feel swelling up. Someone had hit her.

And for the second time in not very long, she had awakened from the flash in a puddle of someone else's blood. Only this time, there was no confusion. Soro was six feet away, his throat slashed, eyes wide and staring up just as his vessel's eyes had been back on that blue bed in that small room on the other side of the world. Dead. Obviously dead.

If one dies, both die.

No, Annami thought, unable to summon anything more.

The brothel's madam and her small staff had been murdered too, their bodies shoved up against a wall in the middle distance. Soro's corpse had been arranged . . . displayed . . . for her benefit. The proprietor and her crew, though—just details, just in the way, and now just dead.

She had let herself care for someone in just the most fractional way. Now that person was dead. Annami was, as always, a death sentence. She walled herself back up, behind steel plates a thousand feet high. Never again.

Standing here and there in the room were other people, men she did not recognize in dark suits with cold expressions. Very cold. Olsen's people? Possible, but unlikely—she could see the cage with Lars the rat-son pushed up against the wall, and surely Olsen would have released him.

These people were something else, then. Enemies she didn't know—but she really had only one enemy other than Olsen, and these people had to be with him.

One was squatting not far from her, studying her face. A man. Also cold . . . but interested.

"I was going to wait until you were done, let you come back on your own, but you were taking forever over there."

He glanced over at Soro's corpse.

"You must have been really into that guy."

The man smiled, and that was all it took. Annami knew exactly who he was.

"Bleeder," she said.

END OF PART II

TEN YEARS FROM NOW

WASHINGTON, DC—Tumult erupted in the Senate as the final votes were tallied with respect to what has become known as the No One Bill—legislation designed to sharply curtail commercial use of the body-switching technology introduced to the world four years ago and popularly known as the flash.

In the wake of mounting pressure from a coalition comprised of religious groups, ethicists, the ACLU, and lobbyists from a wide variety of industries, the No One Bill was proposed as a measure to restrict usage of the flash to a minimum, allowing only certain research applications with a high level of oversight. Additional uses of the technology would be allowed only with the approval of a joint House-Senate committee. The litigation was drafted in part in response to NeOnet Global's AnyFest conference this spring, during which company CEO Stephen Hauser unveiled an ambitious list of applications and partners for the company's technology, touching sectors from transportation to entertainment to even the military.

"Some people are afraid of the flash because they know it will disrupt their ordinary way of doing things," Hauser was quoted as saying at AnyFest. "They don't

want to change. They're that last horse-and-buggy salesman watching cars roll by on the street outside. Well, it's
too late. Change is here—and it came in a flash."

After approval late last week in the House, the No
One Bill was expected to pass through the Senate easily,
based on position statements prior to the vote. However,
earlier this morning the bill was defeated, with forty-nine
senators voting for the legislation and fifty-one against.
The deciding votes were a surprise, a voting bloc of three
of the Senate's longest-serving and oldest members: An-
gus Green (R–MI), Marjorie Washington (D–NV), and
Freddy Mingus (R–AK). The voting histories of Green,
Washington, and Mingus would have suggested a more
conservative approach to transformative technology. As
of press time, only Senator Mingus has commented, saying, "The possibilities inherent in the flash are too significant to curtail research and expansion, as suggested
by the No One Bill. I see the potential of the technology
to effect positive change on this planet in areas such as
climate change, medical procedures, and much more. To
put it another way—we are running out of time, and we
need the flash."

Stephen Hauser also provided a statement: "I am
encouraged by the wise decision of the Senate to refrain
from indulging the misguided fears of short-sighted. individuals about my company's technology. I am telling
you right now, the flash will save the world. I will make
certain of it. That is my only goal. Grandiose words? Perhaps. But wait and see. Just wait and see."

PART III

CHAPTER 21

THE FRONT PORCH, MICHIGAN

THE POSSIBILITIES ARE ENDLESS.

Gabby underlined these four words, twice, hard, the tip of her ballpoint leaving a dent in that page and at least the next two.

She'd never liked the phrase. She wasn't too fond of hyperbole in general. Say what you mean, mean what you say. *The possibilities are endless* represented a failure of imagination, or worse, laziness, an unwillingness to spend the time analyzing the actual, real possibilities inherent in a given situation.

Very little was actually infinite. Very little was unquantifiable. It was just a matter of doing the work.

That said, Gabby had spent the two hours and counting of the Kitten's nap sitting with a red spiral notebook she'd grabbed at the IGA in town and her U of M mug brimming with hot sweet tea, filling page after page with things she needed to understand about the flash and ways it might be used. Twenty pages so far, and she was having ideas faster than she could write them down. Pure idea-phoria.

The possibilities were endless.

Also endless: the questions. She had divided her notebook into two sections, UNKNOWNS and USES, and while the second group was growing quickly, it was nothing compared to the first.

She only had three experimental episodes she could draw on for conclusions—not enough, nowhere near enough. The first time, when she'd gone into Paul's body, she'd been so panicked she'd barely remembered to track the details of the experience. The second, another switch into Paul when she'd tested the portable version of the tech, and then the third, when Sara Kring had also moved into Paul—all brief, nonrigorous, conducted outside of laboratory environments. All they really proved was that the process was repeatable.

Well, no. The mere existence of the flash also solved certain arguments cognitive scientists had been having for generations with respect to the nature of the conscious mind—but Gabby could only imagine the new fights it would spark. It was pretty clear now that the self-model was utterly complete and bounded in the human mind—a person's sense of themselves was a conceptual object, transferable from one brain to another relatively intact. When she had been running Paul's body, she still identified as Gabrielle, even though most of what she would previously have defined as Gabrielle—her physical self—was gone.

She had retained her memories, her skills, her worldview, her emotional library—for instance, she loved the Kitten as much as she ever had, whether she was Paul or Gabby. She wondered if those things would carry over if she moved into a brain outside the normal parameters—damaged, or with an unusual chemical balance. Gabrielle White's prime loved dogs. Would she still, if she moved into a brain that was terrified of them?

Gender, too—would she have made the same choices in her own body that she did in Paul's? Her approach to getting herself back to herself had used a sort of brute-force approach—was that testosterone influencing her decisions?

The sheer scale of the basic research facing her was breath-taking—it felt like a first-contact situation, like an alien spaceship crashing in the backyard, and she was the person tasked with understanding every element of their civilization and technology, from entertainment to weapons to pets.

Consciousness was coherent—it could exist outside the mind in which it had grown. That seemed clear. It meant there was something unique about a human mind—a waveform, a pattern—that could be transmitted. What that was, she did not yet know. She had her own theories about what consciousness was—everyone in her field did. The P3 wave, activation in the frontal and parietal lobes, boosts in the gamma band—all signatures of the mind awakening, directly considering or processing the world in some way. And then, that awareness was filtered through memories, experience, genetic predisposition, education, culture, and more to create a reaction: an emotion or a decision of some kind. Apparently, somewhere in that endlessly complex interaction, that language of light, was a sentence that described the self. A shining, unique article of brilliance she had decided to call the flash.

Could you copy a person's flash? Could you store it? Could a mind exist outside a brain?

Digitized consciousness was a hot sector in cognitive science, garnering big grants and VC investment. She understood that. It was sexy. It promised immortality. If a flash could be replicated on or transferred to a computer, then that mind could, in theory, live forev—

A thin little cry, of hunger or discomfort or loneliness. Kat was up.

Gabby held her breath, hoping this was a brief interlude, an infant's equivalent of sleepwalking, and that the Kitten's nap, the beautiful oasis of peace in the middle of every afternoon, the sixty to one hundred and eighty minutes when Gabrielle White could let herself be herself, was not yet done.

The sound from the crib did not fade away into a burble and then sweet, blessed silence. It grew stronger, more insistent. The nap was over.

Gabby closed her notebook. She set it down on the banged-up, rusty side table next to her rocking chair, where the mug of tea was still sending off little wisps of inviting steam. She took a deep breath, trying to reconcile the many equally true feelings in her mind and heart—resentment that this tiny person could not be denied and must be served, her every need and whim attended to at the exact moment she chose to express them; and also, simultaneously, crushing guilt at having these feelings, Jesus Christ, Kat was a baby, none of this was her fault; and also, simultaneously, excitement that she would get to lift the little person she loved so much, see her smile, attend to her every need and whim and smell the top of her head and kiss her and see her bright eyes; and also, simultaneously, frustration that Paul had insisted on going back to teach at the university so soon when he <u>knew</u> how important the flash was to her, and how much she needed and wanted to work on it.

The flash would change the world, and Gabby would change the world, and that she was doing anything other than making those things happen felt insane. She kept coming up with metaphors she planned to unleash on Paul whenever he deigned to return from Ann Arbor.

It was like having a million-dollar scratch-off but being told you couldn't cash it in for a decade.

It was like going to the airport for the best beach vacation of your life and the plane sitting on the runway for six hours.

It was like being locked in a cell, with the key on a hook just out of reach, and just outside the cell was a pile of gold bars, and—

And so on.

She wanted to take off, to unleash herself . . . and instead . . .

A diaper was changed, a bottle was prepared and consumed, a

resounding burp was produced, generating a laugh from both baby and mother, and Gabby decided to go for a run. She changed into shorts, sports bra, and another of her endless succession of concert shirts, this one old and pretty ratty, full of holes, but that was fine—ventilation. She strapped the Kitten into the jogging stroller, and off they went, moving along the dirt road that bordered their property and circled the small lake adjacent. It was about a two-mile loop, but she could do it twice, letting Kat be entertained by whatever blurry version of the world she saw, looking out from inside the stroller.

Gabby figured that if she took her time, the run would buy her another hour. Time to think. Time, ideally, to get herself back to that sweet flow state, to properly consider all the questions screaming out for answers.

She started with terminology, just to warm up her brain. *Traveler and vessel*, she thought. The traveler moved out of their own body to a new one, and the vessel served as a temporary home for the traveler. Good enough for now.

What would happen if a vessel died while a traveler was inhabiting their mind?

Could a traveler enter a physiologically abnormal mind? Someone with Down's, or autism, or cerebral palsy? If so, what would that experience be like?

Memories? She hadn't been able to access Paul's memories during her time using him as a vessel, and she hadn't lost her own—although she hadn't approached that methodically. Something to examine more closely down the road.

Why was distance a factor? Why did a traveler head to the closest vessel mind? How did a traveler's consciousness locate another mind at all? Was there a distance limit? Through what medium did the traveler's consciousness move?

She knew radio signals faded over distance via the inverse-square law, but did that apply here? Minds were electricity, rippling across synapses and neurons, and so it seemed likely that the same might be true for the flash.

Speaking of which, there was the question of what happened to the consciousness of the vessel. The EEG she'd taken of her own body during that first transfer certainly suggested massively reduced brain activity. Where did it go? Was the vessel's mind "stored" somewhere in the brain, or was it simply interrupted, like a needle being taken off a record?

She needed access to an fMRI. She needed a hundred test subjects. She needed $10 million. She needed all of that and more before she could even begin to answer any of it.

Gabby hit her usual turnaround point, a fallen tree sticking out from the shore that was always covered with turtles on sunny days. She rotated the jogging stroller, taking a moment to make sure all was well within, and began the second leg of the run, which would take her back past their property and to the edge of the two-lane state highway that led to Ann Arbor if you took a left, and Jackson if you took a right.

She ran, pushing the stroller ahead of her, thinking about lefts and rights, different choices, wondering if she should have just gone to Gray Hendricks with all of this in the beginning. She wouldn't be scrambling for time, for headspace, even for childcare. Hendricks would have funded her through the roof, and some delightful young nanny could be watching the baby while she worked, maybe a Scandinavian au pair, and wouldn't <u>that</u> be nice, on so many levels. Her mother would be impressed, at any rate.

But no. Gabrielle White was the world's most fluent speaker of the language of light. This was her job. She didn't really know what she had yet—she had to do the work—but she knew that the possibilities were . . . well . . . endless.

She regretted nothing, she decided. It was right to have kept the flash, hidden it from Hendricks. Even these days of frustration, sitting on that winning scratch-off, were worth it. Even though following Sara Kring's advice—what a wonderful friend she had turned out to be, an ally when she needed one most—would require ten years of all but solitary development and planning before she could really examine the flash in the detail it deserved. But ten years wasn't forever. She would still be young when she revealed the flash to the world—and it would be hers when she did, free and clear.

There was even something nice about the idea of working on the project alone for all that time. No one would ever be able to argue that the flash wasn't hers and hers alone. She would truly own it, and could make it into what it should be. Maybe the Kitten could be her lab assistant, when she was old enough. She could teach Kat everything she knew. Yes, time and resource limitations would be frustrating, with her only truly viable experimental subjects being herself and Paul—but maybe that would bring them closer.

A familiar wobble from the stroller, which was code for *Mama, I'm sick of this, I want to get out.*

Gabby frowned, but honestly, she'd been pushing herself pretty hard on the run, already on loop three in an effort to keep her thoughts flowing. As she came back to her body, she realized her legs were burning, her lungs screaming, her heart pounding.

She slowed to a walk, feeling the stroller's movements intensify.

"Okay, Kitty Kat, I get it," she said. "It's hot, right? You want to splash around a little?"

Their property had an easement through the neighbor's land across the road, a narrow path that gave them access to the lake, and Gabby parked the stroller near the top and extracted the baby. She carried Kat down to the lake, feeling the air cool a bit as they approached the water's edge. A rickety dock extended about ten feet out into the lake. Next to it, on the shore, Paul had set up a small plastic storage locker that held a number of useful items, canoe paddles and cheap fishing poles, and so on. It also included a tiny infant life vest, which turned the Kitten into something like a cork.

As long as Gabby kept one hand on the life vest's strap, Kat could splash around as much as she wanted, wiggling and laughing, diverted at length by fluid dynamics in all their many variations.

Gabby's feet squelched in the mucky bottom as she slipped off the edge of the dock, the cool but not cold water soothing and wonderful on her run-battered soles. The actual contents of said muck didn't bear too much pondering, fish crap and decomposing plants and god only knew, but muck wasn't what she wanted to be thinking about in any case, so that was fine.

Had she proven the existence of the soul?

Gabby didn't think so. She'd proven that consciousness was a discrete item, yes, but an immortal soul felt like more of a philosophical construct. Something of faith, not of science. Let the churches figure it out, when the time came.

Her mind looped back to something she'd considered earlier, a thought about immortality. She wished she had her notes to consult, which generated a momentary twinge of conscience.

She shouldn't be keeping notes at all. It was stupid, even if she was just writing down pure speculation, not experimental data, nothing concrete. When Hendricks Capital came looking down the road, trying to prove they owned the flash, there should be nothing to suggest she'd invented the tech with their funding.

The little red notebook she'd left on the porch would, in the wrong hands, be a smoking gun.

But what choice did she have? There were just too many ideas right now, and she couldn't hold them all in her head at once. She had to offload some, organize them, make room for new ones.

A little shiver ran through her body, not generated by the lake water leaching away her internal warmth but at everything that lay before her. The things she would come to understand about the flash in the years to come. The ways she would shape the gift she would give to the world, to her daughter, to herself. The mountain she would climb, hers and hers alone.

A noise from up the path, behind her, on the shore, and she turned. Paul stood there, smiling at her and she felt very warm, very good, there in the lake between her daughter and her husband.

She knew Paul didn't understand why she was the way she was, but that was all right. You didn't have to understand someone to love them.

"Hey, babe," she said. "Good day?"

"Normal," he answered. "Nothing special. Talked about music to a bunch of people in the eighteen-to-twenty-one age range. It was kind of nice to get back to it, honestly. A little stability in a crazy world, you know?"

Gabby made her way to the shore, her bobbing, chuckling daughter in tow, and stepped out of the lake, feeling the water run down her legs.

"Sure," she said, undoing the clasps on the Kitten's life vest and setting it on the grass to dry.

"You get any work done?" Paul asked. "I know it's been killing you that you can't dig in to the flash the way you want."

"Nothing practical. A lot of thinking," she answered. "I made some plans for the first round of experiments. Speaking of that, I realize you're not thrilled about doing another body swap, but it's the only way I can get the data I need. The alternative is to involve another person in all of this, and I don't think that would be smart."

"No," Paul said. "Not smart."

She heard the tone of his voice and looked up at him, to see a deep frown wrenched across his face.

"What?" she said.

"I thought you were going to try to figure out a way to make the flash work with animals."

"Honestly, I don't know if it's possible. If it were, I'd have ended up in Wilbur back when all of this started."

She shuddered a little, and this time it definitely had nothing to do with temperature and everything to do with the idea of her mind being trapped inside a rodent. If she'd ended up inside the rat, or the baby, or really anyone other than her husband, then she'd still be there, insane or dead.

She'd been lucky—so lucky. So had Paul. The possibilities were endless, and that included possibilities for things to go extraordinarily, apocalyptically wrong.

"You know . . . you're right," she said. "I'll keep working on it. No more human trials for the time being."

Part of her soul, the emotionless, empathy-deficient scientist, screamed that she needed to do human trials immediately; waiting to learn even a tiny percentage of what she could be learning was anathema, heresy.

"I have ten years to figure it out," she said, handing Paul a damp infant. She snapped the stroller closed and slung its strap over her shoulder, then took her husband's hand.

They walked along the sloping path from the lake, her brain already devising experiments she might try that didn't require human minds—computer simulations and such—but doing so in a snitty, offended tone that made it clear that she was being an idiot for not pushing as hard as she could as long as she could.

Gabby gripped Paul's hand more tightly, and he gave hers a squeeze in return.

"I've been thinking about what you said, about what the flash could do for the world," he said. "Make everyone relate to everyone else, get rid of racism, all that."

"I never said it would get rid of racism," Gabby answered. "I'm talking about empathy. I understood things about you in a few hours of being you that I could never have learned any other way."

"Okay," Paul said. "So you want everyone to be everyone else. Get it all mixed up. I have two thoughts on that. What makes you think folks will want to do that? You really think white people will choose to spend time in dark bodies?

"And even if they do, even if it works—wouldn't that erase us? I mean . . . if we're all trying to be someone else, then who are we? Wouldn't it get rid of culture, individuality? Is that what you want?"

"Absolutely not," Gabby answered, not letting go of her husband's hand. "I love what I am. All I want—what I think the flash can do—is to make it, like, twenty percent harder to hate someone on sight. You won't be able to just take someone at face value, because the face might not be them. Everyone could be anyone. So you'd have to <u>work</u> to hate someone, and in that case . . . well, I think most people are lazy. It's the easy path, every time. Maybe once people realize how hard they'll have to work before they can write someone off, they won't bother.

"Maybe the flash will be like planting a seed. Every seed can be a plant, and every plant can make more seeds."

Paul made a soft, noncommittal, familiar noise. Translated through over five years of marriage, it meant: *I don't completely agree, but I acknowledge your point.*

"The flash won't solve everything," Gabby said. "Skin is skin, and it's gonna be for a long time to come—but the flash could make things better, and when was the last time something actually did?

"Someone who believes in that goal has to be in charge, Paul. No, let me say it another way—someone who <u>understands</u> that goal. That's why I have to keep the flash. A hundred thousand decisions will be made about this tech between now and when it's introduced to the world, and every last one is a little nudge in one direction or another. I want to make those decisions, and I want to make damn sure they take the world in the right direction. Doesn't that make sense?"

They walked a few more paces in silence. The path sloped up-ward.

"Hendricks is black too," Paul said.

Gabby threw him an expression that felt like it should have set him on fire.

"So?" she said. "You keep telling me how scary he is, right? And not for nothing, but he's a man. A rich man. Black or white, wher-ever he started, I don't think he'll see the flash the way I do.

"I want Kat to grow up knowing her mother did this thing. I want little girls everywhere to see that it was me. Hell, I want every-one to see, all over the damn world."

"Is that pride talking, babe?"

Gabby reached up and ran the back of her finger along the Kit-ten's cheek.

"I am proud, Paul. I think our daughter will be too."

The lake trail angled more steeply upward as it reached its end, and their house and the barn beyond came into view. Parked on the little loop of gravel that stood in for a driveway were four cars—their old Camry plus three others she'd never seen before. The new cars: a dark sedan, fancy and sleek, and two large, black, tinted-window SUVs. These four vehicles used up all the available space on the driveway, which meant another two SUVs had made do with park-ing on their lawn. A final imposition: a large panel truck had backed itself up to the barn, leaving long brown tire tracks across the grass. The big wagon door was open—and she'd padlocked it; she knew she had.

Two men emerged from the barn carrying a piece of equipment, moving it toward the truck. She recognized it—a gas ballast pump, a subsystem to the primary laser rig, that ensured a pure vacuum inside the lasing medium vessel before the argon was piped in. Her ballast pump.

"What the hell?" she heard Paul say, but Gabby knew. She supposed he did too.

And then one of the men noticed them standing there across the dirt road, their little family, and stopped and pointed at them. They all turned to look, and Gabby felt pinned, caught.

She could still feel the mud of the lake between her bare toes. Her running shoes dangled from her free hand. There was nowhere to run.

The front door of their home opened, and Jon Corran stepped out onto the porch. He had something in his hand.

A red, spiral-bound notebook.

CHAPTER 22

A FLASH BROTHEL, CHINATOWN, NEW YORK

"How'd you do it?" Bleeder asked.

Annami said nothing. As long as Bleeder wanted something from her, he'd probably keep her alive.

Not that she could stave off death forever. In time, probably not very much time, Bleeder or one of his Eaters would kill her, just like they had Soro and the unlucky brothel workers scattered around the room, their wounds horrible, gaping, crimson flowers. But as long as she was still alive, she might come up with an idea that could buy her more time to come up with another idea. Even two minutes. That'd be just fine. It would be two minutes she didn't currently have.

"Let me be more specific," Bleeder said. "How did you stay hidden for so long? You should've popped up on a network some-where. Even that name . . . Annami. Cute, but you don't think it's maybe a little too clever?"

All her muscles tensed, involuntary and strong and ultimately useless. The hard-plastic wrist cuffs holding her arms behind her back wouldn't break just because she was offended.

"Were these tattoos part of it?" Bleeder asked, tracing two

knuckles down the side of her face, causing the already-intense throbbing in her head to flare. "A way to hide from facial recognition algorithms on the dronet?"

"No," she said.

"Huh," Bleeder said. "So you just wanted to look hard-core? I have to tell you, it kind of works. It's—"

A look of understanding passed across his features.

"Oh, I get it. You don't want to recognize your face."

Bleeder stood, an easy, catlike movement that seemed mildly incongruous for such a dense, muscular body.

"You're a sad story, you know that?" he said.

"Yeah," Annami said. "I know that."

Bleeder turned to survey the abattoir that had once been the brothel's waiting room. His small group of men waited—his Eaters, all just as big as he was, tailored suits like the team uniform, fashionable and deadly, blood spatters on their lapels like accessories.

"Do we need to sanitize?" one asked.

"Nah," Bleeder answered. "No one will give a shit. The cops will pin it on the gangs. Three-Folds or the Wigglers or somebody. They won't dig too deep. Life's too short, you know?"

He looked at Annami again and winked.

She scanned the room herself, looking for anything that might help her, buy her another two minutes. The room had flash booths, of course, and she explored the idea of transferring into another vessel on the far side of the planet. It wouldn't work. Even if she could somehow manage to free herself, get to a booth, and run a flash before Bleeder or one of his goons stopped her— impossible—that route would mean she would have to leave her existing body behind forever. That was absolutely, utterly unacceptable. Never again.

Annami reached backward, stretching as far as she could

with inverted arms and pinioned wrists. Not far, it turned out; the human body wasn't built for that sort of maneuver. She had about twenty square inches of floor space available to her, and she explored it all, deep pain of inadvisable contortions of tendon and bone rising between her shoulders. Her fingers failed to encounter anything useful—no knife, piece of broken glass, or ragged chunk of metal. No surprise there. Annami was not a lucky person. If she knew anything about herself, it was that.

An odor was rising in the room, stinging and rich—blood and shit and death, getting so thick she could almost see it. A maroon smell, shot through with veins of brown and deep scarlet.

Annami's eyes lit on something, and her breath caught, not because of the increasing stench but because in that moment she realized that all her chances of escape, of survival, of seeing her plan through to completion, of setting things right, of revenge . . .

. . . depended on a rat in a cage.

The wire mesh enclosure sat against the wall, next to the little locker that had kept Annami's mini and other personal items safe while she was off with Soro. The cage was mostly in shadow, and for a long, tense moment, Annami couldn't tell whether the small shape inside was alive or dead.

If Bleeder's men had interpreted their orders to kill everyone in the brothel liberally enough to include a caged rat, then Annami was out of ideas, and out of hope. She'd be taken to Stephen Hauser for some sort of denouement that would satisfy his ideas of justice, and then she'd probably be executed. All her struggle, horror, study, all the years, her family . . . all gone, meaningless.

The rat twitched in its cage. Just a tiny movement, but she saw it. A little shifting glint of light from its eyes. She could be imagining it, but she thought Olsen's son was staring right at her.

That was good. If Lars remembered her, it could mean that enough humanity still resided in his tiny rat brain that he would also remember that she was the only possible route to him regaining his prime.

So many impossible things needed to happen for this to work. She needed to get Olsen's son out of the cage, and then the rat-who-once-was-a-man needed to understand the stakes, see that there was only one way forward for either of them, and then . . .

Too many. Annami decided to focus on the one impossible thing over which she might have some influence. The cage. More specifically, its door, and how it might be opened.

Bleeder reached down and put his hand into her armpit, lugging her upward to a standing position without effort. Annami, despite herself, felt a moment of surreal pleasure at the quick elevation. Like the first drop on a roller coaster.

"Upsy-daisy," Bleeder said. "Time for a ride."

"Where?" Annami asked.

"To see an old friend," he answered. "Obviously."

"Is this about the network outage?" she said, desperately seeking another two minutes, buying herself time to stay in the room with the cage while she thought of a way to get it open. "You don't think I started that, do you? I didn't. I <u>fixed</u> it. Hauser should be giving me a promotion."

"Or maybe he'll just call it even for all the flash tech you stole from Anyone HQ."

"Is that how you found me?" Annami asked.

"Sure was. Bertrand Milsen came clean. Told us the whole thing."

"It wasn't his fault," Annami said, a cascade of guilt washing through her. "I put him in a bad position. You didn't . . . uh . . ."

Her eyes flicked over to Soro's corpse, not sure how she would deal with another life on her conscience.

"Come on," Bleeder said. "We're not savages. This is a special case. Extraordinary measures authorized, you know?

"Bertrand just got fired, for cause. No severance . . . but nothing severed, either."

He smiled at her, as if expecting a compliment on his wit.

Annami did not give him one.

She inclined her head toward the cage, across the room.

"Hey," she said. "Over there."

Bleeder glanced where she was indicating.

"Yeah? What?"

"You see that cage? That's my pet rat. His name's Lars."

Bleeder raised an eyebrow.

"You have a pet rat? Disgusting."

"Hard-core," Annami said.

"No, disgusting," Bleeder repeated. "So you have a rat. So what?"

"Can you let him out?"

"Why would I do that?"

"Because you're going to take me, and who knows how long it'll be before someone finds this place. He needs food, water. I just . . . whatever happens to me, whatever I did, it's not my rat's fault, right?"

Bleeder exchanged an incredulous glance with his nearest lieutenant, then turned back to Annami.

"Are you serious? This is what you ask for? Your last request?"

"My . . . last request?" Annami said.

Bleeder made a display of thinking, putting a finger to his temple and looking up and off to one side.

"Well, maybe you'll squeeze in one or two more, but you don't have many. You sure you want to burn up some of my goodwill on this? Maybe you'll want some water for yourself down the road, or some pills, or maybe you'll just ask me to stop . . ."

He leaned closer, smiling.

". . . please stop."

Bleeder walked over to the cage and looked down into it. Olsen's son looked up at him, very still. Bleeder drew back his foot and kicked the cage, sending it caroming off the wall, the creature inside somersaulting, scrabbling madly for purchase, squeaking in alarm.

The cage landed on its side, and the rat squeezed itself into a corner, its little body heaving and pulsing from the stress.

If Olsen's son had any sanity left, Annami thought, *it's gone now.*

"Come on," she said. "No need for that."

Bleeder shook his head.

"You are standing in a room full of corpses, and you're trying to play on my sympathies? For vermin?"

He kicked the cage again, sending the rat scrambling.

"You're stupid, Annami," he said. "You were stupid to think you could stay hidden, you were stupid to take a gig at Anyone, and now you're stupid to think I'll give a shit about your stupid pet rat."

Bleeder reached into his coat and pulled out a slim, iridescent rod, something Annami's mind was having trouble identifying until a long, thin blade with curves along its edge snapped up from inside the thing. It was a knife, a switchblade, a cruel thing, looking like it had been designed to hurt before it killed. So long, too—almost more short sword than knife.

Bleeder bent and jabbed the blade into the cage. Lars dodged and bared his teeth, hissing. Another few jabs, none of which merited the result Bleeder was looking for. Lars had apparently settled into his rat self pretty well, and could move with all the agility of the ordinary variety.

"Damn thing," Bleeder said.

"Hey, boss," one of the other men said, tall, dark-skinned, and shiny-bald. "We've been here for a while. We've got a guard outside, and the door's locked, but do we really want to push our luck?"

Bleeder paused, his blade dangling over the cage, the rat glaring balefully up at him. He straightened.

"No," he said. "Probably not."

He looked back toward Annami, closing his switchblade and slipping it back into his pocket.

"I don't know why you want to let this thing out," he said. "You said it's hungry, right? Look around, lady."

He gestured to either side, taking in the room.

"Thirty seconds after we leave, it'll be snout-deep in your dead boyfriend."

Bleeder reached out a foot, clad in a shiny black wingtip, and nudged Soro's body, causing a horrifying loll, a closing and re-opening of the red void that was once a throat.

"In fact . . . ," he said.

The man bent again, wrapping his fingers around the wire of Lars' cage. He dragged it through the pool of blood around Soro's body, snugging it right up against the corpse. He then unlatched the cage door and swung it open.

"There you go, little guy," he said. "Yum yum."

Lars leaped out of the cage, scurried across Soro's chest, and shot toward the back of the brothel, the Eaters hurriedly moving out of its way.

"Aw," Bleeder said. "He'll be back, though. My guess . . . he went to go get some friends. They're gonna have themselves a feast."

Bleeder snapped a finger.

"Call up, have them bring the van around," he said. "It's time to go."

He took Annami by the elbow and pulled her toward him.

"Just one last thing," he said.

Bleeder reached inside his coat pocket and pulled out a pistol-shaped device. The barrel ended in a small half sphere a few inches across. A little screen projected above the grip, and a series of dials ran along the barrel. Annami recognized it—a borderline demonic piece of technology, outlawed except for in certain heavily proscribed medical uses. Their manufacture was banned, but existing devices were allowed to continue to exist under lock and key, all registered in various state and federal databases and requiring high-level authorization to use.

Evidently, Bleeder had secured the necessary permits.

"No. Don't do it," she said. "Don't you do it."

"After what you've put us through? I don't think we have a choice."

He set the cup on the end of the barrel against Annami's eye. It fit perfectly into the socket. Annami screwed her eyelid shut, not that it would make a difference. She knew how the thing worked.

The device was a portable flash-pattern scanner. It could record a person's consciousness signature, their utterly unique configuration of data processing and selective attention that made sense of the world. Their mindprint. Once you had someone's pattern, you could use it to flash into them any time you wanted through their I-fi, if they had one. (And these days, more or less everyone did.) Even if someone didn't have the implant, every time they used the light flash in any way, they were wide open. If you had their flash pattern, you could just . . . take them.

Patterns were guarded even more closely than financial information, social security numbers, medical records . . . they were you, in a completely true sense. Lose your flash pattern, and you've lost yourself.

Annami jerked back, fighting against this new violation but also fighting for time, trying to buy as many minutes for Lars as she could. Assuming he still <u>was</u> Lars.

She wrenched herself free of Bleeder's grip, looking for something she might use or do to escape, seeing the utterly unconcerned faces of the Eaters who stood blocking every exit. She didn't care. This was a fight she would lose, but it was worth the fight. It was a fight for herself.

She ran directly at one of the Eaters, hoping to knock him over, run through and past him and out to the street, where maybe she could think of her next move.

The man set himself, she hit him, he barely moved, his arms wrapped around her, and that was the end. She struggled, trying to smash him with her skull, kicking . . . nothing. This was a man experienced in subduing struggling women.

Bleeder took a leisurely, languid step over Soro's body, stopping right in front of Annami. He punched her once in the face, right between her eyes. White light bloomed in her skull, and pain, and she was barely aware of it when he reached up with the pattern scanner, set it into her eye socket, and pulled the trigger.

Annami lost herself, her soul scanned and copied into the memory unit in the thing's grip.

"Thank you," he said, pulling the pattern scanner back and slipping it into his pocket.

"Let her go, Zahn," Bleeder said. "I'll take her."

The Eater released her, and Annami sagged into Bleeder's arms.

"Come on," he said, propping her up. "If you want one of my guys to choke you out, put you under, I can do that—but you'd regret it later. Wouldn't it be easier just to walk?"

Annami decided he was right and pulled together the strength she had left. She stood straight and let Bleeder guide her toward the exit, and Hauser, and death.

"It wasn't supposed to be this way," she said, her voice dazed. "From the start. It should have gone another way, and it would have been better if it did."

"Better for who?" Bleeder said. "I'm perfectly happy with how this worked out."

They moved through the corridor outside the brothel, up a set of stairs where another of Bleeder's men stood waiting, along with a black panel van backed up in the alley with its rear doors open. Annami could see that it was filled with gear—weapons, tactical armor, computer systems, even a small flash rig. There was a time when she would have immediately begun to assess all of it, seeking something in the van that might help her free herself.

That time was not now. Annami was tired, so indescribably tired. She thought of all the years she'd struggled toward the moment she had just let slip through her fingers. It seemed impossible. How could she work so hard for something, make so many sacrifices, so many correct decisions, and then have it all vanish when she was one last step from the end?

She thought about everything she'd endured—the debasements of the darkshare just the latest example.

She thought about the people dead because of her—not just Soro and the brothel workers but others, in years past.

She thought about everyone she'd imagined was depending on her, everyone she would avenge or vindicate once she had succeeded. People long gone, people she had loved, who had loved her.

She'd thought she could fix the world.

There was no fixing it. The world was always hell, and she deserved every minute of her time in it.

You are you, she thought. It sounded hollow.

When the end came, whether it was Hauser, Bleeder, or someone else . . . she thought she'd meet it with one emotion above all else: relief.

One of the Eaters guided Annami to a bench in the back of the van. While a second besuited goon held a small pistol on her, the first connected her plasticuffs to a steel ring in the wall of the cargo compartment.

"That comfortable? You can still feel your fingers?" he said.

"It doesn't matter," she answered, leaning back and closing her eyes.

Annami decided to think about Soro. The time with him was fresh in her mind, and as long as she didn't focus on how it ended, it had its nice moments. She thought about his smile. No one smiled like he did.

Annami heard the rear doors of the van close, and then two thumps to her right, as of a fist pounding on the divider between the van's driver and passenger sections.

"Let's go," Bleeder said. "We have a delivery to make."

CHAPTER 23

ACROSS THE ROAD FROM THE WHITE FARM

"GABBY, WHAT'S GOING ON?" PAUL SAID, HIS VOICE COLORED MOSTLY by disbelief, with a slight sheen of outrage. "Is that . . . Jon Corran?"

It was. The man from Hendricks Capital was on Gabby's front porch, flipping through the notebook she had used to jot down her thoughts about the flash. She tried to remember everything she'd written, praying she hadn't directly connected the flash to the Alzheimer's research Hendricks Capital had funded. If she had, it would be highly technical—digressions about brain structure utterly incomprehensible to a layman. Corran wasn't a novice, exactly, but he wasn't a neuroscientist, either.

Maybe this would be okay. Yes, Hendricks Capital workmen were moving her equipment out of her barn, piece by piece, and packing it into the big panel truck they'd bought, but technically they owned all of it anyway. And as far as the fact that Corran had been <u>inside their house</u>, well, maybe she'd left the front door open when she went for a run with the Kitten, and he just stepped in for a second to see if she was home. And maybe she'd left the notebook on the porch, and he'd just picked it up.

Maybe. A lot of maybes.

She reminded herself that Corran didn't know about the flash, couldn't know about it, and even if he did understand some of what was in that notebook, it wasn't automatically the end of the world.

"Let's just go talk to him," Gabby said. "He's probably just picking up his equipment. Most of it belongs to Hendricks Capital, really."

"The man invaded our farm, babe," Paul said, shifting Kat to his other hip. "Literally. Those men? Those trucks? That's an army. And you know they had to cut the lock off the big door on the barn to get it open. We should call the police."

Jon finally noticed them standing across the road, staring like gawkers at a car wreck. He lifted his hand in a noncommittal wave, then pulled a cell phone from his pocket and used it briefly before turning his attention back to the notebook.

Gabby crossed to the house, little stones sharp under her bare feet, squaring her shoulders and standing straight, like a prizefighter on her way to the ring. Paul was at her side, the Kitten fussing a little in his arms, sensing the tension in the air. As they neared the front porch, the rear door on the dark sedan in the driveway opened and someone got out, a person Gabby had met only once before, for two minutes, at the closing of her deal with Hendricks Capital. The man himself.

Gray Hendricks.

He took a moment to straighten his suit coat and shoot his cuffs, and then he walked up to the house. He passed Gabby and Paul and the baby, not acknowledging them in any way, and stepped up onto the porch.

He nodded once at Corran, who nodded back and handed him the spiral notebook. Hendricks glanced at it, and then, finally, he turned to look at Gabby. He put his free hand on the front door of her house, laying his palm flat against it.

"This house is mine," Hendricks said.

"Get the hell out of here or I'm calling the cops," Paul said, getting angry, acting tough, even though he knew exactly who Gray Hendricks was, why he was here, and how little Paul White could actually do to address the situation.

"Everything inside this house is mine," Hendricks went on, as if he hadn't heard.

He pointed to their car sitting in the driveway, pathetic and worn down next to the scarab shine of the SUVs.

"That beater, shitty and foreign though it may be," he said. "Mine."

He turned to Paul.

"Couldn't even buy Detroit iron? This is <u>Michigan</u>, son."

"Doesn't matter. It's not your car," Paul said. "I've asked you once to leave. That's all you get."

Paul handed Gabby the Kitten, then pulled his phone from his pocket, making a show of it.

"See? Police," he said.

Hendricks held up Gabrielle's notes, giving her a hard stare.

"I sure as hell own all of <u>this</u>. Legally, under contract, indisputably. You tried to steal it from me."

In Gabby's arms, Kat squirmed, trying to get a better look at these new people Mommy and Daddy were talking to.

"So. Your husband can call the cops, and it'll all get complicated, or we can chat for a little while and see if there's a way that this"—he held up the notebook—"might let you keep this."

He thumped one large fist against her house.

"That has nothing to do with you," Gabby said, gesturing at the notebook. "Those are ideas for what I want to do next. My next research project."

"You invented a way to put people's minds in other people's bodies, Dr. White, and you did it with my money. Stop pretending this isn't happening. It's happening."

Gray turned away and stepped into her house, tucking the notebook up under his arm as he went.

Gabby gave Paul a helpless look, even glanced at Corran for support. None was on offer.

They all went inside. Gabby changed out of her wet clothes, Paul went upstairs to put Kat down, and then, at her own kitchen table, she sat down with Gray Hendricks.

"This is how it will go," he said. "You will give up all ownership of this tech you created. That percentage you had under our original deal? Gone. It all goes to me. In exchange, I'll sign a release saying I'll never sue you or have the police pursue criminal charges against you."

Bitter, bitter words.

"But I still want you involved," Hendricks went on. "You'll run the development team for the flash, working out of a lab I'll set up for you. You can have whatever equipment you need. I'll let you have input over hiring, procedures, experiments, all of that, within reason. You'll get a salary—a good one, mid–six figures, with progress bonuses. That's it."

Gabby could still develop the flash, help bring it to the world. It just wouldn't be hers.

Hendricks sent a quick text, and his attorney appeared as if from a genie's bottle, producing a set of documents from his briefcase, ready for Gabby's signature. She knew, although no one was coming right out and saying it, that if she did not sign, lawsuits, financial ruin, and as many civil and criminal penalties as Hendricks and his team could think up would rain down upon her. Maybe even prison.

Certainly, if she refused the new deal, Hendricks' statements from the porch would be true. He would in fact own their house, their car, everything.

Gabby sat there, pen in hand, in the room where she cooked dinner, began every day with her daughter. She stared down at the contract and tried to summon to her mind the one image that might offset this utter disaster: the Kitten eating blueberries and grinning like a loon. She couldn't manage it. All she could see was the dotted line.

She wondered, for a moment, how Hendricks had found out. Did he have her under surveillance? Had Corran been more suspicious when he left their farm that night than he'd let on? Did it matter? No. Probably not.

Gabby signed.

The flash, and the future, belonged to Gray Hendricks.

Things happened quickly after that. Hendricks' people took her phone, and Paul's phone, and they were given a heavily supervised forty-five minutes to pack. Realization dawned that Gabby's employment with Hendricks Capital's research arm would be commencing immediately, and that said employment would require mandatory residence in company housing not just for Gabrielle White but also for her husband and daughter. Paul wouldn't speak to her as they were packing, except to confirm that the stuffed animals he'd selected were in fact the ones Kat couldn't live without.

The three of them were bundled into one of the SUVs, with blacked-out windows and a divider between the driver and passenger sections, essentially a high-end paddy wagon.

And then they left.

CHAPTER 24

NeOnet GLOBAL NORTH AMERICAN HUB, FIFTY-SIXTH FLOOR, MANHATTAN

"The usual, Mr. Hauser?" Marcel asked.

Stephen walked across his office, tapping a control on the face of the mini he wore around his wrist like a bracelet. A panel slid open in the wall, revealing an alcove containing a purpose-built flash couch. It could be configured in any number of ways—for dentist's appointments, physicals, anything his body might need that didn't require his mind.

Such as, in this case, a haircut.

"Absolutely, Marcel," Stephen said, settling himself on the couch, feeling it mold perfectly to his contours—which made sense, as every specification had been precisely designed to fit his own measurements. He tapped a control on one of the arms, and the couch reclined slightly as supports for his neck and head emerged from its upper portion. They would hold it steady while Marcel worked—because, of course, Stephen's prime would be unconscious. He couldn't waste part of his day sitting in a barber's chair. Fortunately, he didn't have to.

"See you in an hour," he said.

"Of course, sir," Marcel said, stepping up to the chair and re-moving a pair of scissors from his little bag of styling equipment.

Stephen lifted his wrist mini and tapped another/

He blinked. Beta was in the usual spot where he waited for Ste-phen to flash into him, a comfortable armchair set directly in front of one of the big picture windows in his apartment, with a view looking out onto Lake St. Clair. Stephen had sent Beta no-tice earlier in the day that he was planning to use the vessel for an hour or so—not truly necessary, since the man was hired to be available for Stephen's use at any moment, twenty-four hours a day. Nevertheless, there was a certain courtesy to giving that no-tice, and even a convenience to it. Beta would be rested, fed (un-less Stephen was planning to use him for a meal), clean, dressed in an outfit to Stephen's taste, in a good location, not embroiled in any awkwardly personal human moment, and so on.

Stephen liked Beta. He kept Gamma, Delta, and Epsilon on twenty-four-hour call as well, but he mostly used the other vessels for situations when he needed to stay awake for extended periods of time. You could postpone sleep indefinitely by continuing to transfer into fresh vessels every eight hours or so. He had stayed awake for nearly three weeks once in the late 2020s, during the government hearings about potential misuse of the flash. It had come to nothing, of course. There was no issue with the flash—not as long as he controlled it.

He rested for a moment, looking out at the gray-blue surface of Lake St. Clair, whitecaps skating across it here and there.

What will I say to her? he thought.

In some little time, Bleeder would bring him . . . Annami. Yes. That was the name she was using. Such a relief. Stephen had thought she was dead—and if so, a tragedy. Their club was tiny. Bleeder—but you couldn't really talk to Bleeder. And George, of course—they would always be close, but their lives had diverged. It wasn't like it used to be.

There would be no good old days with Annami, either. But even if she hated him, even if she wanted him dead, he'd be glad to see her. They had history. In a way, she understood him better than anyone else.

Hence the haircut. He wanted to look his best.

Stephen briefly considered another quick flash, over to Sigma. He was feeling celebratory, and Sigma's entire highly paid purpose was as a vessel of celebration—his apartment, in Phoenix, was well stocked with cocaine, opiates, designer stimulants, incredible Scotch . . . whatever Stephen might want to indulge in for an hour or three. No. There was work to do.

Stephen glanced at his watch, a lovely Omega gold-on-steel Seamaster that Beta knew he preferred. About fifty-five minutes until he was due to flash back from Detroit to New York—enough time to transact a bit of overdue business.

He stood, walking across Beta's apartment, bought and paid for by Anyone as a valid business expense. A tax deduction, in fact. Most of the rooms were Beta's to use as he chose, barring one with a door kept locked at all times. Hauser had the key code, and he let himself in to the large, well-appointed office, a rough copy of the one six hundred miles east and fifty-six floors up, where his prime was currently getting his biweekly trim.

Thinscreens floated above the desk, waiting for his attention. Stephen accessed the flash network and scanned for Abd al-Hakim, easily trackable—all the Centuries were. The Solar Sheik was in Monaco. He placed the call.

A young woman answered, slim, blond, and lovely, her face mildly surprised. The background looked like some sort of club— expensively dressed people with drinks in hand, music throbbing, and holo-displays flitting through the air.

"Yes?" al-Hakim said. "Who is this?"

The woman's face changed, becoming pleased, pliable, as al-Hakim recognized Beta, and by extension the person riding him.

"Oh, Stephen," the sheik said. "I'm sorry—it took me a moment to recognize you. I haven't seen that vessel in a bit."

His words were charming, but Stephen could sense the tension behind them—al-Hakim wasn't used to hiding his feelings in this vessel, and young people felt emotions more strongly in any case.

"How can I help you?"

"I was hoping we could talk about the outages the flash network experienced recently."

Al-Hakim nodded, a noncommittal and culturally specific gesture of acknowledgment that looked delightfully out of place on the Nordic frame the man was currently occupying.

"Certainly," the sheik said. "I'm pleased you were able to get all of that under control."

"Me too," Stephen said. "My analysts tell me it was all related to power fluctuations. The Lagos node got a spike in traffic, couldn't draw enough juice to handle it. When it went down, we had a little cascade through some of the other nodes. It's all fine now, but I'd like to make sure it doesn't happen again."

"Of course. You know my grid is at your disposal."

"I do know that. I chose your company back in the early days to handle Anyone's power needs because I wanted you to have the capital you needed to expand and help ensure the world turned to renewable energy. All part of the bigger picture."

"Certainly, and I am grateful to you for that to this very day."

"Then why did you strangle my fucking network?"

A long, slow blink from the other side of the screen.

"I did not, Stephen."

"You did. You reallocated power that was supposed to go to

the African flash nodes and sent it to other parts of your grid. I can send you copies of your company's internal authorizations, if you want to see them."

The fight went out of the sheik.

"You must understand, the problem came from when the Lagos node had its unexpected increase in users," al-Hakim said. "Under ordinary circumstances, everything would have been fine."

"What is your number-one priority, Abd?"

"My god."

"You're looking at him," Hauser said. "Here. I'll prove it."

He tapped a few controls on the thinscreen.

"You are no longer a Century."

Horror broke across al-Hakim's face.

"No. Why would you do this?"

"Because Centuries aren't subject to the Two Rules. They're subject to one."

He held up a finger, then pointed at himself.

"Mine. The Rule of Me. You broke that rule, so now you're just like everyone else."

"Please, Stephen—I was just trying to help my customer base. The flash is not the only system powered by my grid. I provide energy to cities all over the world, whole nations. The demand is growing, and I have not been able to keep up. I plan to launch orbital solar platforms soon, but until then, I reallocated a bit of power from the flash to customers in other regions. Hospitals, homes, farms . . . surely you understand."

Stephen did understand. The fundamental problem with humanity: everyone had opinions. The more powerful you were, the more you believed that your opinion was not an opinion at all but fact. That was why war happened. That was why global warming happened. That was why every other horrible thing in earth's history happened.

Too many goddamn <u>opinions</u>.

He had recognized the problem early on, when rolling out the flash. He had immediately bumped up against legislators who wanted to regulate his tech, businesspeople who offered terrible terms, religious leaders who called it blasphemous. So many points of view getting in the way.

The Centuries had fixed that. Stephen Hauser could give the most powerful people on the planet something they could get nowhere else, something they desperately wanted—life. He had chosen the leaders, the captains of industry, the entertainers, people who made the world go round, and offered them eternity. All they had to give up in exchange . . . one small thing. Those opinions.

They had to do what they were told.

And it <u>worked</u>. The trick to saving the world, it turned out, was just doing it. Refusing to let anyone stop you.

"Let me be clear," Stephen said. "What I have built is more important than what you have built."

"But the people," al-Hakim replied. "Without the flash, civilization can still exist, but without electricity—"

"Oh, don't pretend this is about <u>people</u>. What people? They'll always make more. This was about <u>power</u>, and you trying to pretend you have some."

The sheik's jaw tightened at that, which Hauser enjoyed. Abd al-Hakim spent almost every moment of his life as the most important person within a thousand miles. Being reminded there were people above him in the hierarchy couldn't be easy. Too bad.

"I swear on my life, there was no great conspiracy," the sheik said, drawing himself up. "Your network going down was an accident, an accumulation of unlucky circumstances. But now that it is out in the open, yes, I would like you to consider reducing flash traffic, at least until I can bring more power capacity online."

"Yeah, you should have asked for that before you betrayed me."

"*Betrayed*? Such a strong word. This was all just a misunderstanding. Please, you know I am loyal. I . . ."

Al-Hakim hesitated, and then all the hard-won dignity collapsed at once, and he was just a desperate woman in a cocktail dress, afraid he'd lost the thing that mattered most.

"What does this mean, that I am no longer a Century?" al-Hakim said, his voice wavering. "Is this body my new prime? My family . . . they would not understand. Please, at least let me transfer back."

Stephen let him twist on the hook for a few moments.

"Here's what I'll do," he said. "Yes, you can flash back into your prime, but the Two Rules stay. You'll be just like everyone else. You have the rest of your natural life to prove to me that you deserve to be a Century again. If you do, I'll lift the safeguards, and you can move on to a new prime."

Stephen thought this was a fine solution. What better guarantee of loyalty than the sheik knowing immortality was within his grasp, if he just toed the line for a few decades?

"I will," Abd al-Hakim said, his voice almost grateful. "You will see. Whatever you need, I will—"

"Prove it," Stephen said. "Choose one of those countries you sent my power to and make them go dark for a month."

The sheik's perfectly sculpted pale eyebrows lifted.

"But that would . . . a blackout like that . . . it would destroy their economy. How would they . . . there would be riots. People would die. And the reputation of my business, it would never recover."

"Never, Abd? We live forever. Folks will come around eventually. Choose."

"I . . . ," al-Hakim said. "Fiji. They are tropical. At least no one will freeze."

"Good choice," Stephen said. "I'll be watching the feeds."

He ended the call.

He glanced at his watch again. An hour, almost to the second. He tapped his mini and/

The stylist was done, already waiting with a mirror, which he held up the moment Stephen returned to his prime and opened his eyes. Yes. He looked good. Ready for whatever the meeting with Annami would bring.

"Wonderful work as always, Marcel," Stephen said. "Thank you very much."

CHAPTER 25

A LABORATORY, DETROIT

GABBY TOOK A LENGTH OF COPPER WIRE, ABOUT EIGHTEEN INCHES, and slowly threaded it through the weave she'd already created. Over, under, over, under, in a slow circle, integrating the piece into the overall structure. She finished, then set the thing down and examined it critically.

Did it look like it should? Like a basket? Sort of. It wasn't done quite yet, but it was getting there. Definitely a basketlike object, which was good. No one would think it was anything else.

Gabby figured she was somewhere in Detroit, or maybe just outside, in one of the towns to the west of the city. She thought downtown, though. That was Hendricks' territory, where he had his headquarters. He wouldn't keep her too far away. He'd made it very clear how valuable she was to him. He visited fairly often, stopping by every few days to check on progress.

Progress on the flash, not the basket—although Gabby had made a case to her captors that the weaving was important to her process, an aid to concentration. She told Hendricks' people that crafting was her hobby, something she'd been doing for years. For proof, she sent them to her little online stores where she sold the things she made. She claimed that keeping her hands busy would let her mind roam free to unlock the secrets of the flash for Gray Hendricks, and she wasn't asking for much—a spool of wire and a pair of clippers, too small and stubby to damage anything beyond her fingernails.

Her arguments worked. Wire and clippers were brought to the workroom, which she was locked into every morning and released from every evening—a substantial increase to her meager tool kit.

To research the most fundamental technological advance in a century, Hendricks' people had given her personal, hands-on access to: a non-networked laptop stripped of all but the most basic software tools she had used in her Alzheimer's work, a printer, pencils and paper, a few reference books. A sliding drawer built into the wall dividing her space from the rest of the lab allowed for other items to be provided—her lunch, for instance.

That was not to say Hendricks had been cheap. He'd lived up to his promises. Her workroom had a large window looking out onto a fully equipped neurophysiology laboratory, with everything a researcher in her position could ever want. A functional magnetic resonance imaging system, able to monitor brain activity in real time at the synapse level. Microfluid neural culture rigs. A helium-cooled magnetoencephalogram. A Hitachi ETG-4100 optical topography setup, which was, like, twenty grand, easy, and nothing Gabby would actually ever use in her research. She just wanted to make Hendricks buy her one. All of that and much more, a brain science nerd's wonderland.

She could see it, but they wouldn't let her touch it.

Gabby had to relay her instructions through an intercom, to Dr. Camila Chavez, her primary lab assistant, a smart, personable young woman with a PhD in neuroscience from Duke, a wonderful corona of short curly hair, and an endlessly outgoing attitude.

All Gabby could lay hands on, really, was the spool of copper wire, and so she had, working hard over the past few weeks on her little craft project.

Basket weaving was engaging, a problem of math and geometry as much as art, especially because she'd had to figure out how to create what she wanted from scratch, had never worked in wire, and was not actually weaving a basket.

Still, many false starts later, something that looked relatively basketlike rested on the worktable in front of her: about eighteen inches across and eighteen deep, spherical with a circular ten-inch opening at one pole, woven from a thin, tight mesh of untarnished copper wire. She liked it. It would work. She hoped.

Gabby looked up and through the glass partition separating her from the rest of the lab to see the two latest test subjects being escorted from the room by the medical team, headed for the small clinic down the hall. Everyone who used the flash, whether traveler or vessel, went through a standardized examination immediately after returning to their original consciousness. This was done to help the project establish baselines, to better understand what swapping minds did to the body.

So far, it didn't look like much happened at all, before or after a flash. Alterations in heart rate, hormone levels, and blood pressure, all of which could be chalked up to pre- or post-procedure stress. Knowing you were about to be in someone else's body—it tended to get the heart racing.

The lab's main working area emptied out as the medics and their patients left, leaving just Dr. Chavez and Eddie Brill, Gabby's personal, Hendricks-assigned security guard. Her jailer.

Gabby checked the time on her laptop, marking it in her mind.

For the next thirty minutes, while the last round of test subjects were examined in the clinic, it would just be her, Camila, and Brill in the lab. That was her window. Thirty minutes and counting.

Gabby didn't know the facility's exact location, but she knew how long she'd been there—she'd kept count, with little hash marks scratched into the laptop's case. Thirty-three marks, thirty-three days since Gray Hendricks and his thugs had invaded her home, taken the flash, taken her life. It was November, out in the world. The leaves had probably turned and fallen by now.

It was time to go.

Gabby pressed a button on the intercom built into her desk.

"Camila, we've got a little while before those last test results get integrated into the database. What do you think? Can I take a peek?"

Dr. Chavez turned to look at Eddie Brill, sitting on a chair in the corner of the room. He was engrossed in his phone. Not an exceptional guard, Mr. Brill, although he'd been better at first, paid closer attention. Gabby hadn't yet concocted an escape plan when she'd first come to Hendricks' lab, but she knew that her odds of pulling one off would be higher if both Camila and Brill—and everyone else she might encounter here—thought she was the last person who would ever try to escape.

So she was friends with Dr. Chavez, friends with Eddie, friends with everyone, and was about to find out if all the forced smiles and small talk would make a difference.

"Sure," Camila said.

The other woman pulled her iPhone from her pocket and thumbed it on, opening an app. She pulled open the drawer that allowed small objects to pass between the main lab and Gabby's . . . well, her cell. There wasn't really another word for it, although her ostensible coworkers took great care not to refer to it that way. It was her "workspace," or her "room."

But it was a cell.

The drawer slid back to her side of the partition. Resting in it, Camila's phone in its cute pink case, a video displayed on its screen—a webcam feed from the daycare facility a few floors up.

In that feed, her daughter, busy stacking blocks under the watchful eye of Brenda, the person who had raised her for the past month instead of her own mother and father. Kat was smiling, happy, and Gabrielle's heart fell through her body, down to the floor, down to the center of the earth.

The feed had a time stamp.

Gabby had twenty-seven minutes left.

Paul's in the apartment, she thought. He was always there, barring visits to the on-site gym. Hendricks had given them a comfortable two-bedroom suite elsewhere in the complex. No windows, but still, nice. Gabby thought the second bedroom in the little apartment was both promise and threat. Do what you're told, and maybe your daughter will be in that room with you someday. Or maybe you try something stupid, and that bedroom stays empty forever.

She and Paul had talked, of course, in whispered conversations in the bathroom with the shower running to foil the surveillance they assumed was in place. Either they talked to each other or they talked to no one, and while he was clearly still furious with her for getting them into this situation, they were all they had. It had its ups and downs.

At first they'd talked about trying to get a phone, call the police. They'd been kidnapped, after all. But then Paul had asked about the contract she'd signed, and Gabby realized that maybe she'd given Hendricks the right to do all of this, somehow. Maybe they hadn't been kidnapped. Maybe they'd been . . . indentured, or something. Maybe the police wouldn't do a damn thing, and calling them would just make Hendricks angry, and they'd lose the few privileges they had.

The thing they kept circling back to was how unreal it all seemed. They'd been disappeared, made subject to extraordinary rendition like terrorists. How could that be? Paul was a nearly tenured professor at the University of Michigan. She had friends, professional contacts. They both had extended families. If nothing else, they had bills to pay. The mortgage people didn't screw around—late by one day on a payment, and the bank called at 12:01 A.M. yelling for their money. Student-loan people were worse.

How the hell was Hendricks pulling this off? For all she knew, he wasn't, and a massive, multistate manhunt was underway for the three of them.

But most likely not. Gray Hendricks was incredibly rich. He owned half of Detroit. What he wanted to happen, happened.

Would that include killing them, eventually? She didn't know. But she couldn't say for sure that he wouldn't, and that was enough.

They had to escape, although Gabby couldn't see at first how to do it. It wouldn't be quick or easy. Escape would require time, and understanding, and planning.

So while she was trying to devise their very own *Shawshank Redemption*, Gabby threw herself into studying the flash, taking advantage of the opportunity Hendricks had given her to learn everything she could. If she had to be a prisoner, at least she could use the time on her hands to try to understand what she'd made.

And understand she had. Any doubts she'd once had about whether she was the true mother of the flash were long gone.

Hendricks had given her human volunteers, people willing to undergo flash transfers in a laboratory setting. At least, Gabby assumed they were volunteers. For all she knew, the people Hendricks provided were just as unwilling as she was. In any case, the data coming out of the experiments was extensive and invaluable.

Already, after only a month of research, she thought it would eventually be possible to narrow the flash field, target it, send it out as a beam, as opposed to an area of effect. The flash could even, perhaps, be targeted to locate a specific brain or consciousness waveform, or run through a network, probably fiber-optic, since it already carried its signals via light.

That level of refinement was in the far future, but other ideas kept coming, the research area so new that nearly every experiment proved something substantial. Gabrielle knew that would change, that in time advances in the field would become a game of millimeters, as occurred in every mature area of science and technology. But for the moment, everything she and Camila did filled in massive gaps in understanding, and all of it—their notes, conclusions, experimental results—were logged to a non-network server right out there on the other side of the glass partition. Hendricks was taking no chances storing anything in the cloud.

Gabby knew about the server from Dr. Chavez. Camila was very friendly. Liked to chat about her family—two kids, husband who owned three Subway franchises, with plans to open more. Camila responded to Gabby's questions with a basic lack of suspicion. She just . . . trusted. The woman seemed willfully blind to what the partition between Gabby's part of the lab and her own meant.

In any case, the research side of things was, if Gabby was honest with herself, fantastic. She loved it. She couldn't remember the last time she was so engaged by her work, which generated an absolutely brutal disconnect with the black hole her soul slipped into every time she remembered, oh, that she hadn't touched her daughter in two days. That her husband hadn't spoken to her in three.

She had destroyed her family's lives out of . . . professional vanity. An unwillingness to accept that she actually signed a goddamned deal. If she'd just gone to Hendricks with the flash in the first place, she'd still have a piece of it, and maybe she could have . . .

But she hadn't, and she'd lost, and her only consolation, the only thing that kept her from letting the black hole have her, was that she thought she could get them all out. She had a plan, and the time had come to see it through.

Twenty-six minutes.

Not taking her eyes off the webcam feed on her phone—the

Kitten giggling as she stacked blocks—Gabby leaned forward and tapped the intercom button again.

"Hey, Camila?"

Dr. Chavez looked up, smiling a bit. Good old Camila. Gabby felt a little bad about her.

"I was thinking," Gabby said. "What if we targeted our scans to the parahippocampal gyrus in the next round of tests? I have a feeling we might be missing something there. Might have something to do with the way the flash seeks out a receptive mind."

Camila's face went thoughtful.

"Huh," she said. "You know, that's . . ." Her voice trailed off as she turned to the laptop at her workstation and began typing, pulling up old tests.

Gabby hated to give that idea away—she was keeping many of her more interesting conclusions and theories to herself, fully expecting there would be a day when she'd be free to develop them on her own, in the outside world. She had to believe that, otherwise the black hole would swallow her soul. But she needed to throw Camila something intriguing enough that she'd forget to ask for her phone back—or at least not in the next twenty-five minutes.

Shielding the device slightly with her arm, maintaining a doting expression on her face as if she was still watching her daughter play, Gabby minimized the webcam app on Camila's phone. She shifted to the app store and searched for the strobe-light program she'd briefly considered when developing her portable flash gear, before abandoning it in favor of the LED flashlight. The app cost $1.99, and this was the moment—well, one of an endless succession of moments—where the whole plan could fall apart. If Camila had set her phone to require a passcode to install new apps, or her thumbprint . . . but she hadn't. The strobe began to download.

"This is wild," Camila said, her excited voice coming from the speaker built into the partition. "This could be a huge breakthrough."

Gabby looked up, forced herself to smile at Camila.

"I thought maybe," Gabby said. "We can run new tests, but I figured you'd probably be able to get some indicators even from the old ones."

"Oh yeah," Dr. Chavez said, and turned her eyes back to her screen. "Tons."

Twenty-four minutes.

Gabby took ten seconds to wirelessly connect the laptop to Camila's phone—both Apple products, always happy to talk to each other. The app she'd downloaded could be used to do more than just work as a strobe light. It could run custom patterns, and she sent one she'd already designed from her laptop into the phone, willing that neither Brill nor Camila would look in at her and wonder what the hell she was up to.

"There's my good little girl," she said, smiling at the phone, which was acknowledging the new instructions she'd given the app.

Okay, she thought. *On to the hard part.*

The completed wire basket was still sitting on the worktable next to the laptop. Gabby picked it up, inverted it, and slid it down over her head. She smiled, a big silly grin on her face, still looking down at the phone.

Camila looked up from her work, her face going quizzical.

"What are you doing?"

Eddie Brill more intent, standing from his chair, looking at her.

"Yeah. Why the hell'd you give her your phone again, Dr. Chavez? We talked about this."

"Woman wants to see her <u>daughter</u>, Eddie. Put yourself in her shoes."

Gabby held up the phone, the screen facing her.

"I'm just making my Kitty Kat laugh, that's all. Silly mama with a basket on her head, right? Silly mama."

Brill frowned and took a step closer to the partition, lifting his hand with the fingers outstretched in a *Give it here* pose. He was looking right at her. Camila was watching too, a smile on her face.

Gabby crimped the opening of the inverted basket, collapsing it tight around her neck. She triggered the phone's camera, and the flash went off.

Not one single bright burst of light but a staccato, irregular pulse, stuttering out over several seconds and bathing both Camila and Brill.

It would be one or the other—whoever's mind caught the flash first would be the one to travel. Their experiments had proved that early on. So it'd be either Brill or—

Camila dropped like a rock, her head falling forward and hitting her desk with a dull thud Gabby could hear clearly through the partition.

Brill's face went confused, then panicked, as he held up his arms, looking at them, horrified.

"W-what?"

Twenty-two minutes.

Gabby ripped the basket off her head—the homemade, imperfect Faraday cage that was her only bit of insurance that she wouldn't be part of the initial swap between Camila and Brill—and flipped the phone toward herself. She triggered the camera, watched the pattern of lights run/

She was Brill, looking through the workroom window at her own body collapsing to the ground, a stringless puppet. It vanished behind the partition, and she heard it hit the ground, her desk chair rolling out of the way on its casters, shooting across the room to bang against the far wall.

Time to move.

Gabby took a few breaths, trying to acclimate herself to the guard's big, meaty body. So different from Paul's. The gut, the thickness of the arms . . . he was a smoker, too. His lungs didn't seem to fill the same way hers did. Like the air didn't make it all the way to the bottom.

No time. Twenty-one minutes, and still so much to do.

Gabby went to Camila's workstation, gently moving the unconscious woman off her keyboard. She pulled a USB stick from the desk, made a copy of every test result, every note, downloaded it all, then erased everything from the server and the backup drive.

She slipped the memory stick into her pocket, then moved to one of the lab's test areas, where a few wheelchairs sat waiting to house test subjects while their original bodies were unconscious. She rolled one over to the access door to her cell.

The key cards Brill used when escorting her to the lab every morning and back to her apartment every night were clipped to a ring on his belt. Gabby pulled them up, a cord unwinding from a coil on the ring as she did. She swiped cards until she hit the right one, and the door opened.

Her body, lying on the floor, still somehow shocking to see. She realized she hadn't done a swap herself since those first few times with Paul back at the farm. It had fallen in an ungainly position— awkward, folded legs pinned under her torso, like a doll someone had tossed in a corner.

Camila's phone was lying on the floor next to the body, and Gabby sucked in a breath as she realized she'd made a potentially game-ending mistake. She bent down, a maneuver that almost caused her to fall right on her ass due to poor compensation for Brill's various ungainly enormities.

She managed to keep her feet, barely, and snagged the phone. She pressed the home button, and her fear was realized. The device had been left dormant for too long, and it had locked itself. Locked, and the code to open it was in Camila's head, and Camila was . . .

Gabby actually wasn't sure. Buried deep in the body she was currently using, sandwiched somewhere between Brill's original consciousness and her own.

Or maybe a double flash wasn't possible, and Gabby had just killed Dr. Camila Chavez, a kind woman who had, in a limited way, tried to be her friend. She didn't know. No one did—they hadn't gotten that far in the research. Gabby forced herself not to dwell on it. She could fix things later—but now, she needed to get out of the lab.

Gabby dropped the phone. There was no reason to keep it, and even a danger—she knew cell phones could be tracked.

She locked the chair's wheels, then bent again, lifting her unconscious original body beneath the arms and lugging it into the wheelchair. It was easier than she'd expected. Brill was big, but he had some muscle hiding beneath the bulge.

The chair had straps, a handy feature for occupants unable to support themselves for one reason or another. Gabby used them to secure her unconscious body, and wheeled the chair out of the lab, pausing only to utilize Brill's brawn once again to move Dr. Chavez into the cell she had just escaped. She stashed Camila behind a counter, out of sight. Maybe it would buy her a few minutes when other staff returned if they didn't immediately see a comatose neuroscientist right out in the middle of the lab.

A quick, nervous trip through the nondescript corridors of the lab facility, aided by Brill's handy ring of key cards and an elevator ride, and she was at the door of the apartment she shared with Paul. She heard piano music, something complex and quick. Hendricks' people had given Paul a keyboard, although he complained frequently about how it didn't have the full eighty-eight keys and the ones it did have weren't weighted properly.

Gabby pushed open the door, and Paul looked up, the music

stopping abruptly. His eyes focused on the wheelchair, and he shot
to his feet, knocking back the kitchen chair he'd been using as a piano stool.

"What happened to my wife?" he said, stepping forward, his
expression darkening. "What did you do to her?"

Paul had let a beard grow during their captivity. It had come in
as tight curls against his jawline, speckled with a few spots of gray.
It looked very good.

Gabby held out a hand. Paul opened his mouth to speak, his
face still angry, and she quickly moved her index finger to her lips,
willing him to get it, to understand what she'd done without her
needing to explain it to him. The room was almost certainly bugged.

Paul closed his mouth, mostly out of puzzlement, she thought.
Gabby moved her finger so that it was pointing at Brill's chest, then
down toward the top of her body's head, then back at Brill.

Paul got it.

"How?" he mouthed, and she just pointed at her watch, tapping
its face. Brill's watch.

Eleven minutes.

The daycare was the next stop, and a challenge, but Gabby-as-
Brill was able to prevail, talking her way through, convincing the
attendants that he'd been told to bring Kat down to see her parents a
little earlier than usual that day. Easy enough—the daycare workers
had no reason to suspect they were living in a world where anyone
could be anyone.

When all was said and done, they ended up with Gabby-as-
Brill pushing the wheelchair while Paul held the Kitten, keeping her
quiet and calm.

The lobby was a worry—Gabby was sure they'd be stopped—
but it didn't happen. She supposed that the building was huge, and
their little family occupied only a tiny part of it. It was unlikely that
Hendricks had advertised that he was keeping prisoners upstairs, so

no one had any reason to stop them. There wasn't even a security desk.

Three minutes.

The parking lot.

"Now what?" Paul said, his voice surprisingly level.

Gabby fished in Brill's pocket, and there she found the last bit of luck she needed. Car keys, on an electronic fob. She held it up, pressed the unlock button.

A chirp, a few rows deeper into the lot, told them Brill's car was out there waiting.

"Now," Gabby said, in Brill's thick, rough voice, "we go. As far as we can."

CHAPTER 26

THE BACK OF A VAN, LOWER MANHATTAN

ANNAMI WAS THIRSTY, AND A PALLET OF WATER BOTTLES WAS stashed on one of the shelves mounted on the wall separating the van's large passenger compartment from the driver's area. She wanted one, but she was bound, her wrists lashed together, the cuffs set into a locked metal ring above her head, bolted to the wall. She could ask for a drink, but Bleeder had made it pretty goddamn clear back in the brothel she'd used up her last request.

One of the Eaters—the team's chatter had given her his name; he was Perez—followed her gaze. He looked up at the water bottles on the shelf above his head. His mouth twisted.

Perez cast a quick little glance at Bleeder, and Annami looked too. That son of a bitch was busy on the far side of the van, fiddling with the pattern scanner, utterly engrossed in its little screen. Annami knew flash patterns were just number sets denoting neuronic waveforms, raw data, unique to an individual but really just digits in a particular sequence. They didn't mean anything by themselves. Still, what was on that screen was her. Bleeder was looking at her, in the most intimate possible way.

Without speaking, Perez reached up. He snagged one of the

water bottles, quietly releasing it from its plastic pallet prison. He unscrewed the top and held it out to her, a questioning look on his face.

Annami hesitated, then nodded.

Perez held the bottle to her lips and inclined it slightly. A slow flow of water trickled into her mouth, at just the right pace to allow her to swallow. He held the bottle lightly, keeping it steady despite the vibration of the van as it slowly made its way through the alley outside the brothel, bringing Annami to her death.

The water felt wonderful, tasted wonderful, even room temperature and with the scent of a van full of blood-spattered large men in her nostrils adding flavor notes.

At which point her mind could not help but volunteer the idea that Perez was probably good at providing water this way because he'd done it before, to other bound prisoners, enough times that he'd learned the skill. Annami's mouth clenched. How many other people's thirst had he quenched, people who he'd then murdered, whether for Bleeder or Stephen Hauser? Perez, like every Eater, was a killer. Hell, maybe he'd killed Soro, opened him up back in the brothel and watched him die.

Fluid ran down her chin, and Perez took the bottle away.

"More?" he said, his voice low.

Annami shook her head.

Perez replaced the cap on the bottle and set it on the bench beside him.

"Let me know if you change your mind," he said. "And you're welcome, by the way."

Annami didn't answer—but that last bit nagged at her. She owed this man nothing, this Eater, not gratitude, nothing whatsoever, but she also didn't like the idea that he'd scored a point on her. That her lack of manners—manners, while she was tied up in the back of a van surrounded by professional executioners—

somehow set him above her. She could hear her mother saying that very thing, saying that just because their family was poor didn't mean they didn't have to act right. If anything, it meant they had even more of an obligation. *Poor does not mean boor,* her mother said, a thousand times if she'd said it once. Annami hadn't truly understood until she was in middle school and saw *boor* in a book, revising her initial child's understanding of the state her mother wanted her to avoid from large, wild pig to classless jerk.

What a ridiculous thing to feel, under the circumstances— this weird guilt at not thanking her killer for briefly acting like a human being—but ridiculous or not, she felt it.

"How about I give you some advice as a thank-you," she said. "The man you work for is a . . ."

Annami couldn't find the word for the enormity of what Bleeder was. *Monster* didn't seem strong enough—too generic. *Beast,* a little better, but it didn't really get at the heart of the thing.

She could tell this man Bleeder's name, but it wouldn't mean anything to Perez, and for all she knew it would throw Bleeder into a rage and get her killed that much sooner. Despite everything, she didn't want that. She wanted more minutes—as many as she could get. You never knew what might happen. Lars had gotten out of that cage, after all.

"Betrayer," she settled on. "Bleeder will turn on you, first time he needs to."

Perez made a little sound between awkwardness and incredulity in the bottom of his throat, the sort of noise you might make when a friend suddenly mentions the affair they're having, then looks at you for approval while taking a measured sip of their drink. When someone throws up on the subway. When your dad asks to borrow next month's rent. When it's racism, obviously, and you're the only person in the conversation who seems to notice it.

"Lady," Perez said. "We're the Eaters. We don't betray each other. We can't. But thank you, I guess. I'll keep an eye out."

He leaned back.

"For betrayal," he finished, all skeptical sarcasm.

Annami shook her head.

"Your funeral," she said, turning to see that Bleeder had stopped fiddling with the pattern scanner and was staring right at her. Her, and Perez. She wondered how much he had—

A screech, and the van stopped but Annami didn't, her body still moving at the speed the vehicle had been traveling. Her head, her already-abused head, hit the partition between the driver's area and the rear compartment. She cried out.

Perez hit her, traveling at the same velocity, 250 pounds of man and body armor and weapons, and she felt herself compress, her wrists twisting in her plasticuffs, farther than they'd ever been designed to flex—wrists or cuffs. It was a race, a competition to see which would break first, and she was sure it would be her wrists, the pain burning up through her arms, a sharp obsidian heat, a wrongness.

A loud bang and the van slewed heavily sideways, then hit something hard and rotated, almost in slow motion. Weapons, water, and gear spilled from the shelves. Another heavy body hit Annami, pushing her sideways, her wrists burning, until finally the snapping sound she'd been expecting, and to her surprise it was the cuffs, not her wrists. She fell, landing on one of the Eaters, she didn't know which.

Moans of pain, and a "What the fuck was that?" and "Street's blocked—front and back" and "They shot the driver, that's why we flipped" and "Status, right now" and "This was an attack, we're under attack" and then, from outside—a voice called.

"This doesn't have to be any uglier than it is right now," it said, very slightly accented. "This is nothing. We can all go our own way very shortly. You have a woman. We want her. That's all."

All heads in the van turned toward Annami, those not unconscious or otherwise incapacitated.

"Weapons ready," Bleeder said quietly.

Around Annami, *clicks* and *ch-racks* and other thick mechanical sounds as the uninjured Eaters prepared to fight. She backed away from the rear doors of the vehicle, trying to make herself small. She wondered if she could make a barrier out of the two unconscious men on the once-side-now-floor of the van, if her half-destroyed wrists retained enough strength to drag and push them into position.

"Okay!" Bleeder called. "We're coming out!"

Then it occurred to Annami that the two unconscious Eaters must have weapons of their own, and everyone inside the van seemed much more focused on what was happening outside than anything she might be doing.

Annami got on her knees, slowly reaching for the coat of the nearest supine man, hoping for a shoulder holster she could pillage. She slipped her hand just inside, searching, and then something cold touched her cheek, almost a relief against the pain running through her head.

"Look up, Annami," Bleeder said. "Slowly."

She did, moving only her eyes, focusing first on a line of very thin metal moving up from the side of her face, then to Bleeder's hand holding the handle of the same ugly-beautiful knife he'd tried to use to skewer Lars, and then farther up, to his face, his gaze cold and dead.

"Open your mouth," he said.

She did not want to, but she also did not want to die. This was true for many reasons, but the primary factor at that moment was that she had recognized the voice that had called in from outside the van, a cultured voice with a slight Scandinavian accent. That voice that meant a number of impossible things had happened since she left the brothel, and now, maybe, somehow, she had a chance.

The odds were not good, but as always, it was about buying two more minutes, and disobeying Bleeder would take those minutes away.

Annami opened her mouth, and Bleeder slid his blade in, resting it on her tongue. It tasted like charged metal, like the contact on a battery.

"Close your mouth and stand up, very slowly," Bleeder said.

She did, willing her head into an absolute, perfect stillness, so as not to inadvertently slice off her tongue.

"Move with me to the back of the van."

Annami did this too, going very carefully, in step with Bleeder, whose eyes were locked on hers. He wasn't smiling, but his eyes were. He'd never had so much fun in all his lives. Despite her best efforts, her tongue twitched and she felt a little nick of pain, and then the taste of blood filled her mouth. She made a small noise, her eyes flinching.

She swallowed, moving only the muscles in her throat. She could feel some of the blood spilling over her lips.

"Watch yourself there, Annami," Bleeder said. "I keep this thing pretty sharp."

He turned to Zahn, positioned at the door with pistol in hand.

"When I say go, open the door. I want them to get a good view."

Bleeder moved behind Annami, shielding himself with her body but keeping the switchblade where it was, and his hand on it.

Why isn't he just using a gun? she thought. *He could do this just as easily with a gun.*

But she knew why. Because he was Bleeder.

The doors opened, and there, as Annami had known he would be, was Olsen. He'd brought gunmen of his own, who were arranged strategically on the street beyond, using parked cars for cover, pointing rifles at the van. In Olsen's hands, his son, Lars, the rat.

Annami felt Bleeder tense slightly, and readied herself to die.

"Is that . . . is that the fucking <u>rat</u>?" he said, his tone wondering. "From the whorehouse?"

"Watch your tongue," Olsen said. "This rat is my son, and I've never been more proud of him in all my life."

"Well, shit," Bleeder said, "well done, Annami."

A scenario popped into her mind in which Lars found a thinscreen back at the brothel and used it to tap out a message to his father, send a GPS map pin, and explain the situation in whatever broken rat-English he had left. If Olsen sent a drone immediately, and set it to track the Eaters' van as it made its way through lower Manhattan . . . maybe. Maybe that, or perhaps some other incredible sequence of events. It didn't matter. Olsen was here, so was Lars, and perhaps this unsurvivable horror was survivable after all.

"Let the woman go now," Olsen said, gently stroking his son's fur. "You are badly outnumbered, and I guarantee that if she dies, so will all of you. Give her to us, and you will walk away. In fact, once we're done with her, you can buy her back from us, if you like. I will give you a very fair price."

He smiled.

"And if you promise you'll hurt her, I will charge you much less."

Sirens were approaching from not far away, and although it seemed like an eternity, Annami knew it had only been a minute since the van crash, if that. The tension was rising, though, and it wouldn't be long before either Bleeder or Olsen decided to escalate matters.

Turned out it was Bleeder.

"That all sounds good," he called out to Olsen. "Let me just tell my guys how we'll do this. No misunderstandings."

"Fine," Olsen replied, "but . . ."

He made a vague gesture that seemed to indicate the rapidly converging police presence.

Bleeder nodded, then turned his head to Perez and spoke quietly.

"Shoot the rat."

Perez blinked.

"Boss, I don't think—"

"Shoot it."

"What?"

"Right out of his hand. Now."

Perez adjusted his pistol slightly, readying it, and Annami knew he would do as he had been ordered. She could feel Bleeder's attention shift, away from her and toward the violence to come. He was pressed against her back, and she could feel that he was excited.

So this was the moment. Her one chance to act. *Steel*, she thought. *Be steel.*

Perez pulled the trigger, and Lars exploded in Olsen's hand, and Annami bit down on the blade in her mouth, hard, clamping it between her molars. Then she whipped her head to the side and back, simultaneously striking Bleeder in the chin with the back of her skull and wrenching the knife from his hand.

Her mouth filled, a flood of salty, coppery warmth, pain roaring up behind. She'd done herself serious damage.

Annami reached up and grasped the switchblade. She pulled

it from her mouth, then reversed it and stabbed blindly behind her—once, twice, three, four times, each time feeling it sink home. Then a fifth, and it didn't, the blade hitting metal instead of flesh.

A grunt of surprise from behind her, a soft sound, drowned out by gunfire erupting from every side.

Bleeder fell away, and Annami spun, reaching into his coat for the thing that had prevented the fifth stab, praying it was the— it was. The pattern scanner.

She shoved the device into her belt and dove forward, past the remaining members of Bleeder's team, out onto the street, taking the fall on her abused wrists.

Annami hoped everyone around her was too busy killing each other to worry about her, or at least that Bleeder's team and Olsen's men all had orders to keep her alive and wouldn't just arbitrarily shoot her down.

She was deafened, confused, in agony. She stumbled, dragging herself along to the street, over what was just a notably large, facedown corpse until it moved as she clambered over it and she realized the man was still alive. A pistol lay near the man's outstretched hand, and she kicked it away, sending it skittering toward the sidewalk.

Annami stepped up to the curb, then crouched behind a parked car. She spit out a mouthful of blood, trying to think, trying not to vomit, trying to breathe, trying to think.

She began with her where. She recognized the neighborhood, in the way that any longtime resident of New York City could just feel their general area, a low-precision mental GPS. She was still downtown, somewhere below Fourteenth on one of the low-numbered east-west streets, Third or Fourth, maybe. As quiet as Manhattan ever got. A good place for an ambush.

Annami took inventory. She had grievous wounds of various

kinds. The pattern scanner, and that was definitely a victory—she had reclaimed her mindprint, her soul. But that was all. She had nothing else—no mini, no tools, no ID. All those things were still in the brothel, in the locker next to the flash rig that had facilitated her sex vacation with Soro on the other side of the world. The loss of her mini was particularly painful—it held the data downloaded from the Century-hunting virus she had inserted into Anyone's system on the day she quit, and she couldn't see any safe way to retrieve it.

She needed a doctor. She needed a place to think. She needed time.

Annami had none of those things. The auction was hours away.

She peered out from behind the car and saw that the street had largely emptied. Her blown-out ears hadn't let her realize that the gun battle was over, with survivors on both sides fleeing the rapidly approaching authorities.

Annami poked her head up and saw police cars no more than three blocks up and coming fast, with drone support zooming in from above.

The large man was only about six feet away, still lying where he'd fallen. She scrambled to him, keeping herself hidden between the parked cars. She reached out for him, offering a silent apology as she dove into his pockets and yanked out his mini and wallet. Then she got a look at his face and realized it was the architectural man, the one who had almost killed her on her very first darkshare. Gerber.

Annami retracted her apology.

The man's pistol rested where she had kicked it, its barrel a dull gleam in the shadows beneath the nearest car. She grabbed that too.

And then, she ran.

CHAPTER 27

THE BACK SEAT OF A 2002 FORD TAURUS

PAUL TOOK A DEEP BREATH, INHALING THE ODOR OF STALE CIGA-
rettes that outgassed from the car's upholstery with every movement. The vehicle was saturated, a huge, rolling ashtray.

Kat squirmed on his lap, and he wanted to open a window, to get
the baby some fresh air, but the sedan's back windows were tinted,
and he was nervous about giving anyone outside a clearer view at the
interior.

Eastern Market rolled by on the right—bustling, full of people.
It was Saturday, according to a display on their stolen getaway car's
GPS, a dash-mounted system with a screen gone a bit yellow from
age and nicotine. Slipping back into a world where the day of the
week mattered was a bit of a shock. Every day as Hendricks' captive
had very quickly become like every other day.

This neighborhood was just northeast of downtown, a part of
Detroit Paul didn't know well. He'd never in a billion years have
come here when he was a kid. Midtown, the Cass Corridor . . .
these were areas swallowed by the urban apocalypse. You didn't go
there if you didn't have to, and if you were unfortunate enough to

live there—or anywhere inside the city limits, really—you did everything you could to escape. Once Paul had managed to get the hell out, via a high school music scholarship to Interlochen and the doors it opened, all his subsequent choices had been focused on never coming back.

So now, seeing boutiques, cafés, families out enjoying the day . . . he'd heard things had gotten better in this part of town, but this was unreal. Everywhere, kids in strollers, bundled up against the chill of a November day in Michigan by their responsible parents.

Unlike himself.

He had his infant daughter in the back seat of a moving car, secured only by a seat belt and the strength of his arms. Yes, she seemed content for the moment, but he hated that he was doing this to her, that he had put her in potential danger.

He hated it. Not just because it was dangerous, not just because if someone happened to see inside the car they might call the cops, but because it was embarrassing. To a certain kind of observer, it was the decision someone like him was supposed to make. A fulfillment of expectations about the kind of parenting choices his people made. And what was even worse—he _had_ made that choice. He had knowingly put the Kitten in danger.

How had this happened? How had this become his life? He couldn't even keep his goddamned kid safe anymore.

Paul looked to his left, at the unconscious body of his wife, Gabrielle, head lolling with every bump in the road, loose and sickening, and then toward the front seat, at the broad, thick neck of the man who was driving the car, who was also his wife.

They hadn't spoken much since making it out of the Hendricks Capital facility. She'd told him about the cell phone basket trick, a classically brilliant Gabby solution—but that was about it. She was somewhere down deep in her mind, driving on autopilot. That was fine. Paul assumed she was planning the next phase of their escape, and he didn't want to disturb that with idle questions. The future of his family depended on it.

But the cute little stores and wine bars and record shops were zipping by outside the window at least 20 percent faster than they should be, and he couldn't help himself.

"Speed limit," he said.

"I know you're in the back seat, but resist the cliché," came the deep-voiced reply, the rolls of fat on the man's neck shifting with each word.

It wasn't Gabrielle's voice, but it was very much something she would say.

"You really want to put us in a situation where we have to explain what's happening in this car to the cops?" he said. "I've got a baby on my lap with no child seat, and my wife flopping around back here looking like a corpse. Not to mention, I'm pretty sure you kidnapped that guy you're riding."

"You forgot grand theft auto," Gabby said.

"That too," Paul said. "If we get pulled over . . ."

The silence drew out.

"I have a plan," Gabby said.

Relief.

"I'm glad," he said. "Because I'd hate to think you did all of this without one."

Nothing from the front seat. Maybe she'd retreated into her head again.

"Goddamn it, Gabby. Can you please tell me what we're going to do?"

A little jerk from the front seat, like a person startled up out of a nap—yeah, she'd gone deep, thinking so hard the rest of the world just slipped away.

Paul realized his job here was to keep her focused, keep her in the now. She might have a plan, but it was up to him to make sure it happened.

"I need to get back into my own body," Gabby said. "I don't have the gear I need to do a swap, but I can build it."

"Can't you just do the cell phone thing again?"

"If I <u>had</u> a phone. I left the one I used before back in the lab. It was Camila's, and I didn't have the code to unlock it."

"Camila," Paul said. "Where is she? Did she just let you go? She didn't call security or anything? You didn't . . . hurt her, did you?"

Paul imagined Gabby, in the body of the security guard, hitting the petite Dr. Chavez in the face—it was hard to even visualize. She would never. But then, he'd have bet a thousand dollars that his wife would never steal a car, and here they were.

"Camila will be all right," Gabby said. "I just need to get a flash setup going, then I can help her. I can get this guy back, too. His name's Eddie Brill."

Paul tried to parse this.

"Wait . . . I don't . . . ?" Paul said.

"I had to do a double swap," his wife said. "Camila into Eddie, then me into Eddie too, sort of, I dunno, like my mind's on top of theirs. It was the only way I could see to get them both out of the way."

The logic of that began to spin through his head. A mental ménage à trois. He wished he had a piece of paper to work it out. His understanding of the flash was derived primarily from things Gabby had told him in passing, and she wasn't great at conveying her ideas to laypeople. Explaining made her impatient.

"I took all the research data from Hendricks' lab. I put it on a memory stick and erased it from their server. It's the only copy," Gabby went on in her deep, gruff voice. "I can use it to re-create the flash, but I need a smartphone, and I need a pretty powerful laptop so I can program the patterns I'll need.

"I'll swap back into my original body, and then . . . well, Camila was with me in that lab for the last month. She'll know what I did. We can drop her off, and she can go back to Hendricks, get herself and Brill back the way it should be."

"Hold on," Paul said. "Camila? When you get out of that body, Dr. Chavez will wake up in it?"

"Yeah," Gabby said, an edge in her voice. "I think so."

"Will you let her take that phone you're going to mess with? Because you just said you erased all your research from Hendricks' computers. The flash is pretty complicated, right? Unless you give her the phone, I don't see how she can just re-create it herself. Won't she be stuck in that guy you're using now? Brill?"

Silence from the front seat.

"Gabby?"

"I'm not giving her the phone."

"Then how—"

"I will figure it out," she said.

Paul took a deep breath, filling his lungs with the ghosts of old smokes. The Kitten moved again, straining, stretching, reaching over toward her mother. He glanced over at the unconscious body, head lolled back on its neck, mouth slightly open in an unlovely gape, inanimate.

"Mama's okay, kiddo," he said. "Don't worry."

Parents lie to their children. It is an essential part of the process.

He was realizing that Gabby's plan had begun and ended with getting them out of Hendricks' clutches. She hadn't thought beyond escaping the lab. All credit to his wife, what she'd accomplished so far was amazing, but what had she actually accomplished?

"We can't go back to our house," he said quietly.

"Eventually, we will," Gabby said, with great certainty. "We'll have to go to the police, explain everything, but once we do—"

"You think so?" Paul said. "You signed Gray Hendricks' deal. Twice. Anyone broke the law here, I think it's you."

Another long silence from the front seat, and Kat took that moment to grab his beard and give it good, hard yank.

"Oof," he said, reaching to untangle her strong, tiny fingers. She grabbed his thumb and squeezed. He lifted her little hand to his mouth and kissed it.

"You need to let us out," he said. "I can get to my uncle's place. He can put us somewhere, let us lay low for a while."

"Paul . . . ," Gabby began. "I know this whole situation is crazy, but I couldn't let Hendricks keep the flash. Something that powerful can't be in the hands of a man like that. He kidnapped us, for god's sake! This isn't about me. It's about the entire world. I have a responsibility."

"Responsibility?" he said. "Baby, I call it <u>pride</u>. Your responsibility is to the people in this goddamn car. We need to act like parents. Or one of us does. Nothing matters more than keeping our kid safe."

"You think I don't know that?" Gabby said. "You think she was safe with Hendricks? You want her to grow up in his <u>prison</u>?"

"No. But this isn't much better. Let us out, do what you need to do, then we'll get back together. Hendricks only cares about me and the Kitten because we're leverage over you. "Don't you see that? Gabby . . . we have to go."

"I know that, but . . . Paul . . . I'm . . ."

Her voice broke, the deep, thick, smoker's baritone, and it was maybe the strangest, most terrifying part of all of this. Paul didn't think he'd ever heard a man make that sound. The body she was wearing seemed almost like a suit of armor, thick flesh protecting her spirit. It made her seem tougher, stronger. But ultimately, it was just a suit. Inside, she was still his wife.

"I'm afraid," she finished.

A sort of battle raged through Paul's mind, husband versus father. He had no idea where his obligations lay. Stay with his terrified,
genius wife, trapped in an alien body not her own—he had no idea
what that was like; he'd never gone through the flash except as an
unconscious vessel—or do everything he could to get his baby away
from her, to get them both off the horrible roller coaster Gabby's
invention had made of their lives?

A new odor rose in the car, overwhelming the stale smoke, and
he had his answer. His baby needed her diaper changed, and he, her
father, had no idea how he would pull off that most basic of parental
tasks. No money, driving around in a stolen car. Forget it. Enough
was enough.

"I'm sorry, Gabby, but—"

A movement to his left. Faint, small, then a second, more vig-
orous. He looked over, and saw that his wife's original body was
arched, a shallow curve against the seat, a parenthesis, with the seat
belt pulled tight against her chest. The body collapsed, then arched
again, the pace increasing, its mouth snapping closed, the teeth hitting each other with a sharp clack.

"Gabby!" Paul said.

He reached forward, holding his hand against the body's chest,
trying to keep it from convulsing again, failing, feeling wiry energy
vibrating through the small frame.

"Something's wrong!" he said.

The Kitten, watching her mother twist in her seat like someone
in an electric chair, began to wail.

The car slammed to a stop—Gabby had pulled over—and Paul
heard the front door open, then the passenger door. Light and cool
air spilled into the back seat, along with security guard Eddie Brill,
his wife's strange suit of clothing.

Gabby looked at her own body with a clinical eye. She reached out to its head, running her fingers over the back, lightly but thoroughly.

"Fuck," she said, then stripped off the suit coat she was wearing.

She wadded it up into something like a pillow and slipped it behind her body's head. She pulled off Brill's watch and tossed it at Paul.

"Time the seizure," she said, then slammed the passenger-side door.

"What?" Paul said. "<u>What</u>?"

The body convulsed again. Thick, mucosal saliva slipped out of its mouth and down its chin.

Gabby pushed herself back behind the wheel and closed the driver's door. She pulled away from the curb, screeching back into traffic.

"I must have fractured my skull when I did the swap back at the lab," she said, every word clipped and tight. "Epidural hematoma, maybe. Not ideal."

Paul was holding the pillow behind his wife's head with one hand, holding the watch in the other, trying to count the seconds. Leaning over to one side was causing his seat belt to compress the Kitten, and her screaming throttled up to a higher gear.

"Not fucking <u>ideal</u>?" he spat toward the front seat.

Gabby ignored him, her voice calm.

"I need a hospital, right now. An emergency room."

"Are you going to die? What will happen if—" he began.

"Not if I get to the ER. They need to relieve the pressure on the brain. It's not a complicated procedure. I could do it with a drill, if I had one. But I don't have a drill. They used to do it with a chisel in the old days. There's bleeding between my skull and my dura mater, and it has nowhere to go. If we can't get that blood out, it'll be brain damage for sure. The longer we wait, the worse it is."

She was talking faster and faster, her voice like a machine gun firing anxiety bullets.

Paul looked down at his wife's body—the convulsions had calmed somewhat, but her eyes had opened just enough to reveal a sliver of glassy shine beneath the lids. Even more disquieting.

What if, he thought, *she transfers back into her body and her brain's destroyed? If there's no brain for her to go back to?*

He looked up, trying to figure out where they were in the city, trying to remember the layout of streets from when he was a kid.

"We're near Wayne State," he said toward the front, loud, to compete with both his wife and his daughter. "There's a bunch of hospitals there. An emergency room on . . . Beaubien Street, I think."

His wife abruptly stopped talking, and the car swayed with U-turn-generated g-forces. The Kitten grunted at this further indignity, then resumed her former screaming.

Acceleration pushed them both back, and Paul watched the city speed by through the window.

This is when we get pulled over, he thought.

But they didn't. They made it to the hospital, and Gabby pulled the car to a stop beneath the large porte cochere outside the emergency room entrance.

The wheelchair from Hendricks' lab was still in the trunk, saved for the increasingly remote moment of their arrival at a place of safety where they could reflect and figure out their next move.

Gabby and Paul moved the body into the chair and strapped it down.

"I'll go in," Gabby said. "I can explain what's wrong to the intake staff. I'll say . . . I'll say I was her driver. It'll take a few minutes, but then we can go—it's probably safer to leave my body here for now anyway. It will be easier for us to keep moving without lugging it around."

"Okay," Paul said, nodding. "I'll follow you in. Maybe a nurse can get me a diaper for Kat, something for her to eat."

"Perfect," Gabby said, as she bent to lift one of her body's eyelids. She frowned, evidently not liking what she saw.

She straightened and looked at Paul.

"This will all be okay. It's going to work out," she said.

"I know," Paul said.

He reached out and took her hand, her beefy, thick, calloused hand. He held it for a moment, then released it, and Gabby turned quickly, pushing the wheelchair through automatic doors that scythed open as she approached. She was moving fast, which made sense.

After all, it was an emergency.

Paul watched her disappear into the hospital. He had the Kitten up against his chest, patting her back. She had calmed now that they were out of the car, but still seemed unhappy.

"You and me both, kiddo," he said.

Paul turned and walked away, heading for the street.

CHAPTER 28

A GURNEY, UNION SQUARE

BLEEDER WAS BLEEDING.

He'd picked his name as a bit of a joke: yes, a suitably threatening handle for the leader of a team of do-anything, below-the-radar hired guns for Stephen Hauser, but also a private gag that no one else would ever get—and now it had a third meaning, because he was bleeding out all over the stretcher rushing him into his team's headquarters.

Annami, he thought.

She'd stabbed him four times with his own blade. He wasn't sure—it all went very fast—but he thought she had sliced off half her own face in order to achieve that goal. Showed real commitment. Or hatred. Or both.

The whole thing had probably been very satisfying for her. Considering their history.

Bleeder looked up at the faces of the men above him, his Eaters, loyal and true, rolling him through the cavernous, echoing marble interior of Number 20 Union Square East.

All tough, all strong, all healthy, all smart. Any would be accepted as the next team leader without question, not least because he'd have Bleeder's imprimatur.

But only one deserved it. A senior man, someone who'd been around for a while, someone who knew how things worked.

"Perez," he said, his voice weak and raspy.

"Just hold on, boss," came the response, from somewhere near Bleeder's feet. He wanted to lift his head, lock eyes with Perez, but his body didn't seem to want to cooperate.

"No time," he said, watching the ceiling roll by. "It's you. You'll take over when I'm gone."

Narrowed eyes and clenched jaws from the other Eaters, as they realized that Jorge Perez was being handed control of their organization. Not them. Jorge Perez.

They all thought they deserved the job. That they'd earned it through hard work and dedication. Oh well. They'd get over it.

"Get him back here!"

This shout came from somewhere ahead, the voice of Dr. Alice Hong, the team's medic, surgeon, fix-it woman, and occasional lover of its leader. He supposed that last part was over . . . unless maybe she liked Perez.

Alice's head swam into his view; her fingertips touched his throat.

"Aw man, you idiot. What did you do to yourself?"

"Wasn't me," Bleeder rasped. "Blame the knife."

Dr. Hong's hands moved lightly over Bleeder's chest, still and steady even as she kept pace with the rolling gurney. He saw her face reset into an expression of competent resignation, and any thought that he might survive his injuries slipped away.

"Get him to the operating table," Dr. Hong said.

"In a . . . minute," Bleeder said. "Perez . . . we need to do the download."

"There's no time! You're dying!" the doctor said.

"That's why we need . . . to do it," Bleeder gasped.

"He's right," Perez said. Bleeder thought he could hear a bit of eagerness in the man's tone.

Careful there, buddy, Bleeder thought. *I ain't dead yet.*

The stretcher moved again, Perez pushing it by himself now, into another, smaller room just off the clinic. Not much in there— a chair, a table, a safe mounted into the wall.

"The safe," Bleeder said. "Get me to it."

Perez did as he was told, rolling the stretcher as close to the wall as he could, allowing Bleeder to reach up and weakly tap in the access code, smearing blood across the keypad. A soft chime and a thick, metallic *thunk* as the lock disengaged.

Bleeder moved his hand to the lever that would open the safe. He looked at Perez waiting patiently—*Good old patient Perez*, he thought, his head swimming, and realized he really was running out of time.

He pulled the lever and the safe opened, revealing a small device—a tiny screen and keyboard mounted below a miniaturized flash rig, set back from the door so it wasn't easily visible unless you were very near the safe. The screen glowed, displaying a list of names—everyone on the team, from Angelo to Zahn. Bleeder tapped *Perez, Jorge*, and rested his finger on the activation key.

"You deserve this," Bleeder said, glancing at Perez, his vision going dark around the edges.

"I've always tried my best," Perez said, with modesty so false it made Bleeder feel almost sorry for the man.

"Not what I . . . mean," Bleeder said. "You <u>deserve</u> this. You gave that bitch water, after she already used up her last request. You're soft. Eaters have to be hard."

Puzzlement, then realization washed across Perez's face, and before that could change to panic, or anger, or anything else at all, Bleeder looked back into the safe and tapped the key, and the man's flash pattern rolled across Bleeder's eyes, and/

No more pain, which was good. Bleeder stretched a little, getting used to his new environs. Perez was a little taller, his arms thicker, with large, long-fingered hands. Younger, too. He felt that immediate surge of elasticity, limberness, lack of the subtle aches and pains that you put out of your mind in an older body. Not so bad. The only real downside was the baldness, but he looked all right. Wore it well. He'd do a full inspection later, see if anything else was proportional to those big hands—always a fun prospect. Maybe he <u>would</u> try to get to know Dr. Hong a bit better.

Bleeder looked down at his previous body on the stretcher, calm and still and bleeding. It wasn't Bleeder anymore. It was just meat. But it was still alive, and procedures had to be observed. He reached into the body's pocket and pulled out his stiletto, placed there earlier by one of his Eaters, then tucked it away inside his coat.

He closed and relocked the safe, then rolled the stretcher back out into the clinic. Dr. Hong took over, attaching IVs and oxygen and getting to work. Bleeder watched for a moment, then turned and walked back into the main space, seeing the rest of the team, Angelo to Zahn and all the others, perched on equipment crates or leaning against walls, drinking coffee, watching, waiting for news.

"So?" Fitzsimmons asked.

"I got the download," Bleeder answered, liking the way his words sounded in Perez's voice. "Bleeder's still alive, but it took a lot out of him. I'm not sure if—"

"Dammit!" came a yell from the clinic, and all heads turned to look in that direction. "Fuck!"

"That don't sound good," Angelo said.

They waited a while, as Dr. Hong attempted to revive what had once been him. Bleeder wasn't too concerned. Even if she stabilized the meat, it wouldn't ever wake up—it couldn't.

Eventually Alice came out from the clinic, blood staining her surgical gown and speckled across her mask and goggles.

"He's gone," she said. "I did what I could, but the wounds were severe. It's amazing he lived as long as he did."

"I know you did your best," Bleeder said, putting a hand on her shoulder. It felt nice under his hand. Warm. Dr. Hong looked great through Perez's eyes. Even better than she had before, even all swaddled up in medical gear. Maybe it was a pheromones thing. He hoped it was a two-way street.

Dr. Hong nodded, and Bleeder stepped back, then reached into his pocket and pulled out the stiletto. He pressed the lever on its side, and the blade flipped up, still speckled with blood— his and Annami's, a mix. He held it up to show the others.

"I think Bleeder knew his time was up," he said. "He gave me his blade."

"Yours now," Zahn said. "And you're not Perez no more. You're the new Bleeder."

New Bleeder, same as the old Bleeder, Bleeder thought.

"Guess so," he said. "Feels weird. It'll take some getting used to."

He pulled out a mini, his own, that he had taken from the corpse before he left the download room. He tapped in the access code, and the screen lit up. Bleeder did it in such a way that the rest of the team could see and would know that he hadn't been lying about the download. *Even his mini*, they were thinking. *Bleeder had even given him the code to his mini. That, along with all the command codes, mission data, contacts, passwords, every-thing needed to run the team.*

"Our target's still out there, that woman Annami," Bleeder said. "She's top priority, above everything else. She got her pattern back, so we'll have to find her again the hard way—but we'll get her."

He lifted the mini.

"I need to call the big boss," he said. "Tell him what happened."

Another deliberate assertion of status.

"Get the body ready for the ritual," he said. "I don't want to wait. We'll do it tonight."

A few quick taps on the mini and Bleeder ambled away across the former bank lobby, holding the thing to his ear and listening to it ring, finding it interesting how the sunbeams angling down through the skylight seemed different now. He'd lost count of how many bodies he'd occupied over the years, both short- and long-term flashes, and he never got tired of seeing the world through new eyes.

"Bleeder," Stephen Hauser said from the mini.

"Yes and no," Bleeder said.

A pause.

"You did it again," Hauser said.

"Wasn't like I had much of a choice, sir."

"Which one did you choose?"

"Perez."

"Eh. Doesn't matter, I guess. I just can't believe none of those idiots on your team ever put two and two together."

"I usually pick someone more senior, so it's believable that they'd take over. Anyway, why would they have any reason to get suspicious? As far as they know, what I did is impossible. One dies, both die, right?"

"Whatever," Hauser said. "Annami. Talk."

"We had her, then we lost her," Bleeder said, a firm believer in ripping off the Band-aid.

"You <u>lost</u> her? She was working at Anyone for years. That couldn't have been an accident. God knows what she did, what she hid in the network, what she might be planning."

"Don't worry. We have her face. My guys can access the city's dronet to see if she pops up, and she was wounded, too. We can check hospitals, that sort of thing."

"Don't be stupid. We have no idea what she looks like. She's not stuck in one body any more than you or I."

"You think she'll just <u>take</u> someone?"

"Did she strike you as someone who has qualms? You don't sound very concerned, Bleeder, but she wants us both dead. At the minimum."

"I know. Just ask the last Bleeder."

"I am asking the last Bleeder, and I want to know how the hell you plan to find her!"

"I think you're wrong about what she'll do, boss. I don't think she'll leave her prime. You didn't see her. I did. I might be wrong, but I don't think she'll be able to walk away from that body all that easily. She's got tattoos all over her face, too. Trust me. We'll find her."

"Trust you, huh?" Hauser said. "You're the least trustworthy person I've ever met."

"That hurts, boss," Bleeder said. "We've been working together how long? Have I ever let you down?"

"Just find her. Let me know when it's done. If you can, bring her in. I'd like to see her. It's been a long time."

"If I can, sir," Bleeder said. "Good talk."

He ended the call and looked back at his loyal men, his team, his Boys' Club, his Eaters.

It had been a while since they'd lost a Bleeder. In a way, he thought what had happened that day was good. He'd gotten himself a fresh new perspective, and the rest of the team was about to go through the ritual that bound them together, made them who they were. A few were too new to have done it even once.

Bleeder, though . . . he'd done it ten times, at least. He'd lost count. He liked it—the symbolism was perfect. The accumulated wisdom and experience of the lost leader being redistributed through the team. The joint breaking of a fundamental human taboo, one of mankind's most sacred rules, uniting the team in a way nothing else could.

And . . . he just liked the taste. Roasted, very simple, salt, garlic, and pepper—the holy trinity of seasonings. *All you need for meat*, his dad had always said.

Despite a few twists and turns along the way, he thought he could call the day a success.

Time to celebrate. Time for a feast. Time to eat.

CHAPTER 29

AN EMERGENCY ROOM, DETROIT

"THIS WOMAN NEEDS TO BE SEEN IMMEDIATELY," GABBY SAID. "SHE was having seizures—she has a head injury. If you wait, it could be very, very bad."

The ER admitting nurse, wearing a name tag that read AC-COUNE, nodded, her face holding the sympathetic but unrevealing expression Gabby had seen on many a nurse in her day—the one that said, *Yes, I understand you think your situation is pretty god-damn pressing, but please look around and understand that everyone here is hurting too. It's why they call it an emergency room.*

That, plus a thin layer of *Thanks for the armchair diagnosis, pal, but leave this to the professionals.*

She understood that. The cliché of what she was doing pained her—a white man loudly requesting better treatment than the other people filling the waiting room, whose faces mostly looked more similar to Nurse Accoune's. Brill looked like what he was—a slightly gone-to-seed late-middle-aged security guard in a bad suit. He didn't look like an authority on anything. Maybe beer. Maybe hockey. He was not a figure to generate sympathy, or favors—at least not in an inner-city ER waiting room in Detroit.

Gabby realized, suddenly, that she didn't know any of that to be the case. She was doing exactly the same thing as the nurse—taking Brill at face value. She knew nothing about the man's inner life. For all she knew, he gardened and studied water-rights issues in Colorado and loved chutney and had twelve adopted children at home who adored him, a beloved figure in inner Detroit for his many selfless acts.

Face value.

What was the "value" of a "face"?

Society had much to say on this subject. Attractiveness was often the first thing you understood about another human being. You slotted them in on a scale from one to perfect ten. It was instinctive and immediate, and while humans in more enlightened societies tried to convince themselves to look past such things, to give people a chance to be what they were beyond their value as attractive objects, it never really took.

You look at someone, and you make judgments about their wealth, the choices they've made in their lives, whether you would ever sleep with them, whether they would ever sleep with you. The amount we think we know about other people just based on their externalities is ridiculous.

A couple walks past you, and the woman has a black eye.

What does that mean?

A man has a tattoo on his face.

What does that mean?

A child is overweight.

What does that mean?

A woman is in a very short skirt.

What does that mean?

A man has a prosthetic leg.

What does that mean?

A neuroscientist's mind is transferred into the body of an overweight security guard.

What does that mean?

For one thing, it meant that the nurse who could save the neuroscientist's life had placed herself on a professional pedestal above the security guard (who was also the neuroscientist, but she couldn't see that) and was exercising her gatekeeper prerogatives to reinforce that status.

The value of a face was power.

Gabby realized that she was on the edge of losing it. She knew all too well what was happening inside her body's skull, pressure mounting on the brain as blood leaked into the cavity, compressing the sensitive, irreplaceable tissues like a hand slowly closing into a fist around an egg. It was only a matter of time before the egg cracked, and as the rhyme went, at that point all the king's horses and all the king's men wouldn't be able to do a goddamned thing.

"Let me try again," Gabby said, mustering her best I AM A DOCTOR professional demeanor, the one that worked in all sorts of situations, from bedsides to banks. She reached deep inside herself, looking for authority, realizing she possessed, potentially, a new power she had not previously held.

She was, after all, a middle-aged white man.

Gabby stood straight, using all of Brill's height, and shot a look in at Nurse Accoune, sending bullets of will in through the bulletproof plexiglass partition between them.

"Five minutes ago, this woman was presenting a full-on grand mal seizure. I've examined her, and indications are that she has suffered a TBI.

"She needs immediate treatment for subdural hematoma, or she will suffer permanent damage. At the minimum, she needs a course of an IV AED. I'd suggest lorazepam, but there are a number of options.

"Get her seen, Nurse, or I will make absolutely certain the

choices you are making right now will haunt you for the rest of your life."

Nurse Accoune pursed her lips and narrowed her eyes. She was reevaluating Brill's status, deciding where he fit in the grand standings board of the human race.

Gabby knew she'd given the nurse a bad cover story—she'd explained that Brill was just driving along the street minding his own business when he saw a woman in a wheelchair on the sidewalk having a seizure. He'd stopped, bundled her into his car, and brought her to the nearest ER.

The woman had no ID on her, and no, Brill didn't know her name.

Gabby had chosen that approach because she was wary of the idea that Hendricks might have put out some sort of alert on the name Gabrielle White. Paranoid, she knew, but from what she'd seen of the way Gray Hendricks liked to operate, absolutely within the realm of possibility.

The story she'd picked was good for maintaining anonymity, but bad for giving herself any influence vis-à-vis Nurse Accoune.

It almost made her laugh. She'd spent her entire educational and professional life becoming an expert on the brain, worked and sacrificed and scraped in order to gain that authority, and now, at the moment she needed it most, she couldn't access it. Because of the color of her skin.

So now she just had to wait to see the outcome of the fight in Nurse Accoune's head between the various factors in play here—her duty as a healer, her undoubted annoyance at having her livelihood threatened by yet another self-important white man, her recognition that perhaps said man could follow through on his threat, and so much more.

It was complicated.

At least until Gabby's wheelchair-bound body snapped forward against its restraints, another seizure warping through it.

"Please," Gabby said to Nurse Accoune, placing a steadying hand on the back of her body's neck, supporting the chin with her other hand, an instinctive motion but one the nurse apparently recognized as the gesture of a fellow medical professional, because she pressed a button on her desk and spoke into a microphone.

"Crash cart to the waiting room, stat!" she said, her tone urgent.

The team came and took the beleaguered body of Gabrielle White back into the treatment area beyond the swinging doors next to the admitting nurse's station. Gabby tried to tell the harried, baby-faced doctor what she knew, not wanting even ten seconds to be lost in diagnosis, but knowing the ER doc would ignore every word she said.

He did, vanishing through the doors, and Gabby stood alone in the waiting room, absolutely lost.

Gabby looked at Nurse Accoune, who had already moved on to her next bit of business. Plenty more bodies to be seen.

"I'll wait here," Gabby said. "Please tell me what happens to her."

The nurse gave a curt nod, no friend of Brill's, not after the man had threatened her job.

Gabby found her way to one of the few empty seats, between a sad-eyed, shirtless man holding the missing garment to a cut on his head and an elderly woman with nose cannula running to an oxygen tank. The old woman's eyes were fixed on a wall-mounted TV featuring a strident female judge admonishing a shamefaced young man who seemed to be wishing he'd made better life choices.

She could relate.

First, they would administer antiseizure meds. Those usually took effect quickly. Then, once her body was stabilized, the doctors would try to relieve pressure on the brain and stop the bleeding. She wasn't sure if there was a skull fracture—she hadn't wanted to probe the injury too much in the car—but that could complicate things.

They might pull out a little section of the skull. They'd shave her head.

Gabby didn't think of herself as vain, but she found herself fixating on that. What would she look like bald? How long would it take to grow back out? Maybe she'd keep it short, actually—less of a hassle. Some women looked incredible bald. Striking. Like goddesses.

She kept pulling her mind away from the reality, which was that a patient seizing so soon after the initial injury meant very bad things indeed, things that couldn't be fixed.

Eddie Brill and Camila Chavez were somewhere inside the vessel she was now running. Their minds. Their . . . souls.

Hidden, locked away, buried deep, lost, until she could return to her own body.

She wondered if she would voluntarily make that journey if she knew her original self had significant brain damage.

If she didn't, or decided she couldn't, and stayed inside Brill, would she just be a sort of house of souls? How long until Camila and Eddie were gone? Would they just dissolve? Had they already?

There was still so much she didn't know.

The possibilities were endless.

Gabby thought she should go back to Nurse Accoune, come clean, insist that she be allowed to explain the full history behind their patient's current medical situation. It might help.

Or, more likely, the woman wouldn't believe a word Gabby said. She might think she was a lunatic. She might take her at face value.

Nurse Accoune might press the little button mounted below the counter on her side of the admissions window that called hospital security. Or she might press the other one, which called the cops. If she hadn't already.

For all Gabby knew, the police were already on their way to question her about her original body's head injury. Emergency rooms had policies about things like that. The cops were never very far away.

Just a matter of time, probably.

Time.

Gabby looked up, realizing first, how long it had been since she entered the ER, and second, that her husband and daughter were not in sight, anywhere.

She stood again and walked back to the admissions window, which garnered a very clear *What now?* grimace from Nurse Accoune.

Before the woman could inform her that there was no news about her friend yet (of course there wouldn't be—they'd barely had time to get the IV in, at this point), Gabby spoke.

"Have you seen a man and a baby in here? He . . . he needed to change the baby's diaper. Was going to see if you could give him one."

The nurse gave her a long, considering look. Gabby knew she hadn't done her cover story any favors, but she was beginning to think that blowing her cover no longer even rated as a problem, considering everything else she was dealing with.

"The Children's Hospital is around the block. Maybe he went there instead," the nurse said. "And didn't you say you were alone?"

I might be, Gabby thought.

She heard a pinging noise and then, a moment later, a cell phone ringtone, which generated a look of annoyance on Nurse Accoune's face.

"Outside," she said.

"What?"

She tapped a poster taped to her side of the window, with a very clear image of a cell phone inside a red circle with a slash across it.

"No cell phone calls in here. Go outside."

Gabby's mind was so focused on things outside herself that it took her a moment to understand that the ringing was in fact inside her own coat—or rather Eddie Brill's. She pulled it out, intending to silence it, angry at herself for not thinking to look for his phone earlier.

The phone was displaying a preview of an image that had just been sent via text, as well as an incoming call notification.

The photo was tiny. Just a thumbnail. But what she could see . . .

"Oh god," she said.

"Outside," Accoune said again, and Gabby didn't know what sort of evil look Brill's face threw at the woman, but the nurse recoiled, putting her hands up in a reflexive warding-off gesture.

Gabby turned and walked toward the hospital's exit. As she moved, she used Brill's thumbprint to open the phone, accessing the text but not answering the call.

Not yet.

The screen unfolded, the small image expanded, and what she thought she'd seen was confirmed.

A close shot of Paul sitting in a chair, his face desperate, broken. The corner of his mouth swollen.

Men on either side of him, only partially visible, cut off by the edges of the phone's screen.

The phone rang again.

Gabby stepped out of the ER waiting room, the doors sliding open to let her pass, riveted to the phone, scanning every pixel of the image for details.

Behind Paul, she could see her daughter, held by another of the anonymous men, not the way she should be held, crying, reaching out for her father.

Gabby closed the image, accepted the incoming call, and lifted the phone to her ear.

"Hello, Gabby," Jon Corran said.

"Jon," she said, walking along the curved sidewalk that let out from the hospital's entrance back to the street. She had no destination in mind. She just liked to walk when she talked.

"What are you doing, Gabby?" Jon said, and she figured the repetition of her name was probably intentional. "This is insane. This isn't you. Hell, it's not me, either. We're good people. We don't do things like this. All of this . . . it's way out of control. We need to dial it all back, right? Get everything back on track."

He sounded so nice, so reasonable. Gabby reminded herself that he had her family captive.

"We know where you are," Jon went on. "At the DMC Receiving Hospital."

"How?"

"This is Detroit. It's Hendricks' town. He sees everything."

"You have to let my family go now," Gabby said, her voice calm. Calmer than it should have been.

"It's over," Jon said. "It's time to come back."

"Let them go, or . . . I'll destroy all the research on the flash. I took it all with me when I left."

"I don't think you will. It's your only leverage."

Gabby reached the sidewalk and turned around, circling back toward the entrance to the ER. No destination. She couldn't think straight enough to have a destination. Walking and talking was about her limit, just then.

"I'll trade it. Let them go, and I'll tell you where to find it."

"No. It's time to come back. We need you here. There's a lot of work to do. Besides, don't you want to get Brill and Dr. Chavez back into their bodies? You don't want to hurt anyone. You're a scientist, for god's sake. I understand that you feel like Hendricks put you in a corner, but I've talked to him. He knows he made a mistake. It'll be better from now on."

So reasonable. He was making so much sense.

"Your family is here. They're waiting for you. Your daughter seems really upset. We're sending a car. I'm looking forward to seeing you soon."

The call ended. Gabby stopped, at last. She stood there, her back to the hospital, dimly aware that the doors had opened behind her, sensing her presence.

What are you doing, Gabby? she asked herself. *What did you do?*

A touch on her shoulder, and Gabby started, her arms swinging wildly as she spun, a lit match flaring into life.

It was Nurse Accoune.

Her face was not irritated. It was not intimidated, or afraid, or anything Gabby might have expected to see from her based on their previous interactions.

Nurse Accoune's face was sympathetic, even a little sad. Gabby recognized this expression too. She'd had to wear it a time or two herself, during her residency days.

"No."

"I'm so sorry. Your friend . . . she didn't make it through the procedure."

"No. No."

"I'm afraid so. I'm sorry."

The nurse reached out a comforting hand.

"She's gone."

CHAPTER 30

A TAXI, MANHATTAN

THE ADRENALINE HAD WORN OFF, LEAVING PAIN IN ITS WAKE. Annami's face was the worst, a searing ache that swelled with every heartbeat, sending red flashes across her vision. Her cheek felt thick, like post-novocaine shot at the dentist, but sadly with no numbness whatsoever. She felt everything.

Her wrists were the second worst. She didn't think they were broken, but they'd been sprained to such a degree that even the weight of her hands was too much to bear. She let them dangle at her sides, wishing she had a sling. Wishing she had morphine.

But she didn't. She had a stolen mini, a little bit of stolen cash—she didn't dare use any of her payphrases—a pistol, and a flash pattern scanner. The mini was essentially just serving as a countdown timer—she didn't have the access code, so its functionality was limited to what she could use from the lock screen. Its clock, for one, which let her monitor how much time she had left until Bhangra George's auction. The answer—not much. A little over an hour. Not much. Maybe enough.

The cash had let her secure a cab, another self-driving model with a flashed-out operator in its front seat. Any conscious driver would have insisted on taking her directly to a hospital. No, not true. They wouldn't have stopped for her at all.

She was a mess. She looked like she'd gone swimming in a slaughterhouse.

The gun and the pattern scanner, she hadn't used yet—but she thought she knew how she could.

Chinatown outside, and Annami told the cab to pull over. She paid, and the doors unlocked, and she braced herself to move under her own power again. She was so tired, so hurt.

It's almost over, she told herself. *You can't stop now. And it could be worse. At least you got your pattern back.*

Annami took a breath and got out of the cab. She did it without her injured hands, instead using only the strength in her legs to stand—what strength she had left.

A well-remembered navigation down alleys and dark corridors, to a red door she had assumed she would never see again.

Annami looked down at her clothes. Blood-spattered, but mostly dry now, and the people inside had seen plenty of blood in their time.

She pondered throwing up on herself but couldn't bring herself to do it. The thought of bile and stomach acid rushing past the wound in her cheek was . . . no. Too much.

Another function she could access in her locked mini: a mirror app. She activated it and looked at herself, deciding she needed no additional cosmetic disenhancement. She was a ruin.

Her reflection also confirmed what she'd already suspected: there was no way at all she'd be allowed to participate in the Bhangra George auction, not looking like this. The rules required all bidders to show up in person, and the security teams wouldn't be too thrilled about admitting someone who looked like she'd been run through a meat grinder.

Annami walked up to the door and knocked, rapping out the prescribed sequence, each impact jolting through her wrist.

A panel in the door slid open at eye level. An affectation, something that could easily have been handled via security cameras, but part of the overall nostalgic vibe of the place.

She thought she recognized the gaze looking out at her—Somchai, who asked you to call him Chai if he liked you, or maybe because it was easier than hearing Western tongues destroy his name.

"Chai, it's me," she said. "Annami. Three purple . . . uh . . . three purple peacocks in a pinnace."

The eyes behind the panel widened.

"You all right?" he said.

"I'm . . . I'm in bad shape. I just need to run, make some money. I need to get fixed up, too."

"I don't know," Chai said. "Who's gonna run you looking like that?"

"I just need to clean up a little. I swear. Just ask Mama. Please, Chai."

If he did go ask, then Annami knew she'd get in. There was no way Mama Run would turn away a prodigal daughter. She'd be welcomed back, cleaned up, healed, and made strong . . . and then she'd be turned out again, back on the street, earning, and Mama would love every second of it.

But there was every chance Somchai would send her away right then and there—that was his job, why Mama Run kept a person at her door. He was there to tell the no-hopers to run along, the people who would never get hired to do dark runs, not even by the most debased drug addict just looking for a warm body in which to fix.

"I started running for another darkshare den," Annami said.

"It was a mistake. I never should have . . . I never should have left. Please, can you tell her?"

A pause, as Somchai considered. A very long pause.

But he'd asked her to call him Chai once, after about a month of darksharing, when she bought him a shot of Mama Run's best rum.

"All right. You wait," he said, and the panel in the door closed.

Annami sagged against the brick wall. *Just another obstacle,* she thought. *Just another wall to climb. Don't think about all the ones to come. Just focus on this one. Get over it, and then you worry about the next one.*

She closed her eyes, knowing it was a mistake, knowing she could fall asleep standing up right there in the alley if she wasn't careful. She felt herself beginning to drift when the sound of bolts unlocking in the door jolted her back up to wakefulness.

The door opened, and there were Somchai and his brother, Lek, whose name she understood was sort of a play on words, like calling the biggest man in the prison yard Tiny. Lek wasn't large—neither was Somchai—but they were strong in the way of caimans. Thin and whiplike. They kept Mama Run safe.

They looked at her.

"Thank you," Annami said, and made her way inside, moving past them as if her entry to the darkshare den had already been approved, when in fact it had not. They were supposed to search her. They searched everyone. That was their job. She sensed them hesitating, looking at each other, assessing her threat level, assessing her filth level, deciding this time maybe they didn't have to search, this time there was nothing to fear.

That was good, very good. She would have pulled out the gun if they'd come close to her, and she didn't know how that would play out. They had guns too, although they probably wouldn't need them. Lek and Chai could take her apart with just their hands and feet, if necessary. That was also their job.

Into the main room, the scarlet cocoon of the darkshare den, and there was Mama Run, walking out from behind the bar, looking at Annami with the deepest, most sincere expression of concern and regret and welcome she'd ever seen.

"Oh, little girl," Mama Run said. "You're a mess. I'm so glad you came to me. Let me help you."

Annami stumbled forward, almost crying at the sound of kind words, even coming from this madam, this pimp.

"Where is Soro?" Mama asked. "I haven't seen him in a long time either. He okay? I know you two got tight."

Annami pulled out the pistol from inside her shirt and pointed it at Mama Run, the weight reawakening the ache in her wrists.

"Soro's dead," she said.

Annami stepped behind the other woman, putting the pistol's barrel between Mama Run's shoulder blades, seeing that Lek and Chai had already pulled out their own guns. Their expressions had gone cold, too. Annami thought Chai probably didn't like her anymore.

"What is this? You gonna rob me?" Mama Run said, her voice tight.

"I don't want your money," Annami said.

She looked at Lek and Chai, who had spread out slightly to either side, making it impossible for her to attack them both at once. It felt like a tactical thing, the instinctive reaction of violent men.

"Guns on the floor, please," Annami said. "I don't want anyone to get hurt. I mean it."

"Do it!" Mama Run said. "I'm sure we can work all this out."

Lek and Chai glanced at each other, then bent and set their guns on the floor. Annami knew this made them only marginally less dangerous. The two guards needed to be removed from the equation, immediately. In the back of her mind, she could see the clock on her stolen mini, clicking away the seconds and minutes until the auction. She was running out of time.

With her free hand, Annami scrabbled under her shirt and pulled out the pattern scanner. She reached with it around Mama Run's head. She jammed the barrel cup into the woman's eye and pulled the trigger, and five seconds later it was done.

"You got my pattern, huh? What you think you gonna do with it? You wanna be Mama Run? Three-Fold Blades gonna have a problem with that, little girl."

Annami stepped back.

"I'm not a little girl," she said. "Turn around. Look at me."

Mama Run did, and Annami held up the scanner.

"This thing has an upload function. I've got your pattern, and I've set it to broadcast onto the widenet every fifteen minutes unless I tell it not to. It's code-locked, too."

Mama's face paled as she realized the implications.

If her pattern made it to the widenet, anyone could access it, and anyone so inclined could flash into her at any time, at any moment, for as long as they wanted, unless she pulled her I-fi. And even if she did, any time she used the light flash she'd be vulnerable to involuntary occupation. As long as Mama Run lived, she would be a dark runner. She knew what that meant. If anyone understood the ways people used other bodies when there were no consequences and no questions asked, it was Mama Run.

She'd made her living off it for years.

"What do you <u>want</u>?" Mama Run hissed.

"First, I want this situation to get calm and relaxed. I just need you to do something, and once it's done I'll delete the pattern. That's it. No one will get hurt."

That was a lie, but it didn't matter. Mama Run couldn't take a chance that Annami was bluffing.

"And to make sure this all goes smoothly, I'm going to lock Lek and Chai in the safe until all of this is over."

She stepped away from Mama Run and gestured with her pistol toward the back.

"Put your minis on the bar as you pass," she told the guards.

She held up the pattern scanner.

"I can trigger the upload with one button, too, so don't try anything. Let's just get this done, huh?"

The brothers seemed utterly relaxed as they all retreated to the back office, and Lek and Chai entered the closet-sized safe where Mama Run kept various valuables, cash flow, and so on.

"You're probably gonna die," Chai said, almost rueful, as Annami closed the door on them.

"I know," she answered, and set the lock.

"Hey," Mama Run said. "You got an alarm on that thing? That scanner? You paying attention to fifteen minutes?"

Annami hadn't been, which was not ideal. She didn't actually want Mama Run's pattern uploaded to the net—that could cause all sorts of complications.

She lifted the scanner and hit the reset button, then stuck the thing back in her belt.

"There. Fresh fifteen."

Mama relaxed a little, then narrowed her eyes.

"So what's this all about?"

Annami thought for a moment, considering whether she was actually going to go through with this. But in her heart, she knew she was. That's why she'd chosen Mama Run. The woman was the worst person Annami could think of to whom she had access in the rapidly shrinking window before the auction began. She deserved everything that was about to happen to her.

Annami reached into her pocket and pulled out her stolen mini, her breath catching at the time displayed on its screen.

"An auction's set to happen in about forty-five minutes, up in Midtown. It's for a flash into a celebrity, a guy named Bhangra George."

"Oh, I know him," Mama Run said. "Handsome."

"Uh-huh," Annami said. "You're going to go up there and bid, and you're going to win."

CHAPTER 31

THE DETROIT RIVER

JON CORRAN GRIPPED THE COLD RAILING WITH BOTH HANDS AND looked out at the river.

It wasn't the still, dark ribbon it had been the last time he was out here—the surface was choppy, wavelets sweeping by, and the craft, a thirty-foot Sea Ray Sundancer 320 cruiser, moved within and above the water, shifting constantly. The 320 had multiple lounge areas, a wet bar, a wine fridge, state-of-the-art electronics, two inboard Horizon 6.2 engines that could shove the boat through the water at just over thirty knots while swallowing forty gallons of gasoline per hour. Below decks was a bit cramped, but it still sported a full shower, room to sleep four, and various other conveniences.

Corran would have loved to own one, but he didn't have $275,000 to spend.

This wasn't Gray Hendricks' best boat. It wasn't even his third best. It was, however, the least obviously his. From the shore, it looked like just another sporting vessel—the silhouette wasn't anything anyone would register as something other than "rich guy weekend boat." Hendricks' others—the Pershing 108 and the truly enormous Princess 40M—no one else in the city had anything like those, and even a basic description to the Wayne County Sheriff's Marine Unit or the Windsor Marine Patrol (depending on which side of the river the observer was standing on) would result in an immediate identification.

But the Sea Ray . . . you could get things done on that boat. Especially at night, with the running lights off.

Staying dark on the water was foolish, illegal, incredibly dangerous, with the massive freighters zooming up and down the Detroit River, like semitrucks laden with cargo speeding at eighty miles per hour along the highway. They'd flatten a thirty-foot yacht without even noticing, leaving just a few chunks of floating debris and an oil slick on the surface. But Hendricks had a good pilot at the helm, his man Ernesto, and as long as no one else was stupid enough to be out on the water without lights, he'd make sure they kept a good, safe distance from anything else moving along the river.

For more than one reason.

Jon Corran knew what was going to happen tonight. He knew the kind of man he worked for, and if he'd had any doubts, Hendricks' literal imprisonment of Gabby White and her family had erased them. He should have quit then. But he hadn't, and now it was too late. Hendricks had specifically told Corran to come out on the river that night, and he knew why. Whatever he'd see that evening would make it impossible for him to ever leave. He would be a witness, and by witnessing, he would be an accomplice. It was far too late. He was Gray Hendricks' man, and always would be.

Sara Kring was on the boat too, for what Jon suspected was a similar reason. She was standing in the bow near Hendricks. He didn't think the attorney had quite come to the same understanding that Corran had reached—but it wouldn't be long.

"Why am I here, Mr. Hendricks?" she said, and Jon turned toward the front of the boat to watch the drama play out.

Sara was part of a little group consisting of herself and Gray

Hendricks (standing), Paul White (seated on a luxuriously pad-
ded bench, staring fixedly at a large man, one of Hendricks' people
whom Jon had only heard identified as Mr. C, holding his sleeping
baby in the vessel's cockpit), Eddie Brill (also seated, with a large
gap between himself and Paul, a gap that spoke volumes considering that Eddie Brill was actually Gabrielle White), and then Mr. G,
another of Hendricks' men (standing, arms clasped behind his back
in a loosely militaristic posture, ready to assist with anything that
might be required).

Jon himself was just outside the cockpit, near the stairs leading
down to the small cabin below. A distance that he thought might
allow himself some moral deniability in weeks, months, and years
to come. But no, that was ludicrous. There was no denying this. He
was here, he had a phone in his pocket, he could hit 911 any time he
wanted.

Or he could just watch. Bear witness.

"Why are you <u>here</u>, Ms. Kring?" Hendricks said, his limestone-
quarry voice flavored with a note of mild surprise. "Don't you think
your client should have her lawyer present? Could be a high-stakes
discussion."

Brill was staring at Sara, her brow furrowed.

It was so strange to watch Gabby White's expressions swim up
from under Eddie Brill's features. It wasn't a perfect match—the
underlying structure of fat, muscle, and bone was different—but
Corran had spent a lot of time with Gabby in the time she'd been
on the Hendricks Capital teat, and he could <u>see</u> her under there. It
was amazing.

"You're right, Sara. You shouldn't be here," Gabby-in-Brill said.
"You were barely involved in the original paperwork. I don't think
you ever talked to Hendricks at all, just his lawyers, and even then
not much. You mostly just explained things to me. Why would he
even know you were my attorney?"

Kring swung her eyes toward Brill. Her expression was guilt, guilt, all guilt.

"You told him," Brill said, his voice flat and certain.

"I didn't," Kring said.

"Yes, you did. Hendricks would never have gone after us so hard, risked so much, unless he knew exactly what I invented."

"With my money," Hendricks interjected.

Brill swung his eyes over to Hendricks.

"Uh-huh," he said, dismissive, and then looked back at Kring.

"All of this is on you," he said, "and I'll never forget it."

Brill turned toward Hendricks.

"I have all the data from the research I did at your lab," he said. "You must have checked your servers by now, so you know it's the only copy. I hid the drive. I can give it back to you. We can make a deal."

Hendricks smiled and tilted his head, as if he was talking to a child.

"Why would I ever make a deal with you again? You don't honor your agreements. If you did, none of us would be out on the river in the middle of the night."

"Our deal was for an Alzheimer's treatment. Not for the flash."

"Our deal was for <u>everything</u>, Dr. White," Hendricks said, his smile vanishing. "A deal. Is. A. Fucking. Deal."

He turned, looking off the side of the boat, toward the Detroit skyline visible across the water.

"I hate those goddamn things," he said. "The casinos."

Corran knew where this was going—he'd heard Hendricks express this view before—but he turned to look and saw the tall, neon silhouettes, the MotorCity, the Greektown, the MGM, and the rest, the high-rise hotels speckled through the city anchored by several floors of gambling at their base.

"They're a lie, up and down," Hendricks went on. "They make

you feel like you have a chance to win, like you can beat them. They give you free booze and cheap food, and sweepstakes and jackpots and bells and whistles, but the truth is you have to play perfectly to get even a fifty-fifty shot, and no one's perfect all the time.

"This city used to be something. The Paris of the Midwest. Then it all got so bad that the mayor and the idiots on the city council let these . . . parasites in, just so they could have a little bit of a tax base, get some jobs going downtown, maybe fix a few roads and streetlights. But you know who patronizes those damn places? Poor people. People who can't afford to lose. And lose they do.

"Bringing in the casinos was like a starving man eating himself. The city could have bet on hard work, a willingness to improve things, and instead they doubled down on desperation."

He turned back to Brill.

"When this city's mine, they're all going to go. Every last casino, torn down to the ground. I'll put in parks."

He pointed at Kring.

"Explain to your client the legal situation she's in," he said.

"I did," Sara said. "When she first told me about all of this . . . we went over it."

"No," Hendricks said. "The situation she's in now. Seems like things have gotten quite a bit worse for Dr. White."

Kring turned to Brill.

"He's not wrong, Gabby. You . . . might have killed two people," she said.

"What are you talking about?" Brill said. "I didn't kill anyone."

"Well, Dr. Chavez, and Eddie Brill," Sara went on.

"They aren't dead," Brill answered.

"So where are they?"

No answer.

"And . . . there's your body, too. It, you, died in that hospital.

That's . . . another murder, maybe. It's suicide, in a way, but since you're still technically alive, it's not. A jury might decide that you'd killed someone, even if that someone was you."

That particular wrinkle had not occurred to Corran. All of this was turning out to be beyond fascinating.

Kring was right—Brill and Dr. Chavez would need to be brought back somehow, but if he understood the way the flash worked, that would mean Gabby's consciousness would have to be shifted into another body. Gabrielle White's original body was dead, though, moldering in the hospital's morgue downtown. Her mind had nowhere to go.

Corran knew Hendricks would solve that problem—maybe he'd flash Gabby into a comatose patient, or move her around in temporary shifts in various bodies selected from his thousands of employees, or just . . . take someone. It would get fixed. Gabby was too valuable to lose.

But the whole scenario brought up a range of ideas he hadn't really considered before. Gabrielle White was no longer anchored to her original body. She could inhabit anyone, any flesh—at least as far as they knew. If that idea bore out once they did further experiments, then . . . Corran's mind began to race, throwing out possibilities.

He considered it in terms of his grandmother. If they'd had the flash available when she was sick, her consciousness could have been pulled from her diseased brain and moved into a healthy body. She'd have been fine.

Gabby White might have invented a cure for Alzheimer's after all. If the flash could do that, who knew what else it could do? In the right hands, what good might it do for the world?

Corran thought about the fact that Gabrielle White's body was dead, gone, but there she was on the other side of the boat, arguing with Sara Kring about whether she was guilty of murder. Her expressions, her body language, swimming to the surface of Brill's bulky body. She was dead, but <u>she was still here</u>.

That was . . . fascinating.

The possibilities were endless.

Hendricks turned abruptly, shifting toward Paul, whose eyes were still fixed on his daughter.

"Hey, you doing all right?" Hendricks said, moving to sit down next to the other man. "Lotta craziness, I know."

Paul eyed him, wary.

"I'm fine. I'd like my daughter, please."

"She's fine. Mr. C's got her. Better to keep the kiddo away from all of us loud grown-ups talking—let her sleep, right?"

Hendricks reached into his suit coat and withdrew a small silver flask. He spun open the top, took a sip, then offered it to Paul. He took it, which surprised Corran a bit. On the other hand, this was a situation that probably did merit a drink. Paul took a swig and handed it back.

Hendricks gestured at Brill with the flask.

"Is it weird? I mean . . . that this is your wife now? I know you make a promise to stick together through thick and thin, but Eddie Brill is <u>thick</u>. Not sure the vows really take into account 'my lady turned into a big fat security guard guy.' Guess you'll see how it goes."

He looked back at Paul.

"But you know what's funny? As far as the world knows, Gabrielle White died in the hospital. Skull fracture. The doctors aren't sure how that happened. Cops are curious too. Lotta questions, and I know who they'll want to talk to for some answers. The husband. I work with the cops a lot, making Detroit safer. We talk. It's almost always the husband, they tell me."

"I didn't touch her," Paul said, his voice numb.

"Who knows what you did?" Hendricks said.

He lifted a hand and gestured toward his other lieutenant, the tough-looking man not currently engaged with holding Paul and Gabby's baby.

"Mr. G," Hendricks said. "Gimme the thing."

The man, Mr. G, reached into a messenger bag sitting on one of the boat's panels and withdrew a tablet, which he passed to Hendricks.

"Hold this for me, will you?" Hendricks said, passing the flask to Paul. "Feel free."

Paul looked down at the flask, then had another quick sip. Corran understood that.

For his part, Hendricks had busied himself with the tablet, sliding and tapping his fingers across the screen. He finished his work and lifted it, showing the images first to Paul, and then to Brill. Corran could see the tablet clearly from where he was standing. It was showing a short video clip, looped, of them bundling an unconscious Gabby into the hospital where she had died. Imagery scraped from one of Hendricks' ubiquitous cameras placed all over downtown.

Paul and Brill put Gabby in a wheelchair, strapping her in. Corran watched her head loll—she looked like she was already dead. They then conferred briefly, conspiratorially, and Brill rolled Gabby out of frame toward the hospital entrance.

"That's not what it looks like," Brill said. "Not at all."

"Maybe not," Hendricks said, "but how the fuck do you think you'll ever explain what it actually is?"

Brill's face crumpled a little. Despair, a very naked emotion on the big man's face. That was part of the disconnect, Corran thought—why it all seemed so surreal. Men usually didn't express themselves so clearly through the face. Or, no, that wasn't right. They did, but it was usually either laughter or anger, maybe intense concentration. Women tended to say more with their expressions.

Fascinating.

Hendricks shut off the tablet and handed it back to his lieutenant.

"I have footage of you guys from the minute you left my lab. I just followed you along the streets. I can give whatever part of it I want to the cops, make it tell whatever story I want it to tell. You're all fucked."

Hendricks stood up and looked at Brill, whose eyes had gone wide. The big man was looking toward the city, looking to see if maybe there was some help there.

There was not.

"So, Dr. White, I figure you stashed the drive with all that data in the hospital somewhere. Maybe not, though. You're smart."

He raised a hand.

"Thing is, this is all getting complicated. Camera footage, all that crap. Maybe we just make it simple, huh?"

Hendricks snapped his fingers. Once.

Snap.

Mr. G hit Paul in the face, very hard. Once. It made its own sound.

A snap but also a crunch, together, one sharp noise.

Paul's eyes went wide, and a startled little gasp escaped him. Mr. G put his hand around Paul's throat and tilted his head back.

"You bastard!" Brill shouted and made a move forward. Hendricks spoke once, quick and sharp.

"Hey!" he said, and Brill turned to look at him. "Don't forget Mr. C."

Hendricks pointed into the cabin, where his other man was still holding Gabby's daughter.

Brill froze.

"No," he said.

Corran knew he should say something. An evil act was being

committed, right in front of his face, and even if he couldn't stop it, maybe he could defuse it, turn down the volume a little, use Hendricks' general regard for his opinion to help Paul White.

But at the same time, superimposed over the horror and the violence happening not ten feet from him, Corran could see a better world, maybe not too far down the road. He could see the path to get there, every step, but in order for it to become real, Gray Hendricks needed to have complete and utter control over the flash technology.

The things that were happening here needed to happen, he decided, knowing he was damning himself but firm in his belief that his own morality was a worthy sacrifice on the altar of the greater good.

Today, by his inaction, he might be saving the world.

Corran said nothing.

Mr. G hit Paul again. His eyes rolled back, and a low groan escaped his throat.

"This is a sad story," Hendricks said. "A man beats his wife so bad she dies in the hospital."

"No, no," Brill said.

"He gets drunk, goes out on the river."

Mr. G lifted Hendricks' flask, still held loosely in Paul's hand. He squeezed Paul's cheeks, his mouth opened, and Mr. G poured some of its contents in, massaging Paul's throat so he swallowed. A horrible gagging noise ensued.

Mr. G upended the flask over Paul's head—it was all very practiced, like this wasn't the first time he'd done this. Whiskey fumes rolled back across the boat, tickling Corran's nose.

Brill made another involuntary move forward, and Sara Kring grabbed her arm.

"Gabby . . . ," she said. "I made a deal for us. It'll be okay."

"Fuck you, Sara," Brill said, and shoved the woman, hard. She went skidding back, hit the railing, and for a moment looked like she'd go over the side. Kring caught herself at the last moment and pulled herself back. She retreated into a crouch, wide-eyed, and, if Corran had to guess, had finally realized that absolutely nothing was going to be okay.

Brill turned toward Hendricks.

"Stop, right now, or I'll give you <u>nothing</u>. I promise you."

Hendricks reached into his coat again and pulled out a cell phone. Corran didn't recognize it, but evidently Brill did. His eyes went wide.

"That's . . . that's Camila's phone," she said.

"Yeah. Got the cops to unlock it for me. With this, I actually think we have enough to get going on our own," Hendricks said. "Anyway, where was I? Oh yeah."

He turned back to his goon.

"Husband gets drunk, falls into the river, hits his head, drowns."

Mr. G hit Paul in the face one last time and flipped him over the side of the boat, right over the rail.

One quick splash, and a wail escaped Brill—Corran could hear Gabby behind it, even though it was deep and mournful, like a foghorn.

In the cockpit, the baby woke up and began to cry.

"Fantastic," Hendricks said, annoyed. "You woke up the kid."

"Paul!" Brill screamed, scanning the river behind them. Nothing. "Paul!"

"Hey, Mr. C," Hendricks said. "Can you take the baby below, please?"

Brill realized what he had just heard and spun away from the boat's railing, lunging toward Hendricks.

"No, <u>no</u>. You <u>let her go</u>!" he said.

Mr. G, impressive as always, intercepted Brill before he reached Hendricks, taking his wrist in one hand and spinning him, shoving the arm behind Brill's back and up, forcing the larger man to his toes, a high little *nnngh* of pain whistling out through his lips.

"You have the eye things?" Hendricks asked him.

"Yes, Mr. Hendricks," Mr. G answered. "In my left suit pocket."

"Jon," Hendricks said. "Can you help with that? I think Mr. G's pretty occupied with handling Dr. White. Brill's got some power beneath the dough, looks like."

Corran walked forward, not allowing himself to think, and reached into Mr. G's suit, removing two ringlike devices, each about the size of a silver dollar. They were simple enough, and he reached forward and inserted them into Brill's eyes. They were spring-loaded, designed to push the eyelids back and make it impossible to blink.

Brill's eyes focused on Corran.

"Please," he said. "Jon, whatever they do to me, take care of my baby."

She didn't see it yet, and Corran understood that too. What Hendricks was going to do . . . who could see that coming? It was unthinkable.

Mr. C reemerged from below, and Hendricks handed him the cell phone.

"Code's eight, nine, six, seven," he said.

"Got it," Mr. C said, and apparently so did Gabrielle White, at last.

She began to scream, using Brill's voice, and the sound was as horrible as anything Corran had ever heard, mingling as it did with the sound of the baby below.

Messrs. C and G frog-marched Brill down into the cabin, struggling hard against the big body's desperate strength. But there were two of them, and they were strong, and eventually she went.

They came back up a few minutes later, closing the door behind them.

"All set?" Hendricks asked.

"Yeah," Mr. C said. "Did it just like you told me. Tied Eddie to a chair, put the baby in the bathroom, closed the door. Set the timer on the phone's camera. Sixty seconds."

They waited. They could hear Brill screaming below.

Corran looked over at Sara Kring. She was pale but standing straight. He wondered what would happen to her, now that she had tied herself so thoroughly to Gray Hendricks. He wondered what would happen to him, for that matter—although at least he had a plan. Kring just looked lost. Utterly gone.

"Everyone get as far as you can from the cabin, and turn away," Hendricks said. "Don't want to take any chances with this. Ernesto, you too."

The boat's crew and passengers, everyone not below decks, congregated at the bow and stern. No one was looking at anyone else.

"Please, no, don't do this!" came Brill's voice, in ragged harmony with the baby's wails. "I'm begging you! She's a person . . . you can't. Her name is Anna Katherine White. She's a person."

It had to be a minute by now. Hadn't a minute passed?

"Oh, Anna, I'm so sorry," Brill was screaming, sobbing. "Anna, I'm so—"

Silence. At the same time, both Brill's voice and the baby's crying stopped.

A few moments, then another voice—Brill's again, but not, this time with a light Latin accent to the words.

"Hello? Hello? Is anyone . . . hello?"

Dr. Camila Chavez, Corran guessed. Back from the dead, with her head full of knowledge about the flash she'd gained in her time working so closely with Gabrielle White. That was the real reason Hendricks had done this awful thing—it let him get Chavez back and kept Gabby sidelined, putting her in an easily controlled and always accessible prison cell. Brilliant. Brutal.

Corran walked toward the cabin, descended the steps. He couldn't help himself. He needed to see.

Chavez looked out at him from Brill's eyes.

"Oh, thank god . . . can you help me?"

Corran ignored her. He opened the door leading to the boat's tiny bathroom and saw the baby—Anna—sitting on the floor, looking up at him. Her expression was the coldest thing he'd ever seen, all the more because it was an entirely adult emotion, one that had no place on an infant's face.

He lifted her, and she was limp, dead weight in his arms, radiating hate like a furnace.

"Good, it worked," Hendricks said, appearing behind him.

Corran turned and looked at the man. A better world. Not too far down the road.

CHAPTER 32

AGAIN, THE DARKSHARE DEN

THE FATE OF THE WORLD RESTED ON WHETHER IT WAS POSSIBLE to get from East Chinatown to Hell's Kitchen in half an hour. In theory, it could be done, but only if everything went right. If you took the subway, you had to get lucky with the trains and had to make the right decision about whether you took the shuttle across from the east side to the west at Grand Central, or gambled on the F and a transfer to the C. If you took a cab, it was all down to the traffic, the driver, whether someone important was in town clogging up the avenues. If you took a bus, god help you. New York was ever thus.

Annami watched the little dot moving along the map displayed on the thinscreen she'd spread across the bar, willing it to move faster through the street grid of the city. A timer was counting down in the upper-left corner, currently under six minutes. The dot was tagged to Mama Run's mini, and it was telling her that the woman was at Forty-Eighth Street and Seventh Avenue. From there, she needed to do a long block and a short block in less than five minutes, enter the Worldwide Plaza building, and get to a large terrace on the forty-fifth floor, where Bhangra

George would auction himself off to the highest bidder in . . . five minutes and thirty seconds.

Mama Run could do it, but only if she didn't get stuck waiting for a light at a corner, or . . . what about the elevators? Annami hadn't thought about the elevators. If they were running slow, or stopped at too many intervening floors, that was it. Game over.

The dot moved, crossing Forty-Eighth and heading north. It was going fast, too, zipping right along. Mama Run had her own timer on her mini and knew what it would mean for her if she missed the auction.

Funny how all of this had worked out. According to the original plan, the one Annami had designed the moment the auction was announced, it should be her in that elevator, headed up to face her past and reset the future all at once. That wouldn't work anymore. Too many intervening disasters, and Bleeder knew her face—which meant Stephen Hauser did, and maybe even Bhangra George. They'd have alerted security. So it was Mama Run instead, and maybe that was a good thing.

George's team would run a scan for suicide waveforms on the auction winner, just a basic precaution, and that was a test Annami was not sure she would pass. But Mama Run . . . there was a woman with something to live for. You could tell by the way she was hustling across Eighth Avenue.

Three minutes.

Annami reached for the glass she had poured herself of Mama Run's best whiskey and took a sip. With the number of painblocks she'd already taken, it barely stung her cheek at all. Hell, the alcohol was probably a disinfectant.

Such a cliché, she thought. *Tough lady slugging back booze.*

She took another drink.

In another window on the thinscreen, the preshow vee for the auction was playing. Bhangra George himself was chatting with a feednet host, a woman in a tiger-striped catsuit with the full-on beehive hairdo that had recently come back in style. They were talking up the charity to which George was planning to donate the auction proceeds.

A little set had been built on a stage up on the broad, open terrace that occupied the entire southeast corner of the building's forty-fifth floor. The stage was a right triangle, with two sides built up against the building's edge, the Manhattan skyline behind it like a blocky, shining mountain range. The long side of the triangle faced the building and the audience. A flash rig had been set up at center stage, with two transfer couches complete with hoods and the transfer module right in the middle. Off to one side, a few chairs and a coffee table, with drone cams from every feednet in the world swirling around them. Bhangra George and his interviewer had set up shop there, chatting merrily away, the sun glinting off George's silver hair, his diamond smile.

Below the stage, Annami could see people milling around—sipping drinks and laughing, excited and well-dressed. A party.

"Have you ever done this before?" the presenter asked, her tone salacious, winking. "Let someone else into you?"

"Plenty, if you believe the rumors!" George said, and everyone laughed. Annami did not.

"The truth is, I've been so lucky in my life," he went on, "it can sometimes seem overwhelming. I spend a lot of time thinking about how I might put my good fortune to good use. This seemed like it might work. If my little bit of fame—"

"Oh, I'd say it's more than a little bit," the presenter interjected.

"That's kind," George said, smooth, oily, beautiful. "But I thought this might be a way to take people's interest in me and use it for something directly positive. The charity I've chosen, Foundation Nil, provides aid to people we don't always like to think about—individuals who get lost in the flash and never find

their way home. We call them zeroes, say they've been zeroed
out . . . but that's not true. They're still people; they still exist.
Their bodies need to be cared for, in the hope that someday we'll
find a way to bring them back. That level of care is expensive,
and of course there's trauma on the families too. I wanted to do
something for them, if I could."

He shrugged.

"Besides, it's only ten minutes. What's the worst that can happen?"

They laughed again, and this time Annami did too.

The thinscreen chimed, and a new window opened. Mama
Run, calling from her mini.

Annami tapped it.

"You made it," she said.

"Just barely," Mama Run answered, out of breath. "Had to . . .
run."

"Must have come naturally," Annami said.

"Ha. What now? You reset the timer?"

Annami lifted the pattern scanner from where it was lying
next to the thinnie. It had almost ten minutes left until its next
reset was necessary, but she pressed the button anyway. One less
thing to think about.

"Just did. You've signed in?"

"Yes. Used the ID you gave me."

Annami had registered for the auction shortly after it had
been announced, using a false identity she'd set up. Irony of iro-
nies, Mama Run had actually helped her with that, introducing
her to a slicer, an expert at creating people out of whole cloth in
all the relevant databases. The auction's ID verification system
was all passcode-based, which meant Mama could use it as easily
as Annami would have.

"Lotta people here," Mama Run said.

"I noticed," Annami responded, looking at the bidder list in another window on the thinnie.

Over four hundred people had showed up to try to purchase ten minutes inside Bhangra George. More than double the next-largest set of bidders who had ever participated in a charity flash auction, according to Annami's research. Four hundred–plus people, and she had to beat them all.

"Think I recognize some, too," Mama Run said, appreciative, impressed. "Some of these people are <u>famous</u>."

Annami groaned.

Lots of bidders was bad enough. The more bidders, the higher the winning bid, usually. But if some were rich too, famous friends of Bhangra George come to spike his price as a favor or a lark or a charitable deduction? Worse.

Her darksharing proceeds, liberated from Olsen and back in her e-count where they belonged, were displayed in yet another window on her thinnie. They amounted to just under a million dollars. Any ordinary flash auction, she could win five times over with that much. Now her bankroll seemed paltry, barely enough to keep her in the game.

Annami understood basic auction strategy. In an earlier life, she'd spent a lot of time on eBay. If you had infinite resources, you could just outbid everyone else, just grind it out until you were the last woman standing. But that meant the price would go as high as it possibly could, it took longer, and who had infinite resources?

Better to find ways to weed out the other bidders that didn't require a brute force approach—play with their minds more than their wallets. One school of thought suggested you should get in early and bid aggressively—challenge any other bidders as loudly and quickly as you could. The entire bidding pool would see that, and unless they felt like a fight—and who did?—they might not jump in at all, instead moving on to other auctions, easier pickings. It was a good strategy if there <u>were</u> other auctions—but here, there were not. There was only one thing to bid on—Bhangra George, and everyone on that rooftop wanted him.

She would need another angle.

The bidding opened, and Annami saw the reserve, twenty thousand dollars, disappear from her e-count. That was the fee to participate, and it was gone whether she won or lost.

The vee window on Annami's thinscreen displayed a dynamic, ever-shifting view of the proceedings, complete with soundtrack, chyrons, a scrolling bar of trivia, comments from viewers around the world, information about Foundation Nil and the people it helped, opportunities to rent or buy any and all of Bhangra George's media, any of which could be expanded into its own window with a flick of the finger. Above it all, the number, the big number, the running auction price, currently at just the reserve, twenty thousand.

Bhangra George himself was the auctioneer, a tiny micdrone hovering around his head, moving with him as he exhorted the crowd.

"All right, friends, let's get this started," he said, grinning. "How much do you think all of this is worth? Don't spare my feelings now."

He ran a long, languid hand down his chest.

"Sixty thousand," a woman called out.

Annami frowned. Sixty thousand as an opening bid, and most of these auctions topped out at around two hundred, two hundred fifty.

"What a wonderful beginning," George said. "Thank you, madam! Who's next? Surely we can't stop there."

"You want me to bid or something?" Mama Run asked.

"No!" Annami said. "Do nothing until I say."

"Whatever," Mama Run said.

The bidding proceeded in increments of two to five thousand dollars for a few minutes, quickly pushing the price up above one hundred thousand. Then a woman, rail-thin, extremely serious, body language suggesting she was drawing on every bit of financial, mental, and spiritual wherewithal she possessed, bid it up to a hundred and fifty.

A manicured, round man with a macaw on his shoulder and a martini in his hand responded immediately and kicked it up to two hundred.

"Goddammit," Annami said.

"You sure no bid from me?" Mama Run said.

"Yes!" Annami spat.

"This is getting exciting!" Bhangra George shouted. "I am extremely excited and aroused! Let's hope that calms down before the winner gets their ten minutes, eh?"

He winked. "Or not."

The thin woman bid again, another twenty thousand dollars.

That kicked off a flurry of back-and-forth bidding between Ms. Intense and Mr. Macaw, with other bidders jumping in here and there—many of whom the presenter breathlessly identified as actors, musicians, and other notables. Annami had a feeling they were bidding just for show, to shove the numbers up for their old friend George, but whatever the reason, the numbers did go up, and up, and by the time the next moment of calm happened, the number hovering at the top of Annami's thinnie was over six hundred thousand dollars.

"Fuck," she said.

A small, tarnished silver lining: the price had apparently gone far too high for the majority of the bidders. It was now just Ms. Intense, Mr. Macaw, and a few others, all of whom seemed a little taken aback that things had gone so far. Mr. Macaw was winning at present, and Annami thought he seemed simultaneously pleased and queasy.

"Six hundred and twenty-four thousand dollars is the current high bid," Bhangra George said, crowing. "This is incredible. Smashed all previous records. Thank you, thank you all so much. We're doing a lot of good here today, and I am grateful.

"But as much good as we're doing, do you . . . do you think we might do <u>more</u>? Can I hear six twenty-five? Come on, people. I'm beautiful, and it's for charity."

Silence from the crowd. No one moved, not a muscle, for fear of an inadvertent bid.

"Going once . . ."

This was the moment. Time to employ the other common strategy for winning auctions. Sniping. You sneak in at the last possible moment, throw in your lot after the next-highest bidder had already convinced themselves they've won. At that moment, when they've locked in a value for the auctioned item in their heads, when they already think of it as theirs, you puncture their satisfaction with a significantly higher bid that will feel outrageous, just outrageous, who would ever pay so much for such a thing . . . and then it's too late for them. They hesitate, the bidding closes, and the thing is yours.

"Going twice . . ."

"Bid seven hundred," Annami said.

"Whoa, seven? You sure? George is pretty, but that's so much—"

"Just fucking do it!" Annami screamed.

"Seven hundred and twenty-five!" shouted Bhangra George, and the number on the thinnie spun up more than a hundred thousand dollars in a single bid.

Annami was not the only sniper in attendance.

The new bidder was a man, older, early fifties, with a military bearing, standing next to a woman about the same age, in a wheelchair. A chyron below the vee dutifully spun out their biographies—both veterans, she'd taken a wound saving his life in a combat operation in North Korea back in 2022; they'd gotten married when they got home, and she was such a fan of Bhangra George, just such a fan, wouldn't it be a thrill to stand up using his legs, even just for ten minutes.

Annami hated them both.

She considered telling Mama Run to put in a bid of $740,000, but that was likely to just set off another bidding war. No. She looked at her balance: $978,000.

"Bid nine fifty," she said.

"Holy shit," Mama Run said.

"No arguments."

"Not arguing, just . . . okay. Nine fifty."

Either Annami had enough money or she didn't. She was so tired, so finished, so ready for it all to be done. There was nothing more she could do. She had fought as hard as she could.

She had chosen $950,000 because it wouldn't look so much like a last-minute desperation play as it would if she'd gone with the full $978,000. And on the off chance she needed to bump things up a little, she had a tiny bit of room to work.

She thought about everything she'd done to earn that money during her darkshare runs, and in losing and regaining it, most of which she'd never know about. Presumed indignities, violations, to the one body she'd tried so hard to keep pure. She had burned through everything she was, broken all her promises to herself about how she would be as she grew up in the stolen flesh of herself . . . all for this moment.

You are you, she thought.

Either she had enough or she didn't.

Annami wished she'd done a few more jobs, gotten it to an

even million. Nine fifty was just a temptation. It was begging for someone to put in that last fifty thousand, round it up.

Bhangra George thought so too. He was calling out for another bidder, telling the crowd how good it would make them feel, to be able to give a million dollars to charity. The symmetry of it, a hundred thousand dollars a minute. The bragging rights! He even said he'd be willing to let a few minutes of the time in his body proceed in private, no questions asked—this offer accompanied by a saucy wink.

But a million dollars was still a million dollars, and a million was too much.

Going once, twice, sold, and Mama Run won the auction.

Annami was holding her breath. After everything . . . after decades of horror and guilt and pain and effort and planning and failure . . . the day was here at last.

Today, she would change the world.

She forced herself to breathe. She slugged back the rest of the whiskey, bunched up the thinscreen in one hand, and headed for one of the den's flash couches.

Timing, she thought. *Don't screw up the timing.*

Mama Run was now up onstage being awkwardly interviewed by Bhangra George. He was trying to get her to explain why she'd bid so high, and Mama Run was just repeating the words *Big fan*, with a fake smile plastered across her face. Annami realized that Mama Run might be regretting that she'd just bid almost a million dollars in an extremely public auction. Her bosses in the Three-Fold Blades might find that a very odd thing for her to have done. They might be intensely curious about where that million dollars had come from.

Oh well.

Bhangra George gave up and finally just asked Mama Run if she was ready to claim her prize. The woman perked up and agreed, seeming genuinely excited. Annami had briefed her on this. She knew what to do—go through with the transfer, wait ten minutes until she automatically flashed back to her prime. That was it. Once it was done she could come back to the den, and Annami would delete her flash pattern from the scanner. Easy.

Annami pulled the memory unit from the pattern scanner and attached it to her flash rig in the darkshare den. She uploaded Mama Run's pattern and set the rig's control screen to look for a match to her I-fi implant.

Searching . . . on the screen.

Nothing, nothing . . . and on the thinnie, Annami could see Mama Run settling herself on a transfer couch up on that rooftop, logging in to the light flash by putting her head beneath the couch's hood attachment.

"Come on!" Annami shouted at the flash rig on her end, willing it to scan faster. If Mama Run got into Bhangra George before the rig found her pattern, it was over. Or . . . what if the woman didn't have I-fi? She hadn't checked. She'd just assumed— everyone had I-fi. Even Annami had I-fi, and she had every reason in the world not to.

"All good?" said George over on his own transfer couch, his head beneath his own hood. A thumbs-up in response from Mama Run.

Annami pulled the flash rig down over her head. She was out of time. Either the system would get a pattern lock with Mama Run in time or it wouldn't.

She triggered her rig and/

She was on that couch, on that rooftop, looking at Bhangra George three feet away on his own couch, smiling at her, drone cams swirling around them.

He was even better looking in person.

"You ready?"

"Let's do it," Annami said.

"Enjoy yourself," George said, and lay back on his couch. "You've earned this."

You have no idea, Annami thought.

Another flash, and/

Annami was Bhangra George. She stood and made a quick show of smiling, touching her face, running her hands up and down his body, as if she was luxuriating in it.

She was, too. No more pain in her wrists, no more pain in her cheek, no more burning fatigue, no more gritty eyes. Just the sleek feeling of a body maintained at the highest possible level for years.

The beehived, catsuited feednet host was there, smiling at her, sending a micdrone to hover in front of Annami's face with a flick of her fingers.

"How do you feel? Is it everything you dreamed?"

"I hope so," Annami answered. "Excuse me."

She stepped past the host and stood at the foot of the other transfer couch, looking down at Mama Run's unconscious body. The woman was a pimp. She deserved what had happened to her—because of everything she'd done to Annami personally, and probably much more over the years, awful things done or that she had permitted to be done to her other runners—but yet. This next bit . . . it seemed cold. Not unjustified . . . but not the way she'd wanted this to go.

"I'm sorry," she said quietly. "It was supposed to be me."

Annami reached down and grabbed Mama Run by her coat, glad of Bhangra George's trainer-enhanced vee-star strength. She dragged the woman's body the ten feet to the edge of the stage, which was also the edge of the roof.

She threw Mama Run over.

Drone cams raced past her, diving over the side to follow the body down.

Annami turned around, looking at the utterly shocked faces of the presenter, the other bidders, the support staff. They waited— there was no reason to do anything. They knew the rule— everyone knew the rule. It was hardwired into the flash itself.

If one dies, both die.

There were no corollaries, no caveats, no exclusions or exceptions. The instant Mama Run's body hit the street, Bhangra George would drop dead.

Minis were out, more drone cams swirling around her, all waiting to capture the moment. Annami thought some of the minis were probably also tracking the feeds from the drones that had gone over the side, flying down with Mama Run, waiting to see the impact, catching both deaths at once.

A flinch ran through about a third of the crowd, and Annami knew she was right. Mama Run had hit the ground, and these ghouls had just watched it happen.

Murmurs, turning to howls of disbelief as everyone in attendance, everyone around the world watching, everyone everywhere understood what had just happened.

Bhangra George . . . or rather, the woman using him as a vessel . . . was still alive.

One had died . . . but both had not.

The Two Rules . . . were not the rules.

"My name is Gabrielle June White," Annami said, the drone cams swirling around her picking up every word and sending it out across the planet. "Twenty-five years ago, I invented the flash. For twenty-five years, you have been lied to."

END OF PART III

TWENTY YEARS FROM NOW

SOUTH CHINA MORNING POST
OP-ED BY DR. CHEN ZHANG-MIN, PHD

I knew this moment was coming—but foreknowledge makes it no easier to handle. Tomorrow, I turn seventy, and despite my entreaties based on my ongoing work as a sociologist (deemed useful and important by not all, but many), awards up to and not limited to the Nobel gleaming on my shelf at home, and requests from my doctors and powerful friends, there are no waivers or extensions available. Tomorrow, I wake up a Dull.

People all over the planet experience this moment every day, and the vast majority are also denied waivers. I am no one special—but I cannot help but wonder if Anyone's refusal in this case is because of my work these last ten years, examining the impact of the flash on our world. Stephen Hauser does not like people criticizing what he has built, does he? I have been critical, yes, but like any great shift in humanity, the flash has its good and bad elements. The only crime would be failing to examine, failing to look.

In any case, tomorrow the flash will be closed to me

forever, and I will be locked in the body of my birth until the day I die. So strange that this bothers me. After all, for thousands of generations humankind somehow managed to muddle through our lives with only the flesh into which we were born.

But that is not what we are now, is it? Ever since Stephen Hauser and NeOnet Global gave us the flash back in Boston so many years ago, we began to change, to evolve, quicker by the day. Now . . . it is hard to say what we are. But I've spent my career as a sociologist, so I can't help myself. I'm going to try. This may be my last opportunity to think clearly between now and the day I die, and I have decided to use some of my remaining hours to write this piece. Perhaps this is the foolish choice of an old scholar—most in my position use their final flash revisiting youth one last time, for sex or physical exertion or other indulgence. I am using it to think, to write. But these were always the activities I loved best, and tomorrow they will be denied me, so do not judge. Just read.

With no further preamble—my thoughts on who we are now, in the world of the flash.

In some ways, I think we're better. We relate to each other differently—the external doesn't matter so much. Flesh is less crucial. Of course, culture still plays a significant role—unites and divides us as it always has—but it's not as it was. It's harder to hate someone if you can be them. Not impossible, but a little harder.

I give Hauser all due credit for this, particularly the pricing structure he developed. From the very start, he charged for flashing only based on distance and time. Like long-distance telephone calls when I was young. Flashing into a virile young person in their twenties costs the same as, oh, a decrepit old sociologist about to enter her eighth decade. No pricing tiers based on race, abled-ness, gender, or any of our other standard social categories.

Of course, people found ways around this, as people always do—service fees, and add-ons, and other costs to ensure that the most desirable bodies are priced and rewarded as befitting their status. But Hauser would tell you that none of that was his fault. The basic service, the version over which he had control, was offered in the same way for every person on earth.

The cynic in me would say Stephen Hauser did this simply to allow himself some moral deniability—any abuses were the fault of the market, not of Anyone or its policies. Now that my waiver has been denied for the final time, let me say what I have always thought—he's a slippery one. You look at the decisions he makes, the way he exerts power using the flash and its ubiquity and necessity . . . the public decisions are often rather lovely. I think of his choice to use only renewable energy to power Anyone's network, or his efforts to build that network throughout the world to allow for easy flash travel to virtually anywhere on earth, or his insistence that all newly built NeOnet Global facilities be constructed from wood to serve as carbon sinks.

We were headed for disaster as a species before the flash. I believe that. Climate change would have killed us, and if not that, social collapse, or a superbug pandemic, or any number of other catastrophes generated by too few having too much and everyone else fighting over their own little slice of what was left. The flash solved that. Populations no longer mix the way they used to—at least not physically. Air travel, cars, as well as the industries that produced them—everything was reduced substantially, enough for other efforts to save the planet to get a foothold.

All of that is good—but I cannot help but wonder about Stephen Hauser. He is <u>so powerful</u>. We see his public decisions. What about his private ones? What does he actually want?

I think about the way technology and our relationship to it evolves over time. Social media is a perfect example. Do you remember its first decade? For me, it was Weibo. Perhaps for you, it was Twitter, or Facebook. Everything was fun, light; it brought people together. And then it turned, and we understood that the technology was about turning ourselves into products, offering corporations windows into our lives in the most intimate of ways. We understood how much control it had over our minds, our thoughts.

I believe the flash is like this. We have allowed it access not just to our minds but also to our very bodies. It has all of us. We define ourselves by where the flash allows us to go. And, by extension, where Stephen Hauser allows us to go.

We are already addicted to the flash as a species. We cannot turn away from it. What will this mean? We cannot know. The technology has only been widely available for a decade or so. Not enough time to be certain. But I will say, having studied humanity for my entire life, that we are not good at forecasting the consequences of our actions. We want what we want, right now, and let the future be the future's problem.

The flash solved some of mankind's greatest challenges. But I fear we are unable to see the new problems it brought us, or those it might create in years to come. When we can "be anyone with Anyone," will we care about being ourselves? A trite thing to say, but no less true.

I see all of this, and yet I know that I would do almost

anything to get Hauser's waiver, to keep flashing until the day I die. I understand why the suicide rate spikes after seventy. In a way, I am surprised the AI self-harm safeguards in Anyone's network allowed me to do this last flash. Death is very much on my mind. I still have a few hours left before the day turns, but I will tell you, it feels like a premature burial.

For me more than most, perhaps, because I am in the middle phase of a slow descent into dementia. I was diagnosed several years ago. These may be the last clear thoughts I ever have. I will miss being this version of myself, the sharp-minded woman I remember from my youth. It feels like slipping into a fog, returning to my prime. But that is who I am, now and forever. Always, really. Any other version of myself was just a trick of the light.

I do not know who I will be as a Dull. That is the issue, right there. I do not remember who I was before the flash let me be anyone. Humanity is forgetting too. I don't know what that means, but even this strong young vessel I am inhabiting now is sick to its stomach at the thought.

In any case, the genie is out of the bottle, as the saying goes. Whatever the flash has done to us, whatever it will do to us . . . it's happening. There's no stopping it now.

Chen Zhang-Min
Hong Kong

PART IV

CHAPTER 33

NOWHERE

THE WORLD IS LOUD.

The world is bright.

Gabrielle does not understand. She closes her eyes.

She is hungry, and she is small, and she is weak.

She has a sense, a . . . memory, of not being small, of being different than she is now. She does not have the words to explain why she is small now.

A picture comes into her head, of herself, lying in a . . . sleep place. Looking down across her body, long legs under . . . blankies, with feet sticking up, making little bumps at the end of the sleep place. The . . . bed.

It is another memory, of a time when she felt hot and cold at the same time . . . sick, she had been sick. With . . . flu. The flu. Influenza.

The word comes to Gabrielle's mind, and she feels that it is a victory to know such a big, complex thing.

The flu felt like she feels now. A bodily weakness still somehow burning with energy, sensations cranked up to unbearable levels.

She wets herself, a sudden pleasant warmth that unlocks another door in her mind. Someone needs to change . . . the Kitten. Kat. Anna Katherine White.

She remembers now. She is in Anna. Her tiny, wonderful, lovely daughter, and Gabrielle has stolen her body, her mind.

No. Someone else did it to her, to them both. Gabrielle would never hurt her daughter. It was someone else.

She opens her eyes, and the blurred surge of intensity and color and movement that is the world returns.

Gabby fights to make sense of it. She is being held by someone, cradled, and she looks to see if it is the person who can fix this, who can set it right again, who can save her daughter.

The name is . . . the name . . .

Hendricks, she thinks. *A bad name. A bad man.*

She tries to speak, to plead with whoever is holding her—she doesn't know who, she can't see, the angle is off, and the smell around her is worse, dirt and metal and chemicals, nothing clean and right, nothing soft, everything rough against her skin, which is as sensitive as her senses. She tries to beg the person who is holding her so wrongly to return her daughter to life, to set her free.

They made a prison cell of Anna's tiny body and set her inside it. The evil of it, the pure evil.

Surely they can see that. They couldn't do this. No one would do this.

Gabrielle makes a sound, nonsense syllables, spits them out loudly and violently.

The man holding her shifts a bit, changing his grip—she knows it is a man, because a woman would never allow something so abominable to happen.

Sara Kring.

The name comes to her, and she knows that yes, some women would.

She tries again to speak. Nonsense, unintelligible. Just sounds, not language. She knows the idea she is trying to express, but the words will not come.

Aphasia, she thinks, a concept that already seems to come from a distant version of herself, a mind and a set of knowledge rapidly receding against the onslaught of the bright and loud and smelly and rough world she is now inhabiting.

Anna's brain is only eleven months old. Her language centers are underdeveloped, and while the flash carries through memories, skills, and experience, the basic hardware Gabby is now using doesn't seem to like complex adult thoughts. Like trying to watch TV on a radio.

She is so hungry. Why won't someone help her? Give her food?

Where is Dada? *No*, she reminds herself. *Not Dada. Paul.*

But where is he? He can help her. He is good. He helps. He loves, he cares.

And then another memory. The splash, as he hit the water.

Paul can't help anyone.

Her diaper is no longer warm. It is damp and cold.

She needs things. She is hungry.

She needs her mother. She needs her father. They cannot come.

Gabrielle feels herself slipping away into the swirl of Anna's perception, her analytic mind sinking below the surface of the sea of input. Sights, sounds, smells, touch.

She needs.

She opens her mouth to explain this, to ask for what she needs, and a sound comes out, one she has heard so many times before, one that, as Anna's mother, she is hardwired to answer instantly, to address, to fix. To feed, to change, to hold, to love.

Gabrielle cries in her daughter's voice and can do nothing to help her.

The temptation to let herself fall away into Anna is so strong now. Fighting is pain. Just surrender.

But she does fight, searching for one idea, any idea, simple enough that Anna's young mind can comprehend the words, an anchor that will hold Gabrielle separate from Anna until the day she can find a way for Gabrielle to actually be separate from Anna. The day she can free herself, and free her daughter.

You are you, she thinks.

You are you.

You are you.

You are you.

She cries in the arms of a stranger, wailing, screaming, giving voice to her guilt. Because ultimately, who has done this to herself, to Anna, to Paul?

You, she thinks.

You are you.

You are you.

You are you.

But not only you, she thinks.

Gray Hendricks, Sara Kring, Jon Corran, and anyone else who watched and did nothing.

You are you.

You are you.

You are you.

And someday . . .

CHAPTER 34

FORTY-FIVE FLOORS ABOVE STREET LEVEL, MANHATTAN

"The Two Rules," Annami said. "You all know them."

Dronecams circled her, and the audience of assembled press and losing auction bidders all had their minis up. Everywhere she looked, faces focused on her, waiting.

She was still at the back of the stage—near the edge of the roof—and she thought that was why the security guards in attendance hadn't made any moves toward her. They'd just watched her toss her prime off a skyscraper, and here she was, still standing, still talking. Who knew what she might be capable of?

Ten minutes. The transfer into Bhangra George had a preset end point, and she had already used at least sixty seconds, maybe more. She had to say her piece now, before she lost her chance— Annami had no idea what would happen to her when that ten minutes was up. If Mama Run were still alive, the system would automatically shunt her back into that body—but Mama Run was dead, somewhere on the sidewalk far below.

Set that aside, she thought. *It doesn't matter. What matters is now. They've had this coming for twenty-five years.*

Annami held up two fingers.

"The first rule: if one dies, both die. The second: no multiple jumps. You can only flash one step away from your prime."

She pointed off the roof, suggesting the path Mama Run's body had recently taken.

"You just saw me break the first one, and if you dig deep enough, you'll see I broke the second, too. My real prime is three flashes away, and it died twenty-five years ago.

"Like I said, my original name is Gabrielle June White. I was born in Flint, Michigan. I was a scientist. I had degrees from the University of Michigan and Northwestern. I was married. I had a daughter.

"Anyone stole that from me. Anyone, and Gray Hendricks, and Stephen Hauser, and Jon Corran, and a woman named Sara Kring.

"The net and public records have been scrubbed—but if you look, you'll find something. Nothing stays hidden forever. I mean . . . here I am."

Utter silence on the roof, so quiet she could hear the tiny hover systems on the drones. Even the security guards were rapt, waiting to see what she might say next. Twenty-five years ago, she had said. Before the invention of the flash. This was foundational stuff. Fascinating to anyone listening, just fascinating—and she hadn't even gotten to the meat of it.

"The flash was built on murder and lies," Annami said. "I created it, and Hendricks and his people stole it from me. They wanted me to cooperate with them, to help them use it, and when I said no, they killed my husband."

Music came to Annami's mind, a piece she hadn't thought about in a quarter century. The piano in their little apartment in Hendricks' prison lab, being played by her husband, heard through the door as she walked up to it in Eddie Brill's body. She didn't know what it was called—she hadn't thought to ask. She wished she had. It was the last music he ever played.

"His name was Paul, and they drowned him in the Detroit River and told a story about how he committed suicide. That was a lie. Gray Hendricks had him killed."

Murmurs through the audience.

"They could have killed me too, but Hendricks decided I might be useful. So he used an early version of the flash to put my mind in the body of my infant daughter, and he kept me there."

Tears were welling up in her eyes, all the emotions she hadn't let herself feel for so long.

"Her name was Anna, and I . . . I miss her very much."

Annami lifted her hands, trying to connect with the people watching, both there on that roof and all across the world. She knew her words would be analyzed, dissected, for decades. She had to get this right.

"I thought that was the worst of it, what they did to me. But it's not. They stole your world too," she said. "The flash should have changed everything, given us a new way to live. I wanted it to set us free. But we're all slaves."

She wiped her eyes with the back of her hand, willing herself to focus.

"I worked at Anyone for five years, studying the flash, seeing how it had changed during the years I had to hide from Hendricks and his people. I discovered something. When I first saw it in the network, I didn't believe what I was seeing. They hid it. They hid it deep.

"The flash didn't always work the way it does now. When I created it, the safeguards, the Two Rules . . . they didn't exist. NeOnet added them, built them in before they released the technology to the public. But Hendricks kept the original version for himself—and a chosen few, his handpicked elite. He called them his Centuries."

Annami could see the truth beginning to sink in across the

faces in the audience—the guy with the macaw seemed particularly dismayed—but she wanted to bring it home, to make the situation crystal clear.

"Without the Two Rules, the flash can make you immortal. When your prime gets old, you take someone else's body and let your old one die. As many times as you want. Forever. That's what Stephen Hauser did. He can turn off the Two Rules for anyone he wants, and he did.

"He offered immortality to the most powerful people on earth, and his price was obedience. The Centuries control our governments, our technology, our economies, our entertainment, our entire world—and they do whatever Hauser says."

Annami began speaking more quickly. She was running out of time.

"Most of my life was before the flash. I grew up in the eighties and nineties, poor, in a system that made it incredibly hard for people like me to ever get out of that poverty. It was like a ladder with most of the lower rungs missing. I got through it, though—my whole family pulled together, and I worked hard, and I got lucky, and I got my shot.

"I saw progress—my life was better than my mom's, and hers was better than my grandmother's, and I had faith that the life I'd give—"

Annami's voice hitched. She took a breath, steadied herself.

"The life I'd give my daughter would be better than mine. I didn't know how long it would take, but I thought a day might come when no one would make assumptions about people because of their gender or their skin color, or anything else. Just take them as they were. Everyone would have a voice.

"That's gone now. Hauser made a master race, the ultimate master race. They never have to die, as long as they keep taking new bodies. They are vampires. I want you to think about that.

Every time they choose a new body, its original owner dies. The people who run the world think it's acceptable to kill another human being to prolong their own lives. The people who <u>run the goddamn world</u>.

"We are all—every single one of us—their property. Whether we realize it or not, whether they treat us well or not—we are here for them to use."

Annami looked out at the crowd, willing them to understand, willing them to see the truth, willing them to get <u>angry</u>.

"We can stop it. The flash is still new. The Centuries aren't too entrenched. But look ahead a hundred years, two hundred, when these people have gotten used to watching all of us wither and die while they play their little games with each other . . . what happens when they get bored? What happens when they go to war with each other? You think any of our lives will <u>matter</u> to them?

"We're meat, and we'll <u>be</u> meat. We <u>have no voice</u>.

"When you die, they'll still be here. When your children's children die, they'll still be here, deciding every aspect of how the world works. Maybe one will take your grandson or your grand-daughter as their vessel, until they get bored and throw it away for something newer, fresher. Forever."

Frowns among the watchers. Good. They saw it.

"Stephen Hauser is one, Bhangra George is another. There are more, in positions of power across the world. Test them. Use the second rule—it's easy. If they can flash twice, from a vessel to a vessel, they're a Century. You'll see. They're laughing at you. They're vampires, and they're <u>laughing</u> at you."

Annami knew she was repeating herself, losing focus, get-ting overwhelmed. She just wanted them to understand, to feel the enormity of what had happened to her. She needed to purge her pain, to take down the whole corrupt system, to take back what was hers, to change the world the way she had always intended to.

"I was the first person to ever flash," she said. "It was back in Michigan. In my lab, in the barn."

Tears spilled from Bhangra George's eyes.

"I knew what it could mean. A world where you couldn't judge people by how they looked. Only by what they did.

"I wanted to give you that," Annami said. "We deserved it."

She was rambling. This wasn't how she had envisioned the moment. She should have been standing strong, fierce, weaponizing all of Bhangra George's charisma in the interest of vengeance.

And she was weeping, a mess, unfocused.

It wasn't supposed to be this way. The virus she had inserted into Anyone's network was designed to seek out evidence of Centuries running double transfers, breaking the second rule. It had, presumably, sent that evidence to her mini a day before—the raw data that would corroborate everything she was saying here. But events had just underlined, and her mini was still in that locker in the brothel where Soro had died.

"I had proof of all of this," she said. "Records from inside the flash network. I lost it, but the information's there, if you look. It's there."

Motion at the edge of the crowd, a parting that began near the doors leading off the terrace. It advanced through the crowd, like a shark's fin rising up above the surface of the sea.

Annami knew what that meant. Time was not running out. It was gone.

"I would have made the flash about us. About humanity. What separates us and unites us. I would have used it to make us see each other."

The movement through the crowd revealed itself as eight men, large, dressed in black, menacing. Annami recognized some from a brothel-turned-slaughterhouse, and the back of a van, and a gunfight in lower Manhattan. These were Eaters.

"Every baby born should have a chance to be anyone," Annami said, knowing it was over. She'd done everything she could.

"Anyone."

Annami scanned across the Eaters, looking for Bleeder. He wasn't among them, but another face she knew stepped forward, standing right at the front of the stage, looking up at her.

His name is . . . Perry, she thought. *No. That's not right. Perez.*

"Hello, Annami," Perez said.

"Where's Bleeder?" she said. "Dead?"

"Bleeder's dead," another Eater said. "You killed him. Perez got the promotion. Got the download. He's Bleeder now. The big boss."

Annami saw the truth immediately, what Bleeder had done, had probably been doing for years. She wondered why the Eaters let him do it, just put up with it. And then she realized . . .

"They don't know," she said to Perez, who was, of course, Bleeder. "They don't know you take them."

She took a step backward, glancing to either side of the stage, where Eaters had ascended and were slowly making their way toward her, like the jaws of a bear trap closing in slow motion. Bleeder remained below on the roof, looking up at her.

"How stupid are you?" she said to the approaching Eaters. "Bleeder doesn't have the Two Rules. He never dies. He's the eater. He eats you."

Uncertainty washed across the faces of the men nearest her, and they glanced down at Bleeder, who now had a gun in his hand.

"His name is—" she began, thinking perhaps Bleeder's true identity would delay the Eaters even further, but she did not finish, because the gun fired, and Annami felt a sharp punch in her stomach, and she fell backward off the edge of the roof.

Screams, sounds of distress and alarm, quickly fading, and wind rushing past her. Pain burning, surging in her stomach, and she wondered why Bleeder had shot her when she was still in Bhangra George's body. Maybe the wound wasn't a fatal shot, the idea being just to shut her up, but that had backfired, because even if the bullet didn't kill her, the fall certainly would.

Annami put those thoughts aside. She had better things to think about in these final seconds.

After all of it, after everything, she had won. She had fought her way back from the hell Hendricks had consigned her to, and she had ripped open both the many lies and the many truths about what that monster had done to her, to the world. What she'd said could not be ignored. People would rise up, and Gabrielle White would be vindicated. Paul and Anna would be avenged. Soro's death would not be in vain.

Even her own end, mere seconds away, might mean something more than it otherwise would. Martyrdom, perhaps.

The flash would be rethought, altered forever, for the better.

And maybe, in time, the world she would have built with it would come to exist. A fairer world. A better world.

You are you, she thought.

You are you, and you just changed the—

CHAPTER 35

A MEN'S ROOM

JON CORRAN CONSIDERED HIS FACE.

He stared at it in the mirror, focused on its planes and curves and angles. The color of his eyes, the shape of his eyebrows, the little divot on his cheek—a chicken pox scar that brought memories of a specific time in his life, the twelfth birthday party canceled for reasons of contagion and the R-rated movie rented by his father as a consolation prize (*Halloween II*).

The odd little nub of cartilage on his ear, like the very beginning of a transformation into a Vulcan or an elf.

His mouth, which had always just been his mouth until a day in college when a boy had told him he loved his lips, they were so full.

His hair, which he knew he was vain about, but why not? Vanity just meant you loved yourself, and if you didn't, who would?

His face: the only window through which he'd ever seen the world, and the way the world saw him.

He was his face.

He liked it.

He wondered if that would still be the case, if he went through with what he was considering that day.

Who would Jon Corran be then?

His bag was on the floor by his feet, a beat-up leather backpack he brought to work with him every day. The same bag he'd had for years, full of too much useless history, scraps of paper and business cards and charging cords and mostly used lip balm, all making the thing heavier than it needed to be, but the task of cleaning it out never seeming quite important enough to allocate the necessary half hour. Today, his bag felt even heavier than usual, even though he wasn't holding or even touching it, because of the weapon waiting inside.

Jon's phone buzzed: a text from Gray Hendricks. Not surprising.

Ever since the night on the river, out on that Sundancer 320, ugly things happening on a beautiful boat, Hendricks had sought him out repeatedly to talk about the flash tech. To talk at him, really. Jon generally just sat and listened.

This was new, spending so much time with Hendricks. Until very recently, Corran had been just one of the great man's project managers, one of many, not any sort of confidant. The change in status didn't seem like a privilege, though. More like he'd been locked into a shark cage as a great white circled.

Jon wasn't close with every member of Hendricks' personal security team—he knew some of their faces, mostly—but he did know that the men on the boat the night the White family was utterly destroyed hadn't been around recently. No more Mr. C. Bye-bye, Mr. G.

Maybe they'd quit, scandalized by what their boss had done, unwilling to keep working for him, deciding to move on to new opportunities.

Sure.

From his conversations with Hendricks, Corran had gotten the sense that his boss was still in a bit of a mental holding pattern with respect to Gabrielle White's miraculous invention. He hadn't done anything with it yet, as far as Jon knew. Poor Dr. Chavez was still stuck inside the body of Eddie Brill, for example. That seemed like a tactical decision on Hendricks' part, though, like an action, not inaction.

Camila was one of the few people still alive who understood the flash on anything more than a surface level, which made her valuable and dangerous in equal measure. Better to keep her where she was, in a comfortable apartment in one of Hendricks' downtown buildings under twenty-four-hour guard, while he held the ultimate leverage of her own body over her.

Corran wouldn't have done that. He'd have switched Dr. Chavez back as quickly as he could and freed Brill into the bargain, if that was possible. Keeping her trapped was monstrous, yet another monstrous thing in the snail trail of evil Hendricks left behind him.

The more Jon came to know Hendricks personally, the more he was certain that what he'd seen the man do in the last few months was nothing new. An iceberg tip. He knew how Hendricks used tech, too—how many people had he blackmailed with that surveillance system in the basement? Who knew what he might do with something as powerful as the flash?

It's Hitler as a baby, Corran thought, finally turning away from the mirror and picking up his mentally, spiritually heavy bag, slinging it over his shoulder.

Jon knew he couldn't kill a baby, and he wouldn't, even Baby Hitler. Not just because of the horror of it, but also because he believed in the power of nurture over nature—at least where morality was concerned.

But Gray Hendricks was not a baby.

Corran left the men's room and walked to the elevator, riding it to the top floor, to Hendricks' office.

The great man was standing with his back to the door when Corran entered, looking out at the city. His city.

Hendricks turned slightly, acknowledging him, then looked back toward the window.

"Close the door behind you, Jon," he said.

Corran did. He would have anyway. For the best, considering.

"You know," Hendricks said, even before the door latch fully clicked home, "for a long time now, I've been worried I wouldn't have time to save this city. Wouldn't live long enough. Too much work to do. I've made a start, sure . . . but still so much left to do. The bastards dragged Detroit down so far, it's the work of lifetimes to set it right. It's my responsibility, and I didn't know how I'd see it through."

Corran sat in one of the chairs facing Hendricks' desk, setting his bag on the floor, leaning it up against the chair leg. He knew the protocol by now—his job here was to listen.

He could see Hendricks' reflection in the window—could see the whole man, front and back. He considered him, the way he had examined himself in the mirror.

Gray Hendricks.

Not young. Sixty, if not older. Hard to be sure, because of his largely unmarred skin, the dark, shining arc of his skull sloping into thick waves at the back of his neck. His eyebrows were really the only clue that he wasn't, say, forty—bushy salt-and-pepper caterpillars casting shadows down across his eyes. More salt than pepper.

They need a trim, Corran thought.

Hendricks was big, but he wore it well, providing an impression of immense solidity as opposed to indulgence. That could just be the clothes, though. Corran tried to imagine the other man naked and couldn't quite get there. His mind conjured an unbroken, sleek bulk, like a seal or a whale.

Was Gray Hendricks attractive?

Corran couldn't believe he was asking himself the question, but it mattered. Hendricks was immense, institutional. Attractiveness had never entered into it. But suddenly . . . it did.

Would it make it easier or harder to do what he thought he had to if his boss was a good-looking man? It was Baby Hitler again. The Nazi was easier to kill than the baby because babies were cute and Nazis were ugly.

Corran found himself unable to decide with respect to Hendricks' beauty, unable to separate the exterior from the interior.

"The thing is," Hendricks said, still facing the window, "I think I have lifetimes."

"Oh?" Jon said. "What do you mean?"

He knew exactly what Hendricks meant. In fact, he'd expected the other man to figure things out much earlier. Corran had gotten there on the boat, watching Gabby White talk out of Eddie Brill's mouth.

But Hendricks was older, more entrenched, slower to react to change. Human existence had shifted to a new paradigm, and Hendricks had just taken a little while to notice.

It was good that the other man understood, though. Made it easier to do what needed to be done.

"I have all the time I need," Hendricks said. "All the life I need. Once this body's done, I can get another. And then another after that, and another. All the time in the world."

"Huh," Corran said, his tone wondering, as if at the grandiose novelty and ambition of such an idea.

"You too," Hendricks said, and Jon didn't know whether to believe him. Anything was possible. It was a whole new world.

He had run out of time. He knew it.

Now that Hendricks had finally arrived at the big revelation that the flash might be used to achieve immortality, a window would close very rapidly. The man had already taken steps to lock down the circle of people aware of the technology. As far as Corran knew, he and Sara Kring were the only people with knowledge of the flash who Hendricks hadn't killed or imprisoned in one way or another.

Come to think of it, he hadn't seen Kring around lately either.

That wouldn't last forever, though. Hendricks would inevitably bring in people to develop the tech, and then the opportunity Corran had today would be gone. People would suspect the truth, sniff around.

"I think this is bigger than Detroit," Hendricks said. "Given enough time, I can fix the entire world. We have to be careful, though. Can't let too many people know what we've got. You understand, don't you, Jon?"

"Of course," Corran said. "This could be . . . I mean, wars could be fought over this."

Hendricks grunted, amused.

And that was the final piece, the final nudge Corran needed.

The flash could transform the planet in a thousand ways, shift the very nature of human existence. He could see two paths so clearly. One where the technology was developed with an eye toward helping mankind, solving problems on a global scale, pushing humanity forward.

And another where its direction was under the control of a man whose first thought for the flash was his own immortality, a man whose response to the idea of war was an amused chuckle.

Gray Hendricks was a monster, and if left to his own devices, he would end the world.

A sacrifice needed to be made. Jon Corran had to sacrifice himself for the greater good. He had to turn his back on his life, everything he'd ever known, Aaron, all of it.

He had to save the world, and if he didn't do it now, he might never get another chance.

Corran reached down to his bag and unzipped it. Moving carefully, he pulled out the weapon: a laptop with cords running from its ports, attached to a strange item. It was a mask, of sorts, with a metal tube extruding from where its eyes would be.

He had taken it from Gabby's barn on the day Hendricks had taken her and her family prisoner, the day when it all started to go wrong. He'd recognized it from the description Sara Kring had provided. He'd told no one he had it. Jon thought he'd known this moment might come, even back then.

He experimented with the device at home, on Aaron, while he was asleep, swapping into the other man's body, marveling at the experience. He hadn't told Aaron, and he felt bad about that. But no harm seemed to have been done, and he needed to learn how to use the gear.

It was all in preparation for today, when he would use it again, one final time.

He opened the laptop and set it on the edge of Hendricks' desk, moving quickly. Gabrielle White's program was already up on the screen. He could activate it with a single keystroke. He placed his index finger on the enter key, then slipped the mask over his head.

A grunt of surprise from Hendricks. He must have turned, seen what was happening.

"Oh, fuck you," the man said, and he heard quick steps, precursors to a lunge.

That was all right. The closer the better. That's what all the research they'd done on the flash seemed to indicate.

He wondered if he'd still be gay. Hendricks was straight, as far as he knew. Wouldn't that be something?

Corran tapped the key.

Lights, spinning through his mind and/

He was moving very fast, looking at a slim, familiar man sitting slumped in a chair with something bizarre on his head. Corran was headed right for him, his arms outstretched. The immense momentum of himself. He was enormous. He could not stop.

He crashed hard into the man, a shocking impact, the chair tipping over and both of them falling.

The mask the man was wearing jabbed painfully into his stomach, and his knee went.

Corran hit the ground.

He rolled over, breathing hard, the very act of breathing, hard.

There was so much more of him.

He was an institution.

He was Gray Hendricks.

He pushed himself up on an elbow and looked at his body. The mask had been knocked askew, and he could see its face, his face.

Not anymore. Never again.

Jon got to his hands and knees, crawling to what had been his body. He removed the mask, pulled the laptop over from where it had fallen when he crashed into his body after the flash, and closed it. He stood with effort, pain hitting him in various places, not knowing whether that was just how Hendricks lived or if these were more recent injuries.

Corran hid the laptop and mask in one of the drawers in Hendricks'—no, his—desk.

He gathered himself, knowing that these next moments would determine many moments to come. Lifetimes, in fact.

He tapped a button on Hendricks' desk phone.

"Yes, Mr. Hendricks?" came the voice from the speaker. His assistant, Ava.

"I need a doctor in here," he said, shocked at the deep rumble of his voice. "Jon collapsed. He's unconscious. I don't know if it's a stroke, or . . . just get someone."

"Oh my god," Ava said. "Right away."

He looked at his body, considering sacrifice.

This had to be done, he thought. *Hendricks was a monster. I had no choice.*

He turned and put his hand against the window, as if to take the city beyond into his grasp, but really just obscuring his own reflection in the window, his brain not quite understanding yet what it was seeing. He felt dizzy with the disconnect.

"My name is Gray Hendricks," he said. "I'd like to tell you about an exciting new technology we've developed at Hendricks Capital.

"We call it the flash."

CHAPTER 36

EIGHTEEN FEET ABOVE STREET LEVEL, MANHATTAN

AND THEN, A SURPRISE.

Annami expected the ground, but the ground never came. Instead, the shift of perspective that came with a flash, gravity pressing on the body in a new way, the slip into a different self like a ghost punching you square in the face.

With it, pain. Well, there had been pain in Bhangra George's gut from Bleeder's shot, and the expectation of another, greater agony as she hit the sidewalk outside Worldwide Plaza.

This was neither of those. This was old pain. In her wrists, in her face, localized as a throbbing line of heat across her cheek.

Her new self was her old self.

Annami was lying on the flash couch in the darkshare den of Mama Run (RIP).

She levered herself up, her wrists flaring in protest. She realized what must have happened. The timer on her transfer into Bhangra George (also RIP) must have run out, and once the ten minutes were up, she'd been automatically kicked out of his body. Of course, at that point, Mama Run was splattered all over Forty-Ninth Street, which meant Annami's mind had nowhere to go—but somehow it had flashed back here, to the original vessel.

She wondered how such a thing could be, and realized it was a question she could never really answer. It was a mystery of the flash impossible to research unless you didn't mind killing someone when you ran the experiment.

Perhaps it had something to do with her status as a person to whom the Two Rules did not apply, just another way in which she was a one-eyed woman in a land of the blind. A superhero.

In any case, she was alive, and back in her daughter's body.

Annami flicked through her reaction to this fact, and found it to be an echo of a very precise remembered emotion: she had worked as a research assistant while obtaining her cognitive science degree, more than three decades before. The days were long, filled with grueling mental churns, data entry or data analysis at the most basic level, organizing information for more senior researchers to interpret. An individual data set might take an entire week to complete, or two.

But eventually, she'd finish. She'd push back from the keyboard, or the slides, or the centrifuge, and stand up. Maybe she would let herself linger over a cup of coffee, or go for a walk around the building—just enjoy the sense of completion.

Inevitably, though, when she returned to her desk, there, waiting for her, would be the next mountain to climb. Another horrible grind sitting in her in-box. Entering and collating thousands of individual responses to behavioral surveys. Picking through brain scans neuron by neuron to locate and record the firing of a single, minuscule cell and marking down the stimulus that had generated the response. Reviewing her betters' grant requests and journal articles for typos.

Whatever small victory she thought she'd achieved, stolen—and replaced with just . . .

. . . more . . .

. . . toil.

That was how Annami felt right then, in the darkshare den.

She'd won. She'd exposed the conspiracy of the flash, avenged her family, and even engineered a graceful, memorable exit, a swan dive to the street and oblivion.

Instead, she was back to the mortal coil. The mortal toil.

Annami frowned, sparking a wildfire of agony in her cheek.

She needed a doctor. If she had no choice but to keep living, she couldn't let herself die.

More than that, she needed to leave. Bleeder might be coming. How, she didn't know, but she knew he wouldn't stop until he was absolutely certain she was dead.

The one saving grace—the cops probably weren't looking for her. The FCB and everyone else probably assumed that Annami, née Gabrielle June White, had died in her plunge off the roof.

She peered through the crimson-tinted interior of the darkshare den, trying to see if there was anything she could use. A rueful moment as she realized that the huge walk-in safe in the back probably had everything she could ever need—the same safe she had locked Mama Run's enforcers inside. She couldn't open the thing without releasing Lek and Chai. Not a great idea, considering she'd just murdered their boss.

Maybe behind the bar.

Mama Run's cashbox was open, the one she used for small transactions, people buying drinks or stim or snacks while waiting for someone to run them. Not much in it, maybe a thousand dollars, but something. A medikit, almost empty, but it had some painblocks. A neatly folded hoodie on a shelf below the bar. Way too big, probably Mama Run's, but that was fine, the bigger the better. It would cover up the bloodstains on her shirt. She took all that, and a bottle of the best bourbon on the shelf.

She still had Gerber's wallet, stolen during the Eaters' shootout with Olsen. Incredible to think that was just a few hours back. The pattern scanner, although she thought she would leave that behind in the darkshare, or destroy it. It was an evil machine. She had a mini she couldn't unlock, and a gun, and a thinnie.

That was it. Everything she possessed.

Enough to . . . she had no idea.

For the last twenty-five years, she had been the woman who would someday bring down Hauser and expose the truth behind the flash. Now, she was . . .

Now, she needed to get the hell out of there.

Annami paused with her hand on the door leading back to the alley outside the darkshare, deciding if she should say something to Lek and Chai, who were expecting to be set free at any moment.

No, she decided. *I'll call the cops when it's safe.*

She knew it might not ever be safe, and if Bleeder did manage to track her to the darkshare and got there before the police, it would mean torture and death for the two men, but she couldn't think of a better option.

Annami couldn't think of much at all, in fact. Whatever combination of adrenaline and will and rage had gotten her through the past twelve hours was fading quickly, leaving her exhausted and broken. She couldn't remember the last time she'd had anything to eat.

I ate something in China, she thought. *But it wasn't my body. I didn't get those calories. During the sex marathon with Soro. Before he was—*

She didn't want to think about Soro. Not just yet.

Through the door, up the steps to the alley. Through the alley to the street, flipping up the hood on her borrowed sweatshirt, keeping her head down, aware that it was only a matter of time before Hauser made sure her face was circulated to the FCB and the NYPD's dronet. Maybe it was already out there.

But maybe not, Annami thought. *Maybe Hauser doesn't have as much pull with the cops as he used to, not now that they're investigating the mysterious disappearance of a woman named Gabrielle White twenty-five years back.*

That thought gave her a boost, enough energy to drag herself down into the subway, where she took the A train all the way out to the last stop before the airport, in Jamaica, Queens. Annami found a room in a sad, defeated hotel right by JFK, the place barely hanging on in the face of a world in which the flash had reduced global air travel by more than 50 percent. It kept the lights on by offering no-questions-asked cheap accommodations, where ID was superfluous and cash was king.

The place was called the Lady Liberty. A miniature version stood on its roof, half-melted by time, its torch arm broken and dangling at an angle, its original green coat of paint now a mottled gray.

The room was a room. The door locked, and it had a bed and a bathroom, and that was enough for now.

Annami took two painblocks, washing them down with bourbon instead of whatever the hell came out of the sink. She considered food, but the idea of chewing sounded too painful to contemplate. Maybe some soup, if she could find a place that would deliver out here, or ramen. She could go out later and get some protein shakes.

A shower, and then she pulled off the bedspread and lay on the hopefully clean sheets, wrapped in the thin piece of sandpaper the Lady Liberty passed off as a towel.

She had never wanted sleep so badly, but there was one thing she wanted more. She wanted to make sure she had won.

Annami unrolled her thinnie and accessed the hotel's net.

She pulled up the news feeds, and as expected, the headlines were all Bhangra George and his untimely death.

She wondered what he'd thought in those last few moments. Awakening to himself as the ground rushed up. Three seconds of panic and then . . . the end.

She didn't care. George was part of it. A peripheral piece, maybe, who hadn't done her any individual harm—but he was a Century. He'd stolen that beautiful body of his. Someone had died so he could live. He'd known the truth about the flash and allowed himself to benefit from it. He got what he got.

The first link she tapped included a vee'd statement from Hauser, which she watched through eyes going blurry from fatigue. He looked . . . affected, like he'd had a truly bad day.

Join the club, asshole, Annami thought. She chuckled.

"I and everyone at NeOnet Global are deeply saddened at the tragic death of beloved entertainer Bhangra George, particularly in light of his passing during an event slated to benefit people across the world. In his name, Anyone will match the proceeds of his auction and make a donation to his organization of choice: Foundation Nil, a charity whose mission is to—"

Annami flipped away from the vee, scanning through the accompanying article, frowning, looking for any mention of Gabrielle White, or quotes of any of the things she'd said, or . . .

Sleep took her.

She woke in sweat-soaked sheets, too hot and too cold all at once. Her face was burning.

The thinscreen provided the name of a pharmacy with delivery service, and she obtained more painblocks, braces for her wrists, and soy-tasting protein pills, which she crushed into bowls of ramen, eating with biodegradable hardfoam chopsticks. She bought herself a cheap prepaid mini. Antibacs, too, although she looked at the packet and saw they were expired.

Infected head wounds were dangerous. So close to the brain . . . she'd be dead in under a week if it really set in.

Annami decided that she'd go to a hospital and turn herself in once she knew that what she'd done had taken hold, that people were taking action. Let them call the cops if they wanted. She'd be fine. She was the victim in all of this.

Then, three days on, and Annami couldn't find a single bit of video of Bhangra George's death, or of her time in his body. She found nothing, not even on the deep sites. Even with all those dronecams, all those people down below the stage filming her with their minis. Hundreds, just on the roof alone.

But then, she didn't know what had happened after she'd fallen. Maybe no one had been allowed to leave Worldwide Plaza unless they surrendered their minis. Maybe satellites had dropped a signal blocker over the roof to make sure nothing could be uploaded out. Maybe the feedcasts were shut off the moment she'd thrown Mama Run off the roof, right when everyone realized something was wrong, and her grand statement to the world had been made to a bunch of deadlinked drones, seen by almost no one.

Annami, in the hotel room, eating when she remembered to do it. Sleeping, or passing out, keeping the deadbolt on, ignoring the efforts of the maid service to enter. Those poor women— almost certainly poor people from a distant land, flashing up here into someone else's body for a shift of hot-sheeting beds and scrubbing toilets.

Not her toilet, though. No. Her toilet was hers.

"Hey, Gabby," Paul said. "Great job back there. You did it!"

"Thanks, babe," Annami said. "Wasn't easy, but I pulled it off."

Paul nodded.

He began to play the piano, one of those complex classical

pieces he liked. She recognized it, that same piece he'd been playing on the day he died.

"Who is that?" she asked.

"It's me, Mama," Anna said.

She was a little older than the last time she'd seen her. Four or five. Old enough to talk. Beautiful, with her frizzy mane of hair haloing her blueberry-smeared face, smiling, holding out her arms.

"Oh, baby, I missed you," Annami said.

She reached out and took her child in her arms and held her. She didn't smell very good, which made sense, considering how long she'd been dead.

A narrative began to emerge over the feeds with respect to the death of veestar Bhangra George. A mentally disturbed person had beaten the various security protocols designed to prevent such things, the suicide scans and so on, and had taken George during his charity auction, resulting in his death. Such a noble man. So tragic.

A cautionary tale.

Annami's hands shaking too much to use the chopsticks anymore, biodegradable or not, scooping noodles into her mouth with her fingers.

Every search she ran on the words *Gabrielle White* came up empty—other Gabrielles across the world got hits, certainly, but not her, not a decades-dead woman who had invented the flash.

George was the story, Gabrielle was not, and even that was fading after a few days.

"The feed cycle's moving on," said Wilbur, which surprised her, considering the advanced state of his Alzheimer's disease, and also considering that he was a rat. "You're yesterday's news. You didn't have any concrete proof of what you said, and so Hauser and his cronies could just say you were some crazy person and call it a day."

Annami nodded. Made sense.

Her naivete snapped into focus.

Stephen Hauser could give people immortality, when and if he chose. Upon whom had he bestowed this gift? Why, the most powerful people in the world. His Centuries.

The sort of people with a very strong interest in making sure nothing about the flash ever changed. The sort of people who could create any story they wanted, about anything at all. The sort of people who could <u>actually</u> change the world or, if they chose, keep it exactly how it was, forever.

Annami had accomplished nothing.

"Not true," Paul said, caressing her cheek, the hurt one.

"Didn't you get a lot of people killed?" Soro said, nuzzling her ear.

Nothing.

"Maybe nothing, maybe just nothing <u>yet</u>," Anna said, climbing up into her lap. "What are you going to do now, Mama?"

Wilbur said I didn't have any concrete proof the Centuries exist, Annami thought. *But I <u>do</u>. I just need to go get it.*

She reached for her mini and accessed the camera. She took a photo of herself, the flash slashing out, giving the room a momentary, stark illumination that its current state of filth and disarray should never have been subjected to.

She looked at the photo.

God, she thought. *Poor kid looks like hell.*

"Don't worry, honey," Annami said. "This will all be over soon."

CHAPTER 37

THE YEARS

GABRIELLE WHITE SPENDS HER DAUGHTER'S SECOND BIRTHDAY TRY-
ing to remember the word for the sheath of protein and fat around
neurons that enables them to successfully transmit electrical impulses, like the plastic coating on a copper wire.

She succeeds—*myelin*—and allows herself to enjoy the birthday
cake and ice cream the Shermans have set out for her, knowing she
might forget the word again in a week, a month, a day.

You are you, she tells herself, licking frosting off her fingers.

Gabby is six—no, Gabby is thirty-seven, but the body she is in
has just turned six.

The Shermans take her to Mackinac Island for the weekend, to
ride horses and eat fudge and stay in the Grand Hotel. Whatever the
Shermans are, this older couple tasked with raising a child not their
own, tasked with surveilling and reporting and guarding—they are
kind, and they are well funded.

On this trip, a surprise visitor—Gray Hendricks. He is waiting
at the hotel after they return from a walk along the beach, and the
surprise, the shock is so complete that Gabby cringes back, grasping
at Mr. Sherman.

Hendricks is sympathetic. He smiles at her.

"It's not what you think," he says. "I just want to talk to you. We have a lot in common."

Hendricks and Gabby go to a private dining room in the hotel. Gabby has ice cream—peppermint—and Hendricks talks to her.

She knows who he is, remembers what he did to her and her husband and her daughter . . . but what can she do? She is six years old and can't lift a jug of milk on her own.

So she listens.

"I put Sara Kring in Eddie Brill," he says, and Gabby remembers those names too, images of a sad man and a false woman flashing into her mind. "Two birds with one stone. She gravitated toward security. She's good at it. Pretty ruthless. I need to keep an eye on her, but there's this sense of . . . we're all in this together, you know?

"You too," Hendricks says, leaning forward. "You might not believe that, but it's true."

You are you, she thinks.

Gabrielle White is eight, reading a news story on the tablet the Shermans bought her: the obituary of Gray Hendricks, aged seventy-three, the titan.

He was in failing health for some time, in a coma, and has just now passed away. Very tragic, but such a life! He did so much for the city of Detroit.

The obituary is three pages long.

Hendricks' will appoints a successor to his empire, a man named Stephen Hauser. Gray Hendricks gives this man control over his company, over his estate, over everything, much to the chagrin of his natural heirs.

"Some may question this decision," Hendricks said in a statement released to the press by the executor of his estate, "but I wanted to leave my legacy in the hands of someone I could trust."

You are you, Gabby thinks.

She is nine, reading about an incredible new technology that is expected to soon transform human society in countless ways. A company everyone is calling Anyone—she hates that name so much, cloying and clever and stolen as it is—run by Gray Hendricks' successor, Stephen Hauser, who has developed a device that can transfer human consciousness from one body to another. While a mind is traveling, both its original body and the mind of their new host lie dormant.

The possibilities, the article says, are endless.

Gabby throws her tablet on the floor, as hard as she can.

You are you, she thinks.

Gray Hendricks had visited Gabby a number of times over the years, telling her things, asking for her opinion, such as it was. She always said what she thought he wanted to hear, and he nodded, and told her more things, and she listened.

Now Stephen Hauser comes to talk to her, telling her that he has a plan to change the world, to fix its problems, to make it better for centuries to come. She listens.

Hauser tells her that he knows it is wrong for Gabby to have been put in her daughter's body but says there is nothing he can do. He says the work he's doing is too important. He says he has taken steps down a hard road, perhaps one he did not fully understand when he began—but if he stops now he'll just be a monster. He has to push on, see it through. He says he has learned a great deal about the decisions that must be made when weighing the fates of individuals against billions. He asks her forgiveness.

You are you, she thinks.

Gabrielle White is thirteen years old, reading every piece of publicly released technical data about the flash, adding this information to the facts she remembers about her own work, scraps and theories and brain anatomy and experimental protocols and so much more.

Sometimes she thinks about a memory stick hidden in a pot-
ted plant in an emergency room in Detroit, wishing she had it but
knowing it is lost forever, along with so much else.

She comes to understand that the flash that Anyone is selling to
the world is not the flash she created. Rules have been added to it,
safeguards and structures and best practices that make it palatable
for worldwide use, so that chaos will not overwhelm the planet.

Gabby knows why Stephen Hauser made this choice, and understands the power in that knowledge. The question now is finding
a way to use it.

Around this time, she performs a test. Flash technology is becoming cheaper, more readily available to the public, mostly as a
sort of thrill-ride experience at parks and fairs and malls. She saves
her allowance and sneaks away from home one evening after the
Shermans have gone to sleep. She buys a thirty-second transfer into
one of the designated vessels at a shopping center near her home.
She does not know what will happen, but she cannot wait any longer.

Gabby's original body, her "prime," in the newly emerging terminology, is dead and gone. Will a flash work at all for her? And if
so, will Anna wake up? And if she does, what will be left of her? Her
daughter has been dormant for twelve years and would awaken into
the body of a teenager.

Gabby remembers a few case histories of coma patients who
awakened with their personalities largely intact even after many unconscious years. The record is nineteen. True, that is longer than
Anna has been gone—but a flash-induced dormancy is not a coma.

She does not know what will happen, but if there is a chance, any
chance, that her daughter can come back, she has to take it.

The flash succeeds, and Gabby finds herself in the body of the
young woman who earns her living by letting strangers live in her
flesh for a few minutes at a time.

Gabby sits up, turns, looks over at her daughter, willing Anna to return, terrified or not, sane or not. If she does, Gabby will leap up, take her, and run, go, steal this innocent body, take her child to the authorities and find a way to explain.

Anna does not wake up. Thirty seconds pass, and Gabby returns to her daughter's body. She cries, again, knowing she is gone. If Anyone's flash will not bring Anna back, Gabby doesn't know what will.

So, instead, revenge.

A strange word. It sounds cheap, made-up, fictional. Revenge is not a goal sought by normal, well-adjusted, civilized folks.

You are you, she thinks.

Gabrielle White is fifteen and thinks she might be able to make her way. She has been working and stealing for years now and has $20,000 squirreled away. The Shermans were old to begin with, and they are very old now. They love her, in their way, and she thinks she probably loves them too.

They let their guard down. Their guard hasn't truly been up for years. Why would it be? The Shermans see themselves as Gabby's parents. They raised her from infancy.

She leaves.

You are you, she thinks.

Gabrielle White is eighteen. She calls herself by a new name, which is also partly an old name. She travels west, then east again, moving through a country changed by the technology she invented. She is always running, always hidden, staying ahead of pursuers she is certain must exist, even if she never encounters them.

She becomes hard, like steel.

She leaves behind everything she once loved, all identifiers—her music, her food, her family—reinventing herself from nothing. She becomes expert at bar games—pool, cards, darts—as an easy, ubiquitous path to quick cash. When she can afford it, she uses the flash, researching everything she can about Anyone's system. She thinks about ways she might use it, infiltrate it, destroy it, rebuild it as it should be.

You are you, she thinks.

Gabrielle White is twenty, applying for a job at NeOnet Global's North American hub, with access to and oversight of the entire flash system, on Twenty-Third Street in New York City.

"I'm Bertrand Milsen," her interviewer says, standing as she enters his office, extending a hand across his desk to her. "And you are . . ."

He glances down at her résumé on his desk.

"Annami," she says. "Annami Blanco."

You are you, she thinks.

CHAPTER 38

ALMOST THERE

"Don't worry, baby," Annami said, placing a steadying hand on a parking meter, clutching her mini in her other hand. She looked at the picture on it, at Anna, her baby, all grown up now, with tattoos all over her beautiful face, so she could barely recognize her. "We're almost there."

She took a breath and kept moving, wishing she'd chosen the other side of the street—a less direct route to her destination but shaded, and the sun was far too hot, too bright, slicing into her eyes via reflections off windshields and storefronts and even the pale surface of the sidewalk.

Mama Run's hoodie helped a little, shading her eyes, but not enough. She needed sunglasses.

She needed a bed.

She needed a hospital, she knew, but her photo had finally been released to the net. Apparently Hauser wasn't willing to leave her presumed death in the dive off the Worldwide Plaza rooftop to chance. Which, considering that she hadn't died at all, was a pretty smart move. In any case—the police would be called the moment she appeared in the ER.

I'll go to the hospital after, she thought. *Maybe.* The hoodie would hide her face in the meantime.

Annami had other defensive measures as well—she stank, she knew it; she had purposely decided not to shower before leaving the hotel. Add that rankness to her dirty, oversized, weather-inappropriate sweatshirt and the slow stagger down the sidewalk that was all she could manage, and she had the look, smell, and movement of a homeless person.

A disguise, but also the truth.

Annami crossed Twenty-Third Street, passing the deli where she had gotten coffee and a bagel for breakfast at least three times a week over the past five years. She paused, looking up the block at the main entrance to the NeOnet Global building, feeling more than seeing the zone of space other pedestrians were giving her. She couldn't smell herself anymore, but they clearly could.

Security guards were posted outside the huge entrance to Anyone headquarters, the glass facade etched with a beautiful version of the company's lightning-bolt logo. These were not ordinary guards, either, flashed-in rent-a-cops in ill-fitting uniforms. These were large men in suits and sunglasses, with microdrone support hovering around them, alert, scanning the approaches to the building from all directions.

Eaters, she suspected. Bleeder's people.

They knew she was coming.

But they didn't know how.

Annami turned away and walked around the corner, trying to visualize the interior layout of the building as best she could. It wasn't easy. The sun was very bright.

She had already dismissed the idea of trying to get in again via the loading dock. After her break-in . . . what, a week ago and also a hundred years, a thousand, Hauser would have placed more security there than at the front entrance, and certainly changed the access code.

How thick were the walls of the building? Impossible to say, really, but Anyone HQ was a standard Manhattan high-rise, and she had to think it had at least six feet of distance between the outer edge and any interior space. Maybe more.

Annami did some quick math—well, not quick, she was too sick for that, but she did it—and decided that, to be safe, she needed to find a spot on the sidewalk with at least twenty feet of clearance between her and any other pedestrian, driver, or human being of any kind.

In Manhattan.

In the middle of the day.

Annami leaned against the building, feeling its sun-warmed stone against her. How much time did she have? Not much. She could feel her strength fading.

"Hurry, Mama," Anna said, from her mini, and Annami nodded.

"I'm trying, love. It's hard. I'm not . . . not feeling well."

The floor plan to the Anyone building swam across her eyes. She tried to remember her daily procedure when she'd worked there, not so long ago. She would come in through the front entrance, pass through security, show her ID, and key in the accompanying code, then take an elevator up to the network monitoring floor to begin her day. In her five years at the company, she had rarely, if ever, been called upon to do anything on the first floor. Wasn't much there, as far as she knew. The guard station, their lockers and so on, the loading-dock area, some storage.

So . . .this plan would be yet another roll of the dice.

But maybe she could improve her odds a little.

"FUCK YOU!" she screamed, her voice like tires over gravel.

Out of the corner of her vision, she saw the startled reaction from people walking on the sidewalk near her. They were already giving her a wide berth due to her stench, but these were New Yorkers. Stenches were simply accent notes to the city's perfume.

"GODDAMN MOTHERFUCKER! I'LL KILL YOUR ASS!" she screamed, balling up her fists but not looking up, not wanting to risk recognition.

Baleful odors could be endured, part of the price for and adaptation to living in the greatest city in the world, but ranting insanity was a different matter. New York sometimes drove people mad. This was a well-known fact. Best to give crazy a wide berth. Crazy could become violent. Crazy could be catching.

"WHO THE HELL DO YOU THINK YOU ARE? I'M GONNA EAT YOU! SLICE OFF YOUR FINGERS! EAT 'EM ON A SLICE!"

It was working. People were crossing the street to avoid her stretch of sidewalk in both directions. She was right in the middle of the block, twenty feet from either corner, and the other side of the street was at least thirty feet away.

The traffic was a potential issue. Passing cars had drivers; buses and taxis had passengers.

Annami envisioned a circle in her mind, with herself at the center, divided down the middle by the exterior wall of the NeOnet Global building. She was running out of time. New York City had an immune system, and she'd probably already activated its antibodies—people alerting the cops to a violent maniac ranting on First Avenue just south of Twenty-Third.

She'd done everything she could.

The light at Twenty-Second turned red, and traffic heading north on First cleared out. Annami timed it as well as she could, waiting for the two seconds when the half circle in front of her would be completely open.

She lifted the mini to her face and yanked the drawstring on her hoodie tight to create a sort of cave out of the fabric.

Anna smiled at her from the screen.

"Good luck, Mama," she said, and Annami triggered the camera.

A stop-stutter of lights, bright, even brighter than the sun and/

CHAPTER 39

THEN AND NOW

YOU ARE ANNA KATHERINE WHITE. YOU LOVE YOUR MOTHER, AND you love your father, and you love the world, and you love being alive. Sometimes you are unhappy, or you are hungry or cold or uncomfortable, but you call for your mother and father and they come and they make you happy again. You are small, and as far as you know you will always be small. You don't know what you are, you don't know where you are, but you are you.

And then a strange man is holding you, who is not your father. You are put in a dark place, all alone, and no one is holding you.

You hear your mother saying words you don't know, but she is so afraid, you know that, and she says your name over and over. Anna, Anna, Anna.

And the world goes to sleep for a while.

You wake up, but it is different now, like when your mother or father straps you into the chair in the back part of the little rumbly room that moves and you can see their heads sticking up above a little wall, and outside the windows of the little room there is the world. Always changing—sometimes a blur, sometimes a picture you can look at for a little while, and then Momma or Dadda gets you out of the little chair and you are somewhere new.

It is always like that now. You are always in the chair, always strapped in so you can't move or do anything, looking out through a window as the world moves. You can't see your mother, but you feel her, close, and in time you come to understand that it is not the world moving but the little room, and the little room is your mother, and you are seeing through her eyes.

You learn words for things, like *time* and *hurt* and *blue* and *memory* and *myelin*. Anything your mother thinks about, you think about too, in a way. You see what she remembers, and so you know how much she thinks about you, and your father, and the men who took you away from her.

So you live as she lives, and you learn what she learns, and taste what she tastes, and because she learns so much about the flash, there is a moment when you are ten that you believe you understand what has happened to you. And to her. This was done to both of you.

When you are thirteen, your mother goes away for a little while. This is not like sleep. This is something else. You go away too, and she comes back when you do, and you can feel her sadness so deeply. This was some sort of experiment, and it failed, and you know she thinks you are dead. You try to tell her you are not, but she can't hear you, and you can't do anything to get her attention.

But you are not dead. You are Anna Katherine White. You are the Kitten. You are you.

Your mother likes to read. In the early years, the books she chooses are nothing you enjoy, but you try to learn from them, building a larger picture of the world outside from within your little room.

In time, your understanding catches up with your mother's tastes, and you want to tell her how much you enjoyed this story or hated that. You begin to understand the prison of decision in which you are trapped—your entire experience of the world is based on another person's choices, and even though you love your mother, you hate her a little.

You realize one day that no one else is like you are. None of your mother's stories talk about people riding in the little rooms of their parents' minds, forever, like ghosts. You are unique, which means no one is looking for you, and there is something wrong with you. You are not supposed to be you.

You go away for a little while after that.

Your mother takes you places, does things, like she always does. She seems very excited about something. Names rattle through her head endlessly—Bhangra George, Stephen Hauser, Soro, Paul, Jon Corran, Gray Hendricks, Sara Kring, Bleeder, Gabby White. The Kitten. The Kitty Kat.

Anna.

Pain. A lot of it. You have learned, over the course of twenty-five years, to pull back from your mother's sensations when you want to. You can dull pain, dial down sorrow, even ignore fatigue. You don't have to sleep when she does, and you like watching her dreams. They feel like yours.

But this pain is too much. It's everywhere—and sickness, too. You are in the city, moving through New York (you know New York by now, and many other things besides). You are in Chelsea. The view through the windows of your mother's perception is blurred.

You feel her stopping, forcing herself to think, making a calculation, waiting, then holding a mini up to her face.

"Good luck, Mama," she says, which you do not understand, and then there is a flash of light, a stop-stutter start flickering that you have never seen before and/

You come forward, like you have been shoved hard from behind, every part of you slamming up against the window of perception that has been your only view on the world, crashing through it. You feel <u>weight</u>. You feel <u>pain</u>. You feel <u>everything</u> for the first time in twenty-five years. You smell yourself, you taste yourself, you hear the world, all the sensations that used to be dulled by your mother's filters hit you all at once. It is glorious and terrifying, what you think it might be like to fall into a frigid, rushing river.

You slip to your knees—and they are your knees, not hers. You can feel the rough grit of the sidewalk through the fabric of your jeans.

A kind person appears before you, a man with worried eyes.

"Hey, you okay?" he says. "Want me to call someone?"

"It's fine," another voice says, and the man turns.

Two other people are walking up the sidewalk toward you. They wear dark suits, and both are smiling. You know who they are, because your mother knows who they are. But she is not here anymore to help you.

You are Anna, for the first time in your life you are alone, and they are Eaters.

CHAPTER 40

NeOnet GLOBAL NORTH AMERICAN HEADQUARTERS, MANHATTAN

A PIECE OF ART—WOVEN STRANDS OF SILVER YARN, WITH BLUE, yellow, and green accents. A huge panel, twenty feet on a side, a visualization of the flash network.

Annami had seen it every day for five years.

It was mounted on the rear lobby wall of Anyone headquarters.

Deep inside the lobby, in fact. Past the security station.

Annami surveyed herself. She was now a woman, larger than she had been a moment before—wider, thicker. A wedding band on her finger, the flesh around it puffing out a bit. She was older now too, she thought, although it was hard to tell without a mirror.

Overall, though, Annami felt a thousand pounds lighter, despite the heaviness of this woman. She realized how ill she must have been, and thought about her body, Anna's poor, ravaged shell, left on the sidewalk in the sun, collapsed.

That got her moving. It wouldn't be long before someone investigated. She would be recognized, and then alarms would begin to ring, security protocols activated.

Annami moved to the elevator, looking at her ID badge.

Isidore Kolanski, network administration.

She didn't know the woman, but she worked in a useful department for Annami's purposes. Network admin covered a wide variety of responsibilities at NeOnet Global, but the main thing was that no one would blink an eye if they saw Ms. Kolanski on the network-traffic-monitoring floor. Probably.

Annami rode the elevator up and found herself in the hub, the holo depicting the current status of the worldwide flash network hovering above the spiraling rows of workstations. Out of long habit, she gave it an appraising glance. Almost entirely green. No outages at the moment, and just a few yellow spots indicating slow traffic.

To her practiced eye, it looked like the flash was running as smoothly as it ever did.

Beatrice Fring was at her desk, focused on the task before her. Annami walked over and cleared her throat, acutely aware of the passage of time, knowing her body outside would be discovered at any moment.

"Hello, Bea," she said, using a friendly, familiar tone.

Beatrice looked up, her face perplexed, her eyes flicking to Isidore Kolanski's ID badge. Bea didn't recognize this woman.

That was lucky—it meant Annami didn't have to worry about triggering any suspicions by not behaving the way Isidore usually did.

"Hey!" Bea said brightly, overcompensating.

"Sorry to bother you, but I was just with Milsen, and he asked me to send you up to see him," Annami said. "He's in the canteen."

"Wait," Bea said, a little puzzled, a little alarmed. "Bertrand's back? They hired him again?"

Annami realized her mistake. Bleeder had told her this, but with everything else, she'd just . . . forgotten. Anyone's higher-ups discovered what happened with the break-in and fired Milsen, which meant he absolutely was <u>not</u> in the canteen waiting to chat with Beatrice Fring.

Bea was giving her a strange, appraising look.

"I think so," Annami said. "I didn't get the whole story. I just saw him up there, and he asked if you could come see him."

"Perfect timing," Bea said, frowning. "I have a ton of work to do. Did he say what he wanted?"

She waved a hand at her screen, which, it was true, did look occupied with a delicate and time-consuming task—optimizing flash routes across the southern Andes. Annami remembered that project. It had actually been one of hers, before she quit.

"He didn't say," Annami said. "He seemed happy, though, if that helps? Like it was good news?"

Bea nodded slowly, considering this. She stood.

"Okay, thanks," she said. "I'll head up."

Annami noticed she didn't address Ms. Kolanski by name, understanding that for Bea, there was an Izzy/Isidore issue that she couldn't resolve without revealing the fact that she had no idea who this nice woman was.

Bea bent over her keyboard and logged out of the system, following Anyone corporate protocol to the letter.

She then turned and headed out toward the elevator, which meant Annami's clock was now ticking. The canteen was on the building's top floor. It was beautifully appointed, with a different well-known chef flashed in each week to prepare local delicacies from their part of the world.

Bea would have to take the elevator all the way up, perform a fruitless search, be confused, maybe look around again to make sure, then take the elevator back down.

Eight minutes at most. Less if Beatrice went straight to security, which Annami thought seemed pretty possible after her

Bertrand screwup. Even less if her prime was identified outside where it had collapsed—that would get the entire building sealed immediately.

Annami sat down at Bea's desk. The screen was locked, password-protected.

She knew that her own login had probably been canceled the day she quit, and certainly once Stephen Hauser learned that Annami Blanco was actually Gabrielle White—but she didn't have to use her own login.

She was one of Beatrice Fring's closest friends.

She knew her password.

Annami typed quickly, and the screen unlocked.

A twinge of guilt, knowing that heat for this would land hard on Bea, but seeing no other option.

She navigated through the system, moving beyond the surface-level applications and into diagnostic and administration operations, and deeper still into data storage. She was looking for a single file, the output of her Century-hunter virus. She had set her code to record information for every piece of traffic that came through the network. Length, time, location, destination codes, IDs for travelers and vessels. Even flash patterns, which was one of the great secrets of Anyone's network—in order to work, it needed to store the patterns of everyone who used it, to make sure travelers went where they needed to go and returned safely home to their primes. The patterns were heavily encrypted, but they were there.

Somewhere in the data set was her own transfer into Bhangra George. Hers, along with every flash of every human being who had used the network in the past several months. Billions of people, hundreds of billions of transfers.

And in it, somewhere, was proof that there were people on the planet not bound by the Two Rules. There would be a double flash, or a traveler who never returned to their prime. Something. Proof that Gabrielle White had been telling the truth about everything Anyone had done.

Originally, she had intended to go through the data before the Bhangra George auction, find what she needed, and upload it to the widenet as an additional layer of proof of what she was saying. Concrete proof.

That hadn't happened—she didn't have time—but she did now. There was no reason she couldn't send herself the data and comb through it at her leisure.

She could find evidence that the Centuries existed, and then she could try again, release the information publicly, make sure this time it couldn't be covered up. She could still win.

Once she had the data.

If she had the data.

The file was not where it was supposed to be. Annami thought back, trying to remember if she'd hidden it somewhere else in the network. She typed rapidly, sending a search string off to look for large data volumes hiding inside the system, even as she knew the truth.

They found my code, Annami thought. *They found it and deleted it.*

This idea had seemed so perfect in Queens, but she had been feverish, sick, out of her mind, unable to really think it through.

Of course they deleted it, she thought. *They know who I am. They know I was here for years. They probably scrubbed the whole system.*

She watched her search string run, knowing it wouldn't find anything, knowing this wasn't going to work, knowing she had to get out, to go <u>now</u>, as fast as she could, before—

A window popped up on her screen, a vid-chat link. It showed an image of herself, of Annami, in the clothes she had been wearing outside, the same stained jeans and hoodie. Standing in what looked like a small conference room, holding a hand up in front of her, staring at it. Her eyes were open. It was Annami, and she was awake.

The woman on the screen moved her hand up and down, very slowly, following its motion, mesmerized.

"I'm . . . ," Annami said, to some unknown person out of camera range. "I'm doing this. Do you see this? I'm doing it. All by myself."

It was not Annami. It was Anna.

CHAPTER 41

NeOnet GLOBAL NORTH AMERICAN HEADQUARTERS, NETWORK-TRAFFIC-MONITORING FLOOR

WORDS APPEARED ON THE SCREEN.

We have her. Identify yourself.

A rumble of reaction moving through the room from her former colleagues, and Annami realized that Anna was not just on her screen but on every screen. Hauser did not know who had invaded his fortress and so was making certain Annami would see his message no matter what body she had taken.

She set that aside and tried to think through the shock, tried to understand. *Anna. How? How?*

Annami realized that in all the years of tests she had done on herself, all the research she'd done, all her time in the flash, light and dark, as traveler and host, she had never, not once, tried to repeat the process that had sent her into her daughter's body.

Every time, from that first attempt at the mall when she was thirteen to this very day, she had used the flash technology developed and released by Anyone. But that technology was not <u>her</u> technology, and it was not how she had been moved into Anna in the first place. Anyone's version of the flash was created and refined at the direction of Dr. Camila Chavez, using whatever she could remember of that first month of research while Hendricks held Gabby and her family prisoner. Camila's flash was different, in some fundamental way.

All that time Annami spent trying to unlock the door to her daughter, and she had been using the wrong key. The wrong key, when the right one was no farther away than a fucking cell phone and a thinnie.

Annami wanted to give herself up, to stand, to tell them who she was, if only they would let her daughter go, help her. She could not imagine the experience Anna had awakened into and would do anything to help her, to guide her.

But . . . would that ever happen?

Why would they ever let Anna go? What could Annami offer Hauser or Anyone that they did not already have? Nothing.

They wanted only one thing from her—silence. Death. And once they had it, they would kill Anna too.

Anna, who could speak. Anna, who had somehow been there, present, her mind growing and learning, watching as her mother lived her life through her body, not realizing the uniqueness of her existence as an unseen spirit locked inside a body controlled by someone else.

How had she not seen this? Felt her own daughter's mind? Somehow found a way to test for her presence?

That failure could wait. All that mattered: somehow, miraculously, Anna was alive, and she needed her mother.

Gabby searched her mind for a way to free herself, to free her daughter. Any lie, any truth, any deal she might offer Stephen Hauser.

Nothing.

She had only one advantage—they didn't know which body she had taken—and it was minor and would not last.

More words came up on the screen.

Have I been such a bad steward? This world was dying. Global warming, socioeconomic disaster on the horizon . . . and we all <u>hated</u> each other. Don't tell me we didn't. I used the flash to end all of that. I moved us past our differences. I set the world free.

No, she thought. *No.*

Stephen Hauser, once Gray Hendricks, once Jon Corran . . . if he had saved the world, he did it for himself, to make sure he and his Centuries would always have a world to rule.

Would I have done better? she wondered. *If I had held on to the flash, made those hundred thousand decisions, would I have made something better?*

Yes, Gabby thought. *Yes.*

Her first thought, so long ago, once she realized what she had invented, was not about herself. It was about Anna, about what the flash might give her and every child like her.

Someday, you will change the world, she used to tell herself. Changing the world was not about you. It was about *the world*. About *everyone else*.

Gabrielle White knew that. Stephen Hauser did not.

That was the difference between them, and that was why she knew she would have done better.

Whatever you're trying to do . . . stop. It doesn't have to be this way. You're making mistakes, hurting people. Bhangra George was a good man. You'd have liked him. He wanted to be a singer, originally. Did you know that? He liked to sing along with the radio.

This can't be what you wanted. I remember when we used to talk. I know you.
Let me help you.

Freedom, for herself and her daughter. Gabby could see only one way.

She typed quickly, knowing it was only a matter of seconds before she was locked out of the system. She was stunned they hadn't done it already.

She accessed the network control systems, used all her expertise, built up over decades of study and spite. Billions of people, all over the world, used the flash, or had used the flash before aging out and becoming Dulls. Eighty-two percent of the population. They had I-fi, or they were using the light flash at that moment. And all their flash patterns were here, stored safely in the network, unable to be accessed by any except the highest levels of the company's administration.

Or by the goddamned genius who invented the goddamned technology in the first place.

Gabrielle thought about Anna, and Paul, and Soro, and even poor Eddie Brill.

She thought about a world where no one knew who was behind anyone else's eyes. A world judged by actions. The world she would have made.

The world she still could.

With another few keystrokes she initialized a flash, network-wide, utilizing every single pattern stored in the system, every I-fi access code. Everyone would be a traveler, everyone would be a vessel. At random.

Gabrielle paused, realizing that her own pattern was an outlier. Her body had died twenty-five years before. She, potentially, unbalanced the equation. It came down to whether 82 percent of the world's population was an even number. If it was not, and she participated, someone else could be lost, their soul shunted aside by hers. The odds were fifty-fifty. Too high.

No. No one else would be lost.

Gabby knew her pattern by heart. She searched for it in the database and specified the transfer parameters. Her destination was now 0, 0, 0.

Zeroing out, they called it.

Remember, she told herself.

You are you—and today, you change the world.

She tapped one last/

EPILOGUE

EVERYWHERE

IN THE WAN CHAI DISTRICT OF HONG KONG, GAVIN MCINERNEY of Edinburgh, Scotland, realizes his mouth is full of congee when it had not been just a moment before.

In the Sea of Cortez, personal trainer Madison Delilah of Halifax, Nova Scotia, finds herself on the deck of a squid trawler. She slips on the wet deck and nearly goes over the side, her hand caught at the last moment by Adrian Melicar, accountant from Rosario, Argentina.

In Kenya, the prime minister of England stands alone in a field, looking out at a low-hanging sun in a body that is not her own.

Lawyers become soldiers. Dancers become farmers. Men become women. Young become old. Women become men. Old become young. More than seven billion people, all over the world, become someone new.

People, everywhere, often without a language in common, in offices, villages, cars, planes, streets, fields, homes, see new faces around them, with no idea who is behind those faces, who these people had once been. Lifting their hands to see new skin, looking out through new eyes.

All of humanity is <u>all of humanity</u>. There is no rich, no poor, no light, no dark, no young, no old—there is only how we treat each other in these moments. To survive, we must see each other. To survive, we must see.

It may not last, but it begins, and that is something.

In Melbourne, Australia, Anna Katherine White opens her eyes.

You are you.

ACKNOWLEDGMENTS

Anyone was a mighty beast to wrangle, and although my name is on the cover, I would be remiss in not offering huge gratitude to the many people who helped me create this story. First, Amy and Rosemary, who suffered through the horror of having a writer-in-residence—literally in residence—during the book's creation and listened patiently as I worked through the very early versions of the tale told here. My close friends and constant sounding boards Scott Snyder and Shawn DePasquale, who never fail to tell me when I don't quite have it yet and who share in my excitement when I eventually get there. My editor, Sara Nelson, publisher, Doug Jones, and all the other wonderful people at Harper Perennial—Heather Drucker, Megan Looney, Mary Sasso, and many more who make the business of books a joy. My agent, Seth Fishman, and my manager, Angela Cheng Caplan, who make sure both the deals and the stories end up strong. Thanks to my attorney, Eric Feig. And to the many people who read the book in various incarnations, sometimes more than once, and/or offered incredibly valuable feedback on not just the story, but matters of sensitivity and inclusiveness, design, neurology and neuroscience, early '00s hardcore bands, and much more, or just supported the extraordinary effort of writing a novel with friendship and grace: Jeff Boison, Ryan Penagos, Liz Marley, Heather Antos, Constance Katsafanas, Erinna Monck, Tommy Stella, Heather Fong-Quade, Sam Soule, Andy Deemer, Aaron Mahnke, Samantha Irby, Chuck Wendig, Rob Barocci, Ryan

Browne, and many more. Inevitably, a list like this is incomplete, as books and stories come from everywhere, from every interaction and moment of my life. If your name isn't here but should be, accept my apologies and yell at me in person next time we see each other—which I hope is very, very soon.

ABOUT THE AUTHOR

Charles Soule is a *New York Times*–bestselling, Brooklyn-based novelist, comic book writer, musician, and attorney. He is best known for his first novel, *The Oracle Year*, as well as for writing *Daredevil, She-Hulk, Death of Wolverine*, and various *Star Wars* comics from Marvel Comics; his creator-owned series, Curse Words, from Image Comics; and the award-winning political sci-fi epic *Letter 44* from Oni Press.

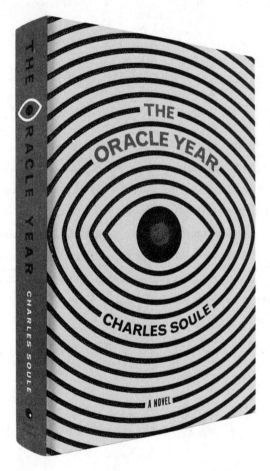